# THE PSYCHIC

## Books by Nancy Bush

CANDY APPLE RED
ELECTRIC BLUE
ULTRAVIOLET
WICKED GAME
WICKED LIES
SOMETHING WICKED
WICKED WAYS
WICKED DREAMS
UNSEEN
BLIND SPOT
HUSH
NOWHERE TO RUN
NOWHERE TO HIDE
NOWHERE SAFE
SINISTER
I'LL FIND YOU
YOU CAN'T ESCAPE
YOU DON'T KNOW ME
THE KILLING GAME
DANGEROUS BEHAVIOR
OMINOUS
NO TURNING BACK
ONE LAST BREATH
JEALOUSY
BAD THINGS
THE BABYSITTER
THE GOSSIP
THE NEIGHBORS
THE CAMP
THE SORORITY
THE PSYCHIC

Published by Kensington Publishing Corp.

# THE PSYCHIC

# NANCY BUSH

Zebra Books
Kensington Publishing Corp.
kensingtonbooks.com

ZEBRA BOOKS are published by

Kensington Publishing Corp.
900 Third Avenue
New York, NY 10022

Copyright © 2025 by Nancy Bush

This book is a work of fiction. Names, characters, businesses, organizations, places, events, and incidents either are the product of the author's imagination or are used fictitiously. Any resemblance to actual persons, living or dead, events, or locales is entirely coincidental.

To the extent that the image or images on the cover of this book depict a person or persons, such person or persons are merely models, and are not intended to portray any character or characters featured in the book.

All rights reserved. No part of this book may be reproduced in any form or by any means without the prior written consent of the Publisher, excepting brief quotes used in reviews.

Without limiting the author's and publisher's exclusive rights, any unauthorized use of this publication to train generative artificial intelligence (AI) technologies is expressly prohibited.

All Kensington titles, imprints, and distributed lines are available at special quantity discounts for bulk purchases for sales promotion, premiums, fundraising, educational, or institutional use.

Special book excerpts or customized printings can also be created to fit specific needs. For details, write or phone the office of the Kensington Sales Manager: Attn.: Sales Department. Kensington Publishing Corp., 900 Third Avenue, New York, NY 10022. Phone: 1-800-221-2647.

Zebra and the Z logo Reg. U.S. Pat. & TM Off.

ISBN: 978-1-4201-5573-0 (ebook)
ISBN: 978-1-4201-5572-3

First Zebra Trade Paperback Edition: October 2025

10 9 8 7 6 5 4 3 2 1

Printed in the United States of America

The authorized representative in the EU for product safety and compliance
is eucomply OU, Parnu mnt 139b-14, Apt 123
Tallinn, Berlin 11317, hello@eucompliancepartner.com

To John S.

For all the years of hard work.

Thank you.

# Prologue

Ronnie looked in the mirror and examined her scowling face. Straight, light brown hair with bangs that were hanging in her eyes just long enough to make Dad mad. White teeth. *You should smile more.* Dad, of course. Blue eyes, which Aunt Kat said were her best feature, well, except for that thing they didn't talk about. Not exactly a feature. *A curse. Stop encouraging her, Katarina.* Dad, again. Ronnie's gift was NOT TALKED ABOUT.

She forced a smile, then stopped herself. It looked fake and scary. The only time it looked natural was when she was with her friends because that's when she was HAPPY. Living with her father was *a trial*. Aunt Kat's favorite term. She, along with Ronnie, felt Jonas Quick was a *trial*. And he was. He might be her father but he'd always been remote and exacting and *determined to mold his daughter in his own image* — Aunt Kat's words again — not her mother's, whose death still haunted the empty places inside Ronnie's heart. That was her own saying, sort of. Maybe she read it in a book, but it was sure true. She missed Mom terribly and it had been years since she'd been gone.

But enough of all that. Today was her tenth birthday and

Brandy and Melissa, the best, *bestest* friends anyone could have, were coming over to celebrate. They were bringing cupcakes and a picnic basket full of candy and little sandwiches with the crusts cut off. Brandy's brother, Clint, was taking them all to The Pond, which was really just a bend of the East Glen River, a place that spread out between the banks, and they were spending the afternoon there. Beneath her shorts and shirt, Ronnie was wearing her blue, one-piece swimsuit with crisscross straps that ran over her back.

She shivered as she waited. She only wanted to think about her birthday and all the fun she was going to have... but that familiar bad, bad feeling was creeping over her. That special feature, that *curse*... It sometimes developed when she thought about her mother, even though Mom had died when Ronnie was barely four. She didn't remember Mom all that good... all that well, she mentally corrected herself. When Mom died it was as if all the bad things escaped, like Pandora's box. Though most of the time Ronnie pushed the bad things away, sometimes, like today, they seemed to hover just outside of her vision, she could sense them, but when she turned to look, they were gone.

Poof.

As if they'd never existed.

She sat down at the table to wait and laid her head on her arms. Sliding a look out of the side of her eyes she wondered, sort of hoped, that she might actually *see* Mom. Why not? She'd seen other things at other times. Once, while going into the grocery store with Gabrielle, her babysitter, Ronnie had spotted a girl lying on the pavement in the parking lot. Freaked, Ronnie had grabbed Gabrielle's arm and pointed, whispering she thought the girl was dead. Gabrielle had glanced to the spot, then shot Ronnie a warning glare as she'd yanked her arm from Ronnie's panicked grasp. "There's nothing there!" she'd whispered harshly. "Stop playing games!"

Ronnie had glared back at Gabrielle, ready to argue. At sixteen, Gabrielle thought she knew everything.

But when Ronnie glanced back to the spot in the parking lot where the girl had been sprawled, she was gone.

"She was there!" Ronnie insisted, clenching her fists.

But Gabrielle had just rolled her big eyes as if Ronnie was just a drama queen, seeking attention. Gabrielle hadn't believed her. No one believed her. They never, ever believed her. It was *a living hell*, a phrase Brandy liked to say.

It all made Ronnie try to hide what she saw but it was really, really hard. Aunt Kat was the only one who ever seemed to understand, but even she shushed Ronnie whenever Ronnie insisted and pointed out there was something *there*.

Now anger and frustration boiled up inside her and she pressed her lips together, fighting tears. Her dad was at work, like always, which was fine, because he never believed her, either. Gabrielle was somewhere in the house listening to music on her iPod—Kelly Clarkson, by the sound of it—which was really all Gabrielle ever did. Ronnie could be babysitting herself, for all the good it did.

The lyrics to "Since U Been Gone" floated through the room. Ronnie wouldn't mind having an iPod, but Dad didn't have much use for anything except for asking her about her studies. He was always about that.

"How's that book report coming?" he'd ask. Or, "How'd you do on that presentation on Oregon? Did you write down all the fun facts we looked up?"

Right.

Or, worse yet, "We still need to work on your thematic writing skills. I don't think McDaniels is pushing you enough..."

Luckily, school had ended weeks ago and his questions had fallen off a bit.

"A living hell," Ronnie muttered, repeating Brandy's favorite phrase. Even though Ronnie tried to relax, she was jumping out of her skin and she just wanted to *go*.

She closed her eyes to calm herself.

But behind her eyelids she suddenly saw someone falling,

falling, *falling* off a cliff. Heard the hard thwack of a body hitting water. Smelled something dank and muddy.

*Don't go in the water.*

Her eyes flew open and she inhaled sharply. Was that warning for her? It sounded like... Mom... maybe? Sometimes the bad feeling crept into her brain and left scattered pictures around that she couldn't piece together and didn't know what to do with. Like a *body* hitting *water*. Was that a scene from the cliff above The Pond?

Ronnie breathed deeply, in and out for several minutes, calming herself down, bringing herself back to the here and now, the summer-warm house and everything familiar. Patrice, the therapist her father had agreed to let her see when Aunt Kat insisted that "the girl needs help, Jonas," had taught her how to pull herself "back from the brink" of her visions. Patrice said they were figments of her imagination, which made Ronnie skeptical of the therapist. The pictures, thoughts and feelings that sometimes flooded her mind were not figments of her imagination. They were something more. She just didn't know what.

She blinked several times... that falling body... that awful *thwack* when it hit the water. It sounded like... death. Was it something about to happen at the river? She grew cold all over and hunched her shoulders. She hadn't told her dad where they were going. He didn't like water and had ordered tons of swimming lessons for her to keep her safe, and if he knew she was going with Brandy's brother he would have a *shit fit*. Brandy, again. Aunt Kat tsk-tsked that Brandy was a victim of her older brother's bad influence, even though Aunt Kat could swear like a—

*Honk! Honk!*

Ronnie glanced upstairs, wondering if Gabrielle had heard.

No footsteps or shouts. Quickly Ronnie snagged her tote bag and dashed for the door. Through the side window panes she saw Brandy's brother Clint's SUV wheel into the driveway, sunlight glinting off the windshield. A Trailblazer, Brandy had told her.

Ronnie stopped at the door, chewing on her lip. Dad was at work and Gabrielle was on her phone, so she could just go . . . maybe. But Gabrielle would have a fit and blame Ronnie and everyone would get upset. Both her father and Gabrielle thought she was going to the Mercers' house and she didn't want Gabrielle to see that Brandy's brother was driving because Ronnie had failed to mention that little fact and she didn't want to have to explain.

And she really wanted to *go*!

She threw open the door, ready to sprint to the driveway, but stopped short upon spying her two besties climbing out of the black SUV. Brandy and Mel both smiling broadly, Brandy with a bag slung over her shoulder, Mel balancing three cupcakes with pink icing as they hurried across the dry lawn to the front door.

What? No. Ronnie stood at the threshold, then stepped back to make room for them to hurry inside.

A mistake. "Hey, maybe we should go now and—" Ronnie started, her eyes on the stairs as her friends rushed past her to the kitchen, where they set the cupcakes on the counter.

No, no, no! Ronnie heard the floorboards creaking overhead. Gabrielle was walking from one room to the other. Possibly heading for the staircase.

"And what?" Mel asked.

"Just leave," Ronnie said, nervous.

"Wait a sec," ordered Brandy. She whipped out ten tiny candles from her bag, then retrieved one of those long, skinny lighters.

Ronnie clenched her teeth into a smile as Mel stuck groups of candles in each of the three cupcakes while Brandy lit the wicks with the tiny wobbling flame from the lighter.

"Happy birthday to you! Happy birthday to you! Happy birthday, dear Ronnie! Happy birthday to you . . . !" her friends screamed, trying to out-yell each other and laughing hard. Despite her worries, Ronnie couldn't help but laugh, too.

"We've got ten. There are seven more cupcakes in the picnic basket, if Clint and Evan haven't eaten them," said Brandy. She shot a dark look toward the still open front door, as if she thought her brother and his friend were already doing just that.

Mel piped in, "One for each year."

Ronnie looked across the flickering candles at her friends. Bright pink frosting slopped across small spice cakes. They had made the cupcakes themselves, Ronnie bet, because Mel loved everything pink and Brandy liked spice cake better than chocolate. The candlelight sparkled against Mel's necklace. All three of them were wearing their pieces of the silver BFF necklace that had come broken into thirds, one for each of them.

"Blow 'em out," ordered Brandy, nodding toward the candles. Ronnie leaned forward, sucked in a huge breath and *whooshed* out all ten. She felt a bit lightheaded afterwards, it was a big breath, but Brandy and Mel were clapping wildly, so Ronnie grinned. Though her wish had been to just leave and save the partying till they got to The Pond, she appreciated her friends' enthusiasm.

A dark whisper stole across the back of her brain and she felt a deep and familiar chill. Was it something about The Pond? No. Couldn't be. It was too bright out. A brilliant, hot, summer day. This vision was dark and gloomy.

*But that's how the bad things start . . .*

"Let's go!" Ronnie urged, hearing footsteps overhead and practically thrusting the cupcakes back into her friends' hands and pushing them toward the front door.

"I want to save one for Clint," said Mel, who thought Brandy's older brother was cute and cool.

Brandy declared, "He can get his own. And probably already has!"

"Well, it's good to share," said Mel defensively.

Brandy rolled her eyes toward Ronnie. They both knew about Mel's crush on Brandy's brother. But Ronnie was still focused on getting away before Gabrielle came downstairs and started asking questions.

They all crammed into the back seat of Clint's SUV with Mel in the middle. Mel was the cutest of them, Ronnie thought. Blond, with big brown eyes like a deer, she was starting to develop breasts. Booblets, according to Brandy, who was pancake flat like Ronnie. Brandy wore her dark hair in a ponytail most of the time to keep it out of her face. She was cute, too, just not as adorable as Mel, but funnier. Ronnie leaned into their friendship the most because Brandy was dead honest about what she felt. Mel was sweeter, but kind of not as dependable.

Wearing sunglasses, Clint was behind the wheel of the Trailblazer. Seated next to him in the passenger seat, his friend Evan messed with the radio. Clint looked back at the three of the girls and said, "Took you long enough," as he shoved the gearshift into reverse and stepped on the gas.

"We were celebrating. I told you," Brandy shot back. She flung her ponytail over her shoulder and crossed her hazel eyes at the back of his head.

"Sit down and shut up," he said, but it wasn't too mean. Just the way he and Brandy talked to each other.

Suddenly Gabrielle was running from the house and screaming, "Veronica! Veronica! WAIT!"

*Uh-oh . . .*

Ronnie dropped her chin to her chest. *Caught.*

Clint muttered something under his breath, but hit the brakes and slipped the SUV out of gear before it reached the street.

Reluctantly, Ronnie, her cheeks growing hot, pressed the button to lower her window, which was facing the house and closest to Gabrielle. "What?"

"Did you call your father?" Gabrielle stared Ronnie down.

"He knows where I'm going," she lied, adding, "He's at *work*."

Gabrielle moved her stare from Ronnie to Evan, who lowered the passenger window and said, "Hey, Gabby."

The three teenagers were all about the same age, but Brandy had heard that Gabrielle thought Evan wasn't cool enough to even talk to. "Call him," Gabrielle ordered Ronnie without taking her eyes off Evan. When she finally looked past him to Clint she added, "This better be okay, and you better take good care of her."

"Aye, aye, Captain," he answered with a brisk salute.

Gabrielle managed a little smile for him because Clint was cool.

Evan, not so much. His nose was too big and his neck was kind of long. He looked sort of like a scarecrow with hair that stuck out above his ears.

"Call him." Gabrielle pointed at Ronnie as she backed away from the SUV.

Ronnie swallowed hard and Gabrielle said loudly to Clint, "Drive safe," as Clint rammed the SUV into gear again.

Gabrielle turned toward the house. Sliding her phone from the back pocket of her cut-off denim shorts, she sauntered slowly toward the front door.

"Let's go," ordered Brandy.

"Bitch," muttered Evan admiringly. His gaze lingered on Gabrielle's butt cheeks in her tight cutoffs.

"Should I wait?" Clint turned to look directly at Ronnie. "In case you can't go."

"She *can* go!" Brandy glared at her brother. "Just drive!"

"I can go," Ronnie agreed. "I'll call my dad." She'd already reached into her bag and pulled out the cell phone she'd gotten for her birthday. She knew how to use it because it was identical to her father's. Still, she almost didn't call, knowing she would be in trouble either way. Jonas Quick didn't like being bothered at work, but he'd also made it clear he wanted to know where she was at all times. After a short debate with herself, she punched the buttons, then crossed her fingers and readied the lie.

She was put through to his desk phone, but luckily only heard his voice mail. With enthusiasm she said, "Hi, Dad, it's Ronnie. I'm with Brandy and Melissa and we're going to Brandy's house. Be back later. Bye. Love you!"

Evan half turned in his seat, smiling as she clicked off. "So, you're a liar."

"I didn't say *when* I was going to Brandy's. I just said I was going."

Evan snorted and sing-songed, "Aannnddd you're going to be a lawyer just like your dad."

Clint eased the SUV onto the street and muttered, "God, I hope Shana's there."

"Shana has big boobs," Brandy related to Melissa and Ronnie.

"Epic casabas," agreed Evan as they drove through the neighborhood.

"Epic?" Brandy snorted. "Big," she corrected.

Clint grinned and Mel's lips tightened, but Ronnie wasn't listening any longer as she stared sightlessly out the window. The bad feeling was pressing down on her and she had to take a couple of deep breaths, in and out. Luckily her friends were too excited to notice.

Staring out the window, not seeing the town give way to countryside, Ronnie was desperate to clamp down on her brain and keep the creeping dark from spoiling the moment as it had in the past. Her father hated it whenever she complained about the bad feeling coming over her, so she didn't anymore because everyone acted like she was crazy whenever she mentioned it. Worse yet, Dad seemed to blame Mom for it even though Ronnie's memory of her mother was that Winnie Quick was always singing or humming to her. It had really been nice. Soothing.

"You are not like your mother," Jonas would say in that warning voice, whenever Ronnie mentioned the oppressive sensation. "Whatever you're feeling, or seeing or whatever, it's not real."

"Mom saw things, too?"

"Your mother wasn't well and it killed her," he always snapped back, and then he would shut down. He'd been shut down for a while now. Wouldn't talk about Mom at all.

Over the years Ronnie had tried to talk to her Aunt Kat, who was Mom's sister and had taken care of Ronnie for a time after Mom died. But Aunt Kat would just hug her and tell her everything was going to be all right. Aunt Kat was the one who directed her to Patrice, but Ronnie couldn't really talk to the therapist, as Patrice seemed to only be interested in exploring Ronnie's emotions. Was she sad? Did she blame anyone for her mother's death? Did she think about death herself? Her questions just made Ronnie want to clap her hands over her ears and scream. If she tried to explain the pictures of the badness, they all looked at her as if she were crazy, so she just stopped. Not even confiding in Patrice.

Now the only people she confided in were Brandy and Mel and they kind of got quiet whenever she told them about her "dreams," so she limited her confessions to them, too. And she never mentioned that the dreams sometimes happened when she was awake . . . and that they sometimes came true. She kept that information to herself rather than have either of them thinking she was weird and risking their friendship.

Not worth it.

When Clint parked in the gravel-strewn lot at The Pond, the river and shoreline were already teeming with kids. There was hardly a free stretch of sand, but Ronnie spied a space that was barely big enough for their blanket and picnic basket right near the river's edge, in the shadow of a tall cliff. It meant they were going to have to walk over small, jagged stones to set up camp on the hard, bumpy ground. Still, it was just good to be here. The damp smell of the river filled her nostrils while the rush of the rapids upstream was nearly drowned out by the sounds of laughter and splashes and conversation.

Clint had carried three sand chairs from the back of the SUV and now he dumped them at their camp. Then, as if staking his claim, he threw down his T-shirt and stood in his green swim trunks near their blanket. He did stuff like mowing lawns and so his arms and chest were tan and strong.

Mel couldn't stop staring at him like he was a *god*, which really bugged Brandy. Ronnie totally understood. It was annoying. And Clint was always yelling at Brandy, telling her what to do, which made Ronnie want to yell back at him. Not that she needed to. Brandy could take care of herself. She always ignored her brother, and once while they were hanging out at Brandy's house, Clint had really pissed her off. Brandy even gave him the finger, which only served to make him see red.

Mel had been horrified, but Ronnie had been forced to bite her lip to keep from laughing. Clint had howled in outrage, then chased Brandy around their house. Brandy was quick, and clever, dashing away from him, keeping furniture between them until he calmed down. He never caught her, which was probably a really good thing.

Lately, though, the two of them had seemed to be getting along better, so that was why Clint had agreed to bring them all to the river today.

So now their camp was crowded against the big rocky cliff where the older kids ignored the signs not to jump off into the river. They always did anyway, as if leaping into the depths of The Pond was some secret rite of passage.

Clint's gaze lifted to the top of the rock face where a group of his friends were standing at the edge, ready to leap off. Someone had thrown a T-shirt over the sign that told everyone not to jump.

"Don't go up there," Brandy warned her brother. "Mom would kill you if you died."

"Well, then I would already be dead, wouldn't I?" Clint mocked.

"You'd be deader!"

"There is no such thing." He laughed and threw his sunglasses down on the blanket.

Brandy wasn't convinced. Through clenched teeth she said, "Clint, I mean it!"

"I'm not going up there." He made a "duh" face at her. "I'm getting paid to take care of you kiddies, but I don't have all day. You get an hour, then I'm taking you home."

"Two hours!" declared Brandy.

"Fuck it. Whatever."

Mel looked a little disturbed, her blond brow furrowing. "I wish he didn't swear," she said, looking after him longingly as he wandered back toward the base of the rock to stand next to Shana Lloyd of the big casabas. Mel, squinting, was pointing upward to the top of the rock ledge.

Ronnie followed the direction of Mel's finger and saw one of Clint and Evan's friends standing at the edge. "Heart" something, she thought his name was. He had dark hair that flopped over his forehead as he glanced down at Shana. They were boyfriend and girlfriend, at least that's what Ronnie had gathered from Clint and Evan's conversation.

"Don't let Clint's language bother you," Brandy advised Mel. "He always talks like that when I'm right." She grinned and wrinkled her nose. "And I'm right a lot."

The three of them unfolded their chairs and straightened the blanket as best they could over the rocks. Then they set up their extra cupcakes and opened the basket that was full of chips, 3 Musketeers candy bars, orange sections, apple slices and water bottles.

"Where's the cooler?" Brandy asked her brother.

Clint glanced back, muttered something under his breath and reluctantly left Shana's side to hike back to the SUV. Minutes later he lugged the cooler filled with sodas and juice boxes back to their makeshift camp, thumping the Igloo down on the ground beside them.

Before Brandy could utter thanks, Clint grinned wickedly and grabbed two of the cupcakes.

"Hey, wait—" Brandy said just as Evan, who'd been missing, suddenly appeared and snagged a couple more. Brandy shrieked at them, but they dashed away, grinning like goblins.

"Assholes," muttered Brandy, almost to herself, as Ronnie settled into her chair and glanced down at her one-piece where her nipples were kind of visible. Just barely. She felt her face flush in embarrassment and hoped no one else would notice. Her nipples had been growing lately and she didn't want them to show through.

Shifting in the chair, she wondered how Shana—who'd now moved to the base of the trail and was smiling up at all the guys, her breasts nearly spilling out of a tiny black swim bra—hid hers. Ronnie had examined herself in the mirror closely before they took off, and she'd thought she looked okay so far. Nothing *too* noticeable.

Brandy didn't have her problem. Her red two-piece from last year was a bit tight on her now, but she hadn't started developing at all.

Then there was Mel . . . Her hot pink one-piece couldn't disguise her booblets, which Brandy had pointed out a couple of times and which Mel didn't appreciate. At all.

Still, the three of them were besties. If they joined the notched pieces of silver dangling at the end of their three necklaces, they would fit neatly together to make a heart that spelled out BFF, one letter on each section.

The day they'd gotten their necklaces Ronnie had announced, "All for one and one for all. That's us. *The Three Musketeers!*"

"The what?" asked Mel.

"The Three Musketeers," Ronnie told her. "You know, the swashbucklers with swords and hats with feathers? Great friends. Out for big adventures!"

"Oh," said Mel, but she really hadn't been paying attention.

"It's a story," Ronnie went on. "They fight for honor."

Mel slid her gaze to Brandy who said firmly, "Three Musketeers is a candy bar."

"*And* a story. A story first," Ronnie responded just as firmly. "They named the candy bar later. My mom told me about it."

When Ronnie spoke about her mother, her friends always grew as quiet as they did whenever she mentioned her "dreams." She knew they felt uncomfortable around her because they had moms and she didn't. In truth, she didn't remember her mom telling her about *The Three Musketeers*; she'd seen pictures of her reading to her, and one of the books in the stack beside her was a kid's version of the story. Later on Ronnie had picked up the real deal from the library and though it was kind of hard to read, she'd gotten the gist of it.

That conversation with her friends had been about two years ago and since then, they'd made it a point to always bring 3 Musketeers candy bars with them on every adventure. Personally, it wasn't Ronnie's favorite treat, but in loyalty to her friends, she pretended to love the gooey chocolate bars whenever they were together, like today.

"Uh-oh," Brandy said.

Ronnie looked up just in time to see the "Heart" guy leap off the top of the cliff. She held her breath as he clamped his arms to his sides and directed his toes downward... falling, falling,

falling... until his body knifed into the water far below. She shuddered, glad to see his dark head break the surface, slightly entranced by his white smile as he flipped wet hair away from his face.

"I'd like to do that," said Brandy, watching as Heart swam toward the bank.

Ronnie glanced at her friend. "Don't."

"Yeah, don't," repeated Mel.

"His name's Heart?" asked Ronnie. "Like—?"

"Sloan H-A-R-T." Brandy seemed somewhat mesmerized by him. "He's Shana's boyfriend."

Ronnie looked back at Shana, who was flirting with the idea of going up the cliff. Sloan Hart picked his way across the stony beach and when he reached her, he swept her up into his arms. She squealed and laughed and pretended to slap at him but she was enjoying herself.

Sloan set Shana firmly on her feet away from the trail leading upward. She pretended to try and go around him, but he shook his head. He might be fooling around with her, but he was serious; he didn't want her to go up on the rock. That much was obvious. He said something to her that Ronnie couldn't catch and she lifted her hands and backed away kind of sexily.

Feeling like there was a dark pit way down in her stomach, Ronnie tore her gaze from them. Brandy and Mel were both staring off to the left where Clint and Evan were pushing each other, knocking shoulders a bit, both heading for the trail.

Sloan joined them. Like Clint he had a hard, strong body. Beside them, Evan looked like a bean pole.

Brandy suddenly shrieked. "DON'T GO UP THERE!"

"I'm not," Clint yelled back, goofing around with his friends. "Shut up, Hart," he said good-naturedly to whatever Sloan was saying. "Let her go if she wants to."

"You tell him!" yelled Shana, grinning.

"Hey, Shana. Show your tits!" Evan waggled his brows at her.

Shana immediately gave him the finger.

Sloan smiled, shook his head and worked his way up the

trail. There was a moment of hesitation, where Clint threw a glance their way and Evan looked like he might ditch his friends and stay with Shana, then both Clint and Evan charged up the trail after Sloan.

Oh. No.

"Asshole!" Brandy declared.

Ronnie sucked in a breath and searched for Sloan. She could only see the top of his head as he got closer to the top.

This was no good.

*Don't go in the water.*

That phrase. That warning. Heart thudding, she leapt to her feet, suddenly certain there was about to be an accident.

Brandy burst out, "He promised he wouldn't go up there!"

"Oh, Clint!" Mel's hands were at her mouth.

"We've got to stop them!" blurted Ronnie.

Brandy tore after her brother, hampered a little by the sharp stones beneath her flip-flops. Clint and Evan were already halfway up the trail by the time Brandy reached the base of the rock. Ronnie was right on Brandy's heels with Mel coming up behind.

Mel was echoing Brandy. "He said he wouldn't go up there! He said he wouldn't go up there! He said he wouldn't go up there!"

"Well, he did!" Ronnie threw over her shoulder.

They all charged up the dusty path. It was rocky and steep enough to steal their breath as they climbed frantically. "Wait for me!" Mel yelled.

Ronnie and Brandy didn't.

By the time they reached the crest Ronnie's chest was heaving, her thoughts a jumble. The sky stretched out before her, the river a green snaking swirl a dizzying, long drop below. Ronnie slowed and took in deep breaths while Brandy, at the cliff's rim, was already arguing with Clint, her face red, her body taut as she yelled at him. With one hand, she pointed toward The Pond far beneath them.

"Are you crazy?" she screamed. "You can't jump off! Something really, really awful could happen. Don't do it, Clint. Don't!"

Sloan was standing near, in a cluster of boys about the same age, all in swim trunks or cutoffs, all hooting and whistling and teasing Clint for getting yelled at by his little sister.

"You gonna take that?" one guy taunted.

"Shut up, Townsend," muttered Clint.

The guy he meant pointed to his own chest and mimed, "Who, me?"

Clint didn't appreciate any of it. "Get away from me, Brandy. Go back down before you hurt yourself!"

"You said you wouldn't come up here!" Brandy screamed. "I'm *telling*, Clint! I'm *telling*!"

"Tell away!" he roared, getting nose to nose with her. "Be a little snitch! I don't care!"

"Slow it down, Mercer," suggested Sloan. He looked like he might try to intervene as Mel finally reached the summit.

"Brother and sisterly love," remarked Evan with an exaggerated yawn.

"You're lucky you don't have a sister," Clint threw at Sloan, as if all the drama was his fault. Then to his sister, "Brandy. Goddamn it! Get off this cliff before I throw you off!"

"If you jump, I jump!" Brandy shot back. One of her legs was trembling, and Ronnie knew her well enough to see past the bravado to how scared she was.

But still, Brandy rarely backed down from a fight. Even a stupid one. "Brandy, come on," Ronnie coaxed. "Let's go back."

"Goddamn babies are coming up here," muttered one of the other guys, rolling his eyes toward Townsend and his other friends. They all chorused, "Yeah!"

"You said you wouldn't," Mel also reminded Clint in a quavery voice.

He threw up his arms. "Okay, fine. Fine! Let's all go back down the cliff!"

Relieved, Ronnie started to turn to go, Brandy and Mel behind her. But a flash of movement stopped her. Clint had suddenly whipped around, legs churning as he raced for the edge.

*No! Oh, God, no!*

Brandy shrieked and half-lunged for her brother. She gathered speed, kicking off her flip-flops as she ran after him.

Clint suddenly leapt into the air.

Brandy slipped at the edge. Flailing, she started to tumble off the cliff.

Ronnie and Mel screamed as one.

Sloan's hand shot out. He grabbed Brandy's arm, yanking her to safety, holding her fast. "Don't!" he warned as she struggled to get free. "Damn it," he muttered through gritted teeth. Still holding tight to Brandy, he shouted down at Clint, "You're an ass, Mercer! You hear me? An ass!"

"Yeah!" Evan seconded, peering over the edge. He tsk-tsked with his finger, staring downward.

"You can't tell me what to do!" Brandy snapped, trying to rip her arm back from Sloan.

He wouldn't let go.

"Where's Clint, man?" one of the other guys asked. He, too, was peeking over the edge downward, searching the water far below.

Evan, inching closer to the edge had grown sober. "I don't know," he said. "I can't see him."

Ronnie hurried forward. She forgot to be scared of the height because she was suddenly so scared for Clint. Frantically, she surveyed the river—the kids on rafts, the swimmers, but . . . but there was no sign of Clint. His head didn't surface, not beneath the rock. Not downriver. Not anywhere.

Her heart clutched.

The other boys, too, eyed the river. All the teasing and joking had stopped. Their faces paled. Their brows drew together.

"Where is he?" Brandy demanded, but she read their worried expressions. "No," she whispered, shaking her head, her ponytail swishing across her shoulders. "No . . . oh, no." Her eyes rounded and then she suddenly burst into tears.

Mel, too, was crying, starting to sniff loudly.

Ronnie just stood near the edge of the ledge and quivered from head to toe.

Evan kept straining to see, half bent forward, leaning over the precipice. Then as he looked over his shoulder, his foot slid in the dirt, his weight shifted and suddenly his arms started pinwheeling, his feet sliding perilously close to the edge.

*Oh, no!*

Sloan was still looking at Brandy. One of the other guys said something like "Whoa!" Without thinking Ronnie leapt forward and clawed for Evan's hand. His fingers surrounded hers, squeezing hard.

Someone—Sloan, maybe?—barked in fear at her. "Hey, stop! What the—?"

"Oh, fuck," Evan gritted out. For a moment he seemed to catch himself, but too late. Overbalanced, he tipped over the edge, seemingly in slow motion. Ronnie tried to wrench her hand free, but Evan held on with a death grip.

Her feet slid atop the rock, little pebbles loosened, released over the edge, sprinkling down, down, down like raindrops.

She felt someone reach for her, almost catch her by the hair . . . Sloan . . .

Then she was falling, falling, *falling* . . .

The wind whistled by her ears. Somewhere along that forever fall Evan released her hand. She heard a faraway voice telling her to knife in. Straightening, she made herself as narrow as possible, holding her arms down, pointing her toes, closing her eyes.

It seemed forever before she plunged into the river, the water closing over her head, the cold enveloping her. She opened her eyes but it was too murky and dark to see. She squeezed her lids tightly shut. Swallowed water. Couldn't hold her breath. She kicked but her legs wouldn't move. They felt wound up, caught in something. Panic was ice in her veins. *I can't breathe! I can't breathe!*

In a black distance, far away, she saw indistinct figures. Heard them arguing. Ronnie tried to speak but couldn't. She needed to talk to them, have them hear her. She needed help! The big darkness was coming toward her, fingers of it clawing forward.

*Don't go in the water.*

*I'm already in the water!* she wanted to scream at them, but were they even real? Was she even in the water? Where was she? It felt like she was floating.

*Am I dying?*

"Veronica!"

*Am I dying?*

A deep calm descended on her. *Yes*, she thought... *I'm dying. I'll die and then I'll be with Mom.*

The darkness slowly shifted to a blue haze. Someone was coming out of the haze toward her, a man, a man in a gray suit. His strong arms wrapped around her and he lifted her up. She was all in white and there were yellow roses and sunshine. He was whispering in her ear, telling her wonderful things... that he would be with her... that she was the one... she could smell the roses. It was beautiful and—

"VERONICA!"

She came to with a full body spasm at Mel's cry. Her eyes flew open and she stared into the blue sky above and the blasting, bright sun but there was something in the way. Some*one*. A dark shadow above her. Mel and Brandy were both screaming. It was dizzying. Someone was pounding on her chest, blocking the light, blowing into her mouth, pressing her into the sharp rocks beneath her back.

At The Pond... they were at The Pond... Her head was full of noise. It was TOO LOUD! Her chest hurt. She felt sick.

Her body convulsed and she coughed. The pounding stopped. Hands roughly turned her to one side and she threw up a flood of water. Over and over again. Retching violently.

The screaming changed to cheers.

"She's okay? She's okay?" That was Brandy.

"She's okay!" Mel repeated, crying with relief.

"I got him, I got him, I got him...!" a male voice suddenly yelled.

Clint... Clint's voice, Ronnie realized dully. She tried to focus. His voice was coming from somewhere beyond the shore, in the river. Her eyelids felt weighted down by stones, but she forced them open again and saw Clint dragging Evan's limp body out of the river. Others came to help him. All the guys who'd been on the rock cliff were now on the pebbled shore, a crowd of horrified onlookers surrounding them. The boys stretched Evan out beside her. His face was dead white. He didn't seem to be breathing.

Clint thunked his fist down on Evan's chest. Hard.

Ronnie felt woozy. Brandy was yelling. Mel's crying increased. Everyone's voices were thundering in her ears.

She realized Sloan was hovering over her, his attention now on Evan. He'd been the one to block out the sun, the one to save her, the one to pound on her chest and press his lips to hers as he blew in her mouth.

All as if in a dream—

With a rattling cough, Evan started choking and sputtering near her.

Ronnie could feel Sloan's relief, telegraphed from his body to hers. He turned to her again, gray eyes searching hers, his dark hair dripping water onto her cheeks.

"You okay?" he rasped.

Ronnie swallowed and tried to nod, though she wasn't okay, not really. But she would be. She would be. She would make herself be.

She forced herself not to cry. She should've listened to the warning. She should've known not to come to The Pond.

But the white dress, the candles, the kiss . . .

As Sloan glanced over at Evan, she announced, "I'm going to marry you," knowing it to be a fact.

Sloan shot her a quick, baffled look, but then his attention turned back to his friend. All around them there were snickers, chuckles, even a big guffaw. And it was catching. More laughter, lots and *lots* of laughter. From the "friends," the "bros." They were nervous, relieved, glad to have something else to think about.

*Thunk, thunk, thunk.* Clint pounded with more force on Evan's chest. She heard a *crack*, cartilage or bone.

She cringed.

The laughter died.

"Come on. Evan, come on!" Clint pushed rhythmically on Evan's chest, willing life into his friend.

Evan's head was turned in Ronnie's direction.

Slowly his eyes opened and he stared at her. Through her. A smile full of secrets crossed his face.

A shudder ran through her.

No one else seemed to notice.

She wanted to let everyone know that he was awake. She tried to speak but somehow couldn't.

"I'll take a turn," Sloan ordered Clint.

"Nah, I got it." Clint was determined.

Evan's eyes were wide and dark. Not their usual blue. He stared at Ronnie and silently said: *It should have been you, not me.*

Ronnie blinked. *Did* he say that? Did he? His lips hadn't moved. Or had they?

The darkness she'd felt came upon her again and it was suddenly everywhere. Engulfing her. She knew she was fading into unconsciousness and struggled to stay awake.

Evan's spirit rose outside of his body.

Ronnie watched it slowly dissipate in the air above him, all except that Cheshire cat grin.

The cold wrapped its arms around her, dragging her into its black depths.

She screamed and screamed and screamed as the darkness pulled her under.

# Chapter 1

**Twenty years later...**

*Hot, damp breath... panting... smell of wet fur... whining... scratching...*

*Ravaged hands... a body... a woman's body... lying in a clearing... and pounding, pounding, POUNDING!*

Ronnie came to on a gasp.

Blinking, disoriented, she realized she was standing in her kitchen, hand on the refrigerator handle.

And someone was slamming their fist against her apartment door.

How long had she been out? A minute? Two? Longer? Whenever she had a vision she lost time, the amount hard to measure. But she'd certainly been having a vision. The force of this one had been like a punch to the chest, which meant it might be real, and it took her a moment to "re-combobulate."

She took in a long, shaky breath and glanced out the window.

It was five o'clock at night, dark as a cauldron, and she was alone in the apartment, the unit she'd rented six months earlier when she and Galen had separated... after she'd had enough of his lies and he'd had enough of her weirdness. He'd married her because she was the boss's daughter and she'd married him because . . . God, she couldn't even remember and it had only been two years.

"I'm coming!" she yelled to the increased pounding. Sheesh. Everybody was so impatient these days.

She walked the six steps to the front door and cautiously pulled it open. On the other side was a white-faced, anxious-looking woman. Her dark hair was threaded with fine silver hair filaments, though she didn't look like she was much into her thirties. She wore a black rain jacket, no hood, beads of rainwater competing with the silvery strands. Her makeup was heavily applied, her dark eyes rimmed in black. One arm was straight down, locked to her side, the opposite hand reached up to touch her face as if suddenly wondering what she looked like.

"Veronica Quick?" she asked tensely.

"Yes?"

Familiar. She was so familiar, but Ronnie didn't think she knew her. Behind her rain was pouring from the skies in sheets and a cold burst of wet December air swept inside the apartment, an eager, uninvited guest. The woman reached inside her jacket with the hand that had touched her face, pulled out a large, manila envelope and thrust it forward. Ronnie's hand came up automatically as the woman slapped the envelope down hard, declaring, "You've been served."

*Galen beat me to the punch.*

Ronnie was almost impressed by his speed. She suspected she was holding divorce papers and couldn't decide if her anger was at her soon-to-be ex because he was such an all-around shit, or because she'd been cheated out of serving him first. Probably a little of both. Her gaze dropped briefly to the envelope, then upward to the deliverer, who was eyeing Ronnie as if she were memorizing her face.

The woman looked like someone she should know, but Ronnie wondered if that were true. She'd experienced the consequences of engaging with people who might have heard something about her psychic ability and were seeking her out because of it. Yes, her "gift" was known around River Glen, maybe all of Oregon and beyond, for all she knew, as was the fact that Veronica Quick was a certified nutcase. Didn't matter to some that she worked hard to pretend and deny this extra ability since more often than not it got her into trouble.

Ronnie tried to place the woman. She looked like someone from one of her visions, in that watery sort of way that always irked her. If you're given a gift, shouldn't it be more reliable? Something you could actually *use*?

*Bark, bark, bark.* Ronnie turned to her right, recognizing the sound as the dog from her dream, though she didn't see it.

"What?" the woman on her doorstep demanded.

"Nothing. The dog."

"I don't like dogs. Keep it away from me," she muttered, then turned on the heels of her black Doc Martens and stomped toward the stairs that led to the parking lot. Ronnie watched her progress through the incessant downpour. She was bareheaded and apparently oblivious to the rain. In the lot below, she splashed through the shallow puddles on the tarmac, the overhead lights marking her progress as she headed for a gray Ford Explorer. Ronnie noted the license plate, a habit, and as soon as she was back inside, wrote it down on a piece of scratch paper.

She might be considered a psychic but she could forget data as well as the next person.

She finally looked down at the now wet envelope in her right hand. It was from a different law firm than Tormelle & Quick. No surprise there; it was from Galen's new firm. He'd sexted too many women online while at Tormelle & Quick, which had caused his firing. Most of the firm believed it was because he'd cheated on her, but the sexting was what really chafed her father. Jonas felt betrayed as he'd initially been Galen's champion. Ronnie felt he'd wanted to unload responsibility for her, even while always telling her what he wanted her to do with her life.

"Time to go back to law school," Jonas had told her when she and Galen had separated, which, as ever, had irked Ronnie.

Maybe it was a function of her father's overbearing plans that had made her deaf to his pleas. She liked being an assistant at the firm. It kept those who felt uneasy over her extra "ability" feeling safe and maybe a little superior. As long as the boss's daughter with her strange woo-woo stayed out of the legal limelight, she could be tolerated.

An ear-splitting squeal of brakes from the highway rang through the apartment. It came from behind the complex. Ronnie froze, listening hard at the drawn-out shriek from the tires.

*CRASH!!!*

Tossing down the envelope unopened, she leapt across the living room toward the small rear balcony of her apartment, throwing open the sliding door and stepping onto the slick, wooden deck boards. Rain splashed onto her head from a listing gutter and ran down the front of her shirt and jeans into her black ankle boots. She leaned over the railing, swiping moisture from her face. The highway below was known for speeders clipping each other. Sporadic serious accidents occurred. She could smell the wet bark and earth as she peered through the bare tree limbs of the deciduous trees that ran down the hill toward the highway. Cockeyed headlights flooded the area where a pileup of cars was already stopping traffic. Vehicles were every which way. Crumpled metal flashed under the myriad headlights.

There was a gray SUV turned sideways. Like the one her messenger had driven.

Rain poured down from the skies.

*Shit . . .*

Racing back inside, Ronnie swept wet strands of hair from her forehead. She grabbed her coat and cross-body purse and racewalked to her own SUV, a dark blue Ford Escape. Slamming the door, she pushed the button to engage the engine and the Escape roared to life. She drove directly into the traffic jam, which was already backing up, nearly stopping. There was enough room for vehicles to still creep around on the shoulder and she followed after them, much to the fury of the drivers stuck in the inside lanes who honked madly at the moving cars.

Sirens sounded in the distance as she followed the slow-moving line. When the makeshift lane suddenly stopped, she pulled as far off onto the shoulder as possible. In front of her the road was completely blocked by the mangled cars. Rain blew over them in curtains as she stepped out, bending her head against the wind as she pushed forward.

A man holding a cell phone to his ear stood outside a red Tesla. "Get back in your car! I called 911!" he yelled.

"I know her," said Ronnie, pointing to the gray Explorer. Its front end was demolished. The woman who'd served her papers must have slammed her foot to the accelerator as soon as she hit the highway to cause that much damage.

"Ma'am, get back in your car. It's not safe."

As if the gods heard his words a small pickup zigzagged around the stopped cars, suddenly racing toward them, clipping one car and taking out the front bumper of another as it aimed forward like a bullet. Tesla-guy grabbed Ronnie and practically threw them both toward the deep ditch running along the highway. She slid into icy water, but somehow remained upright, her boots drowning in the small running stream that had developed from the rain. She sank ankle-deep into the mud.

At the last minute the driver had yanked his steering wheel in order to miss Ronnie's Escape—thank the gods—but it plowed into the back of a white Prius that was still trying to inch forward in traffic. Ronnie could see that the woman inside the Prius was thrown against the dash, then back again. She lifted a hand to the blood forming from a gash on her forehead and started screaming, the sound tinny, barely audible, behind her windows.

*Bark, bark, bark, bark!*

Ronnie glanced around, wondering which car had the dog.

Tesla-man said, "Fuck me," under his breath, releasing his hold on Ronnie before climbing back up the incline to the road. Ronnie scrunched her feet inside her boots to increase her grip as she tried to pull each foot out of the mucky stream. Slowly, the boots released with a sucking noise and she worked her way up the slope as well.

The two cars that had apparently created the initial crash were locked together like two bull rams, squaring off. The drivers were outside, staring at the mess while the icy December rain bore down.

The woman process server managed to wrench open the door of her gray SUV and climbed outside. She swayed for a bit in the rushing wind. She, too, had a gash across her forehead and regarded Ronnie dazedly. She'd opened her coat and her large breasts were already drenched with rain.

"You all right?" Ronnie asked, though clearly she wasn't.

She looked around as if she hadn't heard. She was—

*Shana. From The Pond all those years ago. Shana Lloyd and Sloan Hart.*

That's why she seemed so familiar. She was Sloan Hart's high school girlfriend. Now a process server? Twenty years on she'd aged hard.

And she was about to walk into traffic, while the drivers of the first two cars were still just standing in the rain and the sound of sirens' wails grew closer.

Shana took a step toward the road.

"Stop!" Ronnie grabbed for her. Missed her arm, but Shana seemed to hear because she suddenly froze, though her legs wobbled. She turned her head to look at Ronnie, her eyes moving like they were in a game of marbles.

Ronnie suddenly felt a flood of emotion. Desire and love and sadness. Coming from Shana. A full-on sensory rush that narrowed into a picture of Shana in a wood-paneled office, kneeling beneath a desk, Galen in the chair with her head bobbing up and down as she pleasured him, his head thrown back, eyes closed, his hands in her hair. Shana . . . and *Galen*?

Ronnie saw Shana running her fingers through Ronnie's soon-to-be ex's prematurely gray hair, her head thrown back, mewling cries issuing from her parted lips. Or . . . what?

Ronnie blinked against the rain.

The vision blew apart like fairy dust. Instead Shana stood in front of Ronnie, wet and bedraggled, blood running down her cheek from the gash on her head.

Immediately Ronnie wasn't sure of what she'd seen. The vision didn't have that sensation of something creeping out of the dark to leave its ominous message. This one was more... indistinct. Something maybe true, maybe not. The visions that were real had heft to them.

Ronnie had visited a psychic once herself, kind of as a joke, kind of as a tutorial. She'd been curious about what the seer would say, which had been that Ronnie would have one child with the love of her life. However, the psychic Ronnie had seen had since been mentioned in a lawsuit in which another client, a woman, had learned in the session that she would live a long and healthy life. Within six months that client had died in a mountain climbing accident.

"Do you see her?" Shana asked.

"What? Who?"

She took another step forward, walking directly in front of a car that was edging around the mess of traffic, just as that driver hit the gas. Ronnie screamed at the same moment the driver slammed on his brakes.

Untouched, nevertheless Shana collapsed in a heap onto the wet and muddy shoulder.

Ronnie jumped forward but Tesla-man was faster and was at Shana's side in a flash. He bent over her as Shana lay on the ground, staring up at the sky, rain running down her head as people, victims and onlookers, gathered around.

Then the scene changed.

For a heartbeat the woman lying in the clearing from Ronnie's earlier vision was superimposed over Shana's body. Familiar... so familiar. And somewhere a dog was barking.

Ronnie held her breath. In her mind's eye, she saw the two women as one, a weird vision that was so damned real. She half expected the vision to play out, to say something to her, to *mean* something. But no. It remained unchanged. Nothing happened.

In a blink, it was gone—the woman from the clearing having vanished.

Shana was back to looking like Shana. Not moving. Quiet.

Tesla-man was leaning over her. The dog had traded barking for howling. Ronnie's heart galloped as if it were trying to escape her rib cage.

"She's breathing," said Tesla-man. "She's alive! Come on, lady. You're okay. Come back! Can you hear me? You're okay."

And still the dog howled incessantly.

"Can someone help that dog?" Ronnie muttered, glancing around at the various knots of people who were either in the accident or had stopped to help. "Maybe it's trapped."

"Hey, we got a real situation here. This woman needs help." Tesla-man gave Ronnie a scrutinizing glare before turning his attention to the fast approaching rescue vehicles.

"I know. But it sounds like it's in pain."

His dark eyes clapped back to her. "I don't hear any dog, ma'am."

It was Ronnie's turn to stare. "You don't?"

"No, ma'am." His eyes narrowed as he studied her, assessing. "Are you all right?"

"I wasn't in the accident. I'm here to help," Ronnie assured him, but was starting to feel that sense of unease that crept over her when she couldn't tell what was real and what wasn't. It happened rarely. Most of the time when she surfaced from a vision she was fully aware again. Now, though, Tesla-man was regarding her in that way that said they were experiencing two different realities.

And the pained yowls of the dog had stopped. Ronnie swallowed hard, trying to concentrate on what was really happening. The wail of the sirens cut off as if strangled as the ambulances arrived on scene. The moment their tires stopped, paramedics leapt from their vehicles to take charge.

Thank God.

Still wondering about the vision, Ronnie waited while Shana was tucked into an ambulance, and then returned to her Escape. Drenched and shivering, rain still running down her face, she thought of the dead woman in the clearing. The black void was sending her a message that she wasn't getting.

Who was she?

What had happened to her?

Why had her image melded with Shana's as she lay on the cold, wet shoulder of the road?

And what, if anything, should Ronnie do next?

There was no clear answer.

*The night was dark and cold. The cabin was a little more than a lean-to shelter these days. The woman shivered and counted her many sins. She'd made mistakes, vast mistakes as it turned out. She wasn't good at reading human nature and it was going to kill her... maybe... if she didn't think of a plan of escape.*

*The dog whined softly and she pulled it close. It wasn't her dog but she'd taken it with her for protection.*

*A chilly wind clattered against the cabin, trembling the walls. She could smell dirt and damp weeds, saw tendrils reaching from beneath the rotting floorboards. She couldn't stay here long. She had to move... run... She'd racked her brain. Who could she call to help her? Dear God, there was no good answer.*

*The only person, and it was an insane longshot, the longshot of longshots, was Veronica.*

*Clutching the dog, burying her face in its black fur, she sent a message into the universe:*

*I'm in trouble. He's coming to kill me. I don't want to die. Help me!*

*Was that a car engine? She raised her head in alarm, heart galumphing. She didn't move. The dog growled low in its throat and she quietly shushed it. They'd bonded in their short time together and the animal complied, softly snuffling her ear.*

*She couldn't hear the engine now.*

*Was it real?*

*Had someone cut it?*

*Were those footsteps?*

*Panicked, she strained to listen.*

The door of the cabin had a latch on the inside.
Not much to keep her safe. But something.
And yet...
To her horror she watched as a small stick was inserted beneath the latch and pushed upward, releasing it with a small metallic click.

She trembled. Her hand moved to clasp the rock she'd placed beside herself. If the dog couldn't save her, it would be her last defense.

The dog was quivering all over. Its skin sliding beneath her other hand, beneath its soft fur. The door opened and a black figure stood there. "You called?" said a voice filled with real concern.

Surprise flooded her. Then shock. Full on shock. "You...? You... found me?"

The dog started barking. Sharp. Insistent. Barking and barking.
Slam!
The world went black.

The next thing she knew she was lying face up in a clearing. A faint moon glowed behind a cloud, a momentary respite from the rain. She wanted that rain now. Desperately. Wanted its cold wash on her face. Needed it to clear her mind. She envisioned diamond droplets falling on her face, rinsing all the bad stuff away.

Then hands circled her throat. Gloved hands. "Why?" she asked but it might have been in her mind.

The last thing she remembered was the frenzied barking of the dog, somewhere far away...

# Chapter 2

Ronnie woke on a strangled gasp, the fragmented dark images of a nightmare slipping away even as she tried to mentally grab them, unsure of their import. She took a couple of deep breaths, coming into focus. Had she seen the woman in the clearing again? It felt like it, but she couldn't quite put it together.

*Tell the police about her...*

She snorted at herself as she got out of bed and headed for the shower. Oh, sure. That had worked so well last time when she'd showed up at the River Glen Police Department to warn them that Edmond Olman was going to attempt to murder his ex-wife and they'd better put him under surveillance, maybe even arrest him on some dummied-up charge, just to keep him from killing her.

Detective Elena Verbena had regarded her soberly and, to her credit, had increased patrol cars to drive by the Olman house, but it hadn't helped because Olman had already beaten his wife within an inch of her life. She very nearly died in the days in between the time Ronnie warned the police about him and her unconscious body was discovered.

Olman was now in jail and Ronnie had been grilled long into

the night by River Glen's finest. Only her father's charge to her rescue had gotten her released. They were sure she knew something more, was somehow involved. She'd heard the incredulity in the voice of one of cops who'd interviewed her at the time. "You say a vision just came to you?" Needless to say, the River Glen P.D. had come to view Veronica Quick as someone to be wary of. The wife moved back in with family in Minnesota and Ronnie's uneasy relationship with the police grew uneasier.

Galen was no help at all. He'd never believed much in her abilities and his lack of coming to her aid was another reason the marriage failed so quickly. After that Ronnie had doubled down on her decision to keep her "possible idiopathic neural abnormality" (idiopathic meaning no discernible cause) to herself.

As she was getting ready for work today, she called Dawn at the front desk and left a message that she would be late. She planned to check on Shana before heading to the office. Ronnie had watched her being loaded into an ambulance and felt oddly connected to her.

Now, thinking of how the dead woman's image had been superimposed over Shana's face, Ronnie's mind flicked to another recent bout of extrasensory information that had taken her over.

Barely weeks ago she'd seen trouble coming for P.I. Jesse James Taft, who'd been in the line of sight of two murderous females aiming for his demise.

Ronnie had perceived a mental image of Taft's sister, his *dead* sister, Helene to be precise, who just happened to be his personal muse, and one he apparently saw from time to time himself. Whether Taft actually did see her was yet to be determined, but her "ghost" was someone he talked to.

Ronnie, on the other hand, had gotten a very clear message from Helene that Taft was in danger. Serious danger. When Taft recognized that Ronnie had actually *seen* his sister, he'd been gobsmacked. He hadn't believed it and consequently hadn't listened to Ronnie as carefully as he should have.

Taft was so grounded in reality that the idea Helene could be something more than just a memory was anathema. He'd even thought the times he'd envisioned her were just his mind playing tricks on him.

There was only so much Ronnie could do to explain her "gift," especially since she didn't really understand it herself. She had passed on the message from Helene, that Taft was in danger and left him to deal with it.

That he'd nearly been killed and her vision had proved true probably left him with more questions than answers. She didn't know because she'd avoided Taft ever since, not wanting to have a post mortem on exactly what she'd seen, felt and known was going to happen to him. He was just the latest who'd sparked a vision.

Until the dead woman in the clearing.

After checking her black slacks, jacket and white collarless blouse in the mirror, she glanced out the window. Gray clouds hung low in the sky, but the rain was holding off for the moment. Her boots were sitting by the back door, still caked with half-wet muck, so she slipped on black flats, then took the boots outside, knocking them against the rail that ran along this second level above the parking lot.

Angel Vasquero, Ronnie's neighbor, was already leaning against that rail in a pair of low-hung jeans and a gray T-shirt, barefoot. He watched the little flakes of mud from her boots dropping down to the parking lot below, then eyed her with a slight smile. They didn't know each other well, but the vibe he gave off was always lazy amusement.

"Hey, pretty lady."

Ronnie gave him a look. Angel worked hard to give her the impression that he was an idle Hispanic just hanging around between gigs, but there was a lot more going on with him than he wanted her to know. She suspected he was either an informant for the police, or a cop himself, because he'd appeared shortly after she'd rented her apartment. This had been a few weeks after she'd related her suspicions about Edmond Olman to the police, so it was a pretty good bet there was something there. His living next to her was more than mere coincidence.

Angel lackadaisically gestured toward her boots. "Looks like you ran into some trouble."

"Something like that."

His dark hair was slicked back, still wet from an apparent shower. "How's the lawyering going?"

"I'm not a lawyer. I'm an assistant." As she'd explained to him before.

"Whose old man owns the place."

"Still an assistant."

She wished she would be hit with some kind of mental background on him, but that's not how her gift worked. She had no control over when and how something from the dark void would creep over her, replacing what her eyes saw with an inner screen. The more intense the image, the more credible the vision. Sometimes, if she closed her eyes, let herself relax, made a point of opening up her mind . . . sometimes she could coax it forward. Sometimes . . . not often.

And sometimes what she saw was utter bullshit.

"You know Daria Armenton?" Angel asked now.

"Yes, I do," Ronnie said, in some surprise.

Daria Armenton was one of the heirs to a fortune of the newly deceased Frank Rollberson, who'd bought certain stocks in the nineties that had increased in value nearly twenty-five times, leaving him a very rich man with no children. Daria was the young Hispanic woman who'd taken care of Rollberson for the last ten years or so and she was being sued by Rollberson's myriad shoestring relatives who'd only received small amounts and felt Daria's piece belonged to them, too. Rollberson's estate lawyer, Martin Calgheny, was with Tormelle & Quick and had asked Ronnie to attend the reading of the will, which she had several months earlier.

"She's my cousin," Angel informed her. "She's being hassled. Some lawyer's coming after her."

Had she been wrong about Angel? She didn't think so . . . but . . . ?

"She might need someone to defend her," he added.

"She should talk to Martin Calgheny. He's the one who handled the distribution of the estate. Martin would be best to find someone to repre—"

"Daria said you were there, too, though," he interrupted, straightening, suddenly all business. "She came by the other day, saw you, remembered you. I told her I'd talk to you."

"I'm not a lawyer," Ronnie repeated. "But I'll talk to Martin."

"Will you?" Angel's dark eyes said he doubted that she would.

"Yes. I will," she said firmly, then headed down the stairs to her SUV.

River Glen General Hospital's main parking lot was nearly full when Ronnie pulled in and she had to circle around and squeeze into a spot that made it hard to open her door. She managed to climb out without too much car dirt transferring to her jacket, then hurried around the puddles to the front doors, which slid open as she approached.

She asked to see Shana Lloyd and was directed to an elevator to the fourth floor. She'd had a lie all ready on her tongue, planning to say she was a family friend and Shana's lawyer, but she didn't need to use it. She was actually a good liar, having been forced to cover up her occasional lapses that made everyone uncomfortable. Far easier than trying to explain she was merely "lost in the psychic moment." She might have been able to pull that off if her predictions were always accurate, but since that wasn't the case . . . lying . . .

On the fourth floor, the elevator doors opened and Ronnie faced a nurse in light blue scrubs and a low ponytail who was waiting to enter. She netted a small smile from the woman who barely glanced at her before trading places with Ronnie and heading into the elevator. The doors had closed behind her before Ronnie's brain clicked into gear.

*Brandy.*

Ronnie quickly looked back at the elevator's blank doors, but Brandy's car was already moving downward. She should've recognized the dark ponytail, the intent look Brandy wore most times.

*You didn't recognize Shana at first.*

Well, that was true, but she hadn't known Shana all that well, whereas Brandy . . .

One thing was for certain: It was fast becoming old home week. She hadn't seen Brandy Mercer since they were in high school and even then their elementary-school friendship had turned into little more than an acquaintanceship in their upper grades. She was aware Brandy had become a nurse, but she hadn't known she was back in River Glen. The last she'd heard, which was admittedly a while ago, Brandy had been living in Arizona. And Mel . . . she'd gotten married to some guy in tech and moved to the Bay Area for a while, she thought.

Shana was alone when Ronnie entered, pressed up against pillows, awake and almost as pale as the white pillowcase and bandage that ran over the gash on her forehead and covered her left eyebrow. Her breasts pressed against the hospital gown. Ronnie had a moment of recalling the image she'd had of her kneeling in front of Galen's chair, but pushed it aside. Galen was history. Her pride might be bruised that he'd only chosen her because she was Jonas Quick's daughter, but hadn't she really suspected that all along at some level? If she really wanted to drill down on it, she would find she'd wanted to get married and Galen had crossed her path at the right time . . . and, lame as it was, one small reason she'd wanted to wed was to abolish that damn prediction she'd made about marrying Sloan Hart.

She scowled at the thought as Shana gazed up at her blankly.

"You're Veronica Hillyard," she said, as if they'd just met.

"Veronica Quick," Ronnie corrected. "You got it right the first time. Hillyard's my soon-to-be ex's name."

A bit of color swept into Shana's cheeks. Guilt, maybe, over her intimate knowledge of Galen? If that vision was accurate?

"You're the psychic," she stated.

"I'm an assistant in my father's law firm," she corrected.

"And psychic."

"Not completely accurate." If she could count the times

she'd had to say that... "I've had some... success in predicting things. But it's more about studying human nature than any real ability." *What a load of crap.* She sounded like she was launching into a TED Talk. But it was still easier than admitting she occasionally had episodes, fugue states, lost time... whatever...

Luckily, Shana had lost interest. "Looks like I'm going to be okay. They were worried about my head. I am having a little trouble remembering things, but I remember being at your apartment."

"Serving me divorce papers."

She grimaced, then sucked a bit of air between her teeth at the pain that moving those muscles in her face apparently gave her. "Yeah."

"I heard the crash after you left my door and I went to investigate. You collapsed while we were talking at the crash site. I wanted to stop by and make sure you were okay."

She blinked. "We were... talking at the crash site?"

"You don't remember?"

"No..." She carefully reached a hand up to her face to trace the white bandage.

"You took quite a hit," Ronnie commiserated, knowing that even without a blow to the head it sometimes took time to recall things that happened during extreme stress.

"I remember... being mad." Her fingers dropped from the bandage to pluck at the white covers of her bed sheets.

"Being mad?"

"Being mad about everything." Her gaze grew belligerent. "Things turned out for you, didn't they? But they sure didn't for me. That's the way it always is, isn't it? The rich get richer. The rest of us... eat shit. But you wouldn't know because your daddy's a big deal."

Ronnie felt a spurt of annoyance but held it back. "My *father* is part owner of the law firm where I work. We all have something that's not always perfect." Twice in one morning her relationship to her father had come into play. She felt the urge to explain that she and Jonas really didn't get along, how she was sick of him tinkering in her life, how she'd dropped out of law school primarily to rebel, how she felt he was trying to relive his own life through hers. Never mind that she was "only hurting yourself." She'd heard that one more than a few times, too.

"I was happy to serve you divorce papers." She lifted her chin a bit. "I did it as a favor to Galen."

"You know him well?"

She seemed to collect herself. "He's an asshole. Sorry. I know he's your husband."

"Something we agree on." Had she got it wrong about Galen and Shana? She was glad she hadn't said anything on the subject.

Shana shot her a sideways look. "What are you doing here?"

*I don't really know.* "As I said, just wanted to make sure you were okay."

Unbidden, a recollection of Shana and Sloan Hart came to mind. It was around the time the two of them were graduating high school. Ronnie had been in middle school and the year was just ending. She was with her father and they'd just pulled into the parking lot of the River Glen Grill. Shana and Sloan were standing by his car and Shana was crying, mad crying, ugly crying, looking up at Sloan as if he'd utterly betrayed her. Ronnie had stared out the passenger window at them, eager for a glimpse. River Glen High's hot couple. Miserable. She'd certainly felt a bit of schadenfreude at seeing the supposed lovebirds in a big fight. Then Shana hauled off and slapped Sloan, right in front of Ronnie's eyes, and she'd gasped aloud. That wasn't okay!

Sloan didn't react apart from a thinning of his lips. He turned away and immediately Shana ran after him, grabbing for his arm, begging for him to, "Look at me! Look at me!"

Jonas had been getting out of the car at that moment and missed the scene entirely, except for Shana's screaming pleas. "What's going on there?" he asked, looking around, but Ronnie had whipped around the car and placed herself in front of him, deliberately blocking her father's vision of the scene.

"I don't know." A breakup of some kind, she thought—hoped?

Jonas made a disparaging sound. Though he didn't say it, she could read a snide—*Teenagers*—in his expression as he strode toward the restaurant, Ronnie on his heels.

Ronnie had glanced back before she followed her father inside, but Sloan and Shana had disappeared into his car.

*A lot of years since then*, she thought now.

"You're the one who said she was going to marry Sloan Hart," said Shana.

Clearly it didn't amuse Shana, even after all this time. "Yes, unfortunately. And I've gotten a lot of grief about it over the years."

"Really."

"Yep."

"So did Sloan."

"I was ten. It was just a dumb moment."

"Yeah, sometimes those stick with you." Shana looked away. "Does Galen know?"

"Come on. It's not worth knowing about."

"But does he know? I just was wondering, if that's why he pursued me."

"He pursued you?"

"That's what it feels like. We met at a bar. I was with friends and I swear he knew who I was already. He said he was married to Veronica Quick, the psychic. I didn't tell him about that day at The Pond, but now that I think about it, I think he knew all along. He wanted to"—her dark eyes swept upward—"get to you."

Ronnie didn't like the sound of that. It was too . . . petty . . . and weird. Did Galen know about what she'd said to Sloan? She'd never mentioned it. She'd told him about nearly dying at The Pond, but she'd left out the part about Sloan because it was pointless and had embarrassed her.

"We're all just lucky we survived," she said.

"It bothered Sloan. I mean, really. We all teased him . . . well,

I didn't think it was so funny, but his friends did. And then there was Evan."

Evan. He'd survived the trauma of the fall, but afterwards was confined to a wheelchair. Ronnie could remember everything that had happened that day in excruciating detail—her embarrassing blurt about marrying Sloan, Evan's near-death experience that had stolen his ability to walk, her own heart-stuttering fall, and the laughter and jeers after the marriage prediction—it was as if it were outlined in her mind in black Sharpie.

"He was never the same afterwards," Shana said matter-of-factly.

Ronnie nodded. "I think Evan's a whiz on the computer. That's kind of what he said, when I saw him—"

"Not Evan," Shana cut in and rolled her eyes as if Ronnie was a complete idiot. "*Sloan*. Right from that moment at The Pond. He was never the same. *We* were never the same after that day. And everything went to shit after that. You know he's a policeman now? He's a detective, happily married to that—well, I don't know her. Her name's Tara. They met when he was working in Los Angeles."

"I thought he was divorced."

"Really?" She perked up. "Where'd you hear that? Is that new?"

"I don't know if it's even true. Just something I heard." Ronnie backpedaled. She was getting in way too deep with Shana over a secret crush on Sloan that should have died out years before.

Unexpectedly, Shana's eyes suddenly filled with tears. "I'm . . . just getting by, and that's why I let Galen talk me into serving you. I'm sorry."

"No need to be. Here." Ronnie leaned over and grabbed a tissue from the box on the rolling table beside the bed, handing it to her. Shana just held it in a limp hand, her eyes focused on the past.

"Evan told me it was because of what you said. Everybody laughed so hard when you said it. It was so . . . just so stupid, but it bothered Sloan a lot. All of a sudden he didn't want to hang with us anymore."

"That's not because of me. That's... I don't know what you're thinking but that's too ridiculous. Your class was horrified about what happened to Evan. He nearly died that day. It was totally traumatic for anyone who was there. I was barely even aware of what was going on. We all were all traumatized and—"

"We never really broke up, you know. Sloan and me. We fought, but... we never really ended it. But then high school was over and he was just gone. If he really divorced Tara, I sure would like to see him."

"Shana, I don't know if they're divorced. Don't trust what I said."

"I'll ask Evan. He should know."

"You're still friends?"

"Yeah." She made a face, felt the pain again, sucked air. "Damn it," she whispered. "Did you know he's in a wheelchair?"

"Yes."

"He hit his head or something on a submerged rock. We talk sometimes... He looks out for me some. We commiserate. Two losers, I guess." She sighed.

"I don't believe that."

Ronnie had run across Evan a couple of times through the intervening years and knew he lived in an apartment complex on the south side of River Glen, a nice place with a pool, which he used for physical therapy, or at least he had. She didn't know if he still resided there. Sloan had moved on long ago. Someone in the law firm had mentioned he was with Portland P.D., but that, too, was news from a few years back.

"They want to do more tests on me," Shana complained, moving uncomfortably beneath the sheets. "I just want to get out of here."

"They want to make certain you're okay and that your collapse was a onetime thing."

"What collapse?" She regarded Ronnie with vague alarm,

which was probably echoed on Ronnie's own face as they'd already gone over this. "What?" she demanded.

Ronnie dodged the direct question and said, "They'll send you home when they're sure you're okay."

There was something vaguely exotic about Shana even now, even with deep lines on her face that seemed like they belonged to someone much older than herself.

Ronnie explained further about how Shana had gone down at the crash site, practically falling at her feet.

"I'm sorry," Shana said again, when Ronnie finished.

Ronnie nodded. Time to put their shared history back in the past where it belonged and head to the office. She was probably already going to be late if she got going. Not that anyone paid much attention to when the boss's daughter showed up. She couldn't decide whether that was a good thing or a bad thing. Maybe she should care that they just assumed she could do whatever she wanted. Jonas certainly didn't feel she had free rein. He was, and always had been, very specific about what he did and didn't want from his daughter.

"Do you ever see Sloan?" Shana blurted as Ronnie shifted toward the door.

"I don't even know him, Shana," she answered truthfully.

"What about Clint? You were friends with his sister, right?"

"Brandy and I were friends in elementary school."

"Not anymore?"

"School was a long time ago."

"I thought you might still be connected to them. I'd like to get in contact with Sloan again."

"Well, as you said . . . Evan," Ronnie pointed out.

"He'll razz me about wanting to see Sloan, and I don't feel strong enough to take it."

"Well, I can't help you there. I'll look over the divorce papers and talk to Galen. Thanks for bringing them to me," she added a bit awkwardly.

"He used to work at your dad's firm, and I knew you were there, so . . . I said I'd do it. Bring the papers to you."

"Okay." Ronnie wanted to just edge out the door. She was already regretting stopping by.

"I always kind of thought you were the enemy," she threw out in a rush. "So, I listened to Galen."

"Your enemy? Why? You can't... this can't go back to that day at The Pond...?"

"You ruined my life with those five little words."

Ronnie snorted. There was no way, *no way*, any of that could matter to anyone but herself. "Come on."

"It's true. And by the way, your husband's a real piece of work. He says you're a crazy bitch. Like... *Cray. Zee.* Psychic weirdo."

That, she believed. Galen was a name-caller. Something she'd learned after their marriage. Feeling her temperature rise, she teetered with the urge to lean in to the *Cray. Zee.* She would love nothing more than to pop out with some amazing nugget of information from Shana's own past to impress her with awe-inspiring psychic skills. Give her some dire prediction about her future. Freak her out with words of caution and symbols of death.

But... nothing good ever came of fooling around with her uncertain psychic skills. If she wanted to be believed... and the vision of the dead woman in the clearing was definitely something she wanted to be believed... then she had to rise above Shana's baiting words.

"You never got with Sloan?" Shana asked now, really looking at Ronnie.

"You're kidding."

"I just thought that, after your prediction, you'd follow him around."

"Why is this even a conversation?"

"Okay, well, I get why you're getting a divorce."

"Galen's all yours," Ronnie said lightly.

"I just told you what I think of him."

But was that the truth? "Glad it looks like you're going to be okay," she said, slipping through the door and into the outer hallway.

# Chapter 3

Ronnie drove into the basement lot beneath her father's law office building, a four-story brick structure with a garage built into the hillside at the rear of the building, the visitors' parking spilling from the covered back lot into the open air like some giant gray tongue. She managed to find a parking spot, selecting a space near the stairwell, then as the engine cooled and ticked, she took a moment to collect her thoughts.

The manila envelope Shana had handed Ronnie was now lying on the passenger seat. Heaving a sigh, Ronnie reached for it. Might as well see what it said.

Opening the flap, she pulled out the thin stack of papers. She flipped through and saw Galen's signature already on the bottom with a flourish. He had a tendency to overstate his position on everything. That was another thing that had gotten him in trouble at Tormelle & Quick: his ego. She suspected he would piss off everyone at his new firm soon enough.

*Was he really with Shana under his desk?* It didn't really feel like it anymore.

"This is why I can't trust myself," she muttered aloud.

It didn't take that long to read through the document because basically Galen wanted to divide everything between them evenly and equally. Good on him. Not that they had that much. Some savings was all. Though he'd pressed her during their short marriage to get her father to kick in for the down payment on a home, Ronnie had resisted. First and foremost, she wasn't going to ask Jonas for anything. His money was his, not hers, and no amount of finagling by her soon-to-be ex was going to get Jonas to bestow money on her—which was just how she wanted to keep it. Secondly, her job at the firm was enough to cover her expenses. Financially, she could take care of herself. Okay, she was wobbling on whether to stay at the firm or not. It felt like it was time for a change. A need to break out. A divorce was a good start, maybe the job was next?

"Use your talents, Veronica!" She could hear her Aunt Kat's booming voice. "Forget what Jonas wants. You're a psychic. Leave that stuffy law job. Go help people!"

"I help people," she'd answered, though she'd known what her aunt meant.

"You take after your mother. C'mon, girl."

Like her mother . . . who apparently was the source of her aggravating gift.

Meanwhile, Aunt Kat didn't like Jonas one bit. Never had. She was her mother's sister and ran a small apple farm about an hour or so northeast of River Glen. Ronnie had spent a lot of summer days at Aunt Kat's in her youth and away from her father's iron rule.

"You're not like him, you're like Wynona," her aunt had told her more times than she could count.

"Because I see things?"

"Because you have a heart."

After the near tragedy at The Pond she'd tried to tell Aunt Kat that she'd seen her mother, or heard her, or something. She'd been stunned when her aunt had responded smartly, "That's foolishness, dear."

"I thought I was like my mom. You said that—"

"Oh, sure, Winnie had the same gift, but you can't make up things, Veronica."

"I'm not making it up. I saw her!"

Aunt Kat had shaken her head and shut down as if she'd turned to stone, leaving Ronnie bereft. Her aunt's reaction, coupled with her own embarrassment and that... evil... she'd seen rising from Evan Caldwell... That's when she'd started keeping her sightings to herself... mostly... except for the ones that portended imminent harm to someone. Even then, she was extremely reluctant to predict.

*Yeah, but what about Marian Langdorf? Broke your rules on that one, didn't you?*

True enough. She'd warned the older woman to see a doctor, having caught a glimpse of her on a gurney, eyes closed, mouth open, past saving. All she'd said to Marian was, "You need to see a doctor," and... okay, yes... she'd pressed her hand hard and told her to check out that pain she sometimes felt in her lower right side. She'd figured if she was wrong, Marian Langdorf would be just one more person who thought she was nutty.

But she'd been right that time. And now, after removal of part of her liver, Marian Langdorf kept calling her and calling her, wanting her to be some kind of personal psychic.

*She's wealthy and determined and you could leave this office and Jonas behind.*

Ronnie made a noise in the back of her throat as she put the divorce papers back in the envelope. If she agreed to work for Marian Langford, the woman's nephew and only living heir, Carlton Langdorf, would have an absolute shit fit. Carlton was Marian's constant companion, driving his aunt everywhere, making sure he was indispensable. The last time the woman had stopped in to see her lawyer, Albert Tormelle, it had seemed more like Marian's excuse to see Ronnie than actual estate business, and Carlton hadn't liked it at all. He'd stood back, arms folded over his chest, his expression blank, but Ronnie hadn't missed the hostility.

She headed up the stairs to the reception area. The building lay in a U-shape with the more senior lawyers and their staff at the two ends of the corridors; reception at the front curve.

Dawn Michaels was not at the reception desk, but her latte from Bean There, Done That, a local coffee bar, was. Ronnie was friends with Dawn, about the only coworker she could say that about, but was glad nonetheless to sneak to her office down the east side corridor unobserved. She had some thinking to do. The same thinking she'd been indulging in before Shana had pounded on her door.

*Who was the woman in the clearing? Was she dead? Was it real?*

*And why did you see her superimposed on Shana at the crash site?*

Tossing the manila envelope atop her desk's walnut surface, she watched it skid to the edge. She walked to the window. On her side of the building a narrow alley ran between Tormelle & Quick Law Firm and the nearly twin office building next door. Those red brick offices were four stories high, almost as tall as the River Glen Penthouses, on the far end of the main street, with two more stories than their own building.

She could hear a muffled conversation going on in the office next to hers, Martin Calgheny's. Martin was an estate lawyer and the only one at the firm who actively sought out Ronnie's help on cases. He liked to have her with him when interviewing a prospective client or when he was giving heirs the good or bad news about an inheritance. Twice while they'd been holding a meeting about the division of an estate Ronnie had known what was going to happen, in her psychic way. Twice she'd seen the future spool out and had tried to do something about it. Twice no one had paid attention to her warnings, and that included P.I. Jesse James Taft who, she thought, was lucky to still be above ground with the murderous intent those women had in for him weeks earlier.

Snatching up the divorce paper file again, Ronnie flipped it open, grabbed a pen from her desk drawer and signed her name in a small, precise hand, as un-flourishy as possible. She then grabbed her cell and texted Galen: **I've signed.**

Immediately she got a response: **Bring the file over at noon and I'll take you to lunch.**

She scoffed. **I'll leave it at the front desk. Pick it up whenever. Please, Veronica. Pretty, pretty please.**

Asshole.

**When you put it that way . . . no.**

**Oh, come on. I owe you a big apology.**

Well, there was a new one. He did owe her an apology, but that didn't mean he had the wherewithal to figure that out. What was he playing at?

She gazed hard at the text, trying to see behind the words, but though she waited several minutes there was no help from the psychic world. Figured.

She made a snap decision: **I'll be there.**

In the waiting room of Tormelle & Quick Law Firm, Detective Cooper Haynes's phone buzzed in his pocket. Pulling out the cell, he glanced at the caller. Taft, returning his call. Without hesitation he slid the button to *off*. He'd wanted to talk to Taft before he entered the law offices, but it was too late now. Now, the receptionist—young, tall and commanding—whose nameplate read Dawn Michaels, was seated at her desk and seemingly busy with scheduling, glancing repeatedly at her computer screen, scribbling notes and pressing her lips together as if in annoyance at what she was viewing. Cooper had caught a glance at that screen and seen her juggling names and appointment times before she'd looked up at him and asked how she could help him.

"Cooper Haynes to see Paula Prescott," he'd told her with a smile. He'd been told more than once that his "cop" presence had grown too noticeable and off-putting, so he was working to curb that.

She looked at her screen and nodded. "She'll be right with you."

He watched her from his seat as he waited. She was dark-skinned and dark-eyed and reminded him of his partner, Elena Verbena, oozing with no-nonsense, "don't waste my time" attitude. The lawyer he was meeting was of the same mold, a fifty-something white woman with short, blond-gray hair, a habit of staring hard while she listened to what you said, as if she were cataloguing every syllable, and a surgically precise way of speaking that let you know who was in charge. He'd known Paula for years but this was the first time he'd come to her for personal advice.

"Check with Veronica Quick. Jonas Quick's daughter," Taft had suggested. "Tormelle and Quick Law Firm," when he'd learned of Cooper's dilemma.

Cooper had immediately wished he hadn't told Taft about Mary Jo's disappearance. He'd responded to the P.I., "I need a lawyer." *Not a supposed psychic.*

Taft, an ex-cop who, as a rule, lived in the same cold, hard reality Cooper did, had shaken his head and lifted his hands. "While you're at the firm, talk to her. She's not a kook. You want to find this woman. Use everything you got."

A week earlier, Mary Jo Kirshner, their surrogate who was eight months pregnant with Cooper and Jamie's baby, had walked out of the home that she lived in with her husband and her own two children, leaving a note that said she needed to be alone for a while. Stephen Kirshner, the woman's husband, told Cooper his wife had a tendency to do this kind of thing and not to worry. Mary Jo had been a surrogate before. It was all perfectly normal.

Not from where Cooper sat. Mary Jo was carrying a child that wasn't hers and she'd disappeared to God knew where.

So, he'd demanded to know her whereabouts, but Kirshner said he didn't know where she was. Though Cooper had pressed, the man seemed honestly bewildered . . . and maybe more scared than he was admitting. Maybe it wasn't "perfectly normal." Maybe his "business as usual" attitude was a facade. From Cooper's point of view, Stephen Kirshner had no idea where his wife was, but since she was calling in occasionally, her disappearance hadn't quite risen to the level of a missing person.

That didn't stop Cooper from turning to his River Glen P.D. partner, Elena Verbena, for help. Temporarily *ex*-partner, actually, as Cooper was currently on leave with the department for breaking expected political rules by investigating some of the wealthiest and supposedly most untouchable people around town. The chief had put Cooper on administrative leave, hoping it would all blow over.

But since Jamie was also pregnant—a crazy surprise after Cooper was told there was virtually no chance his wife could conceive—it looked like Cooper might be moving into paternity leave as well. Generous of Chief Duncan, but he knew it was really to keep him out of range for a good, long time—exactly what he didn't want right now.

But Verbena understood his frustration. She had also checked with Kirshner, who'd been somewhat alarmed the police were involved now. Verbena had simply told the man that he'd be wise to get his wife to come home before it looked like she was possibly stealing the baby, but it had thrown a scare into the man. Kirshner assured both Cooper and Verbena that he was speaking to Mary Jo regularly, but that she didn't really want to talk to any of them, not Cooper, not Verbena and not Jamie.

To add to the overall tension of the last months of the two pregnancies, Jamie was in the midst of medically prescribed bed rest, a precaution to make sure she carried to full term. She was frustrated and "had a million things to do," as the holidays were fast approaching.

Which was why Cooper had yet to tell her the full extent of Mary Jo's disappearance. He'd mentioned she'd been gone a few days, missing, taking some time to herself before the delivery. Jamie had been alarmed at the news, but Cooper had said he was on it, everything was going to be fine. He needed more information, something concrete, before he told his wife the true extent of Mary Jo's disappearance, that she was basically MIA.

And the hell of it was, Jamie had never quite trusted Mary Jo in the first place. She'd felt the woman was too . . . flaky, for want of a better term. Now Cooper, who'd pushed for Mary Jo, was going to have to admit she'd been right to worry after all.

Kirshner had continued to assert that Mary Jo was just seeking solace and quietude at the end of her pregnancy, something she'd done during her two other surrogacies.

*Would have been nice to know, Steve. And the tightening of your skin when you said that? And the fact that you're the only one who's talked to her? That she hasn't spoken to either of her biological children or anyone else? Well, that's a big problem.*

Now Cooper shifted in his chair. He was meeting with Prescott to determine what his legal standing was concerning his and Jamie's baby should Mary Jo do anything that would unintentionally harm it. Though he was alarmed by her sudden departure, he truly did not believe Mary Jo would hurt an unborn child. She was unsteady, not evil.

At least that's what he told himself.

He checked the time on his phone and inhaled slowly. Dawn looked over at him. "Would you like some water?" she asked.

"No. Thanks."

He'd initially wanted a full-on manhunt to find Mary Jo. Chief Duncan, nicknamed Humph for his long-faced Humphrey Bogart appearance, had pointed out that she was in contact with her husband, so was she really missing? But then, though he didn't show it, he was deeply angry with Cooper for putting the mayor and her well-connected friends under the microscope. Didn't matter that Cooper was just doing his job. He was paying the price.

He got up, stretched his arms, thought about heading outside for a short walk, but didn't trust that they would wait for him should Paula Prescott call his name, so he returned to his seat.

Dawn had apparently finished with scheduling and was taking calls. The elevator bell dinged just as Cooper reseated himself, and the doors slid open. An older woman, hair wrapped in a scarf, makeup a little too thick and garish for her age, thumped a cane imperiously against the oak floor as she strode forward, a young man busying himself around her as if worried she might topple over.

"I'm here to see Veronica Quick," she announced regally.

Dawn smiled, nodded, but was on the phone again, making

an appointment. The younger man said to the woman, "Let's take a seat."

"I'm going to stand right here until I'm heard," she snapped.

Dawn quickly ended her call, scribbling something down before giving the woman her most beaming smile. "Hello, Mrs. Langdorf. Let me check the appointment log. I'm not sure I saw your name."

"You won't find it. I told Veronica I would see her this week. I know she's busy, but she saved my life, you know. Now, I just want a few moments with her. Please let her know I'm here."

*Respected client*, Cooper decided. *Likely pain in the ass. Wealthy. Lackey beside her working hard to get some of that money. What was his relationship to her? Assistant? Son? Lover?*

Dawn's dark eyes revealed little of what she was thinking as she picked up the phone and pressed a button.

The young man sat down in a chair on the opposite side of the room from Cooper. Mrs. Langdorf stayed exactly where she was.

Cooper's phone buzzed silently in his pocket. He pulled it out again and saw that Jamie had texted him: **Where are you? Coming back soon?**

He'd been unspecific about his destination on purpose. Didn't want to worry her. He couldn't decide whether it was a good thing or a bad thing that he was on leave from the department. A bad thing because he didn't have work to occupy his mind. A good thing because he didn't have his job getting in the way of finding Mary Jo, although apart from choking the information out of Stephen Kirshner he really didn't have a further plan. And though choking Kirshner might work in the short run, the department probably wouldn't look favorably upon it . . .

"It's her own vision quest. Communing with herself," Kirshner had told him.

Bullshit. A vision quest was a whole lot more than that, Cooper had thought at the time. Although it could be for anyone, he supposed, it was generally considered a ceremony practiced by certain Indigenous peoples as a means of reconnecting with their history and making a connection to the spiritual world. Cooper knew Mary Jo had once had ties to a splintered commune who practiced their own rituals. Not a cult per se, though some of its own members seemed to take it that way. But it was not a group of Indigenous people.

And it was not without its own secrets.

Mrs. Langdorf glanced pointedly at her bejeweled gold watch.

Cooper texted Jamie back: **About an hour.**

Fifteen minutes later Paula Prescott walked into reception and in her raspy voice asked him to join her in her office. He followed her down a hallway that branched into an office with a large window that looked toward the East Glen River, not visible from this distance but he could make out the row of trees that lined its banks. Only about a block away he could see a top-floor community room that was often booked for weddings and other large groups. It sat above floors of luxury condominiums, which in turn rose above the ground level River Glen Grill. Through the gray and slanting rain he could make out blurry, twinkling multicolored Christmas lights. Maybe someone had rented the room for a party, or maybe it was just festooned with general pre-holiday decorations. In the uncertain late-morning light the illumination seemed dull and a bit sad.

"Let's go over your contract with Ms. Kirshner," Paula said briskly, having already been alerted to Cooper's concerns. "Make sure its ironclad."

The Bernard K. Waters Law Firm was a four-person operation in a silver building of corrugated metal. The siding was clearly designed to look strong and industrial but it appeared more like a repurposed garbage can desperately trying to be chic. Ronnie yanked open the heavy wooden door with its tiny window that resembled a welder's mask, and entered a concrete foyer with a wide counter desk, its support a curve of matching corrugated metal.

A young woman with dyed black hair that seemed to swallow the light from the overhead crystal chandeliers looked up from a cell phone that she surreptitiously slid to one side as Ronnie entered.

"Galen Hillyard," said Ronnie.

"I'm not sure he's in, he's—"

"He is expecting me."

"You're . . . ?"

"Veronica Quick."

Her brow furrowed. Ronnie wasn't certain she knew she was Galen's wife, but somehow didn't want to get into it all, especially given the circumstances of their upcoming meeting.

The receptionist picked up the desk phone, pressed a button and said, "A Veronica Click is here to see you." A moment later she hung up and said, "He is in his office, apparently. First door down the hall." She swept a languid arm toward the right.

Ronnie passed through a glass door that swung inward and down the charcoal-gray carpeted hallway to the rough wooden door with Galen's name beside it. The Bernard K. Waters Law Firm was fairly new in River Glen. Waters himself was a lawyer whose fortunes had been made from a business his family had owned for three generations and that Bernard K. Waters had driven into bankruptcy in quick order as soon as he gained control. This firm was the phoenix born from the ashes of the original and, though it brandished Waters's name, was apparently owned by one of the firm's other attorneys whose money was really behind it. She didn't know how adept a lawyer any of them were, but their style and decor was the polar opposite of the venerated halls of Tormelle & Quick.

Galen opened the door at Ronnie's knock. "Don't you look lovely," he greeted her.

He made a move as if to hug her and she automatically stiffened.

"Oh, is that the way it's going to be?" He feigned disappointment.

"Here." She handed him the envelope. "Maybe you should have your lawyer make sure everything's in order."

"A joke?" He grinned, showing an actual smile, the smile

that had won her over in a past life where now she wondered if she'd been unconsciously taking some kind of hallucinogenic drug that had skewed reality.

She looked past him to his desk and realized it was exactly as her mind had made it: the dark wood, the black chair, the space beneath where Shana had been crouching. A gentle fizzing ran along her nerves.

"What?" Galen asked, regarding her closely.

Ronnie inhaled sharply. No. It hadn't been Shana. It was someone else kneeling in front of Galen. Similar body type, but not Shana. Someone else . . .

Mrs. Bernard K. Waters.

Oh.

"Having one of your 'moments'?" Galen asked, long-suffering. "Can't we forgo all that and have a nice lunch? There's a bistro across the street. Nothing fancy. Just somewhere we can be civilized and toast the end of our marriage."

"Why would you even care?"

"I'm trying to be nice here, Ronnie."

"Why start now?"

"You always have to be such a fucking bitch, don't you?" he said on a sigh. "You whined to your father and he kicked me out. Okay. One of us, at least, is trying to put it all behind us."

"That's not why he asked you to leave."

"Asked me to leave?" He scoffed. "I could sue him for nearly ruining my reputation. Luckily, Bernard saw my potential. I didn't want to leave River Glen, but I almost had to, thanks to Jonas and you."

"You did that all by yourself. Although, looks like you've been having some recent help."

"What do you mean? No. Keep it to yourself. I've had enough of your predictions."

"Blow jobs under the desk? Not sure Bernard's going to like that one."

"More aspersions. You're making it hard to stay nice."

"Who did the interior design work here?"

"Why?"

"Maybe Mrs. Bernard K. Waters? Just kneeling on the carpet to test its weave?"

A flush crept up Galen's neck. He lifted a finger, as if he wanted to shake it in front of her face. A moment later he collected himself, turned away and snipped, "Okay. Fine. I'll get this filed immediately."

"So . . . no lunch?"

"Goodbye, Veronica."

"It's Ms. Quick to you."

She found herself smiling a little as she hurried through the rain to her car.

# Chapter 4

Cooper walked through Tormelle & Quick's covered parking area to his Explorer, looking toward the main outside lot which was currently being doused by almost biblical rain. Sheets of it poured down, row after row in wind-driven sweeps, like a rushing army. The kind of rain that sloughed away banks of the East Glen River in a muddy torrent. Made him think of the houses perched precariously on cliffs above the river. Hopefully most were constructed on granite.

So much for the light drizzle that had drifted down earlier today.

He drew a breath and exhaled slowly. His lawyer had come to the same conclusion he had: There was nothing in the paperwork he and Jamie had signed with Mary Jo Kirshner that precluded her from being gone for unspecified periods of time. At this late date, she needed to keep in contact with Cooper and Jamie, but it wasn't dictated exactly how often. Still . . . he might have the power to sic the law on her. Tricky stuff in a court of law, but he was past caring about the future fallout. He wanted Mary Jo back *now*.

But it wasn't going to happen. She was on her own time frame, though that time was ticking away fast until her due date. The idea that Mary Jo had maybe joined a would-be cult again scared him shitless. The legal wrangle could take years and there was a baby's health—*their* baby's health—in the balance.

Plucking out his cell, Cooper started to call Jamie to tell her he was on his way home when he saw a vehicle pull into the lot, nearly obscured by rain, and slow down as it approached the covered area. There were no more spots available inside and the driver must've recognized that fact because he pulled into an empty spot in the uncovered lot, the car curtained with rain.

He immediately opened his driver's door to get inside, figuring he'd better get going and give up his spot.

But the new visitor's door opened and slammed shut, the sound barely discernible in the loud roar of the deluge.

Bare head bent, Veronica Quick walked with purpose toward him, drenching herself.

She stopped just under the covered lot ceiling, soaking wet. But she seemed . . . happy?

Cooper said, "I'm just leaving so a spot's opening up. I might have an umbrella in my car if you want to move inside."

"Too late for that. Thank you. It's fine. The skies'll clear sometime. Maybe even today."

"You're Veronica Quick," he said, his voice raised against the thundering rain.

She swept a hand across her forehead to push back her hair and gazed at him out of cautious blue eyes. "Yes?"

"Cooper Haynes," he introduced himself and stuck out his hand.

"Mine's wet," she warned as they shook hands.

He explained about having met with Paula Prescott . . . and then made the mistake of bringing up Jesse Taft and his half belief in her supposed psychic talents.

"Ah," she said. A wealth of meaning in that one word.

She was pretty. A kind of girl-next-door look. Unconcerned about the rain that had soaked her light brown hair and drenched her from head to foot. Contained, but he had the sense of bubbling lava inside. He'd met a lot of people during his years on the force, but some stood out. Some, who you just knew something big was going on inside them, a depth of personality they maybe didn't much like to share.

"You're a police detective with River Glen P.D.," she said suddenly, surprising him. "I've spoken with your partner, Detective Verbena."

"Right."

Quick had once predicted a crime to Verbena, which had made Verbena suspicious of her possible involvement in it. Cooper had only been peripherally aware of the events at the time, although it had since become buzz around the squad room.

"You here on police business?"

"Personal. I'm on administrative leave," he admitted.

"What happened?"

He kind of liked that she asked straight out. "I pissed off the wrong people in town."

"Like Mr. Taft does?" She grabbed her hair with both hands and squeezed water to the parking lot floor. "He's wrong about me, by the way. I'm no psychic. I just knew he was in trouble."

Cooper nodded.

She glanced toward the rain-blurred outdoor lot. "You'll be back on the force soon."

"You just said you're no psychic," he reminded lightly. And he wasn't sure she was right. The chief would have to ignore the politics and back Cooper's investigative efforts into a lot of withheld secrets and lies.

"You seem capable. You don't have to be a psychic to see that."

"'All signs point to yes'?"

She actually laughed and Cooper broke into a smile himself. But then she caught herself up on a small intake of breath.

"What?" he asked, feeling the hairs lift on his arms in spite of himself.

"Nothing." She glanced toward the stairs.

"No, what were you going to say?"

He could see her clench her teeth, as if she were forcibly holding back whatever it was.

"Tell me," he coaxed.

"You're looking for someone?" she asked cautiously.

He felt a rushing in his ears. She couldn't have talked to Paula. She was just arriving. Unless maybe Paula had mentioned his case earlier? In her hearing? After he'd called but before they had their meeting? "Paula told you that."

"Never mind. It doesn't matter."

Her psychic abilities had been discussed and joked about. Verbena's skepticism had run through the rank and file, though someone had once suggested they could use her to solve cases. He'd have to think about who that was. Cooper hadn't paid much attention at the time. Cops talked and joked about a lot of things. But no harm in telling her the truth now, he figured. "I'm looking for the surrogate who's having my wife's and my baby. She took off about a week ago and her husband says it's normal, but it doesn't feel that way to me."

She keyed in on him so he gave her the bullet points of his and Jamie's trials and tribulations on getting pregnant. How Jamie had had a daughter with her first husband. How that daughter, Harley, who was now in college, was thinking about going into law enforcement. How he, Cooper, had never had a child of his own, but had raised his ex's daughter, Marissa, throughout most of her life and considered her more daughter than stepdaughter. How Jamie had been told she was very unlikely to get pregnant again and so they'd hired a surrogate. How just after that surrogate announced a viable pregnancy, Jamie herself had learned that she was having a baby. And how Jamie was now bedridden and how the surrogate had gone . . . on a vision quest, according to her husband.

Quick shifted her gaze from his back to the rain, but she was clearly engaged. When he finished, she glanced back at him, those blue eyes gravely intent.

"Is your surrogate's name Rebekkah? Two *k*'s, one *h*?"

Well, that was specific. "No . . . it's Mary Jo Kirshner."

She shook her head in annoyance. "Sorry."

"Nothing to be sorry about."

"That's debatable," she scoffed, turning toward the stairs. "Nice talking to you, Detective."

"You did warn Taft that he was in danger," he said, feeling she needed some support even if he wasn't a believer himself.

"Yeah, well. Anyone could've made that guess."

Marian Langdorf and Carlton were in the waiting room when Ronnie entered reception from the stairway.

Nightmare.

Dawn took one look at her and said, "Ah . . . let me get you a towel."

"I'm fine. I just need a few minutes to dry out."

"You had no umbrella?" Marian demanded. She was standing directly in front of Dawn's desk, listing to one side, leaning heavily on a cane.

"Just got caught in the rain."

Carlton leapt up from where he'd been perched on the edge of his seat, as if he couldn't make up his mind whether to stand or sit. He seemed to want to grab Marian but her frozen gaze warned him to stay back.

Ronnie said, "Take a seat and I'll be right with you. I just need to freshen up."

"All right," said Marian as Ronnie headed toward the door that led to the inner offices, but she sounded none too pleased.

As soon as she was out of sight, Ronnie pushed into the women's restroom. She stared at herself in the mirror. What a mess. Her shoulder-length hair was plastered to her head. She finger-combed it, then looked inside her drenched cross-body purse for a brush, knowing she didn't have one with her. The shoulders of her raincoat were soaked, but at least her jacket and blouse were dry underneath. Her pant legs and shoes were another matter. Ah, well. She knew what Mrs. Langdorf wanted and she was determined to gently ease her on her way.

When Ronnie returned to reception, Carlton said, "She wouldn't sit down until you got here. Insisted on standing. I tried to reason with her, but she's stubborn. I did get her her cane, but she won't take care of herself."

Annoyance crossed Marian's face. He was right, clearly, but the older woman didn't want to hear it.

She was leaning heavily on the cane's carved silver handle, which Ronnie saw was designed as a wolf's head with glaring red gem eyes. Marian Langdorf was nothing if not dramatic.

Ronnie's gaze had just turned from the wolf's head when a dog started barking, somewhere to her right, outdoors. She looked through the window, in the direction of the sound, but no one else seemed to notice. Great.

*Am I the only one who hears it?*

"Do you hear anything?" Ronnie asked.

Behind the desk, Dawn glanced to Ronnie's right. "The dog?"

"Yes, the dog," Ronnie said in relief.

"Why?" Marian cocked her head. "Is it yours?"

"No, I just . . . hope its owner finds out why it's barking. Are you here to see Albert?" She hoped against hope she was wrong about the woman's intentions.

"No, darling, I came to see you. Do you mind? I need somewhere to sit down."

There it was. "Of course. Let's go to the conference room." Ronnie glanced to Dawn for confirmation that the conference room was free. Dawn nodded once, emphatically, clearly glad to remove Mrs. Langdorf from reception.

Carlton leapt up and offered his arm, practically muscling Ronnie out of the way. Marian ignored him and deliberately thumped her cane onto the carpet ahead of them as the three made their way to the narrow, rectangular room with the row of windows and the carved wooden table that could seat up to thirty, if necessary. Today the rain was obscuring the panes, running in rivulets that blurred the view of the now skeletal trees that lined the street. Marian sat herself on the end. Carlton quickly chose her right; Ronnie on her left.

While Marian settled herself, Ronnie thought about her recent conversation with Detective Haynes. She was a bit embarrassed about saying Rebekkah. She'd seen the name—*Rebekkah, two k's and an* h—floating in her mind, but she'd been wrong. This happened enough that she shouldn't be embarrassed about it any longer, but well, she was.

*Maybe it's the name of the woman in the clearing . . . ?*

Or more likely, nothing at all.

"You've been avoiding me," Marian tsk-tsked as she crossed her arms on the tabletop and leaned in to Ronnie.

"I haven't meant to." A blatant lie.

"You save my life, and this is how you treat me? Come on, Veronica. You know I want you to work for me. This law job . . ." She made a face and looked around. "What are you getting paid? I'll double it."

Carlton choked and coughed, his face turning red. Mrs. Langdorf regarded him imperiously, her mouth turning down.

That one vision of Marian Langdorf had proved correct. Ronnie had seen her gray face, slack jaw and terrified eyes as she'd been on a gurney, raced by EMTs across Glen Gen Emergency's white tile floor. The feeling of rushing speed, the squeaking and clattering of wheels, the odor of antiseptic and stale green beans. A hospital, she'd realized, and had warned her to see a doctor and check her right side before blurting, "I don't want to see you on a gurney being raced into Glen Gen Emergency."

In the moment, Marian had pulled back slowly from Ronnie as if she smelled bad, and had left quickly, one hand gripped hard on her sycophantic nephew's arm. She'd called Jonas within the hour and accused Ronnie of being the crackpot everyone said she was. Forty-eight hours later she'd ended up in the emergency room at Glen Gen and it was nip and tuck for a while before they operated on her liver.

So, she called up Jonas, this time singing Ronnie's praises.

Now she said, "Let's not argue about it. Let me be clear. You know I think you're wasting your talents here. I want you to come work for me, from my home. There's an upstairs suite that you can use as an office, decorate any way you wish. I want you to be comfortable. As I said, I will pay you double what you're making here, as long as it's within reason. I don't want you to take on other clients. Oh, and I would prefer it just be you. Nothing against your husband, but I need a personal aide whose attention will be solely on me. It's the second floor of my house, where my bedroom is and—"

Here, Carlton made a choking sound. His skin had whitened and it looked as if it was all he could do to not clamp his hand over his ears, or maybe Marian's mouth.

"—your suite is just down the hall. I think you can understand I wouldn't want a man on the same floor. No one has been since Howell died," she said, the corners of her mouth turning down at the mention of her deceased husband.

"Look, Mrs. Langdorf—"

"It's Marian. Please."

"Marian," Ronnie began again. "I—"

Carlton broke in. "Aunt Marian, it's a lot to ask right off the bat. Maybe a trial period is in order?"

Ronnie tried to interject, "I was going to say, I don't think—"

"Carlton." Marian turned her hard gaze on him. "Your displeasure has been noted many times. This is my life we're talking about. The life that I still have because of Veronica."

"All she did was tell you to see a doctor," he said faintly.

"Before. My. Liver. Failed." Her voice was a knife, slicing off each word. "I could be dead, except for her."

Carlton shot Ronnie a flash of resentment, before dropping his gaze. He was Mrs. Langdorf's heir, as far as Ronnie knew. She could look up that information as a member of the firm, but she'd tried to stay away from any and all possible conflicts, especially since the woman had decided Ronnie was her savior. Carlton was feeling the sting of Marian's shift of interest and was likely worried his inheritance could be in jeopardy.

"I can't do it, Mrs. Langdorf," Ronnie said quickly. "This is where I work."

"And you detest it, I know, dear. I may not have your abilities, but I can see your unhappiness. You are unfulfilled. This is an opportunity for both of us."

"She doesn't want it," urged Carlton. "It's not—"

"Carlton..." The warning in her tone stopped him from whatever he was going to add. She turned back to Ronnie. "I know you say you have no ability in the psychic realm, but that's not really true, is it? Your reputation precedes you, whether you like it or not."

"I'm not always accurate. You know that. A lot of my reputation is hype."

"You saved me. And I heard about you saving that man's life, too."

Ronnie hesitated. What man? she wanted to ask, but that would be just playing into her hands. Taft? That wasn't public knowledge, was it? Detective Haynes knew, but was there anyone else? Taft's partner, yes, but...

*There are other incidents*, her conscience reminded her. That broken latch on the gate to the pool at the Morrows' house? The one you saw after that vision of a child's body floating in the pool, surrounded by a corona of her dark, waving hair? Carrie Morrow had confided weeks later that she had found their daughter in the pool not long after Ronnie's warning. She'd planned on getting the latch fixed, but it had taken a bit of time. Luckily, Ronnie's warning had made her hypervigilant about her daughter's whereabouts and she'd kept close tabs on the girl minute by minute. Sure enough, the child had found her way into the pool, but luckily Carrie was right behind her and pulled her out immediately.

But maybe the man Marian Langdorf meant was Albert Tormelle's grandson. Ronnie had told Albert not to allow him to go on an upcoming ski trip. Albert had half listened to her, and suggested the tween boy be kept home, which had not gone over well, to put it mildly. She'd been ignored and the boy had fallen from the ski lift and cracked several vertebrae. Since then he'd had a number of surgeries and was reportedly fine. Sophomore or junior in high school now, she thought. That was the incident that had really done it. Before that, there were rumors, but Albert Tormelle couldn't shut up about Ronnie's psychic abilities. He might be circumspect regarding his clients' businesses, but he was a big, voluble man who'd stoked the myth about her reputation so hard that it left anyone who encountered her unsure how to treat her.

And then, of course, there was the time she'd warned the River Glen police that Edmond Olman was going to kill his wife.

"Mr. Lockenbill," Marian said by way of explanation.

Well, that was unexpected. Ronnie said carefully, "Norm Lockenbill wanted to talk to his dead wife and he wanted a seance. That never happened."

"But he saw her, after he talked to you. She visited him."

"I can't verify that," said Ronnie. It was amazing how hard it was to keep the facts from turning into epic fiction.

*This all started at The Pond.*

Clint Mercer had spread the tale of her screaming about Evan Caldwell's ghost and then asking Sloan to marry her. She'd tried to explain, which only made things worse, that she hadn't *asked* to marry him. She'd *seen* it. The white dress. Candlelight. ". . . kiss the bride . . ." And Sloan Hart doing just that.

*I'm going to marry you.*

She'd made the mistake of confiding the full vision to Brandy and Mel, once everything had died down. They'd seemed to go along with her, but later she'd seen the sidelong glances they'd given each other when they thought she wasn't looking. And that was the beginning of the end to their friendship.

"God has given you a gift the rest of us don't possess," Mrs. Langdorf insisted. "Use it, my dear. When it's your time, you want to be able to tell your Maker you wielded His gift to the best of your ability. You can't let it be squandered."

Carlton said in a mansplaining voice, "Ms. Quick doesn't appear to be interested in the plan."

"It's more like I don't think I can help you," said Ronnie in a rush. She didn't want either of them speaking for her.

"Don't say no yet. You saved my life. Let me give you this opportunity to embrace yours as it was meant to be. Come by tomorrow. We'll have a light lunch. Carlton won't be there," she added, throwing a look his way. "Or possibly tonight? For dinner?"

Carlton made a protesting peep, but then held back whatever he was going to say. Probably a smart move, though it looked like it was killing him.

"You can bring your husband," the older woman added magnanimously. "So he can see, but I don't want—"

"I signed divorce papers today." Ronnie cut her off. "That's where I was before I walked in. So, there is no husband any longer."

Marian immediately brightened. "Well, okay. I'll see you tonight. After work. Five thirty?"

"Make it six."

"Good." She rapped her cane on the floor once and stood. "I'll see you then." She lifted her chin and sailed out, with Carlton scrambling to catch up with her thumping gait.

Might as well get it over with. Marian wasn't one to put off. She was a woman who was used to getting what she wanted and she wanted Ronnie. So what the hell?

*Should I wear a conical hat decorated with stars and a silver cape and wand?*

Carlton's final warning glare was the icing on the cake. She was going if for nothing more than to thwart him a bit.

Finally, Ronnie retreated to her office. Her desk phone was ringing as she sat down and she reached for the receiver. "Veronica Quick."

"Hi . . . this is Daria Armenton. Angel told me he talked to you about me?"

Daria. Angel's cousin. "Yes, he did. And I told him you needed to talk to Martin Calgheny. He's the lawyer for the Rollberson estate."

"Oh?" She sounded distracted.

Ronnie added, "Angel said that the other heirs want you to give them your part of the inheritance, which sounds like harassment."

"Yeah . . . yeah, it is. Harassment."

"You can call the River Glen Police Department. Or the sheriff's department, if you're in the county."

"I don't want to do that."

"Should I have Martin call you?"

"Can't you do something?" Daria sounded a little desperate.

"I'm not a lawyer." How many times was she going to have to say that?

"But you've helped other people," Daria said.

"Yes..."

"So, can you help me?"

"What kind of help are you looking for?" questioned Ronnie. She knew, but she wanted to have it come from Daria's own lips.

"I just heard that you were... that you could maybe help me... you know, I mean. Like you could know stuff."

"About... the other heirs?"

"Or anybody, really, I guess." Daria let out a puff of air. "You see stuff. You can see into the future, right? I mean, is there a chance you can see how much...? I'd like to plan."

Oh. So that was it. Ronnie said, "I don't know how much you're inheriting, no." She shifted the phone from one ear to the other.

Daria said, "It's just that me and my boyfriend would like to buy a house, but we are trying to figure out how much we'll get."

Ronnie tried to be patient. "Daria," she said, "you really need to talk to your lawyer. Martin Calgheny. If you're being harassed by the other heirs, it could be a matter for the police."

"Oh, no. It's not that. Angel can take care of things. I just thought..." She sighed. "Okay, thanks."

"You're welcome," Ronnie said into the dead line. It irked her how everyone seemed to think she could magically fix all their problems.

She did walk over to Martin's office. He was on a call and looking at his screen at the same time, talking into a headset while inputting notes to himself on his desktop computer. He glanced her way and she nodded that she'd seen how busy he was. She went back to her own office, wrote out a note with Daria's name on it and slipped it in front of Martin's eyes. He nodded back, message received, so she returned to her own office.

Her cell phone rang as she was just settling in. She looked at the name on her cell screen. DOD.

Her shorthand for Dear Old Dad.

# Chapter 5

"Hi, Dad."

Ronnie kept her tone neutral. The less said the better when dealing with Jonas because otherwise they'd end up in a scrap. She would rather live in her one-bedroom apartment with faulty heating, a sensitive toilet and noisy neighbors than let him coax her into moving home. He'd never gotten over the need to direct her every decision. Didn't matter that she was an adult. Didn't matter that she was married. Didn't matter that as soon as he started in, she grew deaf.

"What did Marian Langdorf want?" he demanded.

"I think you can guess."

"She's still going on about you saving her life?"

"More or less."

"And she offered you money to 'predict' for her?"

"Again, more or less."

"You're not taking her seriously, are you?"

She could picture Jonas, gray hair neatly cut around his ears. Piercing hazel eyes surrounded by wire-rim glasses. Strong chin. Stony expression. Though she'd seen him loosen up, he always seemed particularly tense and uptight around her. Like he was afraid she would make one wrong step too many and . . . what? Bring everything crashing down around her? That felt like it had already happened.

"Carlton Langdorf is definitely taking me seriously. I think he'd like it if I disappeared from the planet."

He harrumphed. "That's because you threaten him."

"He's wrong about me. A lot wrong."

"Be careful, that's all I'm saying. Try to minimize Marian's obsession with your supposed skills."

"I always do."

"Okay."

Ronnie tried, and failed, once again to imagine how her tightly wound father and her apparently free-form mother, if you could believe Aunt Kat's description, ever got together. "Combustion," Aunt Kat would say and make the sound of an explosion. "It couldn't last. Winnie just burned out."

"Anything else?" Ronnie asked her father.

"Are you and Martin meeting with the Bentons this afternoon?"

"I'm about to check with him."

"Fine."

He clicked off then, apparently satisfied with her unsatisfactory answers. At least for the moment. Ronnie returned to Martin Calgheny's office and rapped lightly on the door.

"Come on in," he called.

She pushed in, then hung on the knob, poking her head inside. "We heading to the Bentons?"

"Actually, no. That's been postponed till next week." Calgheny, in a tailored suit and tie, didn't look up from his work, just waved a hand across the papers stacked on his desk. "It'll give more time for them to work their problems out."

"You think it'll help?"

He gave a little sarcastic laugh and Ronnie smiled.

The Bentons were another family where the majority of the wealth came from the previous generations and now there were descendants, close and distant, along with dubious friends and acquaintances all lining up for a piece of the pie, especially now that matriarch Dolores "Dolly" Benton was dying... though the woman had been on her death bed enough times that her current cries of "wolf" were being questioned.

"What happened to you?" he asked, finally glancing up and seeing her for the first time.

"Got caught in the rain. I was going to go home and change before we left."

He lifted his brows. "You might still want to do that..."

She remembered how her hair looked in the bathroom mirror. Good point. She had a few more calls to make and contracts to read over and then she would knock off early. She needed to decide what to do about the woman in the clearing. Did she dare go back to the police and talk to Detective Verbena again?

Dear God, that sounded bad.

She'd have to think about it.

Cooper switched off the ignition and waited in his SUV till the interior lights turned off. He was parked in the driveway, behind the garage where Jamie's car now sat. He watched rain drizzle down the windshield that was beginning to fog, then steeled himself. "Now or never," he whispered to himself as he got out of the SUV and walked toward the back steps. He heard Duchess barking inside, and from the frenzied sound of it was pretty sure the dog was trying to get Twinkletoes, the tuxedo cat, into playing with her. Both animals were basically Jamie's sister Emma's, though the menagerie was all part of their household now. Emma had insisted on taking care of Jamie in these last months of pregnancy, but Emma's help was... hard to define. Since the accident in her teens that had mentally compromised her, Emma had required extra care herself.

A few years earlier, upon the death of their mother, Jamie had become responsible for Emma's care. Jamie and her teenaged daughter, Harley, had relocated from Los Angeles back to River Glen and into the house where Jamie and Emma had grown up, the very house where they all lived now. Emma had recently moved in. Before that she had resided in Ridge Pointe Independent and Assisted Living. That's where Emma had first encountered Twink, the "death cat," an animal that seemed to sense when someone was about to die and curled up with them in bed.

Twink's ability to predict when a resident would pass had not gone over well with the facility's administration and Twink was chased out of the building enough times that Emma feared for the cat's life. So, Emma had moved back in the house with Cooper and Jamie, dog, cat and all. At least temporarily.

Emma joined Harley, who was attending Portland State University; Harley's boyfriend, Greer, a constant fixture; and Marissa, Cooper's own stepdaughter, currently back from out-of-state college but staying at her mother's.

Then there was Jamie's prescribed bed rest added to the mix.

Things were a little on the chaotic side.

What would happen when the two babies arrived?

With that he thought about pregnant Mary Jo's disappearance again and his jaw tightened. He'd find her. He would.

As he opened the back door, Cooper heard the skidding of Duchess's claws as the dog wheeled around at his entry. Which is when he remembered it was pizza night and he was in charge of bringing home dinner. Which he'd forgotten.

Great.

"Hey, Duch," he said to the dog, petting her head and absently scratching her ears before he headed down the hallway toward the kitchen.

Everything was quiet, which put his nerves on edge. Where was everyone? The dog was here and yes, there was Twink standing on the front window sill, her back still up from dealing with Duchess, the Christmas tree standing in the corner, lights glowing and reflecting on the array of ornaments collected over the years.

Looking through the window he spied Harley and her boyfriend saying goodbye to each other by Greer's car, which was parked across the street.

Turning around, he started, his muscles tightening for a second.

Emma was standing silently at the bottom of the stairs, her gaze on him.

"Emma," he said in surprise.

She put her finger to her lips and said in her toneless way, "Shh. Jamie's sleeping."

Their bedroom was on the second floor, down the hall and the door was solid core, so he thought Emma might be overreacting a little, but the point was well-taken anyway.

"How's she doing?" he asked.

Emma's eyes were big and blue, her dark blond hair tossed over one shoulder in its ubiquitous single braid. She'd been one of the most popular girls in his high school class before the accident. Afterwards, things like popularity ceased to matter very much. Now her eyes rarely focused on faces; she mostly looked past people when she spoke with them. Her expression rarely changed as well, but it didn't mean she wasn't listening.

"She said it was driving her batshit crazy," Emma revealed in that same flat tone.

Cooper smiled to himself. He could well imagine just how much the confinement bothered his irrepressible wife, though "batshit crazy" sounded rather mild as a description, based on the look on Jamie's face when she'd realized she had at least six more weeks in bed.

"I still gotta pick up the pizza, but I think I'll go see her now."

Duchess followed him up the stairs and stood anxiously outside the bedroom door, toes clicking on hardwood, as Cooper leaned down and warned the dog that she wasn't needed in the room. He then tapped lightly on the door and entered, fighting to keep the dog out while he squeezed in, keeping Duchess's nose just beyond the closing door.

Jamie gave him a "look" as she picked up the remote and switched off the TV.

"Wait, which house did they pick?" Cooper asked, staring at the TV in dismay.

"Ha-ha. That was a cake decorating competition, not HGTV."

But she did manage a smile, then sobered immediately. "Were you at the station?"

He knew she was worried about how he was taking his forced leave. "I'll check in tomorrow."

"What were you doing?"

"Oh . . . I don't know . . ." *You're putting off the inevitable*, he chided himself as he lay down on the bed beside her.

"What is it?" she asked in a voice threaded with alarm.

He was no good at lying to his wife. He never wanted to, and he never could. "Nothing bad." He sent up a prayer that he was right. "I have something to tell you, but I don't want to upset you." He heard her suck in a breath. "It's normal, according to Stephen Kirshner."

"Oh, no . . ." she whispered, eyes wide.

"Baby's fine. It's not that. It's that Mary Jo . . . left . . . about a week ago, and is on her own . . . he called it a vision quest."

"A vision quest? What's that supposed to mean?" she said, a little edge of panic in her voice.

"I don't know but—"

"And don't they last just a few days? What is this?" Jamie's hazel eyes searched his and before he could answer, she asked, "What does 'about a week ago' mean? Over a week?"

"Kirshner says she's done this before."

"Really? While she was pregnant? This is, what? Her normal behavior?" She was getting upset, her voice rising, her body growing stiff.

"I don't know."

"Well, where is she?"

"She hasn't told anyone, but she's called in."

"She 'called in'? Oh, that's just . . . awesome," she said sarcastically, obviously agitated. "We need to know where she is! That's our baby she's carrying! We're the parents! For the love of God, Cooper. She can't just take off and not tell us!"

"I know. I know. You're right. Of course. We need to know," Cooper agreed. He stood up again. Forced himself not to pace. "I went to see Paula Prescott today. She's an attorney with Tormelle and Quick."

"An attorney . . . ? Oh. God." Jamie sank back against the pillows, some of the fight draining from her, replaced, he thought, by a deep fear. "What? Why? Tell me."

"Okay, just stay calm and—"

"I will not!" she said. "Our baby is—Oh, God, we don't know where it is?"

"Jamie."

She held up a hand. Drew in a trembling breath and blinked back tears as she struggled to stay in control. "Damned pregnancy hormones," she said, sniffing and clearing her throat as she pulled herself together.

"Okay," she finally said. "Tell me what the hell's going on."

He did. Cooper quickly and concisely gave her the rundown of his meeting with the lawyer and the uncomfortable conclusion that there wasn't much to do at this point.

"We have rights," he said gently, trying not to upset her or upset her any further than she was already.

"You bet we have rights!"

"But it's a gray area."

"How gray?" Jamie shot back.

"If Mary Jo claims this is for her health and the health of the baby, and, if she feels she needs it for her own mental health, then she probably does."

"But we don't know where she is." She pressed her hands to her cheeks and took a few more deep breaths, as if trying not to totally flip out. "You've been keeping this from me?"

"For a few days," he admitted. "I wanted to speak to Paula before I told you everything."

"Because you didn't want to upset me."

He nodded, regarding her worriedly.

"Cooper, I'm not going to fall apart. Well, not really. I'm not going to get upset, or mad, or crazy. Well, okay, I am upset, really upset, but you're going to find her . . . right?"

"I'm going to do everything I possibly can," he stated firmly.

"But nothing crazy."

"Nothing crazy. Unless you count squeezing Kirshner's

head in a vise until he tells me where she is, or tells me how to find her. He's a . . ."

"Putz?" she offered up when he stopped himself.

"Yeah, that's just what I was going to say." *Or prick or dick or jerk-wad.*

She made a sound between a laugh and a moan.

"You okay?" Cooper felt his heart clutch a bit.

"Yes, yes. I'm fine." It was a lie. They both knew it, but he wasn't going to call her on it. "But please, don't keep things from me. Okay? Just find her. And find her fast!"

"I will," he promised.

She reached a hand out and he clasped it, holding it tight.

It was in the shower, while getting ready to meet Marian Langdorf, that the image came back to her.

Ronnie had stripped out of her clothes and ducked under the hot spray, shampooing her hair and generally warming up from her walk in the rain when she was flooded with the same scene she'd "witnessed" earlier. A woman's body, on the ground in the failing afternoon light, just before evening. Head turned away from her. Wrists bloody, torn and ravaged.

*Where's the dog? I don't hear the dog.*

Who was the woman? Why was she seeing her?

There were other sounds and sights. Trees. Lot of trees, both deciduous and evergreen. Whistle of the wind through the boughs. Gravel under tires? The rev of an engine? Someone leaving the scene?

Ronnie froze in the act of washing her hair, her hands stopped as if a switch was thrown. She could hear the rush of the water from the showerhead, yet her flesh was chilled from a cold wind, blasting through her memory.

She concentrated. Struggled to gaze harder at the image before the edges slipped away and the entire picture floated apart and disappeared, as they always did.

The lean-to shed looked about to fall down. There were gaps in the boards. She sensed confusion and fear. A hand reaching for the dog... and there it was. A low *grrrr* and the raising of hackles, the fur soft beneath tense fingers.

*Who's there?*

Was that the woman's voice? Ronnie's mind went back to her, lying in ice-crusted puddles, hair and clothes splattered or drenched with mud. A winged maple seed clung damply to one cheek. Her shoes were gone, although it looked like a black slip-on was lying on its side near her left foot.

Her left foot... was it *moving*?

Fear shot through Ronnie and the image *poofed* out.

Gone.

Breathing hard and weaving on her feet, Ronnie slammed back to the present. Quickly she shot an arm out to brace herself against the side of the shower and regain her balance. Water ran over her head, cascading. Shampoo slid into her eyes. Though the spray was warm, she shivered from head to foot, her teeth chattering as she reached for a towel.

Damn.

Sometimes it happened this way.

Sometimes all the noise and confusion and messy bits of information, or non-information, as the case may be, transformed into a piercing reality that needed action. She'd felt this way with Jesse James Taft, the certainty that he was in life-threatening danger, that certainty enough to manifest his own long-deceased sister.

But who to tell about this latest vision? The dead or dying person in the clearing needed help. How or why she seemed to be reaching out to Ronnie was a mystery. One she couldn't solve on her own.

*You have to call the police.*

She sighed. Toweling dry, she thought about calling Detective Verbena again, but this afternoon she'd met Detective Cooper Haynes. He was with the department. Except that he'd said he was on leave. Maybe he would be the best choice. Someone connected to the police but one step out?

But Verbena had listened to her. Sure, she'd eyed Ronnie with a careful expression, which meant she was assessing whether

Ronnie was a complete loon or someone with real information wrapped up in woo-woo, maybe as a method to hide her involvement in the very crime she was reporting. In the end, though, Verbena had used police resources to follow Edmond Olman and save his wife.

What to do? Unsure, Ronnie quickly dressed in black pants and a gray turtleneck, finally warming up as she stared at the items spread across her bed: cell phone, purse, laptop. A phone call wasn't going to cut it. She needed to talk to Verbena in person.

And she needed to meet with Marian Langdorf.

Soon.

No. Now.

She threw on her raincoat, then slid her phone into her purse and slung the strap over her shoulder before hurrying down the stairs to her Escape. All the way to her SUV she debated about blowing off the trip to the Langdorfs' in favor of the police station. But now she wasn't sure what she'd actually seen. Was the woman alive? Was she even real?

"Ah, hell . . ." She climbed inside her vehicle. Not knowing what the truth was, was killing her. Muttering aloud, she cranked the wheel in the direction of the Langdorf estate.

In the twenty-five minutes it took to reach the Langdorfs', Ronnie drove by rote, lost in her last vision, still vacillating on what action she should take regarding it. She didn't look forward to the grilling she would take, the sidelong looks, the general feeling that would prevail—that, once again, here was nutty Veronica Quick with another tale, dream, nightmare, vision that warned of impending doom, this time to a woman lying in a clearing somewhere, out in the elements. If the woman was still alive, time was of the essence. But again, was she? Did she even exist?

She turned into the long drive of the Langdorf property. The two-storied house was of gray stone, with gables and chimneys rising from the roof while mullioned windows stared down through the gathering gloom. The house resembled an English manor on a vast estate and she wondered if there was a garden in the back, behind the neat wrought-iron fence with its wicked-looking arrow points marching across the top.

Ronnie parked where the drive looped in front of the mansion. She was going to hurry through this meeting. She shouldn't have agreed to it, since she had no intention of taking Marian up on her offer. On the other hand, it would be easier to say no, now that she'd been introduced to her would-be job in person. She might not know what her future held, but it wasn't going to be as Marian Langdorf's guru.

The wind had dropped to a kicky breeze and she swept a hand across her forehead to hold back whipping, still damp strands of hair. She then pulled her phone from her cross-body purse and glanced at its face. Just after five. She might be a bit early, but she was eager to get this over with.

She rang the bell and waited... rang it again and waited some more. Was she that early? Leaning on the button with one hand, she tried rapping on the panels with the other. As a last resort she pulled out her phone and phoned Marian, but there was no answer.

Huh.

Well, fine.

She was heading down the one step of the porch toward her car when the door suddenly opened and Carlton stood back to allow her entry.

"I was just about to leave," she said, stepping inside and hearing him close the door behind her.

"Marian wouldn't like that," he said without an expression in his face. "She's expecting you."

"Good." Ronnie found herself standing in a foyer that rose two stories to a windowed dome decorated with a chandelier. A large red fleur-de-lis mosaic was inlaid in the center of the marble floor while an intricately carved railing curved upward to her right, the dark wood gleaming under the chandelier's illumination.

Looking around, she could believe in the rumor that Howell Langdorf, the grandson of a timber magnate, had ascribed to the concept that "more is more." His inherited fortune had been whittled down over the years amongst aunts, uncles and siblings, but there had been ample for him and Marian, who'd never had children. Carlton's arm of the family had reputedly squandered their money on ostentatious, expensive and ultimately worthless things, which was why he'd hitched himself onto the widowed Marian as a means of survival.

"Where's Marian?" She looked at Carlton, who was still wearing his suit from earlier in the day.

"She'll be down in a minute. Why don't you follow me?"

He led her through the double doors that led to a short hallway. Through a watery glass inset in a large exterior door at the end of the hall she could see into the backyard. No gardens. Just rolling lawn currently sprinkled with russet and gold and cranberry-colored maple leaves.

He stopped at an open archway that led into a sitting room with a rather old-looking television mounted above a stacked flagstone fireplace. On the opposite side of the hall was an elevator, its door designed in the same paneling as the rest of the house.

"We had that installed for Marian," Carlton said. He then gestured toward the sitting room. "I thought we might have a talk while Marian is getting ready."

Ronnie walked in ahead of him. "I don't mean to be impatient, but I have somewhere I need to be after this, so—"

"This won't take long." He cut her off. "I just need to clarify some things." He turned a palm toward a leather chair, which Ronnie perched upon as Carlton took his place by the fireplace, posing with a hand on the dark wood mantel. "We're all grateful for your help in diagnosing Marian's health issues."

"I just saw her in pain, that's all."

"She believes it's a lot more than that." They both knew that Ronnie had told her to have her liver checked, but Carlton clearly didn't want to belabor the point. "Which is . . . unfortunate, in that she thinks you're some kind of prognosticator, and you know that she wants to hire you. Let me be frank. There's not enough money. My aunt has assets, but they're not liquid. There isn't a lot of cash," he clarified, maybe thinking she didn't understand what he was saying.

Ronnie wanted to assure him she had no interest in whatever Marian Langdorf had cooked up for her, but Carlton's attitude sucked and she clamped her lips together and let him go on.

"So, her offer of a job just isn't going to work."

"She said she'd double whatever I was being paid," Ronnie said, purposely pushing him.

"I know what she said, but it's not true," he snapped back at her.

"Well, I think I should hear that from her."

"I'm leveling with you here. Don't take the job offer, no matter what she says. You won't be doing yourself, or her, any favors. She might be able to get some funds together in the beginning, but she doesn't really know her finances that well."

"You take care of them?"

"We work as a team to keep her solvent. When that fails . . ." He spread his hands.

Ronnie wondered who the "we" were, but decided she didn't care. She'd grown tired of playing Carlton's game already.

"In any case, she's grateful to you," he said in a brittle tone. "Maybe a little more than is reasonable. I'm sure you don't want to impose on that gratitude."

The whir of the elevator prevented Ronnie from answering. They both looked toward the archway. Carlton left his pose to meet the elevator. He helped open the door and offered his arm to Marian, who reluctantly took it, her other hand gripped around the wolf's-head cane.

As soon as she saw Ronnie, she dropped Carlton's arm and leaned on the cane. "Good. You're here. Let's go upstairs." And she turned around and thumped back to the still open elevator car.

". . . and this is your room. Mine's down the hall. I'll show it to you next, but you can see you have your own en suite bath." Marian worked her way across the room. She'd switched on the lights against the fading light. The windows were covered by heavy navy and gold damask curtains. Ronnie peeked through the slit provided and viewed the eastern side of the house's patio and pool, which was covered in debris from the firs, hemlocks and a now leafless weeping willow. More wet, green lawn ran toward a fifteen-foot-high laurel hedge.

Ronnie followed after Marian while Carlton rocked on his feet, hands in his pockets, waiting, staring ahead glassy-eyed. He was having serious trouble allowing his aunt to pursue her goal. Ronnie almost wanted to assure him that she wasn't going along with Marian's plans, that she'd just been playing devil's advocate, but the man did not evoke empathy.

*He wouldn't believe you anyway.*

Marian stood back triumphantly so Ronnie could peek into the bathroom. It was yards of white tile, set off by navy-blue wallpaper matching the design of the drapes, glittering gold fixtures, a nice-sized shower with a pebbled glass door.

Even as Ronnie eyed the room, her mind traveled to the woman in the clearing. Was she alive? Was she even real? She felt a growing urgency to unburden herself to the police. She wanted to leave now, but if she missed this walk-through, Marian would pester her to return, besides which the woman was a Tormelle & Quick client. Ronnie didn't need more fodder in her continuing fight with her father. Better to just get through it.

"If you prefer a bath, there's another bathroom down the hall, between my room and yours with a spa tub." Marian was going on.

Was the woman in the clearing someone she knew? There was such a tantalizing familiarity, something tickling in her memory that she couldn't quite grasp. She must be real, otherwise why would the vision be so vivid? So compelling and—

"Veronica?" Marian bit out.

She jolted to attention as if goosed. "I'm sorry."

"You're woolgathering. Come along."

Ronnie stepped back and then followed her from the bathroom to the bedroom again.

"Carlton, what are you doing?" Marian snapped at him.

Carlton stiffened, a fleeting expression crossing his face of . . . what? Something dark, she thought. Immediately he became overly solicitous to his aunt, fussing about, annoying Marian Langdorf to no end even as she took it as her due. But the baleful stare he leveled at Ronnie when Marian wasn't looking spoke of his true feelings. It curdled any desire she'd had earlier to alleviate his tension. *This is a you problem, Carlton.* Let him stew about it a little longer. She was half inclined to display an enthusiasm she didn't feel, just to piss him off, but that would only give Marian a false impression.

So . . . she and Carlton both just trailed after the older woman and Ronnie mentally checked the time, wondering when she could reasonably beg off.

# Chapter 6

It was completely dark as she drove through the rain-washed streets, precipitation splattering her windshield in deep, persistent plops. It had felt interminable at the Langdorfs' and then she'd had to hem and haw, much to Marian's displeasure, before she'd been allowed to leave. Now she was heading to the River Glen Police Department. Maybe a fool's errand, but she needed to unburden herself, especially if there was any chance the woman in the clearing was alive. She hoped she still had time to catch Detective Verbena at work, though at this hour that particular hope was slim.

She was fighting with the desire to just head home. She could be settling in for the night, nibbling on cheese and crackers and apple slices, her go-to makeshift meal when she wasn't interested in picking something up or using a delivery service. Maybe even some television, and if she were particularly energetic, popcorn.

Her appearance at River Glen P.D. would not be appreciated. The last time she'd approached them she'd been quietly laughed at, and even though she'd eventually been proved right, it didn't mean they really believed or trusted her. She was having enough trouble trusting herself.

As she pulled in to the station lot it felt like the tan brick, squat, one-story building was malevolently watching her, which really didn't help her confidence. She sat for a moment, wondering if she should go through the main doors and battle with the front desk, or try to sneak in through the back where most of the department's employees entered. That would turn a few heads, for sure, however, and she didn't need any more scrutiny.

Stepping into the rain once more, she tiptoed around a deep puddle in the tarmac, remotely locking her car. The last twenty-four hours had been leading to this moment ever since that first message about the woman in the clearing. And then Shana's appearance at her doorstep with divorce papers, the car accident, the trip to the hospital to see Shana, the battle with Galen, running into Detective Cooper Haynes and then Marian and Carlton Langdorf and everything . . . seeing Brandy, however briefly. The argument with her father . . . issues at work . . . No wonder she was starting to feel really tired, damn near bone weary. She needed to get this meeting with the police over with, pass the baton.

She hurried through the rain and pushed inside.

"I'd like to see Detective Verbena, is she here?" she asked the female officer behind the plexiglass at the front desk. Her name tag read *Dennison*.

"I'm sorry, she's not. Is there someone else you want to see, or could I help you?"

She waited a moment. Ronnie vacillated in her mind. Maybe she should find Detective Haynes. Paula Prescott, an attorney at the office, had his information. That would mean waiting till tomorrow, however, unless she could get hold of Paula tonight and she would be willing to help Ronnie out, which would require all kinds of questions, no doubt. So, maybe Officer Dennison was the one to talk to, but she was working the front desk and Ronnie would really prefer somewhere less public than reception.

While she mentally dithered, the door to the inner sanctum buzzed open and a man stepped out. Ronnie half glanced his way but was still processing. "Maybe," she began, but Officer Dennison said brightly, "Looks like Detective Hart is still here. Right here, in fact." She smiled in the direction of the newcomer.

Ronnie felt the woman's words slip into her brain, electrifying her synapses. Detective *Hart? Sloan* Hart? Was there another Detective Hart in the area? Couldn't be. Jesus. *Sloan* . . . *!* My God . . . old home week . . . it was a conspiracy!

She was afraid to turn and look his way. She hadn't dropped her hood, so she felt somewhat protected. Slowly, feeling like she was in a farce, she pivoted ninety degrees to see his face. Her heart was jumping all over her rib cage. Yes. Damn . . . damn . . . damn.

Sloan. Hart.

"What can I help you with?" he asked.

Dark hair. Gray eyes. Strong jaw. More handsome than she remembered. Scarier than she remembered. Sterner. He wore a gray overcoat over a dark blue suit coat, silver tie.

She couldn't find her voice. Had to clear her throat . . . then still couldn't answer. It would be hard enough to say to Detective Verbena: *I'm having a psychic vision of a woman dying or dead and I need you to find her and help her.*

But to Sloan?

"I'm . . . looking for someone," she managed to finally say in a strangled voice.

He thought a moment, then shrugged. "Buzz us back through," he told Officer Dennison.

*Bzzzzzzzz* filled Ronnie's head as Dennison pressed the button to allow entry and Sloan held the door open for her. She preceded him into the squad room on rubber legs. Sinking into the chair beside his desk, the one he kindly told her she should sit in.

He didn't take off his overcoat as he sat down at his desk, wheeling the chair back a bit so that he could get a look at her.

"Let's start with your name and then get to who you're looking for."

Detective Sloan Hart had only been with the River Glen P.D. scant weeks. Initially he hadn't really considered a position in his hometown, more because he didn't think there was an opening than because he didn't want the job. But he had been hired by the Colvin County Sheriff's Department, where they had been looking for someone to take the place of a recently retired detective. When Sloan had walked in, he'd been greeted by an old school buddy, Abel Townsend, who was delighted Sloan was interested in the job.

"Goddamn," Townsend said, grinning. He shook his hand and slapped him hard on the back. "Welcome."

But almost before he'd settled in, Detective Cooper Haynes had been put on administrative leave at RGPD for pissing off the mayor, the city council and his own chief, a situation that was total bullshit according to the rank and file, political high jingo, the kind of thing that makes good officers want to quit. Sloan hadn't really wanted to step into that mess, but Haynes was too good a cop to be let go and from all he'd heard, was planning to return. So, in a deal between the sheriff's department and RGPD, Sloan had temporarily moved over, one foot here, one foot there, a man without a country so to speak. Townsend had been reluctant to let him go, but had chosen to approve the transfer and Chief Duncan's good favor, so voilà... Sloan was currently with the RGPD.

Which left him a short-timer, and that was fine. He'd chosen law enforcement because he found it interesting and was good at it, not because it was going to make him rich, but he was thinking about the next phase of his life and wondering if he should try to find a more lucrative career path. His father had pushed hard, encouraging Sloan, but then his parents had always dreamed their son would work on Wall Street or become some sort of multimillionaire/billionaire, and Sloan just wasn't made that way. His friend, Evan Caldwell, another River Glen grad, was the man who was amassing a fortune, from a wheelchair, in front of an array of monitors that kept track of whatever financial wizards like Evan kept track of.

But that was not Sloan.

His desk was several rows back from Detective Elena Verbena's, Haynes's partner, though he was directly in her line of sight. He hadn't been foolish enough to sit at Detective Haynes's desk, which butted up to hers. He didn't need to ruffle more feathers than had already been ruffled by Chief Marcus Duncan hiring him practically as the door was still shutting on Haynes. Verbena was still a tad tetchy with him, so it was wise to tread carefully, although she was absent a lot herself, looking after her ailing mother.

Sloan had been in Seattle, after a stint in both Los Angeles and Oakland. His relationship with his ex-wife, Tara, hadn't survived the shifting moves. She'd wanted him out of police business entirely and hadn't been shy about saying so. He'd had to keep his own seesawing thoughts about law enforcement to himself, or she would have pounced on his indecision and made future plans for him . . . for them. They'd split while in Seattle and she'd been so angry that she'd hooked up with a friend of his, expecting, apparently, for him to be consumed with jealousy and anger and . . . what? Take her back? Change his mind? All it had served to do was make the break permanent.

The irony was that Tara worked for a vacation rental company that competed with Airbnb, whose headquarters happened to be in Portland, and each move had brought her closer to the mother-ship and, well . . . Portland, or specifically, River Glen, which was where he wanted to be, too. She'd called him the other day, wanting to get together for a drink, or dinner, or just a talk, and he'd eased out of that. But she clearly thought being in the same locale was some kind of sign for the future.

But . . . it wasn't. The marriage was over. He and Tara had different interests and time had eroded that first blush of excitement. If they'd been able to settle into a real friendship they might have had a chance, but as time went on, things went the other way. The fissure between them grew to a chasm and though she'd dragged her feet a bit about getting the divorce, she'd eventually capitulated. If she had other ideas concerning that decision now, Sloan wasn't interested.

Another bit of irony: He was temporarily staying in a You+Me Homes, one he'd booked through Tara's company.

Now, though, he was filling in for both Haynes and Verbena, as the latter's uncertain schedule was another reason Sloan had been shifted over. Chief Duncan was down two detectives—at least, one and a half—and a suspicious death had been reported at the Oak Terrace Apartments this morning. He and Verbena had checked into it just before she left to take care of her mom. She'd tasked Sloan with interviewing witnesses and family members while she was gone and had promised to help him in the investigation as much as she could from her mother's hospital room.

Meanwhile, Townsend seemed to be regretting "loaning" Sloan to RGPD and had said he needed a hard date when Sloan would be coming back. Sloan had protested; he'd barely stuck his head in at River Glen P.D. But Townsend had just growled at him, something about being taken advantage of, which had zero base in reality. Sloan's appointment to River Glen had been as much Townsend's doing as Chief Duncan's.

So, when Colleen Dennison at the front desk told the woman in the black raincoat that he was available instead of Verbena, he'd felt mild annoyance. After a day back and forth with Townsend, he'd barely looked at the woman; his head was full of other stuff. He didn't really see her. And not just because her black hood shadowed her face. His mind was elsewhere and he was already regretting not lamming out when he had the chance.

"I'm . . . looking for someone," she managed to say again, ignoring, for the moment at least, the question of her own identity. Okay—they would get to that.

"Uh-huh. A missing person?" he asked, taking a fresh legal pad from a drawer.

"Yes . . ."

"How long have they been missing?"

"I'm not sure."

"Do you feel this person is in danger?"
"Yes. I think so."
"You do." He'd half expected her to say there'd been some kind of fight and the missing person had walked out on her. There was some tension about her that made him feel she was holding back.
"You don't sound sure."
"I'm sure."
"Okay, what's the missing person's name?" He picked up a pen and clicked it on.

He wanted to tell her to drop the hood, but she seemed skittish and ready to bolt and he would just as soon get everything taken down before that happened and she ended up complaining that no one would help her. He'd been down that road before.
"I don't know."
Sloan leaned back in his chair and studied her. "You don't know the name of the missing person."
"It's a woman. She's in a clearing . . . and there's a shed, and trees, evergreen and deciduous, and there's a shed . . . gray boards. It, uh, doesn't look that sturdy . . . and I think there are tire tracks. It's wet and muddy and she's just lying there, face turned away."
Sloan took that in. "You've seen a picture?" What was this, a ransom attempt?
"Yes . . . yes . . . oh, and there's a dog . . . barking."
"You've seen a picture of a barking dog?"
"No, not exactly. I haven't seen the dog. I just think he's a part of it. Or she, I don't know what the dog is. I know I'm confusing you. I just know that this woman's in trouble and I need to help her somehow."
She sounded impatient.
"How do you know there's a barking dog if he's not in the picture?" Sloan asked slowly.
A long pause.
He felt the hair on his arms rise long before she answered, "Because I heard him."

\* \* \*

She was making a mess of it. She didn't want to talk to Sloan. She wanted to talk to Verbena. She should never have agreed to come into the squad room. She should've turned tail and run as soon as she realized it was Sloan. *Jesus.* Sloan! *Sloan!*

He clearly didn't know who she was, but she was pretty sure when he heard her name he would. And it wouldn't be good. So far, she'd avoided the question of her identity. That wouldn't last long.

"Will Detective Verbena be here tomorrow?" she asked a bit desperately.

"You want to give this report to her then?"

"If . . . if she's going to be here? But I need to . . . you, the police, need to find this woman before it's too late, or maybe it already is. I don't know for sure, but we need to find her."

She was repeating herself and she could hear her voice growing higher with tension over the rumble of warm air flowing through hidden air ducts.

"I can't promise Detective Verbena will be here tomorrow."

His tone said he would be more than happy to be rid of her, and the way he kept his eyes on her emphasized that fact as well. She was afraid to put her hood down, but now he was shrugging out of his coat, as if he'd given up on trying to go home. He already thought she was a crackpot. *Knew* she was a crackpot. But he was going to follow through with taking down her information.

Ronnie let out her breath. The room smelled like dust and a faint hovering perfume, which she associated with Detective Verbena. The desks were butted up to each other and there was a glassed-in office toward the rear that was currently empty, the blinds thrown back to reveal a desk shrouded in shadows. She could hear some conversation going on in another room but she couldn't make out the words. At that moment an officer entered from the back, which she knew contained the break room, and further along, several holding cells. The officer nodded to Sloan, his glance passing over Ronnie.

"You know Detective Verbena," Sloan said, prompting her.

His tie was a bit askew, as if he'd been pulling on it, releasing the top button of his white shirt. She caught a glimpse of the naturally tan column of his throat. The darkened beard shadow on his chin spoke to the later hour. His eyes never let her go.

Carefully, Ronnie pulled back her hood. "We've . . . been involved in a case together," she admitted, keeping her face averted. Her voice sounded like her own again, though her pulse was running light and fast.

"Does she know about this missing person?"

"Not yet. That's why I'm here."

"Okay. Let's start at the beginning. Tell me who you are, and as much about this missing person as you have."

"I already told you as much as I know."

"A picture and a barking dog. A dog that's not in the picture, but you think it belongs in the picture. Have I got that right?"

"I know how it sounds," she said evenly.

"That makes one of us." He was trying to remain neutral, but she was definitely testing his patience.

She admitted, "I haven't given you enough to find her. I know that. I wish I had more."

He swiveled toward his desk and computer screen, clicking the keyboard. "Let's fill out a missing persons report. Give me the information and I'll enter it. Your name?"

Ronnie closed her eyes. If she didn't feel so certain, if the situation wasn't so critical . . . "Veronica . . . Hillyard."

It was a chicken's way out.

He typed it in. "Two *l*'s or one?"

"Two."

"And the woman you're worried about?"

"I don't know her name. I told you all I know. Oh. She has wounds on her arms, her wrists, actually."

His eyebrows drew together. "That was in the picture?"

"Yes. It's cold. The mud puddles are icy, ice-edged."

"Do you have this picture with you?"

Was he playing with her? His tone had grown more and more remote. "In a manner of speaking." Her mouth was cotton.

"Can I see it?" He took his hands off the keyboard and slowly swiveled back to her.

"I think you already know you can't."

They stared at each other. In a distant part of her mind, Ronnie was annoyed that he looked so damn good. Yes, Sloan Hart had always been attractive, but couldn't he have gained weight, lost hair, aged early like Shana had? Instead, he pulled at her in a way she hadn't felt in years... maybe ever.

*I'm going to marry you.* She mentally cringed away from the memory and felt a slight charge in the air. He recognized her.

"Veronica... Quick," he said with a nod.

"That's right. And I'm sure, if you know anything about me, you've got a lot to say about it, but my purpose here is to find the woman in the clearing, and I need the department's help to do that."

"Let me get this straight, then," he said evenly, gray eyes assessing. "Cards on the table. You've seen this person. Not in a photograph, in your... mind..."

She nodded firmly. "I don't recognize her, but there's some reason, some connection, or I wouldn't be getting these messages."

"You've gotten more than one?"

"I've gotten several."

"All the same." His tone was without judgment or skepticism, but still he was appraising her and it was all she could do not to squirm under his gaze.

"Mostly... minor differences... the picture's becoming clearer."

"Okay, Ms. Quick."

"It's Ronnie," she reminded him.

He nodded, said only, "You want me to believe, so convince me."

There was nothing in his demeanor that said he was going to listen to her. She half considered just walking out and taking her chances later with Verbena. Or maybe Haynes, although she'd thought she had some information for him and it had turned to dust.

She was in over her head with Sloan Hart. Way over her head. Convince him? His mind was already made up. Still...

"I've been getting messages about her, possibly from her, I don't know. But she's lying in a clearing with a shed and there's a dog barking. It's frigid cold and—"

"You *hear* the dog," he interrupted.

"I hear the dog, but I don't see him, or her. I don't know what kind of dog it is. It's not a yip, but it's not a really deep bark, either." She hesitated, remembering how she'd thought she heard the dog at Shana's accident and had been looked at by Tesla-man as if she were nuts. He'd thought Ronnie had suffered some kind of head injury.

"Go on."

"Her wrists, her arms and wrists, are bloody and the skin is torn. I think... she might be dead. Strangled." He lifted his brows and she added, "I think there are marks on her neck. Bruising?"

"What's she wearing?" When Ronnie didn't immediately answer, he added, "Or, is she naked?"

"No, no... she's in a dark gray coat and pants and a dark blouse or shirt. Her shoes have come off and her feet are bare. It's cold. It feels really cold."

"So, you can feel it, too?"

She shot him a baleful look. "She's lying in icy mud puddles, so yeah, it's cold. I see the picture and I can feel it. It's December."

"This picture, this vision, doesn't give you a clue where it is?"

"No."

"So, it could be anywhere in the world?"

"I've never seen anything outside of the region I'm in. It's near enough to me for me to be getting the message."

"There are rules, then?" One eyebrow arched.

So he thought she was nuts. Like just about everybody. From down the hall she heard a printer coming to life.

"It's fine that you don't believe me," Ronnie said, more than a little indignant. "You're not the first. All I'm doing is giving you the information."

"Sounds like you've had this kind of thing happen before."

*I'm going to marry you.*

She cleared her throat. "Once or twice."

Another cop waltzed into the room from the back hallway at that moment, rolling the wrapper off an energy bar and biting into the nuts, oats and goo. He looked over at her as she was avoiding Sloan's hard stare and their gazes met.

"Hey." He stopped short. "You're that psychic gal, huh? The one who said Olman was going to kill his wife." He bit off another chunk of his bar, and mumbled around a piece stuffed in his cheek, " 'Course he'd already beaten her up pretty bad by the time you reported it."

Sloan had looked over at him, but his attention boomeranged back to Ronnie. If he'd stared at her hard before, it felt like she was being blasted by flames under his current scorching glare.

He said carefully, "Is this some kind of joke?"

"No."

"You're famous around River Glen."

"Infamous, you mean." She lifted her chin. Man, he was irritating her.

"That, too. But I'm not wasting my time over a pursuit that's all in your head. You don't have information, you have ideas. Maybe this woman is out there and needs help, maybe she isn't. But even if she is, you haven't given me a starting place."

"I wish I could give you more. Believe me."

"But you can't."

"She may be dying, or is dead already. I—I don't know. We just need to help her. She's out there, somewhere. Maybe he'll come back and finish her off if she's not already dead."

"He?"

"I don't know. Maybe it's a she," Ronnie admitted. "The perp. Whoever did this to her, but I don't feel like it is."

"You don't feel like it is," he repeated.

"That's right. I don't *feel* like it is." She stared him down. "Look, I came here to report a crime and that's what I'm doing. Make fun of me all you want, I just want to help a victim."

He held up his hands. "Okay. You clearly believe you've gotten a psychic message, but just wait," he said as she started to protest. "View it from my perspective. You want me to find someone. Someone you don't know, and don't know where they are. And where that place is? Just a description from somewhere in your head. You don't know if this person even really exists. You have no information other than this belief, vision, or whatever. You don't even know the person's name."

"I know she's in terrible trouble. That's what I know."

"It isn't a lot to go on."

She half laughed. "It's nothing to go on. *I know.* But it needs to be said. It needs to be . . ."

"Out in the universe?" he finished for her.

He was trying to make her see how ridiculous she sounded. Well, she already knew. In spades.

"When someone's in trouble, I try to help them. Detective Verbena listened to me about Edmond Olman. She increased patrols around the house after I told her Olman was going to try and kill his wife. I didn't know it had already happened."

The officer munching on the energy bar made a scoffing sound.

Ronnie felt her cheeks heat. She was getting nowhere. Par for the course. She could already feel the anxiety building that reminded her she was going to have to figure this one out for herself.

"Without more to go on, there's nothing we can really do."

At least he wasn't scoffing like the officer. But he didn't look like he believed her at all, either.

*He thinks you're a complete crackpot.*

She looked away from his steady gaze and remembered being beneath him at The Pond, the pebbles digging into her back, his hands on her chest, his mouth on hers . . .

For a moment she was back there. Twenty years past and it felt like it was happening again. She could smell the dank odor of algal water, the sweet aroma of pink cupcake frosting, the sharp, clean scent of fir needles . . . She could feel Sloan's strength, sense his own fear. She remembered that joyful feeling that she was meant to be with him, marry him, that had consumed her when she was *ten years old.*

*Jesus H. Christ. Get OVER it!*

Her throat was hot with embarrassment. She wanted to say something sharp and mean. She'd nurtured the dream that if and when she should ever meet Sloan again that she would be smart, cold, and bitingly clever, put together and completely disinterested in anything he had to say. She would roll her eyes at her own moronic silliness from that day at The Pond and then, because she was a nice, good person at heart, she would thank him again for saving her life, but it would be perfunctory. Duty done.

Never in her imaginings had she seen herself coming to him for help with one of her psychic visions.

And the fact was he wasn't going to help her, so she needed to leave.

As if on cue her cell phone rang. She swept it from her bag and glanced at the number. One she didn't recognize. She didn't answer, but it was a good excuse to act like she had somewhere she had to be.

"I have to leave," she said, getting to her feet as the call went to voice mail.

"I'll walk you out," Sloan said.

"You don't have to."

"Car's out front. I'm going the same way."

# Chapter 7

Ronnie felt Sloan behind her as they headed out of the squad room. He reached around for the door and the heat of his arm lifted the hairs on hers. She had a moment of thinking about her relationship with Galen and realized with a kind of annoyed pang at herself that she'd never been so attuned to Galen as she seemed to be to Sloan Hart. What a cosmic joke.

"You work at your father's law firm," he said as they both prepared for the rain, Ronnie tossing her hood over her head, Sloan stretching his arms through his gray coat.

"You do know about me."

Did he also remember she was the same girl he'd saved at The Pond?

She was trying to figure out how to ask him, when he did it for her. "Glad you and Evan both survived that day on the river."

Ah, yes. He did know. Shana had described his embarrassment at all the teasing he'd endured because of her. But this was an opportunity she'd missed when she was ten. "I never got to really thank you for saving my life, so thank you."

His smile appeared genuine and she felt herself melt a little inside, which pissed her off anew. She'd never gotten over that day, either, and she'd apparently almost granted celebrity status on Sloan, at least where she was concerned, which *really* pissed her off.

"I'll let Detective Verbena know you want to talk to her," he said as he walked toward a black Bronco parked two slots away from her Escape, both spaces empty.

Did he remember what she'd blurted out that day? Did he? It had been so embarrassing for both of them. "How is Evan?" she heard herself ask, knowing she was just trying to keep Sloan from disappearing so soon.

What she'd said was wild, but people came out of dreams, comas and fugue states and often said strange things.

*But . . . you said you were going to* marry *him . . .*

*And then you screamed your head off when you saw Evan's "evil ghost" rising from his body.*

She shook her head against the memories, wanting to physically push them away. They were the first and worst of her prediction failures.

"You okay?" he called to her as he reached his Bronco.

Still skirting puddles, she glanced over at him. "I'm fine." Kind of a lie, she thought as she unlocked the Escape remotely. "Thank you . . . Detective."

"Good. And as for Evan, he's doing all right, I guess. I ask him for help sometimes."

"Help?"

"He's . . . good at computer research." Sloan held up a hand in goodbye.

The dryness of his tone held a wealth of unspoken information.

*Evan's a hacker*, she thought, sliding into her Escape.

She forced herself not to look back at him as she drove away. Her cell phone rang as soon as she was out of the parking lot. Same number as before. The double call suggested someone needed her immediate attention, so she picked up, touching the button for speaker phone as she set the cell in her cup holder.

"Veronica? It's Shana."

"Shana," she repeated, then asked, "How did you get my number?"

"Oh. Galen. Can you come back to the hospital? I think they're going to release me and . . . my car was towed? I don't know where it is. I need a ride."

Galen. It figured. Did Shana have no one else she could depend on? She'd mentioned Evan as a friend, but maybe picking up Shana and driving her around was beyond his scope. "They're releasing you *tonight?* Not tomorrow?"

"I don't have insurance. I don't know what I'm going to do."

For several moments Ronnie stared silently at the rain drizzling down her windshield. It was dark as pitch. No moon. The clouds were low, obscuring the view beyond a few yards from her headlights, turning the sharp edges misty. She really didn't want to take on the responsibility of Sloan's high school girlfriend. What a weird set of circumstances.

"We'll have to check with the police to find out where your car is." *We'll?* "*You'll* have to check with the police. Where do you live?"

"It's not far from you. Closer to the river."

She wanted to tell her to call a cab, hire an Uber, phone a friend . . . but she already sensed that if Shana could possibly do that, she already would have. Somewhat reluctantly, she said, "Okay, I can be at Glen Gen in ten minutes and drive you home."

"Thank you," she said, sounding more sincere and heartfelt than she had at any moment when Ronnie had seen her earlier. Maybe that's what desperation did to you.

Ronnie drove back to the hospital, whose parking lot pole lights cast large pools of misty illumination through the dark, over the soggy asphalt and dreary greenery. She parked as near as possible to the front doors, tossed her hood over her hair again, and walked determinedly forward, head bent to the rain.

She didn't know what she was going to do about the woman in the clearing.

"Now would be a good time for some real help," she muttered aloud to the powers that be who'd blessed her with this curse.

As she entered the building, she stood a moment just inside, wondering if it would be inopportune to shake herself like a dog to throw off the water. She dropped back her hood and headed for the elevator to the fourth floor. When she exited she nearly ran into Brandy again.

Only this time Brandy noticed her and looked very surprised. She stopped short and smiled back at her old friend and classmate. Her eyes were lively with interest.

"Ronnie," she said on a note of discovery.

"Hi, Brandy."

"Wow. You look exactly the same. Well, almost. Are you eating anything? There's a lot less of you."

Ronnie looked down at herself. Was she that skinny? "I'm basically the same."

"Okay, maybe you are. I didn't see you as much in high school. How are you? I was . . . believe it or not, I was just thinking about you."

"Seriously?"

"Yeah. And here you are."

"Maybe you're the psychic."

Brandy bit off a laugh. "Not even. I can hardly tell what time it is when I'm working."

"You're a nurse at Glen Gen?"

She nodded. "I just moved from cardiac. A lot of cranky old people in cardiac. I'm over it."

Ronnie smiled. Brandy hadn't changed.

"Have you got a minute?" she asked.

There was a tension about her that Ronnie recognized had been there when she'd seen her earlier, too, even in those few moments that she was getting on the elevator. Her dark hair was bound back from her face in a tight bun at her nape. Her makeup was faintly smeared, as if she'd been rubbing her eyes, and there were lines of strain around her mouth.

Ronnie pulled her cell from her purse and checked the time. "I think so. I'm here to pick someone up, but I don't know what time she needs to leave."

"Who? This is kind of late."

"I know. That's what I said. I don't know what the reason is, I'm just . . . picking her up, but sure, I guess."

"Good." A half a pace ahead of Ronnie, Brandy led her past a central nurses' station toward an alcove at the end of the hall. Four tan-colored chairs and a table and artwork on the walls filled the niche. "Wait a sec." Brandy, as if an idea had just struck her, stopped short near the alcove and abruptly turned. "You're not picking up Shana Lloyd, are you?"

"One and the same."

"Huh." She sounded nonplussed.

"I know. It's . . . surprising how much involvement I seem to suddenly have with old classmates," Ronnie admitted.

"Okay, well, I don't want to get in the way of that. Can we get together, though. Soon? I'll call you tomorrow?"

"Sure." They exchanged numbers and then Brandy frowned down at the floor, as if she were working herself up to say something else.

"What is it?" asked Ronnie. She had a spidery sense of something coming, so strong that her skin raised in goose bumps. She waited, but Brandy just shook her head and said, "Tomorrow's my day off. Want to meet for coffee? Or lunch?"

The moment passed. It wasn't a premonition, exactly, but it had grabbed Ronnie's attention. "Coffee's fine." Her day was fairly open. "Any hint of what you want to talk about?" Brandy was practically bursting with the need to get something off her chest.

For a moment it seemed like she would unburden herself, but instead she settled for, "It can wait till tomorrow. Let's just say I may need your help."

"Legal help?" Ronnie asked carefully.

"More like your special kind of help." Brandy shot her a weak smile and Ronnie tamped down her disappointment that her old friend was as much a user as everyone else. She wanted something to do with Ronnie's "gift."

*All for one, and one for all.*

"Okay," said Ronnie, and Brandy seemed to breathe easier.

Ronnie's last good deed for the day was dealing with Shana. It turned out the hospital hadn't really released Shana yet, but she was panicked about her rising medical debt and was determined to leave.

Wearing her blood-splattered clothes from the night before, Shana was seated in a wheelchair when Ronnie entered her room.

Shana wasn't happy about it and argued with the aide who insisted on pushing the chair to the front doors, despite Shana's insistence she could walk on her own "just fine." Nonetheless she grudgingly accepted the ride to the portico beyond the sliding glass doors where it was left to Ronnie to make sure Shana made it into her SUV.

"Geez, I'm not that bad," Shana insisted, though it seemed that maybe she was, as she struggled to buckle her seat belt. When it snapped into place, she said, "You think we could stop for coffee on the way?"

Why not?

Ronnie drove through the nearest Starbucks with a drive-through window where holiday lights twinkled around the windows of the shop. They each ordered a small coffee, Ronnie's black, Shana's with cream.

"Thank you," Shana said, cradling the warm cup and sipping in the few minutes it took to drive to her apartment complex, a run-down group of buildings several rungs down in the "deferred maintenance" column from Ronnie's.

"I'll get rid of that," Shana said, grabbing Ronnie's coffee that was only half drunk. Ronnie started to protest, but Shana was determined to carry both cups as she negotiated a weather-beaten wooden stairway to the building's third floor. The place needed new paint, a new roof, new siding and new windows, and that was just the exterior. Inside, Ronnie caught a whiff of dampness and a glance around a tidy but tired living room and open concept kitchen.

"You sure you're okay?" Ronnie asked as Shana set the two paper coffee cups on the chipped Formica counter.

"I told you that Evan can help me from here. Thanks for the ride. I really appreciate it. Evan doesn't drive much."

"Okay."

Shana had given Ronnie a further inside view of her surprising relationship with Evan Caldwell on the ride from the hospital. Though things had faded with Sloan, she'd been there for Evan and he for her, in turn, apparently. Their friendship had endured and strengthened over the years. And though he rarely got behind the wheel of his hand-controlled vehicle, they found ways to get together. Shana went on to reveal that she had worked at a large Portland department store through the years and risen to run the women's department, aided by Evan's business acumen as he grew a regional investment business. When her store merged with another and she lost that job, it was Evan who came to her rescue. Shana was currently seeking a job at Galen's law firm, which is how Galen had roped her into process-serving for the firm and she'd landed on Ronnie's doorstep.

Between the lines there had been another thread running throughout this explanation: Evan was connected to Sloan Hart, their friendship having endured as well, and Shana wanted a connection to Sloan. When Ronnie's name came up she'd been curious to meet her again, the girl who, at barely ten years old had pronounced she was going to marry Sloan Hart.

"I told Evan about you," Shana had admitted. "He remembered you screaming that day. He said it was kind of weird that after all these years I connected with you not long after Sloan moved back to Portland. It's kind of like we're all coming back together in some odd, cosmic way, y'know?"

Ronnie had made appropriate "huh" and "you think so?" comments to what really sounded like Shana still obsessing over Sloan in ways that seemed almost pathological. Ronnie kept her recent meeting with him to herself, sensing that would not be appreciated. Though Shana didn't say it—she didn't have to say it, as it was obvious—the message was Sloan Hart was hers and hers alone.

It seemed like this tale of love and devotion was entirely one-sided.

"Any prescriptions or anything else I can get you?" Ronnie asked, preparing to leave.

"No. Thanks. Evan will help if I need anything."

"You sure?"

"Yeah."

On the way back to her own apartment, Ronnie was overcome by weariness. A long day. A lot of people and a lot of distractions, but still the overriding need was to find the woman in the clearing.

*Maybe there is no one. Maybe it's all just smoke and mirrors. There's nothing you can do about it anyway. In that, Sloan Hart is right.*

"Sloan Hart," she murmured aloud, turning into her apartment complex.

She went to bed still thinking about him and he ended up haunting her dream, a lover who stayed just out of reach.

*What was Mary Jo's transportation?*

The question kept interrupting Cooper's sleep Thursday night and was the one he woke up with in the wee hours of Friday morning. As he lay next to a sleeping Jamie, Cooper thought about what Stephen Kirshner hadn't said—wouldn't say, actually—but Cooper had seen two cars in the Kirshner driveway when he'd stopped in to interrogate Mary Jo's husband about her disappearance. Those were the same two cars he'd seen when he and Jamie had gone to their home to meet with them about Mary Jo's possible surrogacy months earlier.

So . . . how had she left? A lift from a friend? A cab? A ride share? She likely hadn't traveled on foot, at least not far, considering she was eight months pregnant.

What was likely was that Stephen Kirshner knew where she was, but wasn't telling. He acted as if his wife just up and left in the dark of night, or the bright of day or in a puff of smoke . . . as if it were some big mystery. But that's not what happened in real life, and Cooper, who'd tried hard not to strong-arm the man into telling what he knew, or at least suspected, was through messing around. A deadline was approaching. Time quickly passing.

He needed to find Mary Jo and he needed to find her now.

He slid a glance at his wife and saw Jamie was breathing regularly, sleeping peacefully after nearly coming unglued when he'd told her about Mary Jo's disappearance. Not that he blamed Jamie. He, too, was worried and angry and scared. What the hell was up with the surrogate? Where was she? God, he hoped beyond hope that the baby—*his* baby, *Jamie's* baby—was okay.

He'd called Verbena. He'd wanted to ask his partner to check cab companies and ride shares to see if anyone had picked up someone at the Kirshners' address. But Verbena wasn't on the job. She was with her mother, who was not responding well to cancer treatments. The department had a new temporary hire: Detective Sloan Hart. Cooper knew the man slightly. They'd both graduated from River Glen High, about five years apart. But he didn't know him well enough to ask this kind of favor, and he did know better than to leave digital footprints for Chief Duncan to follow and find out he was trying to use department resources for a personal problem.

A personal problem, he thought darkly as he took a shower, dressed and quietly went downstairs in the predawn hours. He didn't want to wake Jamie, or anyone, although he heard Duchess whine from Emma's room. He almost let the dog out but Twink shot out of their bedroom at the same moment and trotted down the stairs ahead of him, so he determined he would get the dog once the cat was taken care of, otherwise the animals' feud, if that's what it was—sometimes he suspected it was just their favorite game—blew up into wild barking and hissing and ended up waking the entire household.

Twink cried at the back door and Cooper let her out. Jamie wanted him to cut a cat door somewhere in the house, but he hadn't gotten around to it yet. Now, he started making coffee.

A scramble of wild claws on hardwood announced that Duchess was wide-awake and was suddenly running down the stairs. No doubt Emma had released her.

Duchess bounded into the kitchen, wagging her tail wildly and wiggling, a flurry of brown fur. "Hey, girl."

Whining softly, she placed her head under his hand, demanding to be petted. He rubbed her ears then opened the back door to let her outside. As he did the cat whizzed back inside, making a beeline for the Christmas tree.

"Three-ring circus," Cooper muttered as Duchess galloped outside to the black morning. No sign of light yet, but at least the icy rain had stopped, however briefly.

He snapped on the porch light and watched as the dog did several loops around the wet grass of the back yard. She romped and chased a scolding squirrel that scurried up the gnarled bark of a fir tree.

Cooper took a minute, breathing in moist air thick with the scents of fir and pine and the dank loam and grass. He needed to remain calm and steady, have a clear head and not let his emotions get in the way as he tracked down Mary Jo.

When the dog had quit her morning explorations, he wiped off her muddy feet and opened the door for her to go back inside where Twink, thankfully, had not climbed the Christmas tree, nor disturbed any of the low-hanging ornaments.

He finished scooping fresh grounds into the coffeemaker, pushed the button, and as the machine began to gurgle and hiss, he considered what he'd have for breakfast for what he suspected was going to be a long day.

Cereal, he decided, then filled a bowl and added milk before pouring himself a cup of the coffee that had finished brewing. After a few sips, he measured kibbles into Duchess's bowl which she, ever ravenous, pounced upon.

They ate in relative silence apart from the crunching of their meals and he considered the day to come, how he was going to find Mary Jo.

For starters, as soon as the sun came up, he was going to begin canvassing the rural neighborhood around the Kirshner home and see if anyone had noticed anything about Mary Jo's sudden departure.

Ronnie woke up to the sounds of her own strangled moaning and the fading memory of Evan Caldwell's leering ghost, rising from his body.

*Don't go in the water...*

Her heart was pounding triple time. She hadn't had that particular dream in years, but it still could blast her sleep to smithereens. And the admonition to stay out of the water... it was a woman's voice. Like it was that day at The Pond. Was it her mother's? That's how she'd viewed it as a ten-year-old, but had that just been a young girl's deepest wish?

She lay in the dark, staring at the ceiling, willing her heartbeat to slow down. She supposed she'd manifested this particular dream because of Shana's comments about Evan.

*Or, maybe coming face-to-face with Sloan did it?*

Throwing back the covers, she headed for the bathroom and a shower. Half an hour later she was dressed and ready to go. She had time to stop by Lucille's, the diner in Laurelton, the bedroom community next door to River Glen, and pick up a coffee or sit down for a plate of hash browns and eggs, a choice she often made when she worked through lunch. Although today she had a date with Brandy... so coffee only.

Twenty minutes later she was standing in line at Lucille's. Glancing through the window she could almost see the Laurelton Police Department; it was that close. She had no history with the Laurelton department as her contact with Detective Verbena was with the River Glen P.D., which kind of made her want to stop in and tell them her tale... but she would just wind up in the same back-and-forth she'd had with Sloan at River Glen.

Taking her to-go cup of coffee back to her car, she sipped carefully of the scalding brew. It felt wrong to just head into work and do nothing about the dying or dead woman, so she sat for several minutes, going over what she'd seen in her mind, attempting to suss out more information.

Nothing.

Just the same image of the woman in the clearing, the mud, the rain...

"Damn it." Ronnie could feel the familiar worry creep in—that she'd made a mistake, missed the signs. She angrily shook it off. Until she knew differently, she was going to assume someone, somehow, was reaching out to her for help. She just needed to stay open, receptive. But she felt the inexorable tick, tick, tick of the clock working against her.

Cooper knocked on four of the Kirshners' neighbors' doors before he got any kind of answer. The neighbors were acres apart and didn't have Ring cameras, or city water and sewer, or sidewalks or traffic or any noise beyond an occasional bugling elk or chickens clucking and scratching in their yards. The rural aspect of their abodes appealed to Cooper's inner self; one of the reasons he'd been so high on choosing Mary Jo as their surrogate. But the acres of land weren't conducive to neighbor "spying" as it were, which was what Cooper had been counting on.

He was already a little discouraged as he drove down the long, gravel entry lane of the fifth neighbor, splashing through chocolate-colored mud puddles along the way. It didn't help that it gave him time to go over the conversation he'd had with Jamie regarding Mary Jo's disappearance. Jamie had wanted to pore over every detail but Cooper had no other answers for her, which only increased her worries. It killed him that she was at a delicate part of her own pregnancy and he couldn't alleviate the worst of her fears. It was his job to keep her from getting up from the bed too much and certainly to keep her from being unduly stressed.

He pulled up beside the circle of gravel surrounding a concrete birdbath, which in turn sat in the center of a shaggy oval of grass. Today there were no birds partaking of the nearly overflowing bath, whose water looked almost as muddy as the puddles studding the drive.

The house was a one-story gray shingled ranch with white

pane windows flanking the front porch. A slab of concrete with one step served as a porch. Cooper walked up to the door and knocked firmly. He half expected to be met with silence, but a woman opened the door. She was still wearing her bathrobe, which she tightened at her throat upon seeing him. She was middle-aged with grayish-blond curls and a round moon face. Her eyes were surprised and looked him up and down without abashment.

"Hello, ma'am. My name's Cooper Haynes and I'm a detective with the River Glen Police Department. I'm checking to see if you noticed anything unusual around your neighbors', the Kirshners', home about a week, week and a half ago." It was a benign, standard line that had gotten him nowhere so far, and it omitted a big chunk of information about his move to administrative leave. He showed her his identification, which she pored over for long seconds, nearly half a minute before she was satisfied. He had already prepared himself for more head shaking, followed by questions about what he was looking for, and should they be concerned, without the offer of any true information. So, it was a surprise when the woman said, "You mean about Mary Jo taking off?"

Cooper nodded slowly, hiding his elation. Maybe she'd seen something. "That's right. You saw her leave?"

"I saw the preacher's van pick her up, if that's what you mean. She was on her walk and there he was."

No one had mentioned Mary Jo went walking. Not any of the neighbors. Not her husband. "You know this preacher?" he asked, mentally holding his breath.

"Atticus?" she remarked with a sniff. "Sure. Who do you think introduced Mary Jo to him?"

"You?"

"Atticus do something wrong?" she suddenly asked, her hand crawling protectively up her neck again.

"Not that I know of. We're just trying to find Mary Jo." This was his vague reference to Stephen, as if he and Mary Jo's husband were working together.

"Well, if she's not at the church, I don't know where she'd be. Do you wanna come in?" she asked after a moment. "If you give me a moment, I'll get decent and we can talk. I got coffee."

"Coffee would be great."

And he waited in the kitchen while she went to "get decent."

Sloan was in the middle of a phone conversation with Detective Verbena about the suspicious death at the Oak Terrace Apartments that occurred earlier in the week. He was outside that apartment now, near the unmarked black sedan he'd chosen for this duty. He'd zeroed in on the victim's estranged husband, who'd been on scene at the time of her death, as possibly contributing to her overdose. The man had declared he'd come to the apartment only after being contacted by other members of the family, that he hadn't seen his ex-wife in months. Sloan had doubted him until he'd happily taken a swab to the inside of his own mouth, then handed over the DNA sample without complaint . . . so . . . maybe not.

"It's looking more like accidental overdose," Sloan told Verbena after he explained about the swab.

"I still want to get the swab checked as fast as possible, just in case he's the weasel I think he is."

"I know someone who can help with that," said Sloan.

"You can get this sample to the front of the queue?" She was skeptical.

"I can get it closer." Sloan knew Inga Pedderson at the state crime lab. They'd met during the course of an investigation when he was still in California and his case spread into Oregon. Their business relationship had morphed into friendship over the years. They'd never dated; he'd been with Tara most of the time, and Inga had married a few years before his divorce. Still, they'd remained close, and Inga complained to Sloan about the assholes she dealt with everyday who pushed her to prioritize their work above anyone else's. But she was more than willing to help someone she liked.

"Do it," Verbena advised. "I want that man's DNA on file."

"On it," said Sloan. He asked her how her mother was doing and she said she was about the same.

"I'm back to work next week full time, unless something dramatic happens. She's stabilized for the moment, so I'm coming back."

"Good . . . there's something else."

"What?"

"Veronica Quick stopped by the station last night, looking for you."

"What did she want?" A note of caution entered her voice.

"To report a missing person." Sloan laid out what Veronica had said in an emotionless voice. He didn't want Verbena to pick up on his own skepticism where Ms. Quick was concerned. He finished with, "I told her I would let you know she wanted to see you."

"You don't have to be so careful, Hart. You're probably feeling a lot the same way I did when she came to me about Edmond Olman." A pause. "That woman is lucky to be alive."

"Olman's wife."

"If Quick hadn't been so adamant, Mrs. Olman would have died before help came. I had patrols cruise by, but they were on again/off again. Just her word wasn't much to go on."

Sloan didn't respond.

"All right. I'll talk to her. Thanks." Verbena hung up.

Sloan climbed into his vehicle and drove back to the station, thinking about Veronica Quick. It was best that he'd passed the information to Verbena, so he could forget about her. Maybe Veronica Quick's guesses were close, but that didn't make her a psychic. That just made her more aware than some.

He had an image of her in his mind from the night before. Wide, suspicious blue eyes, light brown hair, a slight chip on her shoulder about her gift.

He snorted. Gift. It was all blue smoke and mirrors as far as he was concerned. That she was the daughter of the respected Jonas Quick was kind of mind-blowing. Now that had to be a strained relationship. He didn't know the man, but from reputation alone it seemed like Quick wouldn't want his crackpot daughter spouting off the kind of thing she'd spouted to him last night.

What had she said that day at The Pond way back when? Something about marrying him. Words that had made Caldwell and Townsend and others snigger and tease him in a way that had driven Sloan's ex-girlfriend Shana crazy. He hadn't appreciated it much either, but come on. Veronica Quick had just been severely traumatized, a kid who'd nearly drowned. He'd been the one to administer CPR, and her words in the moment had stemmed from gratitude. Maybe in her preteen mind she'd mistaken it for love. Whatever the case, his friends had taken her at her word, and then when it had come out that she believed she had some psychic inner eye, or whatever the hell it was, his friends had doubled down on the joke.

And now she wanted him to find a missing woman from inside her mind? He could just imagine how that would go over with Caldwell and Townsend, if and when they heard about that.

Yep. It was a good thing that next week the Veronica Quick problem would be Detective Verbena's.

# Chapter 8

Ronnie hung her raincoat on a hanger in the employee break room's closet. At least the coat wasn't soaked this morning, as the rain had taken a small break during her drive to work. She returned to her office in time to catch Dawn walking back to the reception desk with a glass of ice water, a lemon slice floating inside. Jonas frowned on anyone at reception eating or drinking at the front desk during business hours. Only water was allowed, so Dawn would practically chug a half cup of coffee during her breaks.

"Coffee's made," she said now to Ronnie. "The one with the gummy smile made it."

Dawn knew perfectly well that their latest intern was named Moira, but she was dismissive of the pretty young women hired by Albert Tormelle in a never-ending parade. Albert was an old-fashioned gentleman who was unfailingly polite, so it was hard to fault him, but she understood how Dawn felt. Her own father had no interest in the interns. His mind was always on business, money, keeping clients happy, and seeking to push Ronnie onto the only career path he deemed suitable, the law.

"You're meeting with Dame Langdorf today?" Dawn asked, lingering at the door to Ronnie's office.

"Took care of that last night," Ronnie said back.

"Oh. Did you give her what she wanted?"

"Am I moving in with her and becoming her personal psychic?"

"Nice house?" Dawn smothered a smile.

"Very nice house. Think I should consider it?"

"And crush your father's dream for you?" she asked, dropping her voice in case anyone should be listening.

"He's already warned me against it. If I was into torturing him, I'd pretend I took the job."

"You're not into torturing him?" She lifted a brow.

"Not that much." Not yet anyway.

Apart from Aunt Kat—and when she was younger, Patrice, her therapist—Dawn was the only person to whom Ronnie had really tried to explain about her visions. Even then it was over enough vodka martinis to later make her head pound as if it were being squeezed in a vise. She wasn't sure Dawn really believed her, but at least Dawn didn't treat her like she was an alternate life form, so that was something.

Ronnie had confessed to Dawn that Jonas acted like she had some fissure in her brain that led to her lapses, or that she was maybe "making it all up." She'd laid out her predictions, the winners and the failures. Ronnie had even told Dawn about Sloan and Evan Caldwell, which she later regretted. At that point Ronnie had determined she was never going to let down her guard again, even though Dawn had never used any of the information against her.

Now she said, "In all seriousness, I've just got to figure out how to turn Marian Langdorf off."

"Good luck with that." Dawn took a sip of her water and kept one eye on the hallway leading to reception.

"You might find it interesting that I ran into Sloan Hart last night."

"*The* Sloan Hart? Your fiancé?" Dawn teased, her attention swinging back to Ronnie.

"Ha ha. He's a police detective, with the River Glen P.D.," and Ronnie went on to explain that her meeting with Sloan was about her latest vision.

Dawn lifted her brows at Ronnie's description of the woman in the clearing as she sipped her lemon water. "This one of your tsunamis?"

Ronnie made a face. Another thing she'd revealed to Dawn was that her visions ranged from small, lapping waves to massive walls of water that sometimes made her feel like she was drowning beneath their weight. It was still sometimes difficult to discern what was important. "Feels like it. It hit a couple of times yesterday, but then . . ." She shrugged.

"You went to the police," Dawn said in a tone that suggested, *That's a surprise.*

"I went to *Sloan Hart.*"

"Did you say anything about that day at The Pond?"

"I thanked him for saving me. Better late than never, I guess."

"Think he remembers what you said?"

"God, I hope not, but maybe . . . probably . . ." Ronnie didn't want to go there.

"It's bound to be a funny joke, by this time."

"Yeah, ha ha. A real riot. Did I also mention I was served divorce papers by Sloan's ex-girlfriend?"

"*Wha-at?*"

"I know. It's been weird how many River Glen alums from back then that I've run into." She then explained about Shana serving Ronnie the divorce papers from Galen, and by the time she was finished Dawn was cradling her head like she couldn't take in any more information while doing a poor job of holding back further laughter. "What the hell, Ronnie? That's more than coincidence!"

"Exactly! That's what happens when you're a lunatic like me. People want to look at you like you're a monkey at the zoo. Also, let me tell you about Galen and his boss's wife . . ."

Dawn was holding her stomach in between howls of laughter

by the time Ronnie finished with that story. "You don't know that! You're making it up!"

"He practically admitted it. See?" Ronnie said with a roll of her eyes. "You see? Everyone thinks I'm batshit crazy, including me."

They both heard the rising elevator and Ronnie put a finger to her lips and slipped into her office as Dawn, water glass in hand, hurried back to her desk before whoever was coming into the firm showed themselves.

What Ronnie had purposely omitted from her narrative was seeing Evan's ghost and the sense of foreboding that particular memory could still evoke. Still, it helped to make light of her "condition," and she felt better than she had in weeks. But then she thought of the woman lying on the cold, wet ground, her bloody wrists, the shed and the trees, and fervently wished she knew if that was a true vision—it felt so real, it had to be. Or was it another red herring?

*You were supposed to die, not me.*

Evan's ghost had said that, too, hadn't it? Or, had she just made that up inside her ten-year-old head because she'd been scared?

Ronnie was deep into the Benton file, ready to take notes for when she and Martin Calgheny met with the heirs, when a chill swept over her, her skin breaking out in gooseflesh. She looked at her pimpled arms, then closed her eyes. This was it, then? Another vision concerning the woman in the clearing?

She waited but nothing happened. She'd read somewhere that gooseflesh was a reaction to cold temperatures or danger, a primal response leftover from the time when humans were covered in fur, the body triggered to make hair stand on end either to add warmth or increase the person's size, the latter a means to scare off predators.

Ronnie started to relax, but then... in her mind's eye she saw Sloan Hart as he'd been, bare chest starred with water drops, more water dripping off his dark hair onto her blue one-piece, strong hands turning her so that she could vomit ignominiously into the pebbles surrounding the spread blanket.

Her heart was thundering in her ears. She saw his concerned gaze through a watery haze. Felt his hands pressing on her chest. Sensed his fear for her.

She shook her head violently, blasting his image away.

She wanted to slap her hand to her forehead.

"What good are you?" she said through gritted teeth, calling out to her psychic awareness as if it were a flesh and blood being.

The woman, Gracie, made a cup of coffee strong enough to put hair on your chest, a phrase Cooper had heard from his Uncle Rodney, the police detective who'd influenced him to seek a career in law enforcement.

Gracie didn't know the Kirshners well. And it didn't appear she liked them much, but then Gracie was an opinionated woman who didn't seem to like anyone much. Or anything, for that matter.

She truly didn't like Atticus Symons, leader of the Heart of Sunshine Church, her voice dripping with sarcasm when she spoke its name.

"He's a pious prick," she said of Symons. "Wraps all his bullshit in gobbledygook words like 'eternal' and 'purism' and 'rapture.' I spent one afternoon there. Sammy's idea, rest his muddled soul. The man found religion a nanosecond before he died, and that's how we ended up there. Didn't take, I guess you can tell." She lifted an eyebrow at him over her cup.

"Where is 'there'?"

They were sitting in her living room. Cooper was trying hard to quell his desire to cut to the chase. Gracie might be entertaining but his inner clock kept ticking out its warning of time speeding by.

"Is it near here?"

"The church is more like a compound. You know the kind? It's about ten miles thataway." She waved toward the west.

Oh, he knew the kind. Apart from himself, his whole family had attended a camp of sorts for varying amounts of time the previous summer, the place where Mary Jo had spent a good portion of her youth. Now it looked like her current vision quest was happening at the same kind of commune... maybe cult, depending on the group's practices and your own outlook.

"You said you recognized the van."

"You can't miss that rattletrap. Not that I have any room to talk, what with what's out in my drive." She snorted. "Sammy didn't know shit about car engines, either, so it's dying just like he did. Atticus's van is white with a big yellow sun with all these lines." She used one hand to sketch a series of lines in the air as if spokes from a central point. "Says something like..." She hesitated a moment, then nodded once. "'God's love is found here.'" She snorted. "And it's got children's handprints on it."

"Do you have an address?"

"I can tell you how to get there." She wagged a finger at him. "Bein' a cop ain't gonna do you any good, though. Atticus will just beam at you and say how great it is to be protected blah, blah, blah. He talks a lot of nothin'."

"Think I should approach him some other way?" asked Cooper. His gut was tight and ice had developed in his veins as he'd listened to the tale of Atticus Symons. The preacher likely had Mary Jo as a member of his flock, and maybe thought he had some influence on the baby inside Mary Jo's womb. All of it made Cooper want to put his fist through a wall. He could feel the strong grip he'd held on his anxiety and rage loosening.

"Oh, yeah. Tell him you're looking to be saved. I don't know if he'll want cha anyway. He likes women... of a certain age, which I'm long past." She smiled thinly. "But tell him you need to be saved. Force him to find a reason not to save you. He had a helluva time with Sammy, who really wanted to believe. We had to leave there and go to a different church. Sammy was baptized long ago, but he never cared until he was near the pearly gates. Then, he cared."

She verbally related the route to Symons's church and grounds. From her description, it sounded like the place had a back building with barracks, which didn't bode well. But if Mary Jo was there, at least Cooper would know where to find her. That was step one. Step two was extracting her and making sure both she and the baby were safe and healthy.

Ten minutes later he was on the road.

Sloan had barely gotten back to his desk when his cell rang and he saw on the small screen that the caller was Abel Townsend. "Sheriff?" he answered.

"You'd better get over here," was the abrupt response.

Immediately, Sloan straightened. "Why? What's up?"

"Meet me at the station. We'll go from there together."

Sloan asked, "Where are you?"

Townsend wasn't usually so mysterious, but then he'd been tougher to talk to ever since Sloan had taken the temp job at River Glen P.D.

"Tell ya all about it when you get to the station." And Townsend hung up.

Ronnie paused in the hallway outside Martin Calgheny's office. His door was ajar, so she rapped lightly, then stuck her head inside. The attorney was at his desk and glanced up, looking over the rims of his glasses.

"So, Monday for the Bentons?" she asked.

"Tuesday afternoon. Collecting heirs never works on a time line."

"Okay." She made a mental note. "Did you talk to Daria Armenton?"

Martin gave her an odd look. "I called her, but she said it was all taken care of."

"Her part of the Rollberson inheritance?"

"That's what she said."

"Huh." The way Angel had talked, it had seemed like a battle royale for Daria's small share, but when Daria had spoken to Ronnie, it sounded like she might have other plans. "Okay, thanks."

She stopped at her office for her purse and cell phone, then grabbed her raincoat from the employee break room. On her way to the elevators, she gave a finger wave to Dawn, who was currently on the phone at her desk, and left the office.

Ronnie was on her way to meet Brandy at a sandwich shop near Glen Gen.

Once in her Escape, Ronnie drove toward the hospital. The gray clouds occasionally offered shafts of bright sunlight before closing together again. It almost seemed purposeful, the little bit of brightness peeking through, only to be swallowed up again.

She found parking on the street and walked to the sandwich shop, its windows surrounded by red and green tinsel, an outdoor menu offering a "holiday" menu. A bell tinkled as she pushed open the door to the smells of baking bread and strong coffee and the buzz of conversation and clatter of flatware. Several tables were occupied, but no Brandy. She was about to sit down and wait when her phone buzzed.

Brandy.

Full of apologies for being late. "We're short-staffed," she said a little breathlessly. "Do you mind having lunch in the cafeteria? I'm sorry. Or, we could forget lunch . . . but I . . ."

"Or, I could bring lunch," Ronnie suggested. "Sandwiches. I'm already here."

"Actually, that would be great." Brandy sounded relieved.

"What would you like?"

Brandy knew the menu and asked for a tuna sandwich, so Ronnie stepped up to the counter and ordered from a blond girl in braids and a red Santa hat.

Fifteen minutes later she headed up the hospital elevator with a white bag containing two tuna salad sandwiches. As soon as Brandy saw her, she asked her to wait in the alcove for a few minutes. "Just got some relief. I'll be ready in a couple minutes and we'll go downstairs to the cafeteria."

"Sure." Ronnie seated herself in one of the tan alcove chairs. Almost immediately her skin prickled. She sat up straight and held her breath. Concentrated. The sounds of the hospital—the rattle of carts and whisper of footsteps and buzz of soft conversation—faded. She bit her lip. Listened more closely. Waited.

She closed her eyes.
Seconds passed.
Nothing.
Not a damned thing.
A minute passed and then another.
No vision appeared.

She slowly opened her eyes, expelled her breath and relaxed into the chair again.

Running her hands through her hair, she glanced around the alcove, her gaze snagging on one of the pieces of alcove artwork, a watercolor portrait done in deep greens, browns and grays hanging on the west wall. She could see the side of a white house in the corner, just a sliver of a building, like it was a mile away. The main focus was of the line of trees behind it. A woods. Douglas firs and pines . . . maybe a Ponderosa pine by its red bark, which were generally seen in central or eastern Oregon, not the Willamette Valley, though there were a few this side of the Cascade mountains.

"I'm ready," called Brandy, waving to her from the nurses' station.

Ronnie left the picture behind and walked with Brandy to the elevator where they took a car down to the first basement level and stepped into the long corridor leading to the cafeteria.

As they stepped through the open doors, the smells of simmering tomato sauce and roasting meat greeted them, floating on a rumble of conversation. Hospital workers in scrubs and name tags joined visitors in separate lines where hot meals or sandwiches or pastries were displayed. At one of the vending machines, Brandy bought them each a bottle of water. She tried to pay for her sandwich, but Ronnie held up a hand. "My treat," she said and Brandy didn't argue.

They each sat in one of the molded green chairs surrounding a four-top table which, if it had been one floor up, would have overlooked the back parking lot. On this level, the view was of diagonal parallel lines in four-inch green stripes running down the one wall, a mood lightener to combat the room's windowless starkness.

Ronnie knew that down the hall and around the corner, on the opposite end of Basement One, the lab and pathology department were housed. Also, the morgue.

Thankfully, this area was made for the living.

"It's a bunker down here, but it suits my mood," said Brandy. She cracked her bottle of water, took a swallow and asked, "What were you doing with Shana?"

"She collapsed at my feet. I guess I felt kind of responsible."

"Sorry. It just seemed weird, along with everything else. Old home week, and not in a good way."

Ronnie had unwrapped her sandwich, wondering what Brandy meant, not sure she wanted to poke around and find out. Taking a bite, she realized Brandy wasn't eating. She was staring down at her sandwich with a frown. Ronnie swallowed and added, "Of course, this was after Shana served me with divorce papers."

"You're getting a divorce? Oh, I'm sorry." Brandy's hazel eyes shadowed a bit. "I didn't know you were married, or maybe I did. I don't know. I've never wanted to make that commitment." She shook her head. "So Shana's a process server?"

"She might have just done it for Galen. Doesn't matter. I signed the papers and we're on our way."

"Marriage . . ." Brandy made a face.

"Divorce," Ronnie countered. "You said you wanted to talk about something?"

"Divorce," she repeated. "Specifically Mel's. You . . . know about her and Hugh?"

Ronnie slowly shook her head, but yes, maybe. She knew Mel had gotten married. She paid attention to her friends, or had. It had mattered once. But she wouldn't have come up with Mel's husband's name.

Brandy suddenly looked up, turning her eyes intensely on Ronnie and said, "I wish we'd stayed friends."

From some deep well she hadn't known existed, Ronnie felt a sudden surge of emotion. It hadn't been her choice that their friendship had ended. Brandy and Melissa had eased themselves away from her: weird Veronica Quick.

*I lost my mother and you abandoned me, too.*

Immediately she quelled that ridiculous thought. They'd been kids. She'd freaked them out. She managed to shrug and say lightly, "Grade school friendships."

"I know. But we did everything together and then it was just over. And then you were so shut down in high school. Mel and I were still friends, but..."

Shut down? She didn't remember that, but she'd spent a lot of time hiding oddness from everyone.

"You know about Mel and Clint, right?" Brandy had unwrapped her sandwich, but stopped and looked up at Ronnie from the tops of her eyes.

"Your brother? No."

"It was because of Clint that Mel and Hugh broke up."

"Oh."

"Yeah, best friends and all that. The three of them together. I'm not trying to make excuses... those things happen. It's just that Clint's a mess, and I don't think he'd do anything wrong. I mean he's an idiot. I love him. He's my brother. But he's an idiot."

Ronnie's mind flew back to that day at The Pond. Mel had been crushing on Clint even then. "Wow," was all she said now.

"I know."

Brandy made a face before biting into her sandwich. She changed the subject to talk about the hospital, then switched the conversation again to the apartment she'd recently given up to move back into her parents' house, the same house she and Clint had grown up in. Brandy's last move had come upon her mother's unexpected death.

"Kinda weird," Brandy admitted. "Being there as kids with the whole family and now... Well, it's just me."

Ronnie thought fleetingly of her own childhood home, the house her father still lived in. And that made her think of Gabrielle, her babysitter, who'd died in a car crash a few years ago, a tragedy that had brought a number of her schoolmates back to River Glen. There had been a service for Gabrielle at the high school, a chance for people to collectively grieve. But when Ronnie stepped through the familiar front doors of the school, she'd gotten such a bad vibe that she'd faltered and left almost immediately, though not before she'd caught a glimpse of Brandy and Clint and Evan.

Brandy and Clint sat in folding chairs, Evan seated in his wheelchair.

For some reason, Ronnie had experienced a sense of what she could only describe as such *wrongness* that crawled up her spine. It had been so intense, she'd immediately skedaddled back out the door, her heart thundering, nearly bowling over a couple of mourners on their way in.

She should have shaken off that feeling and stayed and paid her respects to Gabrielle, even though she'd seen little of the babysitter after her tenth summer. She'd heard that Gabrielle had graduated high school and gone off to some university Ronnie couldn't remember. Then, about the time she should have been graduating from college, Gabrielle had been in a terrible, fatal automobile accident.

She had been with a boyfriend, who was driving. He'd lost control of his car at the highest point above the East Glen River. The car skidded over the edge, tumbling down the river's chasm. Both passengers had died on impact with the river's edge. At least that's what everyone had been told.

Gabrielle's boyfriend hadn't been from River Glen, had just been visiting Gabrielle. Their deaths had shocked the whole community.

Now, in the cafeteria, Ronnie shoved the disturbing memory aside. She tuned back to Brandy, who was waxing nostalgic about their childhood days, and Ronnie found herself growing restless. She didn't like nostalgia. It had a way of making her feel empty.

Brandy had finished half her sandwich and wrapped up the rest while she talked. Ronnie did the same, and put her uneaten half back into the bag.

"I'll have this on break," Brandy interrupted herself to say, touching the red-frilled toothpick she'd stuck through it. She crossed her arms and laid them on the table. "You know there are Three Musketeers bars in the vending machine."

"You want one?"

"You never really liked them," Brandy observed.

"Touché. I was always selling them hard, though."

"All for one and one for all." Brandy smiled a bit wistfully, then she inhaled and exhaled. "I'm mad at Mel and I'm... upset with Clint for getting involved. But it's not his fault."

"You said that."

"Clint didn't really break up Mel's marriage," she said a bit more forcefully. "She wasn't... faithful. There were guys before him. So, it was just a fling. Hugh, of course, being the wronged husband, blames Clint completely."

"What about Mel?" Ronnie asked.

"Well, that's why I wanted to see you. I mean, don't get me wrong. I'm glad to see you anyway. It's just fun, after all these years. Maybe we can make up for lost time. Connect again, as adults."

"But...?"

"Mel's missing and—"

"Missing?"

"—I think it might be because of Clint."

"Missing..." Ronnie repeated, feeling the blood drain from her face.

"Oh, shit, Ronnie. What's wrong?" Brandy stared at her in alarm. "Do you know where she is?"

No... no... the woman in the clearing wasn't Mel. Not Mel. Couldn't be Mel.

*But she looked familiar!*

"Ronnie?" whispered Brandy. "Oh, God. Ronnie! Oh, no. Do you see her? Do you?"

"She's why you wanted to see me..." Ronnie's voice sounded far away to her own ears.

"Yes. Yes! But Mel is okay. Right? She's okay. You just... you're just... this isn't like with Evan. You don't really see anything. Man, I don't like this. This is bullshit. Don't do this. Don't say anything." She held both hands up like a shield.

Brandy's face was drawn in terror. Ronnie looked at her helplessly. The woman on the ground. Her bloody wrists. Head turned ... the blouse ... a faint pink beneath the mud, Mel's favorite color.

And suddenly she understood why the picture she'd seen in the alcove had tugged at her.

"The watercolor upstairs in grays and browns ..." she whispered.

Brandy's eyes stretched wide. "Mel's watercolor?"

*Mel's watercolor.*

"She gave it to me. I put it there so I could see it every day."

"Mel painted it?" Ronnie felt slightly faint, a new clarity barging into her brain. She was glad she was sitting down.

"Yes."

"I know where it is," she admitted, her throat tight, her stomach turning.

"You do?" Brandy wasn't tracking well. She laid her arms out flat across the table.

"You do, too. It's Aunt Kat's place. Where we all used to go to that shed, when it was better. Still had paint ..."

"Oh, God."

"Except the whole area's worse now ... old and dilapidated and yes, she's there."

Brandy lay her head on her arms and gazed at Ronnie with dull eyes. "Please tell me she's all right."

When Ronnie, her throat hot, couldn't answer, tears filled Brandy's eyes. Slowly Ronnie stood up and Brandy lifted her head.

"Where are you going?"

Ronnie was reaching for her phone. "I've got to go there."

"I'm going with you!"

"I don't know if—"

"I'm going WITH YOU!" Brandy insisted, her voice rising.

Heads of the people at nearby tables turned, the buzz of conversation momentarily interrupted.

"I need to call 911 . . ." Ronnie said, lowering her voice and taking a step away from the table as a few of the lunch crowd went back to their meals. A few didn't.

The cell rang in her hand and Ronnie stared at it in wonder. "It's Aunt Kat."

Brandy moaned and looked about to faint. Until this moment, Ronnie had still held out the vain hope that she was wrong. Now, she gave that up.

# Chapter 9

"Aunt Kat?" answered Ronnie, only peripherally aware of the eyes staring at her in the crowded cafeteria. Even Brandy faded into the distance.

"Hi, honey. Are you okay? Police are everywhere. They're going into the woods, and—"

"I know," Ronnie said breathlessly. "I'm on my way. It's the . . . clearing?"

There was a brief moment while Aunt Kat collected herself. Then she said, "Ah, you already got the message. Well, come on then. Tell your dad you have to come to the farm. Don't listen to him when he argues with you."

"I'm on my way," Ronnie repeated. In the back of her mind she recognized that her aunt seemed to be way ahead of the moment, already knowing that the victim was a friend of Ronnie's, already knowing Ronnie needed to be with her. For someone who claimed she had none of her sister's precognition, Aunt Kat seemed to often be a step ahead. There was something there. A silvery thread of intuition. Knowledge before there was evidence. It wasn't just Ronnie's mother who'd had the gift.

"I'll tell them I'm leaving and then I'm coming with you," said Brandy, white-faced but determined. "Let's go!"

Ronnie blinked back to the present and nodded.

As they walked swiftly to the elevators, Ronnie considered calling her father, but let it go. She was certain of what she'd seen, but having trouble processing. The woman in the clearing, the one with the ravaged hands, wrists, lying in the mud was Mel. She could feel it.

*But her hair's dark. Melissa's a blond.*

But maybe not anymore. Or maybe that was mud, dirt, a trick of light...

*You know it's her.*

Ronnie shuddered. No excuses. The dead or dying woman was Melissa.

Brandy stopped by the nurses' station where she worked to explain that she had to leave and met Ronnie at the front doors of the hospital, where a group of carolers in their teens had gathered and were singing the chorus of "Jingle Bells," one lanky kid actually shaking bells.

With a passing look at the singers, Brandy said, "My co-workers didn't like it that I was leaving them, but I'm going with you. I'll make up for it tonight on a later shift, which is when we're the busiest and they'll appreciate it then." She shrugged into her raincoat, flipped up her hood and glanced at Ronnie. "But they'll deal. They have to. This is Mel we're talking about."

"I know." They stepped outside, bending their hooded heads against the scudding rain and wind as they headed to Ronnie's car.

As she threaded her way through traffic, Ronnie's mind stayed on the clearing and the trees, a place where she and her friends had played together as kids. It had to be the same general area as the watercolor. The picture drawn from Mel's memory. The shack had been newer, better, back then, not nearly so dilapidated as it was now. She, Brandy and Melissa would stay at Aunt Kat's and spend hours outside, wandering through the apple orchards or the thick evergreen woods beyond. She couldn't remember when they'd stumbled upon the shed and the small clearing. Their secret place. They hadn't even told Aunt Kat about it. She would've probably worried about them being so deep into the woods.

"Tell me what you see," demanded Brandy as Ronnie negotiated the blustery conditions outside, the wipers rhythmically slapping away the pounding rain. "Mel's not okay, is she? That's what you saw."

"I just know she's hurt . . ." *Dying or dead.*

"What happened?"

"I don't know."

"But she's at your Aunt Kat's . . ."

"Seems that way," Ronnie said grimly.

And the rest of the trip was made in silence.

The harsh December wind was rushing through the surrounding trees as Cooper stood bareheaded outside the Heart of Sunshine Church's massive double doors. The skies had decided to open up again at the exact moment he stepped from his SUV and sleet slid down the back of his neck, chilling him to the bone. He shivered beneath the portico of Atticus Symons's place of worship. Late November had been cold, wet and sometimes threatening snow. December seemed to have decided to take the winter weather one step further, coming in with frigid hammer and tongs. The weather aside, he was inwardly coldly angry after talking to Gracie. All his worry and concern regarding Mary Jo had crystallized into something harder. Normally he had a cop's grip on his emotions, but Gracie's revelation about Mary Jo climbing into the "sunshine van," or whatever the hell, had opened his palm and he'd let go.

Indulging his rage wasn't going to help him, however, so he took a moment to pull himself together before pressing down on one of the two oversized handles. Locked. He tried the other one. The same.

He wanted to rip the doors down with his bare hands.

He'd been focused on just making sure Mary Jo and the baby were okay up to this point. That was still the main objective. But now he was about to blow up. Frustration and fury had taken over and he could only see red.

No... Nope...

*Take a breath... or two or three... don't get yourself in trouble for wanting to strangle the man in charge just because he lives in a commune, cult, whatever. Symons might not know the whole story. Likely doesn't know that your wife is currently bedridden, needing to keep down stress, hoping to birth a healthy baby.*

But he had to know Mary Jo was pregnant. No hiding that at this stage.

*You don't know Mary Jo's here...*

"Yeah, I do," he whispered aloud. He could feel it.

Rapping hard on the panels, he bruised his knuckles. Good. Pain was distraction.

He just needed to know Mary Jo was safe. That she was getting the care she needed these last weeks of her pregnancy. Either way he was also bound and determined to have it out with her about running off.

*She grew up in a similar type of community. She's looking for "community fulfillment," her vision quest.*

Yeah, right.

Cooper was keenly aware of his wife's reservations about Mary Jo. That he had been the one who'd pushed for Mary Jo to become their surrogate. He felt wholly responsible. He needed to be calm and clearheaded when dealing with her. She was too unstable to trust. God knew what fueled her decision-making these days.

*Like the one to abandon her family and run back to cult living? Or the deluded belief that since Cooper and Jamie were having their own baby now, maybe she could keep the one inside her?*

She hadn't said that. That was his own fear talking.

He was so tense his organs felt like they were shrinking and tightening. A warning against that last, hopefully inaccurate, possibility.

Bunching his hand into a fist, he slammed it against the door panels over and over again. The thick oak boards absorbed his rage and turned it into muffled pounding.

Finally he heard footsteps approaching the door and he drew in a lungful of air, a deep, calming breath.

He could hear a large bolt being thrown back from the other side. A man in ivory linen robes stood in the aperture of the opened door. Atticus Symons, he guessed, looking like a being from another age, another place, which was probably the intent. Cooper put him somewhere in his fifties. His graying hair was long and bound back by a rawhide tie. He greeted Cooper with a beatific smile, as if he'd just been waiting for him to appear. Something superior in it that stoked Cooper's simmering anger, reminding him again that the women in his family—Jamie, Harley, Marissa and Emma—had all lived through a nightmare experience at a camp the previous summer, one quasi-connected to another cultlike group. He'd felt powerless then, and he felt powerless now, and though he considered himself rational and fair by nature, he was way out of his lane on this one.

He wanted to rip the bastard's head off.

"Atticus Symons?" asked Cooper, carefully polite.

"At your service, good sir," he said with a deep nod of acknowledgment. "What brings you to our door on this dark afternoon?"

"You're the preacher."

"I am merely a vessel for our Lord, as are we all. I am the person who leads prayer. In that regard, I am the leader of our flock, but—"

"I want to see Mary Jo Kirshner," Cooper cut through. "Tell her Detective Cooper Haynes is here."

A small frown darkened his brow.

"I'm the father of the baby she's carrying," Cooper elucidated.

The frown deepened. "There must be some mistake. There is no Mary Jo here . . . Are you here on official business?"

Cooper counted slowly to five. It was highly possible Mary Jo knew he was on administrative leave. It was public knowledge. Atticus Symons could know it, too. This, then, could be a test of his authority. "Only in the sense that I'm the father of the baby she's carrying. My wife is the mother. Mary Jo is near eight months pregnant. She disappeared about a week ago and I believe she landed here."

Cooper could almost see the wheels turning inside the man's mind.

"I can bring the police," Cooper stated flatly.

"No need, sir. I'd like to help you, if I can. Please come in. It's clear you are in some pain and our mission is to alleviate pain and strife in the world."

"Is she here?"

"All the women, and some men, who stay at Heart of Sunshine are here of their free accord. It is—we are—a sanctuary."

"Is there a pregnant woman here?" Cooper asked, hanging on to his sanity with an effort.

"Come with me, seeker." Symons dipped his chin and spread his hands as he headed inside. *Well, hell,* Cooper thought, entering behind the man.

Beyond the oak doors lay a small vestibule and further beyond rows of plain, pine pews, positioned in front of a raised dais at the end of the room. A peaked ceiling, also all in pine, was scattered with skylights and rose in arched beams overhead. Sleet pinged and skittered across the glass as Cooper breathed in the clean, sharp scent of the wood. Currently the entire space was empty. Atticus Symons walked down the aisle to the three steps that led up to the raised platform where a lectern stood poised and ready, dead center. Presumably this was where Symons led his flock, whether he named himself Pastor, Father, Priest, Leader or whatever.

"Mary Jo is married and has two children of her own who are with her husband," he told the man. "They all want to know where she is and that she's healthy and"—*not held against her will*—"that she's coming home soon."

Symons had stopped near the lectern but had not yet climbed the few steps. He glanced back at Cooper. "This woman's husband . . . is he in custody?"

"No." Cooper frowned. "He's just worried about where his wife is."

"Shouldn't he be here instead of you?"

The quiet way Symons held himself, the clasped hands at his waist . . . had to be an affectation, although maybe his feelings on the subject weren't exactly unbiased. Cooper wanted to mow through everything and everyone to find Mary Jo. "Her husband asked me to bring her back."

Symons said patiently, "Well. We have free rein in this country, Detective."

"But we also have responsibilities to our families. Especially our children. Is Mary Jo here, or not? It's a simple question."

"I've already told you, there's no one here called by that name."

"How about any other name? Do you have any pregnant women here? Maybe you could check with your . . . flock and ask her to come see me."

A bit of color entered the man's cheeks. In a cooler voice, he said, "Please sit down. I will be right back."

Cooper lasted about three minutes after the man had departed. He was torn between following after him and calling his partner, Elena Verbena. He chose the latter, but wasn't surprised when the call went to voice mail. Verbena was out of the job more than in it, at this point in time, owing to her mother's long-term illness.

He couldn't sit still. It felt too . . . passive. He wandered down the aisle between the pews, staring up at the colorful stained glass windows, now rain-lashed, those jewel tones muted against the dark afternoon.

*We should all be home watching TV and eating popcorn,* he thought.

He headed back to the anteroom. There was a pine bench against one wall, and a wooden lectern pushed to the wall beside the double doors. A book lay open on the lectern, a Bible. He glanced at it and saw an open leather folio below it with a number of names listed, a sign-in sheet. He picked up one end of the Bible to look beneath it at the names. Mostly traditionally feminine names popped out at him. Maybe the women under Atticus Symons's care?

He scanned down quickly. No Mary Jo.

But . . .

The hair on the back of his neck rose.

Quickly, he strode back to the pew where he'd been when Symons had left him, waiting, lost in thought. When the pastor returned and told him he'd spoken to his flock and no one knew anything about the pregnant woman he was seeking, he nodded and thanked the man, who'd clearly expected some kind of fight and was puzzled, even maybe slightly alarmed, at his change of attitude.

Didn't matter. Cooper had some thinking to do.

Symons was still staring after him as he left the church.

"Are we almost there?" Brandy asked tensely, staring through the rain-washed windshield past the frantic wipers.

"Almost."

A few more miles passed beneath the SUV's tires, before Brandy burst out, "She always had a crush on Clint, you know. Mel. She always did."

"I remember." Mel had always had a boyfriend in high school. Even though they hadn't been all that close, Ronnie could recall Mel dating a bunch of different guys, flirting with others. None of those relationships had lasted long.

Brandy swore softly, then whispered, "She has to be all right."

Ronnie remained silent, her hands tight on the wheel as gusts of wind buffeted the Escape.

"Maybe it's not what you think. What you . . . saw . . . Maybe she's okay. Maybe she's not even there . . ."

Again Ronnie stayed silent.

"Whatever happened, it wasn't Clint. He would never intentionally hurt her . . . or anyone. He's not made that way."

Ronnie risked a glance at her. Now Brandy was hunched forward, face muscles taut, eyes on the road.

"And Clint is Hugh's friend, or was his friend. The Mel/Clint thing was short-lived but intense . . . Maybe, maybe Hugh did this. He *would* hurt her. He's not a good guy." She was biting at a fingernail as if wrestling with how much to confide. "The thing is, Hugh and Mel were split at the time she was with

Clint, but Hugh is really the jealous type, if you know what I mean." More finger biting until she realized what she was doing and dropped her hand. Turning in her seat to face Ronnie, Brandy said, "It's Hugh. If someone did something to Mel, it was Hugh. She's been missing for a few days, like I said, and I've been worried. When I saw you at the hospital . . ."

"I know."

"I'm sorry about what they say about you. I don't care. I just want to find Mel. I warned her . . . I . . ." She pressed a hand over her mouth.

"You warned her about what?"

"About pissing Hugh off. She . . . wasn't faithful. I told you that. And you know her. She's always been kind of flighty, I guess. There were other guys. It's just been a shit-show and I tried to tell Clint, but he never listens to me. Never."

*In love with love . . .* Ronnie could practically hear Aunt Kat clucking her tongue over some of the girls in Ronnie's high school, girls like Mel, whose heart could be easily won, easily broken, easily mended. Even having such thoughts made Ronnie feel like a traitor when she was so worried for Mel.

Yet, it seemed odd, almost prophetic, that Mel and Clint, Brandy's brother and Mel's grade school crush, had gotten together.

"Clint just got back from a fishing trip in Vancouver, B.C.," added Brandy.

At this time of year? Maybe. Vancouver, Canada, was on the coast about three hundred miles north of River Glen and the weather was iffy at best, dangerous at worst, the beginning of December. "Hope the weather's better there."

"He fishes no matter what. Unless it's really nasty I guess." Brandy checked the dash clock for the umpteenth time. "I know you're driving as fast as you can, but can you step on it?"

"No."

"I know. I know." Her eyes moved nervously as she eyed the storm. "We just gotta get to that clearing. Find her, if she's there. Maybe the police have found her?"

"Maybe it wasn't foul play," Ronnie posed. She wanted to

add, *We don't know that Mel's dead. Let's not think the worst.* But she couldn't.

"Is that what you think?" Brandy asked. "That it's not foul play?"

*No.* "Does she have a dog?"

"A dog?" Brandy shot Ronnie a perplexed glance. "I don't think so. But maybe Hugh has a dog. Why?"

"It's probably nothing," Ronnie said, but she didn't believe it for a second.

It took almost an hour by the time Ronnie was bumping up the long drive to Aunt Kat's white, two-story farmhouse. A sheriff's department vehicle was parked outside, probably answering Aunt Kat's 911 call.

They both hurried inside and Aunt Kat, gray-faced and grim, her silvery hair in a short bob, her rail-thin face as taut as Ronnie had ever seen it, handed Ronnie a green plastic poncho she snatched from a hook by the back door. "I've got another for your friend," she said, nodding to Brandy, who said in a small voice, "It's me, Brandy."

Aunt Kat had already turned toward the kitchen and the back of the house, but now she spun back and put a hand on Brandy's shoulder. "Why, yes, it is you. Brandy. Oh, my. So good to see you again." But there was no life in her expression, her words without any enthusiasm, the situation too dire.

"Do you . . . Do you know if it's Mel out there?" Brandy's voice shook.

Aunt Kat shot Ronnie a quick look. "Let me get you that poncho," she said to Brandy. "Come with me."

They followed her through the kitchen to the storeroom. She opened a tall cabinet which held canning jars, boots, jackets and scarves. "The police left one car here and drove the others to the road that winds into the woods. Sheriff's department and other police. The man that found the body, Randall, is showing them where to go."

"Body?" Ronnie repeated as Brandy pressed her hands to the sides of her face and shook her head.

"No, no, no . . ." Brandy's eyes filled with tears.

"I'm sorry, honey. I thought you knew." Aunt Kat's soulful eyes held Ronnie's gaze.

"I just thought she might still be alive," Ronnie said as Brandy made a little squeak of protest.

"Who's Randall?"

"Randall DeBoer, one of the neighbors. He hikes a lot and gets his own firewood. He generally doesn't come on my property, or at least I thought he didn't, but anyway he came and told me."

"How did you know I'd want to come?" asked Ronnie.

Aunt Kat didn't respond.

Brandy offered hopefully, "Maybe it's not Mel."

Neither Ronnie nor Aunt Kat answered her.

They pulled the ponchos on over their raincoats and Aunt Kat led them off the back porch to the gate that led to the orchard. The trail was already heavily trodden, and veered off to a faint pathway leading into the woods. It was midafternoon but dark enough that when they reached the edge of the forest it felt like night had fallen.

"Just keep following the path," Aunt Kat had instructed when they took off.

Ronnie's heart was heavy. She and Brandy walked in silence, each caught in her own worrisome thoughts. They trudged into the undergrowth, moving as fast as they could, which wasn't saying much, blending into the foliage in their matching dark green ponchos. This was the same path they'd used as young girls when they'd gone exploring and pretending that they were lone survivors, with Mel always certain her Prince Charming would find her, save her, steal her away to her happily ever after.

It was strange, and yet not, being with Brandy after all this time. If she hadn't been so scared and worried, Ronnie would marvel about that.

They shouldered aside wet branches and stepped over exposed roots and mossy rocks for about fifteen minutes as the path threaded through the woods.

The clearing wasn't all that close to Aunt Kat's house. The

shed must've been designed for some kind of storage at one time. Ronnie had never talked to Aunt Kat about it; had kept the shed to herself as the three friends used it as their secret hideout.

They could see illumination glimmering through the trees, could hear men's murmuring voices, as they approached. As they stepped into the clearing they were greeted with white glare from the lights that flooded the area, dissipating the gloom. Their steps slowed in tandem as they emerged into the clearing and about seven or eight officers—men and women—turned to look at them.

Ronnie first saw the shed. In the twenty-some years since she'd last been here, it had deteriorated to the dilapidated, gray shambles it was today. The boards were shrunken and gapped, the edges sharp under the illumination. There was a pop-up canopy in front of, and to one side of, the shed, its blue nylon top offering cover from the rain for the group. The sheriff's department, Aunt Kat had said.

And lying on the sodden ground, just as she'd seen in her visions, was a woman. A dead woman.

Her heart sank, the tiniest bit of hope that had still lingered, extinguishing.

One deputy was bending close to the woman's body, eyeing her. Others were standing back, taking pictures. Another was photographing the ground; tire treads . . . the shed . . . the trees . . . There was someone inside the shed, the beam of their flashlight slicing through the darkness, sending out narrow rays of light through the gaps in the weathered siding.

Brandy made a whimpering sound beside her, her gaze fixed on the body.

Ronnie forced herself to look. Her stomach was a hard knot. Maybe she hadn't recognized Melissa, but Brandy now did. The knowledge left her dazed and dazzled by all the illumination that turned the falling rain to diamond sparks.

"Excuse me. This is a potential crime scene," a gruff male voice ordered. "Stay back!"

The order came from a man in the brown of a sheriff's uniform. He stepped from beneath the canopy, slapping the hat he'd been holding in his hand onto his head to protect him from the continuous rain.

Ronnie and Brandy were hooded and likely looked unisex in the ponchos over their coats. When they didn't immediately respond, he marched their way, his sheriff's star flashing. Ronnie braced herself even while she glanced past him . . . and felt her heart twist.

*What doesn't belong in this picture . . .*

One of the men turned to look at them. *Sloan Hart.* Her insides twisted.

Immediately his eyes narrowed on Ronnie, as if he couldn't believe what he was seeing. *She* couldn't believe what she was seeing, either. What was he doing here? What the hell was he doing here? With the sheriff's department? How had he found Mel?

And how had he gotten here first?

He stalked bare-headed in her direction.

Ronnie fought the urge to run and hide, then berated herself for being such a chicken. She had as much right as anyone to be here, maybe more. Her aunt had called her and this was Aunt Kat's land . . . and the woman lying on the flattened rain-drenched grass was her friend, Melissa Burgham . . . McNulty.

Sloan stopped right in front of her, rain running down his hairline and temples.

Brandy sucked in a breath. Ronnie hoped to God she would say something. Take the pressure off her. But Sloan beat them both to the punch.

"You should have just told me where she was last night," he stated coldly. "Saved us all a lot of trouble."

"I didn't know where she was. I told you that." Ronnie forced herself to stand her ground.

"Do you know who she is?" he demanded.

Was he baring his teeth? No. That's just what it sounded like.

Ronnie looked at Brandy, who had closed her eyes and was swaying a bit. She nodded but didn't say anything.

"Ma'am?" The sheriff, Townsend by his badge, took a step

toward them as Brandy caught herself by grabbing Ronnie's arm. *Townsend*... Sloan's high school friend... one of them at The Pond that day?

Sloan was still waiting for her to answer. "I believe she's Melissa Burgham," Ronnie said, her eyes now on Brandy for confirmation.

"McNulty," Brandy managed to get out. She was pale as death.

"Melissa Burgham McNulty," Ronnie stated for the record, putting an arm around Brandy for support. It felt like she was in rehearsal for a play. Going through the motions. Not really feeling anything yet. Just trying to remember the lines.

"Burgham?" Sloan repeated and then glanced back at the body, his jawline growing hard. He may have thought he'd seen the dead woman before but hadn't been able to place her. "Jesus."

The sheriff's eyes narrowed, as if he were conjuring up a memory.

Brandy was raggedly breathing in and out, fighting to get her bravado back. Fighting and failing. This was Mel, her closest friend from high school. Ronnie felt shattered, too, but if that's the way it was for her, she couldn't imagine how hard it was for Brandy. "Melissa McNulty," Brandy repeated. Then on a half hysterical hiccup, "Unless she changed it back. She said she was going to, but I don't think she had time."

"She was at The Pond that day," Townsend said, surprised, then looked harder at each of them. "You too. You were all there." To Brandy, he said loud enough to be heard over the noise of the storm, "You're Clint Mercer's kid sister. Randi."

"Brandy," Ronnie clarified and Townsend's gaze swung to Ronnie's face.

"You're... you're the one who..."

*Who's the nutcase.*

"Veronica Quick," Sloan cut in.

"Riiiiight." Townsend was nodding. "I remember you."

Of course. They all did. She ignored Townsend's scrutinizing gaze and concentrated on Sloan, watching as rain tracked along his jawline. "Aren't you with River Glen P.D.?" she asked.

"Yes," was Sloan's unilluminating answer.

"Ma'ams..." Townsend blocked their view as much as he could. "We need you to keep clear."

"This is my aunt's land," Ronnie said. "I'm not leaving."

Townsend looked like he was about to come unglued, but Sloan snapped at Brandy, "Stay right here on the periphery." His eyes then bored into Ronnie's. "I want to talk to you. Now." He hooked a thumb toward where a patrol car, its nose pushed into the side of the clearing, its headlights adding to the brightness of the area, sat waiting.

"Walk around the edge. We can take my car back," said Sloan.

"Both of you," ordered Townsend, sliding his finger between Brandy and Ronnie before heading back toward the canopy.

"I said I wasn't leaving," warned Ronnie.

"I suggest you change that," Sloan said grimly. "You described this scenario last night. Said it was a missing person. Didn't mention it was on your aunt's land and that you knew who the person was."

"I didn't know then."

"I knew it was Mel... Melissa," Brandy said in a rush, as if it took her too long to answer she wouldn't be able to.

"I'm not asking," he said, his voice steel.

Ronnie felt herself bristle. She resented his tone. But defying him wasn't going to help Mel or anyone, and one way or another she was going to have to explain her "special ability" again. She nodded curtly, and she and Brandy squished through the mud edging the clearing and past the patrol cars and sheriff's SUVs to a black Bronco that Sloan remotely unlocked with a *beep* and flash of lights.

They both climbed into the back. Brandy said, "I'm going to get mud on your floor mats."

"Fine." From the driver's seat, he slid them both a look in the rearview, then started the engine and slid the Bronco into gear. "Your aunt is Katherine Dubois?"

"Katarina Dubois," corrected Ronnie.

The Bronco splashed along the rutted track and onto the two-lane county road that circled back to her aunt's house. Sloan took the lane up the slight rise, to park behind the patrol car that had been left near the house, next to Ronnie's Escape.

"We should go in from around back," said Ronnie as they climbed out of the Bronco.

Sloan followed Ronnie and Brandy to the rear porch without comment. Aunt Kat was already just inside, opening the door as if expecting them. Ronnie and Brandy took off their ponchos and draped them over an outdoor table at Aunt Kat's direction. She gave them all rags to wipe off their shoes, but Sloan said to Ronnie before they stepped into the house, "I would like to talk to you at the River Glen station."

Of course.

"The crime," she pointed out, "if there was one, happened here, not in your jurisdiction."

"You came to the department yesterday and asked us to find the woman who was discovered by Mr. DeBoer," Sloan stated evenly and from the corner of her eye Ronnie noticed Aunt Kat stiffen.

Sloan went on. "The sheriff called me to the scene at the clearing today. It was exactly as you had described. And then you and Ms. Mercer showed up."

"Abel Townsend's your friend," said Brandy.

"What's going on here?" Aunt Kat asked, worry lines creasing her forehead.

"Just clearing up some jurisdiction issues," Sloan said. "I was with the sheriff's department before River Glen P.D." He was dead serious. Cop mode all the way.

Ronnie's heart sank. Knew she was going to be given the third degree about what she knew when and how. She'd hoped she could save the woman in the clearing, but it had been too late. Now that she knew it was Mel, she was burning for retribution. "All right. I'll take Brandy home and I'll meet you at River Glen P.D. Will that work?"

He hesitated a moment before nodding slowly. "Make sure you show up."

Sounded like a threat. "Oh, I'll be there. You won't have to come looking for me."

"Ronnie?" Aunt Kat cut in worriedly.

But Ronnie wasn't finished. Her voice was as steely as Sloan's had been and she met his hard gaze with her own. "And for the record. It *was* a crime. Your tech team will find the victim was strangled. I want to know who did it as much, or more, than you do."

# Chapter 10

"You don't have to meet with him, you know," Brandy said as they walked back to Ronnie's car. "He can't arrest you or anything."

"Yeah, but I'll just be putting off the inevitable. They're going to want to know how I knew."

They climbed into the Escape and Ronnie backed out of the drive. Sloan's black SUV was just pulling out of sight around a corner as they reached the county road.

"How *did* you know?" asked Brandy.

Ronnie stared straight ahead. "I had a vision."

"Yeah?" She was trying to sound interested, but she was still reeling from seeing Mel. Ronnie felt much the same way, though she'd been somewhat warned by her visions.

"I saw a woman's body in a clearing, her wrists . . . bloody. Head turned away, dirt and ice and rain . . ."

"You said she was strangled."

"And marks on her neck . . . I couldn't see them today. We were too far away, but I know they're there. I know that's what killed her."

Brandy squeezed her eyes shut and shook her head. "You are creepy, Ronnie. You know that, right?"

"Oh, yeah."

"So, she died at the hands of someone, literally."

Ronnie nodded.

"I just want to cry, but I don't know that I can for some reason." She looked out the window, then said, "Sloan Hart. Jesus, what a hard-ass. You sure you're going to marry him?"

*Humor. Good.* "I gave that idea up a long time ago. When I'm right, I'm right. But when I'm wrong, I can be way off."

"You were right this time." Melancholia flavored her words.

"I thought she might be alive. I thought maybe there was movement."

"It wasn't Clint. I'm a broken record, I know, but it wasn't him. You think I should've told Sloan about Hugh?"

"You'll get your chance." Brandy would likely be next on Sloan's acquaintance list. This was a murder investigation, and the authorities would be checking and rechecking everyone connected to Mel.

"What are you going to say?"

"The truth. And they'll all think I'm lying."

"Don't mention Clint, okay? Let me do that."

"I'm only going to tell him what I know." *What I saw.*

At the hospital, Brandy unbuckled her seat belt, then stopped in the act. She looked at Ronnie. "I don't know if I can go back to work. I can't think about anything but Mel."

"I know."

"I'm going to see if I can cut this short. I'll call you later," she said, then shut the car door and walked through the gloom to the brightly lit hospital.

Ronnie took a moment before heading to the police station to meet Sloan. She'd turned her phone off and now picked it up and checked the screen. Six calls. Three from her father. Two from Shana. Maybe she'd made a mistake in exchanging numbers with her. One from Mrs. Langdorf.

She exhaled heavily. Aunt Kat's advice to not call her father was still good. She couldn't tell Jonas what was going on without it pushing every one of his buttons over his concern for her career, her life, her psychic ability, not necessarily in that order.

And Shana . . . ?

It was pretty clear that her interest in Ronnie had to do with her relationship to others: her soon-to-be ex and Sloan Hart, both of which weren't really anything. As for Marian Langdorf, Ronnie wasn't certain she was up to the pressure right now. There was no good reason to call her back because she wasn't going to become her private guru, psychic or Rasputin.

She pulled into the station's front lot, which was where Sloan had parked again.

*Great.*

Stepping from the Escape, she saw he was already outside his own SUV, turning back to remote lock it. His hair was a bit windblown and it made her wonder what her own looked like. She fought the desire to finger-comb her tresses in this rare moment of respite from the rain, knowing he would see. Let the wind do its worst. She wasn't here for a fashion contest.

Still, her shoes were still pretty muddy and her clothes felt damp and cold under her raincoat.

"You don't park in the back," she observed as he waited for her to walk toward him as he was closer to the front door.

"Back parking lot is a mud pit." He half smiled.

"You've taken Detective Haynes's position?" she asked.

His brows lifted as he fell in step beside her and then held the front door for her to enter first.

"You know Haynes?"

"A little. I helped Detective Verbena on a case. Detective Haynes was her partner," she explained.

"Will be again. I'm a temp."

In the vestibule in front of the glassed-in reception area, Sloan gave Colleen behind the desk a high sign and she nodded, then buzzed them through. Sloan held the door and Ronnie preceded him into the squad room. She wasn't fooled by his gallantry. He was seething beneath his manners, undoubtedly certain she was lying to him.

Her eyes turned toward Detective Verbena's desk. No one

there today. She expected Sloan to be taking over Detective Haynes's desk, but he took one back a row and invited Ronnie to take the seat across from it.

She sat down on the visitor chair's edge, facing Sloan, and only then became aware of other officers walking in from the rear of the building. She knew there was an interrogation room down the hall as she'd been there before. Now she almost wished for the privacy.

Sloan asked, "This okay with you?"

"I'd rather be more private."

He glanced around and she sensed he was feeling much the same. Or, maybe he just wanted to hide the fact that he was interviewing the whack job because he said, "There's a room down the hall, or ... we could go somewhere else."

"Like where?"

He shook his head. "Coffee shop?"

"You want to go to a coffee shop?"

He leaned a bit closer to her, to where she could see those gray striations in his eyes. She had an almost visceral memory of that day at The Pond. "I want to go somewhere where I can learn what you know. If that somewhere is outside of the station, then—"

"There's a Starbucks close to my apartment." She forced herself not to pull back from the charged space between them.

"Where is that?"

She gave him her address and explained where the store was in relation to it.

"I'll follow you there." He leaned back, still holding her gaze.

"Okay," she said around a suddenly dry throat.

She hardly remembered the drive. She spent the trip in a nervous state, vacillating from grief to misery to a kind of suspended fear over being with Sloan.

Entering the coffee shop, she smelled the familiar, faintly burned scent of the grounds and heard the constant *pfffssttt* of specialty drink preparation. Behind the counter three baristas were busy taking orders and preparing drinks.

"Tom," one of them called as he placed a large paper cup on the pickup counter and turned back to his next duty. A man with rain-dampened hair and a gray rain jacket scooped up the drink and headed for the door.

Sloan came up behind her. "What'll you have?"

"I don't need anything."

"Latte? Mocha? That pink thing?" He'd pulled out his wallet. "Maybe something to celebrate the season. Peppermint or crème brûlée or—"

"I'm fine." Was he actually teasing her or just being nice? Considering how he'd treated her earlier, she was wary.

"I'm buying."

"Okay, then. Black coffee."

He flicked her a look and then ordered two of the same. Within seconds the barista had poured them each a cup. No waiting.

There was a two-top in the corner, away from the populated tables and chairs. Even with all the other people in the place, it felt a hell of a lot more intimate than the squad room. "Thank you," Ronnie murmured, cradling the warm cup in her still chilled fingers. In fact her whole body was still chilled. She wasn't sure if this was further reaction to the grim scene at the clearing, or the fact that she was so close to Sloan Hart, who'd haunted her thoughts in a way like no other. Silly, but true.

"So, tell me how you knew about the *strangled* woman we found today."

"You know how."

He snorted. "I want to hear you tell me exactly how you knew."

"You want me to tell you about my vision?"

He leaned back in his chair, the cup in one hand, and opened his arms wide, inviting her to just go ahead.

She blew across her cup, then said, "I saw her. I saw the whole tableau, actually. The dark, wet scene, the shed . . . and Mel." She swallowed. "I didn't know it was my Aunt Kat's place until today."

"After you asked me to help you find a missing person."

"If I'd known yesterday I would have gone without asking for help," she said, vaguely aware of the barista calling out customer names.

"So, the place just came to you?"

"No, I figured it out."

"Explain that." He took a swallow of coffee.

Drawing a breath, she told him about going to the hospital and seeing the watercolor and Brandy saying it was Mel's work and suddenly knowing the woman in the clearing was Mel and then Aunt Kat calling and telling her the police were already there.

"We haven't determined that it was death by strangulation," said Sloan once she'd finished.

"I thought you just said it was."

"*You* said it was strangulation," he corrected, "but there's no way you could see that from where you were standing."

"It will be. There were marks on her neck, weren't there?"

He didn't deny it.

"You think I'm involved in this crime somehow, or that I heard about it, or something, but it's none of those things. I saw it. Call it a vision, a dream, a message from another dimension . . . hocus-pocus or a sign from the universe. It happens to me sometimes. Kinda runs in my family, actually."

He didn't change expression. "You're all psychics."

She thought about Aunt Kat . . . her mother. She shook her head. "It just sometimes happens that I get a message. And I'm not always right."

*I'm going to marry you . . .* The words floated across the screen of her mind and she took a long sip of the hot coffee as the doors opened and two thirty-something mothers, toddlers in tow, bustled into the shop. One little girl wearing a fuzzy hood with teddy-bear ears burst through the tables to rush to the glass case where Christmas cookies and muffins were on display. "Cake pop! Mommy. I wants a cake pop!" She looked up eagerly at her mother, reddish curls peeking out from her hood. "Chocklit."

"How do you get a message?" Sloan asked, and she turned her attention back to him.

"It's just there. A thought."

"From... Melissa...?" He was clearly struggling to even humor her with questions as he drank from his cup.

Had Melissa sent that message to her? It felt more... expansive somehow. "I don't know that there's a particular source."

"And this has been with you all your life?"

"As long as I can remember. Look, I know you're trying to act like this is normal and it's not. Believe me, I know. You're thinking, maybe she's been lucky with her guesses. She admits she's not always right. Maybe it's just a kind of intuition. Nothing psychic about it."

His lips faintly quirked. "Something along those lines."

"Okay, fine. Whatever. I just wanted to find the woman in the clearing and now you have."

A gust of cold air rushed inside as the two mothers she'd seen earlier were corralling the toddlers and heading for the door. Ronnie watched the girl with the red curls and teddy-bear hat skip outside. In one chubby fist she clutched a chocolate cake pop.

Sloan said, "In this vision, though, you clearly saw your friend's body and knew she'd been strangled."

"It was a series of... images. I didn't recognize her. I told you that. Oh. And the dog..."

"The dog you heard."

"Yep."

He took another drink. *Giving himself time to think*, she thought, her gaze moving to a nearby table where a bearded man in his twenties was stretched out in a chair, laptop open, earbuds visible as he scrolled with one hand and picked at a bagel with the other.

What was it about the dog in her vision? Why couldn't she see it, just hear its incessant barking—

"What about her bloody wrists?" Sloan asked.

Ronnie blinked back to the here and now and the warm coffee shop. "I don't know. Was she tied? Were they chafed?"

He gazed at her through narrowed eyes. She could tell he was calculating whether to tell her something or not. When he finally spoke, he shocked her. "It looks like they were chewed."

"By . . . by the *dog*? No. The dog is warning us. Telling us to find her. That she's in trouble."

"The dog that you can't see."

"But I can hear him!"

"A male dog?"

"I don't know." Was it? "Yes. A male dog. I think. But it wasn't the dog." On that, Ronnie was certain.

Sloan cocked his head, thinking. "What if the dog was trying to save her?" he suggested. "Pulling her by her wrists?"

Ronnie froze in her seat. He was right. She knew he was right. The dog had tried to help Mel. Maybe it had been tied when she'd been attacked. Had gotten free later. Had tried to pull her to safety.

Tears filled her eyes.

"What?" Sloan demanded. "Are you *seeing* this?"

His tone was so arrogant that she immediately snapped out of her reverie. "No, I'm not seeing it. I'm *feeling* it. I'm feeling sad about my friend and the dog that was trying to save her. It just breaks my heart."

She realized she was on her feet. She was so mad at Sloan. Mad that he was such a prick. He'd shattered all her romantic illusions about him.

He waved her down. "I'm sorry about your friend. This won't take much longer."

"It's not going to take longer at all because I'm leaving."

"Wait . . . please . . . sit."

She almost stormed out. That would feel good. In the moment.

*But it won't help find out who killed Mel.*

She slowly retook her seat, perched on the edge, saw the guy with the laptop close his computer and shove back his chair before donning a wool cap, zipping his jacket and making his way to the door.

Sloan said, "I'd like some background on McNulty."

"Melissa. Mel."

"Mel." He nodded.

Ronnie controlled her anger with an effort. "I don't know a lot. It was seeing Brandy again that made me even realize it was Mel."

He thought about that for a second, then held up a hand. "Let's start over," he suggested. "When was the last time you saw her?" He was trying harder to be . . . not cold. *Difficult for him*, she thought with an inward sneer.

She said, "Years ago. Brandy, Mel and I were grade school friends. Not so much later. I haven't seen either of them in years until I ran into Brandy at the hospital. She and I were in the hospital cafeteria when I realized that the woman I'd been envisioning in that clearing was Mel . . . and you know the rest."

"You didn't go to the hospital to see Brandy because of the 'vision'?"

"No." He waited and Ronnie started to sweat a little. She didn't want to tell him about Shana, the whole story about the divorce papers and accident and driving Shana home. "I was there to see someone else. Unrelated to this story."

"Who?"

"Does it matter?"

"Do you not want to tell me?" he countered, a dark eyebrow arching.

"I don't. And anyway, are you in charge of this investigation? It happened in the county, not River Glen, so how did you get involved?"

In lieu of answering, he said, "It sounds like you've had more than one vision."

"I've had several about Mel. They've grown a little clearer. Or, maybe I'm better at concentrating and see more. I know you can barely listen to me with a straight face, but I'm telling you the truth."

"I don't doubt you believe it."

"Okay," she stated flatly.

Detective Verbena, like Sloan, had pretended to believe her when she'd come to her about Edmond Olman's wife. But Verbena had listened enough to send a patrol to watch the house.

"Is that all you want to say about it?" he asked.

"Yes." She took another swallow of her now tepid coffee.

"All right, then."

"If you want to talk to Brandy," Ronnie said, "she went back to work. At Glen Gen."

"I'll stop by the hospital. I'm talking to Clint later."

"You keep up with him?" she asked, surprised to hear Brandy's brother's name. "Unrelated to this?"

"Him and a few others."

"Let me guess. Evan Caldwell, and Abel—*Sheriff*—Townsend?" she couldn't help throwing in.

"Don't know if you know Abel, but that's a hard one to get used to. Him being the sheriff."

"I know of him. So you—you're all still friends? Like in high school?"

"It's not the same, obviously. But Clint and I have kept in touch."

Ronnie didn't respond.

"What?" Sloan asked suddenly, breaking into her thoughts.

"What do you mean?"

"You looked like you were going to say something."

She'd had Brandy's comments about Clint's innocence on her mind. "Maybe you *should* talk to Brandy."

"What were you going to say?" All of a sudden he was dead serious again.

"No . . . I . . . Brandy knew Mel way better than I did."

"But you were going to say something," he persisted. He was like a dog with a bone. Not giving up.

"No," she said with more force. "All I want to do is help. Judge me if you want, but I want to know what happened to Mel. So please talk to Brandy, and talk to Mel's ex-husband. Like I said, I really didn't know her anymore. We quit hanging out in grade school."

"But somehow you got a message about her."

"Somehow I did. I know you can't use any of this in a court of law, even when and if you find the guy."

"Or woman..."

Ronnie couldn't stop her reaction. No. It wasn't a woman who'd killed Mel.

"You don't believe it's a woman," he pushed, finishing his coffee and crumpling the cup in his fist.

"No."

"What do you think happened?"

"I don't really know. I've... I've told you everything I saw." Her mind wandered back to the images that had appeared to her. "But it seems like it's a crime of passion. Whoever killed her did it because he was in love with her."

His gray eyes didn't miss anything. It felt like they scoured her face, through her skin, into her brain. "That a guess?"

"Call it a deduction. Like I told you, over and over, just talk to Brandy. I've got to go. I've got a lot to do. I... thanks again for the coffee."

She half expected him to stop her again, but this time he simply sat back and let her fly out of the shop. She didn't know who'd killed Mel. She had no idea. But she'd been influenced by Brandy and she didn't want to blurt out Clint's name just because Brandy had been so hell-bent on protecting him and throwing blame on Mel's ex, Hugh. In any case, she *did not know* who it was behind Mel's death, and she'd be damned if she sent the investigation in the wrong direction.

That said, she wasn't going to sit by and expect the police to solve the case. She'd been sent a message and she was going to act on it... somehow.

Sloan watched Veronica Quick scramble away from him as if he were about to arrest her. She was right about one thing: He had no real right to suspect her. But yesterday she'd brought the question of the missing woman to him, and so she was involved at some level.

What that level was, was anyone's guess. Psychic revelation? Message from beyond? Kooky nonanswer that would never pass the smell test if, and when, they caught the bastard who'd killed Melissa Burgham McNulty and tried to take the case to court?

He headed out the door, back to the station. Fresh in his mind was the memory of Veronica Quick from the day before. Seeing her at the crime scene in that soaked poncho, her face half obscured by its hood, he hadn't immediately recognized her. She'd always been more myth than reality. The girl who'd declared she was going to marry him, then developed a reputation for being a nutcase psychic, though her father was a lauded attorney with an eclectic practice, everything from venerated estate lawyers to down and dirty criminal defense ones. Sloan didn't really think Veronica had anything to do with her friend's death, but she knew something. So maybe she knew someone involved? It wouldn't be the first time a person passed off information that they "heard" in an attempt to shield whoever "told" about the crime.

As he entered the squad room he saw that Chief Duncan was in his office. The man had been gone of late, hobnobbing with the mayor and her posse. Well, go ahead, he thought. I've got one foot here and the other with the sheriff's department. Abel Townsend, who'd changed from the massive screwup he'd been in high school, to become a more than capable lawman, a pretty damn good sheriff, was waiting for him to return. But Sloan knew morale was down at the River Glen P.D. ever since the chief had sided with the wealthy rather than the majority of the city's citizens. He also knew that putting Detective Haynes on administrative leave for basically solving the case was assbackwards in every way. So Sloan was a placeholder for Haynes and though he would've liked a full-time position, he was more interested in restoring faith and belief in the system.

Like everyone else here, he was keeping his mouth shut on the issue around the station. Hopefully Haynes would be back at his desk soon, and Verbena's mother's health would improve, though he sensed that wasn't likely. In the meantime the new guy himself was going to do his damnedest to keep the investigative train on track and on time. Might not work, but it wouldn't be for lack of trying.

He hadn't alerted the chief about Melissa McNulty's body being discovered yet. Hadn't seen the chief and, as Quick had pointed out, it wasn't River Glen P.D.'s jurisdiction. The crime would be investigated at the county level and Sloan would just be aiding them as he could. Still, he owed the chief an explanation of where he'd been all day, even though nobody was asking.

With that in mind, he started toward the chief's office, but Duncan—or Humph, as he was called around the station—was already around his desk and heading for his office door, meeting Sloan before he could enter. "I've got a meeting," Humph said. "Can it wait?"

"Just wanted you to know I'm helping Sheriff Townsend on a possible murder case."

"Abel Townsend. Friend of yours?"

"Classmate," he said with a nod. He didn't want to overplay the friend bit with the chief.

"You can tell me about it later." And he was gone.

That done, Sloan was free to follow whatever came next. In River Glen, things had been quiet, pretty much since the moment he'd taken over a desk. He thought about it. Had Clint Mercer's number.

He picked up his cell and put through a call to Mercer. Clint worked in sales for a regional furnace manufacturing company. Sloan waited, but was told by voice mail that Clint was unavailable. He left a message, then decided to look up Brandy Mercer's number. He'd called Clint to clear the way for Sloan to connect with his sister, as he'd picked up that Brandy wasn't wild about being interviewed. But then neither had been Quick.

Briefly he considered calling Quick for Brandy's number, but there was no need. He could find it himself through the department.

*You just want to talk to her again.*

He made a sound in his throat, scoffing at himself. As much

shit as he'd endured from her saying she was going to marry him, by all his friends and acquaintances, Clint Mercer and Abel Townsend included, you'd think he would want to stay as far away as possible.

He thought back to Abel's comments last night about her. They'd planned to meet for a few beers and Sloan had just come from the meeting with Quick in which she had even given him her psychic reveal about the "woman in the clearing." Abel had nearly spit out his Bud.

"So, the rumor's true? She thinks she's a psychic?" He twirled his finger by his ear.

"She helped Elena Verbena on a case. She was accurate." Sloan found himself defending her.

"You're buyin' this?"

*Not really.* "I'm willing to listen."

"If you're bored in that little podunk town where we used to live, in that little podunk police department, come on back," Abel had said before taking a long draught of his beer.

"River Glen's not that podunk. And your department's about the only one in the state of Oregon that's overstaffed. I'll stick it out till Haynes comes back."

"So what fable did she tell ya?" Abel had then asked, switching gears.

Sloan hadn't wanted to reveal Quick's declarations about the crime to Abel. It felt disloyal to her, somehow. He'd therefore reluctantly explained about the unidentified woman in the clearing, how Quick had described her as missing, how she'd wanted some kind of action on the part of the police. He could tell Townsend was ready to go full-on "she's a crackpot" on Quick, and Sloan had been short with Townsend. He didn't want to make Veronica Quick the butt of Townsend's jokes.

This morning when Abel called, all amused barbs were gone. A neighbor had found the body, just as Quick had described it. He and Sloan had then both gone to the site, neither saying what was on his mind. Abel had commented on the raw flesh around the victim's wrists and it was the tech on site who'd suggested dog's teeth had made the wound.

Then Quick had shown up with Brandy Mercer.

Sloan's first thought: *What game is she playing?*

His second: *She knows more than she's telling.*

His third: *She can't really believe this shit, can she?*

Well, now he knew the third was correct. Maybe the second and first, too, for that matter. But whatever the answer, he had his own teeth in this case and he was going to find out who killed that woman in the clearing no matter who, or what, got in his way. Didn't matter whether it was the sheriff's department or River Glen P.D., he was going to insinuate himself into the investigation. Luckily, Townsend was more than amenable. He might have to do a dance with the R.G. chief, but he was already invested, so he'd be dancing like he was aiming for the mirror ball.

# Chapter 11

Ronnie's cell phone rang as she was entering her apartment. Gave it a glance. Dear Old Dad, once more. She let it go to voice mail as she was taking off her shoes and putting them behind the front door. She would deal with their mud later. Then she headed for the shower, stripping off her raincoat and throwing it over the couch on her way.

Twenty minutes later she was towel drying her hair and hearing the phone ring again. Her father. There were still a few hours of work left and she was on her way back; she just wanted to deal with him when she got there, not before. She finished getting dressed again in black slacks and blazer over a cream collarless blouse and headed out. When the phone rang in the car, from where she'd set it in the cup holder, she finally answered.

"Where've you been?" he demanded as a form of greeting.

"Crime scene."

"What do you mean?"

"I'll explain later," she said, feeling the weight of Mel's death overcome her again.

He made a sound of annoyance in his throat. "Veronica, I don't try to tell you what to do."

"Since when?"

"I don't try to force you to make every meeting, but today we had the annual budget meeting and there were questions over some of your expenses."

She'd forgotten about the budget meeting. Mainly because it rarely had much to do with her. It was Albert Tormelle's and her dad's issues, and maybe some of the other lawyers—Galen had sure known how to spend company funds while wining and dining prospective clients. "What are my expenses?"

"I don't want to get into the details over the phone, but you are—"

"Get into the details."

"—coming back to the office, right?"

"On my way, even though the workday's almost done. What are the details?" she demanded as she slowed for a stoplight.

"Just come to my office when you get here."

Yeah, like that was going to go well. It wasn't about her expenses. She didn't have any. He was just pissed she wasn't there when he and Albert tsk-tsked the others, who accepted the reprimands with varying degrees of equanimity or fury. The furious ones left. The ones who stayed either argued that they weren't to blame, or let it roll off their shoulders.

As the light changed and she eased onto the gas again, Ronnie thought it was counterproductive and unnecessary to bring up costs incurred by individuals at the main budget meeting. Put it in a syllabus. Write it in an email. But don't embarrass good attorneys just because you're old-school. Sometimes it felt like her father was deliberately trying to run his business into the ground.

*Or, his nihilism comes from being frustrated at trying to bend your career his way, no matter what.*

How narcissistic. She was almost embarrassed for having the thought. Except it was true.

At the office building she parked in the open as the sheltered lot beneath the upper offices was full. But it wasn't raining anyway, though the air felt poised, just waiting, catching its breath. And for reasons that probably had a lot to do with her recent meeting with Sloan Hart, the day at The Pond flashed across her mind again. She could practically hear those faint figures from her dream whispering about her. See Evan Caldwell's wide-open eyes, remember his words from a mouth that didn't move.

*It should've been you, not me . . .*

What had that meant? She'd gotten over his evil laugh, putting it down to her ten-year-old fears and reaction, but where had that statement come from? She'd never had an opportunity to talk to Evan about their co-near-death-experiences. Probably wouldn't if given the chance. Didn't mean she wasn't curious if he'd experienced some kind of unconscious episode like she had.

Dawn was on the phone as Ronnie appeared, but hitched her chin toward the right-hand corridor behind her, indicating she was to go directly to her father's office. *Fine.*

She saw that his door was ajar, not the usual circumstance for Jonas. She rapped softly, then stuck her head inside. "Okay. I'm here."

"Come in."

Jonas was seated behind his desk, a medium-height man who looked more imposing while seated. His gray hair was a tad longish currently. A fight to hang on to his youth? His hazel eyes were penetrating.

"I'll get right to it. It's game time. No more indecision."

"About my legal career?" Ronnie let just the hint of disbelief enter her voice as she walked to his desk, preferring to stand rather than take a seat in one of the leather side chairs.

"What are you waiting for?" he said, leaning back in his chair, his eyebrows knitting. "I need you to zero in on your future and that starts with going back to law school."

"I don't think that's what I want."

"I don't care what you want!" He slapped his palms on his desk, shocking her. Jonas never displayed out-and-out anger.

"What?"

"Albert is getting divorced and half of this company goes to his wife. I need you to be my successor and I want you to have a law degree because he's planning on hiring his son as soon as he's fresh out of law school. Your capriciousness isn't helping our cause."

Ronnie stared at her father. He'd finally made it abundantly clear that it was really about the company, not her. Had always been. "You encouraged my relationship with Galen because you wanted an heir."

"I want you, Veronica. *You*. In charge. I've always wanted you. You know that."

What she knew was that she was right about Galen, no matter what her father did or didn't say, but she also knew he was right about her. She'd never wanted what he was throwing at her with both hands. When she'd first dated Galen, he'd encouraged the relationship because it had been a sideways attempt to rope her in.

"I can't make myself want something just because you want it."

"We're going to lose everything unless you get in the game."

"You own half of this firm. They can't take that away from you."

"And what happens when I'm gone? Hmm? What happens then?"

Her flesh prickled. "Are you okay?"

He held up a hand, fighting for a calmness he clearly didn't feel. "I'm fine. I want your future settled. Galen was a mistake, I think we both can admit that, but leaning into your mother's . . . side. That's reputation suicide."

"Jonas . . . Dad . . . My reputation—"

"You can't meet with Marian Langdorf. You have to stop that. Can't give the Tormelles more fodder against you. That's all I'm asking."

Ronnie thought back to the clearing . . . Mel's body . . . Sloan Hart, *Detective* Sloan Hart . . . "My reputation is going to take another hit," she said, and then told him about the events of the afternoon.

* * *

Sloan strode toward the sliding entry doors of Glen Gen to see Brandy Mercer. She had been nice enough to call him back and agree to speak with him, but said she was filling in, working an overtime shift, a result of the hospital being chronically understaffed and also to make up for her abrupt departure in the middle of the workday with Veronica Quick.

He was guided to her floor by the front desk and then had to wait in an alcove that sported two chairs and some artwork until Brandy had a break. His eye had just snagged on a picture when Brandy was there in blue scrubs, white-faced and sober, which could either be from some serious situation at the hospital or the fact that she'd earlier seen her friend's dead body.

"I can't believe she's gone," she said, sinking into one of the chairs with a heavy sigh.

That answered that question.

"I can't believe someone hurt her!" she added with more spunk.

"We're going to get to the truth."

Her gaze flicked up to the watercolor picture on the wall. Quick had mentioned the artwork.

"Mel painted that," Brandy clarified. "Ronnie recognized it."

"It's . . . the crime site?"

"Yeah . . . now. Mel gave it to me and said it reminded her of our Three Musketeers days." Sloan almost asked the obvious question, but she went on before he had to. "That's what Ronnie called us. I brought the picture here for times when things get hard and hectic, like today. It's, um, it's calming. At least for me." She swallowed. "It was anyway." She cleared her throat and glanced away, obviously emotional.

"You were the Three Musketeers?" he asked.

"Once upon a time."

"Can you give me some background on Melissa McNulty . . . Mel?"

She laced her fingers together. "Whatever you think, Clint didn't do this. My brother thought he loved her . . . he did love her. The only one who would hurt her was Hugh, her ex-husband."

Clint Mercer was involved with Melissa McNulty? Romantically? Sexually? What? It was clear Brandy Mercer was already protecting Clint and that meant she was worried about her brother. Sloan, too, wanted to strike Clint as a suspect, but he was bound to carry out a thorough investigation and Clint's entanglement with the dead woman didn't look good.

"Let's start with Hugh," said Sloan.

Brandy let out a sigh. "The irony is, Clint introduced them..."

Cooper sat on the living room couch and read through the cold case files he'd taken home before his administrative leave had commenced. His mind wasn't on them. He probably shouldn't have them anyway, but he'd been looking for a distraction. One of them wasn't even a case, more a question from the family about the nature of their child's death.

He'd come home ready to tell Jamie what he'd learned, but her ob-gyn had been with her when he'd returned, which had given him pause. When he'd entered the bedroom, she'd been ebullient about how things were going with her pregnancy and he didn't want to bring her down, so he'd told her he had a line on Mary Jo and left it at that. She'd immediately wanted every bit of news, but he'd managed to stave her off.

"She and the baby are safe," was all he would say, which was really stretching the bounds of truth. But he was pretty sure she was at the Heart of Sunshine Church and there was no reason to believe either Mary Jo or the baby were in danger.

The truth was he was still working through what he'd seen at the church. He was still a bit gobsmacked by one of the names written into the register that sat on the Heart of Sunshine lectern.

*Is your surrogate named Rebekkah? Two k's, one h?*

Rebekkah Parrish had been written in a shaking hand. Mary Jo's signature, maybe. As soon as he was home he'd checked her signature on the legal papers they'd all signed and yes, he thought it could be Mary Jo's handwriting.

But what did that mean? He wondered, and glanced at the

Christmas tree, lights now set in some kind of twinkle mode and reflecting on the window.

Now, while everyone in his household was upstairs except for Duchess, who lay on the carpet by his feet, curled nose to tail, Cooper put in a call to Veronica Quick. *Ronnie*, she'd said. When she didn't immediately answer, he left a brief message: "Hi, it's Cooper Haynes. Give me a call. I'd like to talk to you about Rebekkah . . . .two *k*'s, one *h* . . ." In the moment he'd dismissed her comment as completely off base, but now . . .

"Who're you talking to?"

He startled. Clicked off and turned swiftly at the sudden question to find Jamie's daughter, Harley, walking from the kitchen into the dining area, in line with Cooper's chair.

"Where'd you come from?" He was surprised that he hadn't heard his stepdaughter approach. Losing his touch? Or, just too deeply worried . . .

"Upstairs. I was tiptoeing downstairs because Mom's sleeping now."

He nodded.

"This is weird. What are you hiding? Is it Mary Jo?"

Harley was lean and alert in a way that reminded him of his partner, Elena Verbena. Dark hair and hazel eyes that missed nothing. Like everyone else in the household, she knew Mary Jo was missing, though Cooper had tried to downplay the worry and act like her behavior was normal. Looking at Harley now, he knew he wasn't fooling her.

"I'm leaving a message," he told her and, disturbing Duchess, pushed himself up from the couch. Grudgingly the dog ambled to the fireplace, where she settled once again.

"Who's Rebekkah?" Harley asked.

"Long story."

"Who were you calling?"

*A psychic.* "No one you know."

"Something else is wrong. What is it?"

Cooper had seesawed back and forth about confiding fully in Harley. She was smart and engaged, and flirting with a career in law enforcement. She was also fiercely loyal to both her mother and her Aunt Emma.

But if he was going to reveal all to Harley, he was going to have to tell everything to Jamie first.

"Bring me into the circle of trust," Harley said sternly, folding her arms over her chest.

Cooper smiled. "Or what?"

"Or, I'll find out anyway."

He wasn't sure exactly what she had in mind, but he figured he didn't want to know. Harley was bullheaded and strategic. "I'm going to talk to your mom about a few things."

"Then we can talk?" she clarified, her gaze locked with his.

"Yeah, maybe."

He headed for the stairs and Jamie.

Ronnie was just finishing her last meeting and walking back to her office when her phone rang and she saw it was Brandy.

"Perfect timing," Ronnie answered. "I'm wrapping up for the day." She heard herself and realized how seamlessly she'd turned to trusting Brandy, remembering their long-ago friendship, and wanting it back.

"God, what I wouldn't do for a drink," Brandy said. "Unfortunately I can't."

"You're still at work?"

"So far. I was trying to leave early but we're busy tonight. As always. I had to take a break to meet with Sloan Hart. He scares me a little. Don't hate me, but after I gave him some background on Mel, I turned him back your way."

"What did you say?" she asked, heart clutching a little.

"I told him your visions were real and he should work with you to find Mel's killer. I told him it was probably Hugh. It's gotta be, but I couldn't get a read on Sloan. I told him it wasn't Clint, but of course he's going to talk to him. I mean they're friends . . . so . . . How long does forensics take? I mean, it's fast on television, but I'm guessing that's fake?"

"I'm guessing you're right. Did Sloan say when he was going to call?"

"No, but he's pretty gung-ho. I don't like this at all."

"Neither do I," Ronnie admitted.

"I've gotta get back to work. Tell me what Sloan says."

"I will."

"I'm just so glad to talk to you," Brandy suddenly burst out. "I mean it. It's been too long and I can't even remember why our threesome broke apart."

It was because she was the weird one with her nutso visions, the girl who had been screaming at The Pond that day, the one with visions. Ironic, she thought, now that those very visions had brought them back together, but she just smiled and said, "I'm glad to talk to you, too."

"Okay. Let's keep it going. I just feel numb and achy and drained."

"Me too," admitted Ronnie.

"All right. I'll call you later," Brandy promised before clicking off.

Seeing she had a voice mail, Ronnie pressed the number and listened to Cooper Haynes asking to meet with her. The hair rose on her arms as she heard him spell out "two *k*'s, one *h* . . ." So there was a connection in there somewhere. Maybe Detective Haynes would give her more credit than Detective Hart.

She texted him back **Sometime tomorrow afternoon?**

A little while later she received: **Thanks. I'll text you around noon.**

"Rebekkah?" Jamie asked.

Cooper balanced on the edge of the bed where Jamie sat, propped up by pillows, her eyes gazing hard into his, a line forming between her brows.

She'd awakened after a long nap, stretching like a contented cat, and he'd been hard-pressed to follow through and explain about Mary Jo and Atticus Symons's flock. But she needed to know.

"What kind of place is Heart of Sunshine?" she asked worriedly. "How long's she been there?"

"It's a retreat of some kind."

She drew an unsteady breath. "Like . . . last summer? Like she was in *before*?"

"I don't know," said Cooper. But didn't he? Wasn't that just what Stephen had said? That Mary Jo defaulted to cultlike behavior when she was stressed or pregnant? She'd spent her youth in a sect that had become its own microcosm of society, one dictated by an unyielding ruler, and Mary Jo, despite leaving it all behind, apparently held vestiges of it close to her heart.

"You were there? You didn't see her?" There was an edge to her voice and Cooper knew she was trying to keep her emotions under rein, to not flip out as she had earlier. "Cooper!"

He held up his hands, as it looked like Jamie had given up on keeping cool and was about to jump out of bed. "I haven't seen her, but I'm pretty sure she's there. I'm not losing her, Jamie. I'm just working things out before I go in guns blazing, so to speak."

"Jesus, Mary and Joseph," muttered Jamie.

"She's not taking our baby."

"You're right about that!" she proclaimed, then as if understanding the situation, said, "You think that's what she's trying to do?" Now she sounded downright terrified.

"It's a vision quest, Stephen said, but only Mary Jo knows for sure. You were right about her. We shouldn't have used her as a surrogate. She's too flaky."

"I don't want to be right, I just want my baby back." She sank into the pillows and looked miserable. "And after she has SuzyQ, I may just strangle Mary Jo."

"We're having a girl?" They hadn't wanted to know the sex, the last he'd heard.

"Or two girls," she said, patting her distended abdomen. "Or maybe one of each. Or two boys." She was trying again to keep the conversation light, but she failed and she knew it, so her voice turned serious again. "All I know is they're both ours, no matter who births them. So, if she has *any* thought about keeping *our* baby, the one she's carrying . . ." She left the threat unfinished but her expression said it all.

"She knows she's not keeping it," assured Cooper.

"You sure?"

"If she's fuzzy on it at all, I'll make it clear for her."

His tone warned any attempt to argue with him would be futile. Jamie half smiled, then she fought tears, and it was a losing battle.

"Hey." He brushed back the tresses that fell in her face when she'd collapsed back on the pillows. "Don't worry. River Glen's finest is on the case."

"I hate to remind you you're on leave."

"Still with the force . . . still the finest . . ."

"You are that," she agreed, keeping her eyes closed but turning toward him.

He kissed her on the forehead. "Rest. Take care of SuzyQ One while I make sure SuzyQ Two is okay."

"We're not naming either of them SuzyQ, by the way. Just so you know."

# Chapter 12

Brandy called almost the moment that Ronnie got home from work. "I'm off. I had to beg, borrow and steal, but I got someone to come in. It was all I could do to stay focused. I feel too terrible."

"I know what you mean," admitted Ronnie. "I just got back and I'm drained."

"Any chance you could go with me over to Clint's? He's a mess. Broken up about Mel. He needs me, and I want you there, too. He asked me how you found her and I told him . . . you just knew."

"I thought Sloan was meeting up with him."

"Trying to. Clint's avoiding him. Sloan makes you feel like a criminal. Did you talk to him?"

Ronnie asked, "He hasn't called?"

"He will. He's going to talk to everybody." Brandy sounded certain.

"Well, we'll just be going over what's already been said."

"Maybe he's better than Townsend. I don't know. Why isn't Abel doing the investigation?"

"You'd have to ask him, or Sloan," Ronnie suggested.

"Will you come with me to Clint's?"

"Where does he live?" Ronnie asked, letting her doubts draw out her words. She was ready to call it a day. She needed time to just think things through.

*And maybe hope you get some illuminating message?*

"It's not far. I'll drive. I'll pick you up. You don't have to do anything but go with me."

"All right," she said against her better judgment.

She made herself a tuna and melted Gruyère cheese sandwich and ate half of it, thinking while she chewed. She had a lot to process about Mel... and Sloan. And her father, Albert Tormelle and the business; and Mrs. Langdorf and Carlton; and Cooper Haynes and his missing surrogate...

"Rebekkah," she muttered aloud.

Her cell buzzed and she picked it up with a certain amount of trepidation.

Marian Langdorf's number appeared. "Fabulous," Ronnie muttered, grimacing. She needed to talk to the woman, find a way to convince her that she wasn't going to take up residence with her and become her personal psychic. But not right now.

*You should've been firmer.*

"How many ways can you say no?" she asked the empty room, letting the call go to voice mail.

She changed from her work slacks and blouse into jeans and a heavy sweater. At least it had stopped raining, for the moment.

*Don't go in the water...*

She stopped short in the process of wrapping up the other half of her sandwich. She'd had a lot of psychic moments, messages, the last few days, and it had been raining almost constantly. Could there be a connection? She'd always considered the warning she'd heard when she was ten had something to do with The Pond, and well, that had proved true. But...

She put the wrapped sandwich in the refrigerator and swept up her cell phone, pressing the Favorites button for Aunt Kat.

"Hi, hon," her aunt greeted her, though her voice was a bit more subdued than usual. "How're you doing?"

"I'm operating at a surface level, but anytime I think about Mel . . . I just can't go there. But, I have a question for you."

"Oh?"

"I have a lot of questions, actually. I want to know about how you knew I was going to call. And please don't put me off. You knew. You've got this, too, don't you?"

"By 'this' you mean, the gift . . . that you inherited from your mother?"

"That's exactly what I mean."

"Veronica, I don't really have the same thing."

"But you've got something. How do we have this? Is it genetic? That's what it sounds like."

Aunt Kat heaved a long sigh. "Who knows? Your mother was supremely gifted. She knew things before they happened. She hid it, too. Like you. I don't know if you're the same . . . you've shown that you might be."

"When did it come on with Mom?" Ronnie demanded.

"She seemed to always have it."

"Did Jonas know?"

"You'd have to ask him. As I said, your mother was careful, like you are."

Ronnie had told Aunt Kat about seeing the figures when she was unconscious in The Pond, hearing their voices and their warning. Now she said, "Don't go in the water. I feel like I've been channeling more, with all this rain."

"Never heard that before."

"Maybe not. It just feels like it. And who is it that's trying to tell me something about Mel? Is it Mel herself? Or my mother?"

"I wish I knew, honey. I really do." She sounded sincere.

Ronnie had never gotten so much out of her aunt before. But then she'd never seen an actual death before. Up till now, what she'd seen had been possible futures, warnings of danger, sometimes a possible incident, or random information.

"How did Mom die?"

"Her body just gave out." Aunt Kate heaved a heavy sigh.

"She was at the ocean?"

"That's right. She and your father were staying at a small motel. Winnie hadn't been well for a while."

*The ocean... Don't go in the water.* "She walked into the water."

"That wasn't what killed her. Her organs were shutting down." Aunt Kat was firm but her voice trembled a little. "I hate talking about it. It was such a tragedy." She sounded like she was about to cry.

"I get that. I just... need to know the truth. It's just always been so brushed over, and now I feel like my life is ..." Ronnie couldn't quite explain it. Like everything was moving faster, maybe to some ultimate end.

*Your own death?*

She shuddered.

"Veronica." Aunt Kat sounded alarmed.

"I'm okay. I just... I'm fighting with Jonas. He wants me to become a lawyer and take over the firm ... and he won't talk to me about any of this. Acts like it's not happening. And he's getting worse about telling me what to do. One of the clients, Mrs. Langdorf, asked me to become her personal psychic, and Dad lost it. I wasn't going to take the job, but he forbade me from taking it, which pissed me off."

"Maybe you should," Aunt Kat said tentatively.

"What? Take the psychic job? No."

"Maybe you should get away from your father so he stops trying to shoehorn you into the life he's chosen for you."

"Thank you," Ronnie said, a bit surprised. For all her dislike of Jonas, Aunt Kat had never openly defied his wishes, as far as Ronnie could recall.

"All I want for you is your happiness, Veronica. A happiness that eluded your mother. She ... was failing, before the accident. She had too many ... visions."

Ronnie's heart galumphed. "What?"

"Don't worry. It's not the same as you," she said hurriedly.

"How is it not the same?" demanded Ronnie.

"Winnie started to believe in every message. She had trouble differentiating. To the therapist we sent her to, they were all hallucinations. She didn't like taking the anti-psychotics and . . ."

"She didn't kill herself," Ronnie declared.

"No. Who told you that?" Aunt Kat sounded aghast.

"No one. I just wanted to make sure."

"She did not kill herself," Aunt Kat reiterated.

Ronnie tested the truth of Aunt Kat's words and decided to believe her. "When Mom was okay, though, do you remember what she predicted?"

"I don't," she said quickly. Too quickly. Then added, "I'm sorry, honey."

Now *that* was a lie. Ronnie would bet money on it. But she'd gotten more from her aunt than she ever had before and that was something. She tried to ask more questions, but Aunt Kat didn't seem to have any more answers. Or maybe she was just putting her off. In any case, they ended the call a few minutes later and Ronnie went to the bottom drawer of her dresser and pulled out the scrapbook she had of her mother. Mostly it was pictures of Mom with her father or Aunt Kat. Only a few with her mother and herself.

She stared at the picture of them together long and hard and conjured up the scene at their home. She vaguely remembered the scents of jasmine and lavender, and remembered some of the books lining the bookshelf, just out of the camera's range. She could almost hear Mom singing to her.

A pang of longing cut through her heart and she closed the scrapbook.

Her mind slipped from that memory to one of Mel. In high school. Melissa had been wearing a pink sweater, her hand clasped within a guy's grasp. They were walking away from Ronnie and she focused on her memory of the guy. Not Clint, though Mel had never quite gotten over that crush.

So who—?

Ronnie was still thinking about Mel in that pink sweater, wondering about the boy she couldn't recall, when Brandy came to the door to pick her up.

\* \* \*

Clint Mercer's houselights illuminated the front yard of a small bungalow with what looked like ongoing repairs. There were new fascia boards around the eaves and fresh wood being erected over a scarred and pitted concrete porch. The paint was peeling on the front door and the doorbell didn't respond when Brandy pressed it.

"It was working last week," Brandy muttered.

"Maybe it's part of the remodel."

"Let's hope," she said in a tone that doubted it was. She pounded on the door panels and yelled, "Clint! I'm here. Open the door."

There was a delay and Ronnie looked toward the driveway, which was basically two cracked ribbons of asphalt that led to a detached garage. A large silver GMC truck with a company logo—River Glen Heating and Cooling—painted in black script across the driver's door gleamed in the slanting light from the house. The truck, its tires thick with mud, was parked in front of garage doors that looked like they swung from the center out. Dark shadows covered up its truck bed and even with the momentary lull from the rain, it still was wet.

A male voice called from inside the house. "It's open."

Brandy tried the handle and pushed. "Oh," she said as the door gave.

Ronnie followed her inside where an enormous TV took up one wall. Football players were fighting it out at the scrimmage line. The sound was turned off and there was no one in the room.

"Where are you?" Brandy demanded.

"I'll be there in a minute," Clint called back in a voice that sounded weary beyond words.

"See what I mean?" She hooked a thumb toward the TV. "That's not his favorite team, and still he's watching? Even to kind of try and forget for a little while?" She inhaled and closed her eyes, exhaling on a long breath. "It's just so hard to believe, isn't it . . ."

"Yeah."

In the quiet that followed Brandy looked away from Ronnie

and her eyes swam with tears. Dashing them away almost as soon as they formed, she straightened her shoulders. "You said she was strangled. What about her bloody hands?" Brandy asked. "You don't think she was stabbed or something?"

Ronnie thought of her discussion with Sloan, what they'd concluded. "That looks like maybe from a dog. There actually wasn't a lot of blood so maybe after her death . . ."

"What dog?" he'd asked.

Now, Ronnie shook her head. She hadn't had a real sense of the dog since those first hours, day. And yet she'd heard barking . . .

Clint Mercer entered the room. He looked like someone who'd been in a car wreck. His dark hair was practically standing on end from where he'd obviously run his hands through it. His gray shirt looked like he'd slept in it and its front buttons weren't aligned. Contrary to his shirt, his jeans were pressed and neat. He was barefoot, and his eyes were bloodshot . . . and he smelled like beer.

Seeing him, Brandy lost the fight with her emotions and she cried out and threw herself into his arms. He nodded, as if agreeing with her pain, looking over her head to Ronnie.

"Psychic girl," he said tonelessly.

She shrugged. "Ronnie."

"Okay, okay . . ." He carefully grabbed Brandy's shoulders and pulled back from her. "You okay?"

"Yeah . . . yeah . . . It's just that it's Mel," Brandy said, not sounding convincing.

Clint frowned and looked away. "I know."

"Have you talked to Sloan?" asked Ronnie.

"Not yet. Have you?"

"We both have," said Ronnie, nodding toward Brandy, who had found her way to the couch. Ronnie perched on a cushion beside her while she was sprawled as if her bones had melted. "He's a friend of yours?"

"Doesn't mean I want to talk to him," Clint explained. "Brandy said he's investigating Mel's death. Good. I hope he finds the fucker."

*Well, then why don't you talk to him?*

She'd just had the thought when Clint's cell phone rang. He fished it from his pocket and stared at the screen before clicking off.

"Was that Sloan?" asked Ronnie.

"Don't you know, Miss Psychic?"

"Clint . . ." Brandy murmured, her eyes closed.

"Why don't you want to give him a statement?" asked Ronnie.

Brandy's eyes flew open and she gazed at Ronnie as if she'd betrayed her. "Why is Sloan doing this? Shouldn't it be Abel Townsend?" Brandy asked. "Sloan's with River Glen P.D. and Mel was found outside the city. It's not his jurisdiction."

"He thinks I did it," Clint said in a strangled voice.

"That's not true! You love Mel. Sloan knows that!" Brandy was fierce.

"He doesn't know me. He's been gone for years." Clint took the only other chair, throwing a look at the TV. "We're fucking losing," he said, his voice deep with despair.

"He does know you," argued Brandy.

"He'll want an arrest. He'll say I did it."

"No, he won't!" Brandy had found her feet again. No more throwing herself down in despair. "It's Hugh. I told him it was Hugh. He'll find out that—"

"It's not Hugh." Clint cut her off. "Hugh's been gone since last Saturday. I've tried calling him, but he's not answering. I left him two voice mails. Nothing."

"That's suspicious in itself," insisted Brandy, and Ronnie silently agreed.

Clint explained, "Hugh's out of range. He's hiking on Mt. Hood with a friend. Building snow caves. All that shit. He's not here."

"Maybe he is. Maybe that's a lie." Brandy was adamant.

"You think I did it," Clint realized, his tone changing to betrayal. "That's why you're blaming Hugh."

"No! I know you didn't do it. You couldn't hurt Mel. You love her. And she loves you . . . loved you," she corrected herself.

"Brandy said you 'saw' Mel... in a clearing in the woods. How?" The question was directed at Ronnie as Clint gave her his full attention. There was something furtive in his eyes, which made her heart clutch. He wasn't telling the truth... or at least all of the truth.

She had a sudden image of his truck. Practically printed on her retina. The mud on his tires... Would that tread match the tire tracks left at the clearing?

Her thoughts were but an instant, but Clint must have seen something in her expression because he said, "You... you think I did it, too. Well, I didn't. And none of your hocus-pocus can make me her killer."

"If it wasn't Hugh, who was it?" asked Ronnie.

"I don't know. How should I know? Mel... oh, God." He shook his head as the realization hit. "Listen, the truth is Mel slept with other guys. It's one of them, probably."

Brandy looked from Clint to Ronnie. "You're not taking Sloan's side, are you?"

"There are no sides!" *Sloan's* side. What the hell? "Who else was she seeing? Do you have names?" Ronnie asked him.

"No. I don't know."

"Mel wasn't with anyone while she was with you," said Brandy loyally.

Clint's mouth twisted. "Sure."

"You must have another name," probed Ronnie.

"Well, I don't. That's why I don't want to talk to Sloan. I don't want to have to tell him about Mel's cheating." He ran a finger through his already-mussed hair. "There was always somebody better."

"There's no one better than you," said Brandy.

This time his smile was genuine. "You're such an idiot."

"No, I'm not. I'm the smart one." She looked ready to cry again.

Clint said, "There was one guy... from Laurelton, I think. But if it was anything, it was over quick. She didn't like his dog."

"Dog?" repeated Ronnie.

"'A smelly mutt,' that's what she said about it. We had a big fight, but she never ran off that time."

Ronnie asked, "She ran off before?"

"Sure. Yeah." Then with a scowl added, "You know I introduced her to Hugh? Next thing I know they're getting married and I'm toasting the bride and groom. Didn't realize how I felt about her till she was gone." He shrugged. "As it turned out, she wasn't sure about the marriage, either. Hugh and his bros are extreme outdoors guys. Mel wasn't into that."

Ronnie thought of Mel at the clearing. Even when they were kids she'd been the one who'd tiptoed inside the shed, crossing her arms over her chest and gazing around with trepidation at the cobwebs hiding in the corners, the dirt on the floor, the tendrils of plants reaching inside the walls. No, she wouldn't have a love of the extreme outdoors in common with Hugh.

"Tell me how you really knew Mel was in trouble," said Clint.

"I told you. She sensed it." Brandy shot Ronnie a look for confirmation.

"I just knew."

"When did you know? After she was . . . injured?" He seemed suddenly reluctant to say the word.

"After she was strangled," agreed Ronnie. She could feel herself growing uncomfortable. It always happened when she was pressed about her gift.

"You told that to Sloan?"

"Yes."

Clint's look was ironic. "And he bought it? Doesn't sound like him."

"You should talk to him," Ronnie suggested.

"Maybe he won't go after me, if he's letting you off the hook with that excuse." A pause. A sick smile crossed his lips. "'Course, you are going to marry him."

"Oh, Clint . . ." Brandy sounded tired.

"I didn't say it. She did."

"I'm not marrying Sloan." Ronnie heard the thread of anger

in her voice, but she barreled on. "Call Sloan. Tell him what you know. Get it over with."

She found herself more annoyed than she ought to be. She was an anomaly, a curiosity, a freak, and that hadn't changed over the years. She told Brandy she'd be outside and then left the room and carefully stepped over the wooden stringers laid out for the porch, down the steps and to the yard. The rain was still holding off, but it felt like a cloudburst was coming.

There was a cracked, curving sidewalk that circumvented the porch and Ronnie walked along it toward the truck rather than to Brandy's car. As she neared, outdoor floodlights attached above the garage doors lit up the area like midday.

Ronnie hadn't expected to feel so angry. What was wrong with her?

*You saw your friend dead.*

Yeah, but—

*And you think Clint's involved.*

She made a face. She *was* wondering about Clint. Brandy was, too, by her fearful protestations.

Had Clint driven this truck to the clearing? Had the forensics team taken tire track impressions that would confirm or deny her suspicions? She looked at the truck's tires, then swept her gaze over the cab. She glanced into the truck bed as the floodlights blinked off, leaving her in darkness. Stepping back, she waved her arms, and the floodlights came back on.

She looked in the truck bed. Strewn across the metal flooring were maple whirlies, all damp and stuck in nooks and crannies. Lots of them. As if they'd floated in while the weather was nice, then had been glued down by the incessant water.

*Plants had DNA...*

Brandy stepped outside, and also negotiated the half-formed wooden porch on her way down to street level. "What are you doing?"

"Nothing. Cooling off."

"Ready to go?"

*More than.* "Yes."

By the time Brandy dropped Ronnie off, it was after eight, closing in on nine. She let herself in and took off her wet and muddy boots, then padded sock-footed into the living room, before sinking into her favorite chair. She held the remote in her hand for long minutes without turning on the television. There was too much in her head already, she didn't think she could absorb anything more.

# Chapter 13

Ronnie awoke with a start. She listened, but didn't hear anything. Was that a noise, though? Something?

She threw back the covers and padded barefoot in the dark into the kitchen. What time was it? She looked at the oven clock.

Four a.m.

Nothing seemed off, so after a few minutes she headed back to bed. She lay quietly, willing herself to relax and drift off, but she was wide-awake. Surprising after everything that had transpired over the last few days, but then, maybe not because her head was full of Mel, Brandy and Clint, and her father and work, and Marian Langdorf and Carlton, and . . . hell . . . everything.

Cooper Haynes's call popped up in her Rolodex of events, worries and problems . . . *I'd like to talk to you about Rebekkah . . . two k's . . . one h . . .*

It appeared she'd gotten that one right after all. Haynes had quietly gone on to say he believed Mary Jo was using Rebekkah as her own name. He believed Mary Jo was concealing her identity while living in a religious community called Heart of

Sunshine. He sounded a bit gobsmacked. Maybe at learning she'd had some information that had panned out?

*Don't believe in me too much. My gift seems to boomerang more often than help.*

She punched her pillow and rolled onto her side, seeing the digital face of her alarm clock: 4:45 a.m.

*Sleep*, she silently ordered herself, closing her eyes and setting her jaw.

But her traitorous mind traveled back to the clearing, reviewing Mel's body, her turned-away face, the investigative lights blasting down on the temporary canopy, the glowering trees, the white-suited techs collecting samples from on and around her, Brandy's stuttered breathing . . .

And Sloan interviewing her, basically interrogating her because he didn't believe a word she was saying. Brandy defending Clint . . . Clint's truck with its muddied tires and bed full of soggy maple whirlies.

And her father. Always disappointed in her disinterest in his firm.

*I might not know what I want, but I know what I don't want.*

Which reminded her of Galen. She thought about her vision of him with the boss's wife. *That* was not going to end well. You didn't need to be a psychic to make that prediction.

Lastly, her mind tripped on Marian Langdorf and Carlton. She'd put off calling Marian back because she just didn't want to go another round of *I can't* and *But you must*. She felt a little guilty for not immediately shutting the whole thing down . . . but then Aunt Kat had told her that maybe she should think about it.

"No," she said into the darkness.

At five thirty she gave up on falling back asleep and got up. It was still dark when she was dressed and headed into the kitchen. What a way to start a Saturday. She might as well be going to work, since she was already up, but since it was the weekend and the office was closed, she could get ready for the week ahead from home. She didn't want to give her father the false hope that she'd suddenly developed a gung-ho attitude toward the business.

After making herself a dish of raspberries and plain yogurt, she spent several hours on the computer, reexamining the paperwork on several cases, proofreading files for the Benton estate, the heirs of which she and Martin Calgheny were going to meet with on Tuesday.

Finally she shut down her laptop. The darkness had disappeared, replaced by a dim, gray cloud cover, perfect for jogging. She'd specifically put on running gear when she'd dressed, so now she tied on her Nikes and opened her front door.

A dead bat lay on its back on the outside mat, its wings spread wide, its tiny feet curled up.

Ronnie froze in the doorway.

"What?" This wasn't some random thing. Couldn't be, could it? It felt . . . malevolent. A message . . . that was left for her in the middle of the night . . . Maybe what had woken her?

Heart thudding, she swept her gaze quickly around the long porch and parking lot below, as if she could spot the perpetrator. Of course she saw no one.

Her next-door neighbor's door suddenly swung inward and Angel stepped out. Her brain sizzled with unspoken accusations, but his dark eyes widened in surprise.

"Someone left that for you?" he demanded.

He was so quick to come up with that. Almost too quickly. *Because he'd left it?*

No. It didn't feel right and unless he was a better actor than she believed, the flash of alarm that had crossed his face spoke of his innocence. "Looks that way."

"Don't touch it. I'll get a shovel and get rid of it."

"You don't have to, I can—"

He gave her a look and she lifted her hands in acceptance. "Thank you."

"Go on your run," he said, noticing how she was dressed. He hitched his chin toward the street, silently urging her.

"Okay." She stepped over the bat and hurried down the stairs. Once she landed in the parking area, she took off and jogged at a faster pace than usual, trying to outrun the thoughts that plagued her, thoughts of Mel lying on the wet grass, cold and dead. Sloan eyeing her with suspicion. Brandy protecting Clint, who in turn tried to protect Hugh. A tangled mess . . . and then Rebekkah and . . .

*Stop it!*

She gave herself a silent command and concentrated on the cold wintry morning. Storm clouds were gathering again, threatening rain. She dashed by homes and shops, ran in place at crosswalks, avoided puddles and skimmed the edge of the park, only to reverse her route at the fountain.

Ronnie was breathless by the time she reached her apartment building again. Thankfully, there was no trace of the bat on her doormat, but Angel was still outside, leaning against the rail again. He straightened when she came to a stop at the top of the stairs, taking a moment to catch her breath.

"Got any idea who left you that little present?"

She shook her head. But in her mind's eye she saw Mel's mud- and blood-spattered body again and a shiver ran down Ronnie's spine. A killer *was* out there. Did the bat have anything to do with it?

Her mind jumped to Clint's mud-caked tires . . . the helicopter maple tree whirlies in the truck bed . . .

*Both could be innocent remnants from his work. You're leaping to conclusions. Brandy's protectiveness of her brother got to you . . . made you look at Clint too closely.*

*And what about Sloan Hart and all of his intense questions. Did he believe her? Or was he still skeptical? She'd put money on skeptical. Big-time.*

"You think it's a prank?" asked Angel. Even as he asked the question she could already tell he didn't believe that any more than she did.

"Maybe I've made someone mad."

"You know who?"

She shook her head. The truth was, her mind was spinning too much with thoughts of Sloan to think clearly about who might be threatening her. She didn't want to think about him, but she did. So, he didn't believe her, so what? Didn't make him the enemy. He was one of the good guys. Right? So maybe the killer was Hugh after all. Maybe Clint was wrong to exonerate him. Hugh didn't have to be on some bro adventure. He could have been at the clearing, waiting for Mel.

But would he leave the bat as a message? *How could he know about me? Clint?* Always back to Clint.

She drew a long breath, noticing the clouds beginning to darken and roil overhead.

"What?" demanded Angel.

"Nothing," she lied. "I'll think about it later. Thank you for taking care of the bat."

He waved that away. All in a day's work. "Did you talk to your boss any more about Daria?"

She reached into her zippered joggers pocket for her keys. "Martin's not my boss, but I did talk to him. He said Daria wasn't interested in going any further about the inheritance."

There was a rumble of thunder off to the left and then a sudden deluge of rain. It pounded on the roof above their heads and bounced on the pavement below in silvery arrows.

"Daria wasn't interested?" he repeated.

"That's what Martin said."

"I'll talk to her again." Clearly Angel didn't believe her.

She turned toward her door, thinking about Mel. A flash of lightning and a few seconds later a louder grumble, almost a roar. The rain doubled its efforts, a violent cacophony.

Ronnie fished out her key, her fingers surrounding cold metal.

An image of Shana, her mouth open in a silent scream, her eyes wide and fixated, filled with disbelief and terror. She was lying on a carpeted floor, hands by her side, fingers splayed and digging into the fibers, her skin so white it looked blue.

*Strangled?*

*Hey . . . hey . . .* The voice was tinny. Somewhere in a distant dream.

She saw the bruising around Shana's neck. Yes . . . strangled . . . like Mel. . . .

"Hey!"

This time she heard it through a jangled ringing in her ears.

She was deafened. Her knees giving way. Unable to do anything but let gravity take over as she stumbled forward... *falling... falling...*

Suddenly she was pulled upright, taut arms surrounding her. But her head swooped downward and she was staring at the floor of the porch. Her keys slipped from her fingers, lying on the concrete next to the mat at her front door, inches from where the bat had been earlier.

She tried to find her feet.

Couldn't.

Still Angel's arms were locked around her, making it impossible for her stand on her own.

"I'm okay, I'm okay," she told him, pushing away.

Reluctantly, he let his arms drop.

She glanced at him, her head woozy. In the depths of his dark eyes she registered his alarm. "Happens sometimes..." she murmured. Rarely. At least until recently.

She bent to pick up her keys, felt that same *whoosh*, and had to steady herself a moment by placing her right palm on the concrete. Taking deep breaths she slowly straightened as her cell, zippered into her back pocket, began to ring.

She carefully pulled back the zipper tab on her pocket and withdrew the phone.

*Sloan.*

Brandy had said he was going to call her. Bad timing.

"Hello," she said, feeling that odd, tingly sensation that followed an episode, like a limb waking from an uncomfortable position.

"Ms. Quick?"

"Yes." She blinked, tried to concentrate and found herself leaning against the railing.

"You all right?" asked Angel.

He'd let go of her but was watching her as if expecting her to fall face-first. No wonder. She felt like she might. She nodded at Angel and held up her hand, finally standing without support.

"You saw the news?" asked Sloan.

"Um... no."

"They don't have Melissa McNulty's name yet, but Townsend gave a brief statement to the press about the woman's body found in the clearing."

"Oh. Okay."

"Townsend's leading the investigation. He will want to talk to you."

"Yes... all right."

She was having difficulty threading the key into the lock. Angel took it from her, opened the door, then handed the key back. She nodded her thanks, pushed in and closed the door behind her. There was something about Angel she needed to think about, but she already had too much on her mind.

"What is it?" Sloan suddenly demanded. "Something else you want to tell me?"

Ronnie expelled a pent-up breath. "Not about Mel..."

"What, then?"

"I—it's Shana. I think she's in trouble."

"Shana... Lloyd?"

She could tell she'd thrown him for a loop. Well, yeah, but she was having trouble articulating and she was referring to his old girlfriend. "Yes. She was in a car accident the other night and I took her home from the hospital. But I think something's happened to her now. At her apartment. I think she's in trouble."

"You picked up Shana Lloyd from the hospital and took her home," he repeated.

"I know. It's a long story. But I need to see that she's okay." She pulled herself together with an effort. "I *have* to see she's okay," she added with more determination. "Thanks for updating me on Mel."

"Wait. Don't hang up. What do you mean? What do you think happened to Shana?"

"I'll call you back from the car. I've gotta go."

"What's her address? I'll go with you."

Ronnie held a hand to her head, tried to mentally wipe away the cobwebs clogging her thoughts. All she knew was Shana needed help now.

"If you're going, I want to make sure she's all right, too," he insisted.

"I hope I'm wrong. I really do, but I . . ." *Don't think so.*

"How do you know she's in trouble?" he asked.

She couldn't have this argument. "I don't need your help, Sloan."

"I'll pick you up."

Anger stirred in her breast. She was coming back . . . and worried . . . and she didn't need to explain herself. "I don't need—"

"I'll be there in fifteen, twenty at the latest." He clicked off before she could argue further.

Fine. Let him come. It felt like she was being bombarded with information and she didn't know how to process it all. Normally, she was near someone when she picked up something from them. Not always, but this was different. She almost felt under attack.

Had Mel reached out to her? And now Shana? Or, was it something else?

Ronnie hurriedly headed for a second shower. Turning her face up to the hot spray, she let it warm her from the coldness that had come over her, another symptom of a particularly vivid vision. She was toweling off when her cell rang again. After throwing on a robe, she swept up the phone. A number she didn't recognize. She let it go to voice mail and saw that someone had already left a message. Marian Langdorf. She didn't have time for either of the callers right now.

Quickly she threw on jeans, warm socks and a sweater. The sheets of rain had passed but it was drizzling outside. Plucking her coat from a peg on the wall behind the front door, she slipped her arms through the sleeves. Twenty minutes had passed. Longer than Sloan had said, but she expected him to wheel into her lot any second. Didn't think of him as one to dilly-dally.

\* \* \*

Dealing with all the ins and outs of Veronica Quick's world was like going down a twisting rabbit hole. Visions and memories and danger and even death... *'Twas brillig, and the slithy toves did gyre and gimble in the wabe*... This was his world since reconnecting with Quick: "Jabberwocky" half-words that seemed to almost make sense.

But Melissa McNulty was definitely dead. And Shana Lloyd? His ex-girlfriend from high school? That was out of left field... except Veronica Quick's tone had sent warning messages along his nerves.

He drove straight to her apartment. He'd looked up Quick's address as soon as she'd first stopped by the department to warn the police of the woman in the clearing. Pulling into the apartment's lot, he spied an open space near Quick's Escape and parked, then headed for the stairway to the second floor.

She was clearly waiting for him because she held her hand out from the upper balcony, silently telling him to stay where he was while she came downstairs.

They met at the bottom step, she in jeans and a dark rain coat. Her face was flushed. There was something appealing and fresh about her, something open, that he was drawn to in spite of himself.

*Openly crazy, you mean.*

"You have Shana's address?" he asked as he held the passenger door for her.

She told it to him as he slid into the driver's seat.

"Okay, tell me about Shana," he said as he pulled back onto the street.

"I don't know what to say. Something's happened to her. She looks, it's... she's on the floor and I don't know... if she's even alive." Her voice wobbled slightly and she cleared her throat.

She was taut as a bow string and scared. That seemed real. He pushed back the clamoring voices in his head telling him that this whole thing was insanity. She'd been right about Melissa McNulty. And she clearly believed something had happened to Shana.

"You said she was in a car accident?"

"She came to my door with divorce papers. Galen, my soon-to-be ex, hired her to deliver them and she did. The back of my apartment's right above the road, and after she left I heard the crash. I ran out to help when I saw her car. She was inside but managed to get out, then collapsed right in front of me. It was . . . it was awful." She took a breath. "They sent her to Glen Gen . . . er, the hospital—"

"I know Glen Gen."

"—and she was there about a day. Then she called me and said she needed a ride home."

"You're friends?" Sloan asked.

"Not really. I think she just needed somebody in the moment and recalled that I'd been at the scene of the accident."

"She's friends with Evan," Sloan pointed out.

"She may have tried to reach him. She did say he helped her get her apartment . . . ? But he wasn't available apparently, so she called me."

"On the phone, I assume."

She shot him a dark look, probably sensing this was a jab on her outré ability. "Yes, on the phone," she said shortly.

He didn't think he should be blamed for wondering how she got the information, given that she wanted him to believe in her psychic ability. Letting that go, he said instead, "Caldwell and Shana have helped each other over the years."

"I'm sorry I screamed about him that day at The Pond," she murmured.

"That's long over."

"I know. I just . . . think about it sometimes."

They drove through the rain in silence for a few moments. Thinking of Caldwell, Sloan said, "He does all right. Mostly in a wheelchair, but he can sometimes push himself to walk a few steps."

"I heard he's good with computers."

"He's good with information." *Maybe a little too good.*

Sloan had actually asked Caldwell to find information for him a few times that should have been legally off limits, but was available if you knew how to look for it, which Caldwell did.

"I've seen him a few times," she admitted. "Once at Gabrielle's memorial service."

Sloan hadn't been around for that one. He hadn't known Gabrielle well. She'd been Caldwell's hot crush. Although Gabrielle had never had any use for him.

"You saw Shana on the floor?" he asked. "Injured?"

"Yes... injured." She slid him a reluctant glance.

*And you saw this in your mind???*

He didn't say it, but his face must've given him away, because she pulled back in her seat, as if trying to put as much space between them as possible. She was very touchy about her "extra ability," but he was running an investigation, so...

"The same way you knew about Melissa McNulty?"

"Something like that," she muttered, staring straight ahead through the windshield.

Sloan's continued disbelief came off him in waves. He didn't like what he was hearing. Didn't seem to like her much either, Ronnie suspected. But she was now actually glad he was with her because she didn't want to discover Shana's body alone.

The night of the car accident, she'd seen Shana's body superimposed over Mel's. Had what she'd really seen been Shana's upcoming fate? Could she have stopped it? Was it related to Mel's murder somehow?

*Is it about you? Are both deaths because of you?*

"I'm worried we'll be too late," she said tensely.

"Well, we're going to find out," he muttered as they turned into the parking lot of Shana's apartment complex, a three-story, multi-building affair whose tired face looked out at them with the expression of a beaten dog.

Ronnie stared at the circa 1970s cluster of apartments again and found she suddenly didn't want to go in. Hadn't she just driven Shana here the night before? It felt like an eon ago and she didn't want to face another dead body.

They were parked at the far side of the lot and no one was moving around in the dreary rain. Sloan climbed out of the Bronco and stood outside his vehicle beneath a lightly waving western hemlock branch. Ronnie unbuckled her seat belt and joined him in the cold, damp morning.

They walked up the steps to the top floor of the seen-its-day building and along to Shana's door. Sloan knocked and no one immediately answered. He knocked louder and longer. Ronnie held her breath, both wanting him to hurry and find Shana and wishing to turn back the way they'd come.

Sloan's brows drew together. She should be grateful he believed her in this, she supposed, but she was sick with dread.

"Not answering," he said.

"We need to break in." She knew it wasn't protocol. The police didn't have the authority to burst into someone's home without being invited unless they had reason to suspect there was a crime being committed—and her mental view of Shana's dead body wouldn't pass muster in a court of law.

"You've called her on her phone?"

She could feel her face heat.

"Try her," he drawled, his belief in this rescue clearly fading.

Ronnie collected her phone and quickly pulled up Shana's number, punching the digits, letting the phone ring and ring. No answer. And no sound of a phone ringing from inside the apartment.

"I can get a wellness check," he suggested.

"How long will that take?"

"I'd have to get a team out here."

"I can't wait that long."

"What's your plan, then?"

She had no plan. That was the problem. "I'm going to get into that apartment."

"Breaking in?"

"I know you don't think what I saw was real."

"I know you believe it." His tone, his whole demeanor, had shifted to chilly politeness.

She was used to that. In frustration she rattled the doorknob with vigor. When the door suddenly opened beneath her hand, she didn't hesitate, just pushed in, glancing around uneasily.

It was a studio apartment. And it was empty.

No body on the floor, no body anywhere. She immediately bent to the carpet. There was no imprint where Shana's fingers had dug into the fibers. No tracks where a body may have been dragged. Nothing.

No! It couldn't be. Ronnie had seen Shana. A chill whispered down her spine.

"She was here," she said, pointing to the floor, knowing how feeble that excuse sounded, unable to come up with anything else. "Right here. I saw this carpet."

She could tell Sloan was weighing whether to step across the threshold or slap his hand to his forehead. He had no right to enter Shana's home. But he must've won that argument with himself because he followed Ronnie in and walked through the rooms, checking every corner. He glanced in the bathroom and used the sleeve of his jacket to open the closet door.

Empty. No Shana.

He turned to meet Ronnie's gaze and she saw the same careful "look" she'd been gifted by all disbelievers throughout the years. She felt sick inside, but there was no denying that she'd been wrong. Shana Lloyd's body was not lying on the floor. Her face was not frozen in terrified horror. Her fingers were not digging into the carpet.

Her phone still in her hand, Ronnie took a picture of the room. Sloan didn't object as he followed her out, closing the door behind him, testing to make sure it was locked, though the metal tongue didn't engage properly and probably accounted for the way the handle had just opened beneath Ronnie's hand.

"She was there," Ronnie said for the umpteenth time as Sloan drove her back home. "I know she was there. I saw it. I know you don't believe me, but she *was* there."

"You're positive this time."

She bristled at "this time." "It's not an exact science. Don't say 'pseudo' science. I *know*. Fine. But sometimes things are very clear."

"Like this time."

"She was there!"

"I'm not going to argue with you. I know you've had some success."

She sensed he was trying to be magnanimous, which pissed her off all the more. "But a stopped clock is still right twice a day. I've heard all the clichés."

"I wasn't going to say that."

She snorted, eyeing the traffic on the wet streets.

"The fact is, Quick, she wasn't there. If you're worried, just keep calling her. Maybe she'll eventually pick up."

Ronnie slowly shook her head, angry at her failure. "What about Evan Caldwell? Maybe she got through to him. Maybe he knows what happened to her."

"You want me to call Evan?" He didn't sound like there was an ice cube's chance in hell he believed it would help.

"Yes. I want to know Shana's all right. You don't have to tell Evan I 'saw' her . . . body. Just that we're—*I'm*—worried about her."

His face was granite as he rolled that around. He was undoubtedly rethinking helping the crackpot psychic. He called her Quick instead of Ronnie, or even Veronica, which drew the line between them as something less than friends.

*I'm a person of interest.*

That realization dawned on her. Of course she was, but it now felt doubly depressing. Yesterday he'd at least listened to her. Today, no dice.

So, she was surprised when Sloan plucked his phone from his pocket at the next light, slid his thumb through his Favorites list, pressed Evan's number. Evan answered as if he'd been waiting for the call. Sloan said, "I'm on my way to your place with Veronica Quick. That okay? She's worried about Shana."

"Shana? Really? What happened?" His voice was tinny but Ronnie could easily hear him.

"I'm not sure. She's not at her apartment and... Quick's worried about her."

"Veronica Quick..." His tone turned lightly mocking. "Okay. Come on over. Can't wait to hear how you two hooked up."

Sloan clicked off as the vehicle slid into gear again, then didn't say anything throughout the rest of the ride.

At least he wasn't abandoning her. Yet.

Evan Caldwell lived in a building that looked like an upscale, big city hotel. It was gray stone and rose six stories, high by River Glen standards. The parking lot was on the side, with a levered arm. Sloan took a ticket and they drove into an underground lot. The surrounding vehicles were upper end: Mercedes, Lexus, BMW... and was that a Ferrari in the corner spot?

*Must do well for himself*, Ronnie thought.

They walked toward a bank of two elevators. Their car rose above the parking structure and as they traveled upward offered a windowed view of the pool area, shuttered now with chairs tucked beneath the first floor balconies. The pool's normally aqua water was muted to a dull slate beneath the gray clouds, but she could imagine a bustling bar scene in warm weather with waiters serving tall, cool drinks from trays to various sun worshipers draped on lounge chairs.

They got off on the fourth floor and Sloan led the way to a corner apartment that appeared to back up to the pool area.

Evan Caldwell...

Ronnie hadn't spoken to him since she'd screamed and screamed at his evil, rising ghost at The Pond.

As Sloan knocked on the door, she thought, *Here goes nothing...*

# Chapter 14

Sloan almost wanted to believe Quick. He liked that she was determined and stubborn and goddamned attractive. A figure from his past. A niggle in the brain. An unfulfilled prediction. A moment in time when his life had taken a seismic shift, though he hadn't recognized that fact while he'd been pressing on her chest and blowing into her mouth, the latter a practice that had all but been discontinued but one he'd believed in totally in that moment...

But there was no way she could know the things she did without some involvement. And now this expedition to find Shana... his ex-girlfriend... who'd lied to him about nearly everything, had even pretended to be pregnant, to which he'd asked, "Who's the father?" knowing it couldn't be him.

She'd slapped him on that one, even though he was right.

Still, Quick seemed truly worried about Shana, so he wanted to find her.

He looked around the exterior of the building, trying to focus on the moment. Evan's condominium complex was a series of townhouse units built in a U-shape around a pool/patio area. There was an ADA-compliant lift on the pool's far end, one of the reasons Caldwell had chosen this particular setup, the other being he had a corner unit with more space for his extensive computer and internet setup. Sloan had twice asked his old friend for information when he hadn't necessarily wanted his searches logged to his work account.

Both times Sloan had asked for Caldwell's help was because of suspicious behavior within his own respective police department. He'd thought it was best to check out the activities privately. Caldwell had surprised him with his ability to access supposedly inaccessible information, and the speed with which he'd managed to do it was impressive.

"Don't tell me how," Sloan had warned Evan at the time.

"Oh, I don't let my secrets out," was the drawled reply. "You better keep the faith, too, bro."

*Bro* . . . He and his friends had thrown that word around a lot back in the day. Caldwell and Mercer and Townsend, among others. Bros . . . "Bros over Hos" . . . what a stupid, misogynistic line. It had made him wince at the time, and when one of them would utter it even now, which still did happen, that wince became a groan. It was one of the reasons he'd always been on the fringe of their group of guys. One of the many reasons.

Now, as he heard movement inside the condo, Sloan darted a look toward Quick. Weird that they'd reconnected in the past twenty-four hours. He'd barely noticed her that day at the river until she was underwater and not coming up. The panic he'd felt had driven him to dive in and find her, which he had, but he'd been scared shitless she would die anyway.

Those moments of heroism had changed his life. One instant he'd been toying with thoughts of engineering, or business, or tech . . . lost in all kinds of career paths . . . then after the rescue at The Pond he'd swung toward public service, which had sent him on the path to law enforcement.

Shana had wanted to get married. Right out of high school or during. She didn't care which. Crazy. She'd known he wasn't as into her as she was him, and she'd doubled and redoubled her efforts to force the future she'd planned for herself. But she wasn't pregnant. He wasn't that reckless. Her pressure, desperation and lies had just brought on their inevitable breakup sooner.

And now, all these years later, she'd taken a job to serve Quick with divorce papers? How in God's name had that happened? He didn't talk to Shana anymore. Though she'd reached out to him a number of times, he hadn't responded. Her untrustworthy past was still very present for him. Why had she been the one to serve papers to Quick? There was something missing in that story. Some motivation from Shana . . . something that didn't add up . . .

And he'd be damned if he believed it harkened back to that day at The Pond. Shana hadn't even known who Quick was then. *He* hadn't known who she was, beyond that she was some friend of Clint Mercer's younger sister. They'd only crossed paths now because they lived in the same town. It wasn't some secret plot.

He slid a glance at Quick as they stood in silence at the apartment door. He expected it to take Caldwell a bit, given that he had to wheel himself from wherever he was in the unit, likely too far a distance for the few steps he could sometimes take unaided. While Sloan waited, shifting from one foot to the other, his thoughts turned to Tara, his ex-wife. She, too, had complained about his lack of attention, even when they were married. She'd said it was his fatal flaw, a perpetual disengagement. Maybe she was right, but then she'd gone and slept with someone he'd considered a friend, which had ended any chance of trying to save their marriage. She'd tearfully sworn it didn't mean anything. She was just so frustrated and she wanted him to "wake the fuck up!" but he'd walked away.

*No coming back from that one.*

It was funny, really, when he thought about both Tara and Shana now. They were different, and yet the same.

"You don't care about anyone but yourself!" Tara had accused him, which was diametrically opposed to Shana's, "You care about everybody else but me!"

"Women," Caldwell was fond of quoting from some film. "Can't live with 'em, can't kill 'em." Unlike Sloan, he'd never been in a long-term relationship and was still proud of the fact.

There had been a lot of "asshole," "bastard," even a few "fuckers" thrown at Sloan over the years before either of those two relationships were fully over.

"Coming," Evan called from within his condo. "Hold on a sec."

Sloan didn't look at Quick again, but he could sense her along every nerve. She had a scent. Something kind of clean and light, a brush of some flower. Lilac, maybe? Not rose. Not that deep. Something fainter, breathier . . .

*Don't. Even. Think. It.*

The last thing he needed was to get involved with a nutcase. People had done crazy things for an unstable partner in the name of attraction, and sometimes it ruined their lives.

*You've already stepped into a gray area by bringing her to Caldwell.*

When the investigations currently swirling around her were resolved, he would stay away from her. It was a simple solution.

The locks snapped back and Evan Caldwell, seated in his wheelchair, opened the door inward, his eyes alight with curiosity as he looked them over.

Ronnie didn't waste time as they walked into Evan's apartment. "Has Shana called you?" she asked Evan as he rolled out of the doorway.

"Well, hi to you, too, Ms. Quick." A smile hovered around his lips. "You mean today? No."

Ronnie didn't back down. "Have you seen her recently?"

He turned his wheelchair to look at Sloan. "Who's the cop here? What did Shana do?"

Sloan said, "Nothing that we know of. Quick's just tried to get hold of her, but can't get through."

"You two working together or something?" Evan's sharp gaze moved from Sloan to Ronnie and back again.

"Or something," Ronnie murmured. "I'm worried about Shana."

"Uh-huh. I got that. Why?"

They were standing in Evan's compact foyer, looking straight across a spacious living room and through a sliding glass door which was flanked by floor-to-ceiling windows and opened onto a balcony. Through the glass Ronnie could see the bistro directly across the pool area, its silver and black awnings rolled up and tightly wrapped.

"I feel she's in danger," she managed. She didn't dare look at Sloan. He would know she wasn't eager to tell him how she knew.

Evan's wheels whispered across the hardwood floor as he moved toward a specially designed desk which sported an array of computer monitors, most showing blank screens, as if he'd just switched them all off before their arrival, which he probably had. Soft music was playing from hidden speakers. Something classical, barely audible.

"You feel she's in danger . . . Well, let me say that Shana's a friend, but we're not BFFs. I don't know every little thing she does."

"You help her out," said Sloan.

"Sometimes." Evan was nodding. "You gotta be careful, though. She's kind of needy."

Ronnie walked across the living room and stared out the slider, trying to get her frustration and worry under control. Was she wrong about Shana? Was her "vision" false?

"What do you think?" Evan asked her, nodding his head toward the view.

"Very nice," she murmured distractedly. The pool area was directly below Evan's balcony. Louvered wooden doors covered the outside bar, though the bistro lights were welcoming.

"I don't use the pool much anymore," he admitted.

"You have any kind of guess about where Shana might be?" asked Sloan. He'd followed Evan into the living area and was standing near a bar, a rolling cart that displayed half-full bottles of whiskey.

"Sorry, bro. So, are you going to tell me what's going on, or just ask questions?"

There was a pause and Ronnie turned from the view to look at Sloan, who was clearly waiting for her to explain more.

She was saved from saying more by Evan himself. "Never mind. Let me guess. She's out of money and the rent's due and the landlord is a piece of shit who's offering a discount for a blow job. That sound about right?"

"No." Ronnie was firm.

Evan lifted his brows, waiting for more.

His looks had definitely improved with age. His nose fit his face more and his longish hair, combed away from his face, suited him. He wore jeans and a gray hoodie, his feet clad in designer sneakers. His arm muscles bulged beneath the tight sleeves of the hoodie.

Ronnie said, "I just want to make sure she's alive and okay."

"Okay. Well. Sorry I can't help you there. Haven't seen her in weeks." He swiveled to look at Sloan. "Saw Townsend on the news. You a part of that investigation?"

Sloan nodded.

"Who's the vic? They're going to release the name later today, so don't give me any 'I can't reveal names until the next of kin has been notified' bullshit."

She could see Sloan think that over.

"Seriously, bro?" Evan motioned toward his computer. "I can do some digging and find out the whole story at hyperspeed."

"Melissa Burgham McNulty."

"*What?* Oh, man." Evan blinked a bunch of times, then added, on a whistle of surprise, "Well, fuck me."

"You know her?" asked Ronnie.

He turned his attention back to her. "Clint's sister Brandy's friend? Your friend, too, right? From The Pond? Yeah, I know her. Married Hugh McNulty. She's the vic?"

"Yes," Sloan answered.

"Oh, man . . . and you're here because of Shana?" He gave Ronnie a searching look.

She didn't know how to tell him that she was half-convinced Shana may have suffered the same fate. Just thinking about Mel and possibly Shana made her feel ill.

Evan shook his head as if dispelling cobwebs. "All these years... I don't remember that day very well, when we were all there. And now Melissa McNulty... and what about Shana? Why do you think there's a problem?" He seemed genuinely concerned. His eyes bored into Ronnie's. "Oh, wait." He pointed a finger at her, the light dawning. "You think you saw something. Some danger."

"I just want to make sure Shana's okay," Ronnie repeated, more than a little irritated. "She's not answering her phone."

But his gaze narrowed and Ronnie could almost see the wheels in his mind turning backward to a time she'd rather forget.

Sure enough, he said, "I guess you were screeching that I was evil, or something, that day at The Pond. I never heard it, but I've heard about it for years since. That the kind of thing you're seeing?"

"I don't remember screeching that you were evil, but I've also heard a lot about it over the years as well," said Ronnie in a tight voice as the background music switched to instrumental Christmas carols.

Evan held up a hand. "Okay. Okay. That was then, and this is now." He threw a look at Sloan. "I've known Melissa for a while. Not well. Mostly through Clint. She's his booty call, you know."

Sloan's brows pulled together. "Melissa McNulty was seeing Clint Mercer?"

"Seeing... like dating? More like two rabbits fucking any chance they could get behind her ex's back. You know about him? Hugh McNulty? Piece of shit if there ever was one. He deserved to be cheated on, but I warned Clint to stay away from her anyway. Never ends good. Married women always come with big trouble."

"She was divorced," Ronnie put in defensively.

Evan sent her a look that told her not to be so naïve. "Well, she is *now*. Not always. But... there were others... and maybe the times were a little earlier than the divorce . . ." He sent Ronnie a slow grin. "But I'm not one to name names."

Ronnie held onto her tongue with an effort.

Sloan stated flatly, "You can give me those names."

He held up a hand and said dismissively, "Sure, bro. Whatever. Or, you can ask Clint." Lifting a brow, he changed the subject. "So, you two finally got together. Trying to make the prediction come true? Heard about that, too. Not at the time, of course. Too busy getting saved by Clint. But it sure as shit has made a good story for years."

"So, you haven't heard from Shana." Sloan cut him off. Ronnie wasn't sure whether he'd purposely stopped Evan's musings about that day at The Pond, or whether he just wanted to get back on track.

"Nope. Not since . . . a few weeks back." To Ronnie, he said, "I saw you at Gabrielle's funeral, but you didn't stay."

So, he remembered seeing her peek in the doorway that day. "I was feeling pretty raw. Didn't want to come in."

"It was a bad time," he agreed soberly. "Her and her boyfriend in that accident. Can't remember his name."

"Gerard DeLenka," she said.

Both men looked at Ronnie in surprise.

Evan gave her a thumbs-up. "You have one helluva memory. One would maybe think you're psychic." He paused for comic effect but the joke fell flat. He asked, "So how did you hook up with Shana again? She never mentioned your name before."

"Shana Lloyd was in a car accident three nights ago," Sloan stepped in. "The pileup on 212. She collapsed at Quick's feet."

"You're not calling her by just her first name, like friends usually do?" Eyebrows slamming together, Evan looked from Sloan to Ronnie and back again. "That's twice with the Shana *Lloyd* shit." He scrutinized Sloan. "So wait. Is this an official visit?"

"We're looking for her. That's all."

"Who's the suspect in this caper? You?" He poked a finger in Ronnie's direction.

Her heart clutched a bit. "Maybe." She had no idea what was going on behind the scenes with Sloan's investigation.

"Really?" Evan looked at Sloan, who remained quiet. With puckish amusement, he added, "All right, *Quick*. You tell me what's going on, since Hart's got a stick up his ass."

Despite Evan's attitude and crass remarks, Ronnie needed information. From him. She said, "We went to Shana's apartment—she said you helped her move in—but she wasn't there."

"From this you think there's something wrong?" he scoffed.

"The door doesn't latch well," Ronnie told him. "We easily pushed our way inside."

"Was the place 'tossed'?" Evan asked, more interested now. "In shambles?"

"No," answered Sloan.

"But you still think there's something wrong? The last time I saw her... a few weeks after I gave her money to move in. First and last month's rent's a bitch, isn't it?" He gestured to his wheelchair. "Couldn't really move the furniture for her, but she managed somehow. She might be just out somewhere. Meeting a friend for lunch or drinks. Something like that."

Ronnie realized she wasn't going to get any answers without revealing what had caused her fear for Shana in the first place, so she drew a breath and admitted, "I saw her lying on the floor. On the carpet, of her apartment... anyway I thought it was her apartment... but she's not there now."

"Lying on the carpet?" he repeated. "Through her window?"

"I saw her... in a vision."

There. *Make of that what you will, Evan.*

He turned again to Sloan. "Ah, the truth. So, that's what we're doing. I'm kind of surprised you're in on this."

Sloan's face was stone, so Ronnie cut in, "I just want to make sure she's okay. I can't reach her, that's all. Hoped you could help."

"I'm sure she's fine." Evan swatted away Ronnie's concerns with a hand. "Shana always manages to land on her feet."

"Got any idea how we could reach her?" asked Sloan. "Family or friends?"

"Shana's still got her mom. Doesn't really have a lot of friends." He wheeled away from the desk and closer to Ronnie, who forced herself to stay put as he regarded her with close examination. "So, what did this vision look like? Did you get one for Melissa, too?"

Ronnie looked to Sloan, who was waiting for her answer as well. "Shana was lying on the carpet. On her back." *Looking terrified. Strangled.*

Evan pressed, "Do you get a lot of 'em? The visions?"

Ronnie's mind flew to the image of Mel's body. Her bloody wrists and bruised throat. And then she thought about the scene at the clearing itself. The cops standing in the downpour or beneath the tarp, rain running off their hats . . . the techs in white suits taking physical evidence . . . the canopy holding off the rain . . . the shed . . . the dripping trees . . . the icy cold ground . . . the maple tree helicopter whirlies . . .

She shot another glance at Sloan, who returned a questioning look. He broke eye contact to say to Evan, "Do you have Nadia's address?"

"She still lives off State Street," Evan answered, adding for Ronnie's benefit, "Nadia's Shana's mom. But if you want to know who killed Melissa? Look no further than Hugh McNulty. Not to be confused with 'huge,' according to her." He looked half ashamed for already making jokes, but it didn't stop him. "She told Clint that 'little' story, and he told me."

Ronnie inwardly sighed. Evan Caldwell might be highly successful, but he was still kind of a dick.

"Do you have Nadia's address? I mean her specific street address?" asked Sloan in a cold voice. She suspected he felt something similar. "If not, can you get it?"

"What do you think?" Evan turned back to his desk, punched a few numbers, looked at the screen, then wrote down the address on a piece of paper and held it out. "Here ya go, bro."

Sloan moved forward to take it from him.

"I could call her. See if she answers for me," Evan offered, already pulling out his cell and clicking through his contact list. He pushed the button for her number, and they all waited, but there was no answer. Clicking off, he shrugged. "Nada."

Sloan turned to Ronnie. She wasn't sure if he was ready to leave, but she certainly was. They'd gotten information on Shana's mother, and a little of Evan went a long way. "Let's go," she said.

"Thanks for this." Sloan held up the piece of paper with Nadia's information as he and Ronnie moved toward the door. Evan followed after them, his wheels nearly silent against the hardwood flooring.

"You know, I'm a little psychic myself," he said as Sloan grabbed the door handle.

Here it comes, thought Ronnie. One more person with jokes about her extra ability.

She wasn't disappointed.

Evan waggled his finger between the two of them. "I got this feeling that this is the beginning of something beautiful between the two of you."

"Thanks for the warning," muttered Ronnie.

Sloan shot her a sideways look.

Evan gave a short laugh, then switched gears. "If you're really looking for somebody, you can generally find them if they're inside the downtown River Glen city limits. Cameras everywhere. But if you get on the edges, or the outskirts, no dice. River Glen folks worry about the government spying on them. They vote everything down. And they're smart to do it. Anyway, if she's really missing, you might catch Shana on a Ring camera or something in town. Otherwise, it's a no-go. If you want, I can check the available cameras, but . . ."

"You have access to city cameras?" asked Ronnie as the soft notes of "God Rest Ye Merry, Gentlemen" drifted through the rooms.

"Yeah, but I doubt there are any near her apartment. And I wouldn't bet on any private ones there, either. Not the right caliber of place ... But I'll give it a look." He stopped suddenly and snapped his fingers. "Just remembered a name. Amy Deggars. Shana's mentioned her a few times. I don't know how close they are, but she works at that law firm where your husband works."

Ronnie's brows raised. He knew about Galen?

"Soon-to-be-ex, according to Shana," he added with a smile.

"You knew she was serving me papers? I thought you hadn't talked to her," accused Ronnie.

"I knew she was working with that firm. Didn't know about serving you."

"When did you last see her?" asked Sloan. "Can you remember?"

"There you go, being all official again. Haven't talked to her for weeks, like I said." Then lifted his palms. "Okay, she left a message on the phone from the hospital. I didn't call her back. That's the last I've heard from her."

"You could've led with that," Ronnie let him know.

Evan's smile was cold. "Sloan, my man," he said with a hitch of his chin toward Ronnie. "Be careful with this one. Who knows? She might be telling the truth about that psychic ability." He shook hands with Sloan and winked at Ronnie.

On their way down the elevator, Ronnie said, "Friends, huh?"

"Caldwell likes to play mind games."

"He seems to revel in making himself unlikeable."

Sloan's mouth quirked. "Sometimes," he agreed.

He stopped at the car and looked back the way they'd come. Then he shook his head and hit the remote to open locks. Ronnie climbed into the passenger seat as he got behind the wheel. He started the engine then said, "I'll check with Shana's mom and the lawyer, Deggars."

"When? Now? I'm going with you."

He seemed about to argue, then just shrugged.

She realized he thought he was on a wild-goose chase, but was seeing it through to humor her. Well, fine. As long as she found Shana, that was all right with her.

"Did you connect with Clint last night?" she asked as Sloan drove out of the underground parking lot.

"He was trying to dodge me, but yeah."

"You can be . . . hard to talk to."

He let that one slide as he steered, melding his Bronco into traffic. "He said he'd seen you earlier with Brandy."

"She was going to see him and asked me to go along. He was pretty broken up over Mel."

"How much did he tell you about their relationship?"

She shrugged and looked out the window. Now would be the time to tell him about Clint's truck tires and the maple tree whirlies. *If* she really believed Clint was involved, maybe responsible, for Mel's death. But did she?

*What about when Abel Townsend calls you? What are you going to tell him?*

"I've heard you can get DNA from plants and they're just as individually specific as people," she said.

He took his eyes off the road for a moment to really look at her before turning back. "What are we talking about?"

Feeling a little like a traitor, she nevertheless explained about the maple seeds that she'd seen in Clint's truck and the mud-caked tires. Better than telling Townsend, or holding it back from him, which was what she would do. Like Evan Caldwell, she didn't really trust Townsend. Sheriffs were elected and didn't have to listen to governors and senators and other politicians. They had a kind of fiefdom with a lot of power. She'd dealt with one particularly surly sheriff in the course of a lawsuit once and was leery of all of them.

Sloan flipped on the wipers to combat the drizzle quickly turning to rain. "You saw Clint's truck at his house."

"Yes."

"You think he was at the site where McNulty's body was found."

"Maybe."

"This wasn't any . . . vision."

"No," she bit out. They'd driven several miles, the traffic thinning.

"Okay."

Her cell phone rang, sparing her the smart comeback that had jumped to her tongue. She pulled it from her purse. Saw it was Cooper Haynes's number. Another call she would return later. She didn't know what Haynes wanted, but she could guess, and she didn't want to be conversing with him in front of Sloan. There was no explaining about Rebekkah . . . She'd gotten that one right apparently. But if Haynes wanted her help finding his missing surrogate, she doubted she could offer anything more.

And now she was starting to doubt what she'd seen about Shana. There had been no body in the apartment. Was Shana's terror, her apparent attack, even real? Ronnie had been so sure, but now, after talking with Evan . . .

"This the way to Shana's mom's house?" she asked when it looked suspiciously like he was taking her home.

"No."

"You're trying to drop me off?" Her temper started to rise. "Look, either I'm going with you, or I'm going by myself."

"You know where she lives?"

She hadn't seen the scrap of paper with the address, so no, but she didn't bother answering. "Are you even planning to check on her?" she asked.

"Yes. Since you're so convinced I want—"

"What? To prove me wrong?" she cut in. "Maybe you're right, maybe I'm wrong, but I wasn't wrong about Mel, was I?"

"No."

"Just take me with you then," she insisted. She had to know about Shana.

He turned on his blinker and circled back the way they'd come. With a glance in her direction, he said, "Fine. We're both going to see Nadia."

"Thank you." She wondered belatedly if maybe he just didn't want her by his side when interviewing Shana's mother, who probably had known him pretty well while he and Shana were dating. And Shana had made it clear that she still wanted Sloan . . . and maybe her mother knew that, so Ronnie's appearance would not be welcomed.

Didn't matter. They were on their way now. Which was good. Because as she'd said often enough, the single important fact remained: Ronnie just needed to find Shana.

# Chapter 15

Sloan called ahead and learned that Nadia was home. They walked up the woman's cracked sidewalk together, and Ronnie saw the attempts made to brighten the small two-bedroom house with its now empty window flower boxes.

Nadia Lloyd was thin as a rail and, like her daughter, seemed to have aged unfairly fast. Ronnie put her somewhere in her fifties, based on Shana's age, though that was just a guess. In any case, she looked like mid-seventies. Her hair was steel gray and had the fine, flyaway appearance of spun sugar. Her face was lined and the scent of smoke floated around her as she answered the door.

"Sloan," she said with real warmth.

"Hello, Nadia."

Shana's mother turned dark eyes on Ronnie. The warmth fled. There was something in the way she held her head, her faintly judgmental attitude, that echoed her daughter.

Something calculating and dangerous.

Ronnie mentally shook herself. What was wrong with her that she was seeing enemies everywhere? All she wanted was to know that Shana was all right.

"We're trying to get ahold of Shana but she's not answering her phone. Evan Caldwell suggested we check with you," said Sloan.

Nadia's veined hand strayed self-protectively to her neck. "I haven't talked to her today."

"When was the last time you did?"

"Would you like to come in? I can give her a call. It sounds . . . important?" She directed her conversation to Sloan. Ronnie had the impression she would like to slam the door in her face instead of invite her in.

"Yes, call her. Thank you," answered Ronnie.

Nadia was in the act of opening the door wider and Ronnie could tell she didn't appreciate being dictated to. Sloan could probably get away with it, but not a female stranger.

Nadia picked up a cell phone as Ronnie and Sloan stood in the dark living room of the home. Since Sloan hadn't known where she lived, Ronnie took it that Nadia had moved since Shana was in high school. There were pictures of Nadia and Shana around the room. Nothing of Shana's father.

"She's not answering." She clicked off and slid the phone into her pocket. A line formed between her brows. "We usually talk every day or two. She'll call when she's not busy."

Ronnie concentrated on the vision she'd seen of Shana. It had seemed true. From the same well of information as Mel . . . She shuddered involuntarily and Sloan looked at her. "Cold?" he asked.

"It's warm in here," said Nadia, feathers ruffled as if Ronnie had deliberately maligned her hosting skills.

"Do you know where Shana could be?" Ronnie questioned.

"Well, she's a grown woman. She has a life." She hadn't looked at Ronnie once, her gaze either on Sloan or somewhere else in the room. Now, she asked Sloan, "What's so important?"

"I'm just worried about her well-being," said Sloan.

"I'm sure she's fine. I can't tell you how happy I am that you're back in her life. I confess, I've prayed for this. It's been too long and she's been lost without you."

Sloan kept his face expressionless, but Ronnie felt a jolt of her own heart. She'd brought Shana's problems to Sloan, setting up Nadia's current expectations. "When was the last time you talked to her?" She repeated the question.

"I don't know. Thursday? Maybe Wednesday? Middle of last week." Her attention was still on Sloan. "Give me your phone number and I'll have her call you."

Sloan complied and Nadia put his number into her phone. She tried to keep the conversation going, clearly wanting Sloan to stick around, but there was nothing more they could learn from her so they said their goodbyes.

At his Bronco, Ronnie looked up to find Sloan staring at her. "What?" she asked.

The rain had momentarily stopped and he squinted up at a watery sun peeking through the clouds. "It's Saturday. I could probably get Amy Deggars's number if I went to the department."

At that moment Ronnie felt her cell buzz. Marian Langdorf, or Detective Haynes, or her father, or who knew who else. Whoever it was, she didn't want to have a conversation in front of Sloan Hart.

And she was starting to lose confidence in her vision of Shana. It had been so visceral, and yet there'd been no sign of her at her apartment.

Still . . . "If we could get her number I would feel better."

"I'll take you home."

"Are you going to call her? I want to be a part of that."

"I'll let you know if I learn anything."

Pursing her lips, she leveled her gaze at him. "You don't believe Shana's in trouble."

He didn't answer as he climbed into the Bronco. He didn't have to. She could read his disbelief. Well, fine. She'd been down this road before. In the passenger seat she maintained a stony silence back to her place.

But almost the moment Sloan's SUV's taillights disappeared around the main building of her apartment complex, Ronnie's phone rang again. Marian Langdorf. Holy God, the woman was persistent.

"Hi, Marian," she answered.

"You've been putting me off," the older woman huffed. "Come by this evening. We'll have dinner. I have some questions for you."

Psychic questions? "I know you don't believe me, but I probably can't help you, Marian."

"Just come by. Six o'clock."

"Okay. I'll be there," she said firmly. *And I'll put an end to her obsession about me living with her.*

She walked toward her front door, shooting a glance at her mat. No bat, vermin or other warning lay there. At least that was something. She was glad she hadn't mentioned the bat to Sloan. He already thought she was strange, or deluded, or lying, or just a pain in the ass. Until she had an inkling of what that disturbing message meant, or even if it was a message—though she didn't see how it could be anything else . . . an accidental bat death on her doorstep? Come on. Still, until she knew who left it for her and why it was left, she was keeping its existence to herself.

Once inside her apartment, she listened to her voice mail messages as she examined her texts. Afterward, she texted Detective Haynes that she was free to talk after three if he wanted to call. Then she locked the front door behind her, sank into her favorite chair, grabbed the fuzzy television blanket slung over its back and turned on the TV.

She fell asleep as if drugged and was lost in vaguely threatening dreams where she couldn't open any door in a long, crooked hallway of doors that seemed to stretch to infinity. Though she tried to open each door she came to, the knobs kept twisting and twisting in her hands and gaining no purchase.

Harley Whelan Woodward pressed an ear to her mother's and Cooper's bedroom door and listened hard. Cooper had brought Mom a late lunch and they were quietly talking.

Twinkletoes, the tuxedo cat, usually as quiet as a tomb, started purring and rubbing herself around Harley's legs the moment Harley pressed her ear to the door panel, that purr sounding like a jet engine. She tried to push the cat away, but Twink was having none of it. She started meowing loudly and Harley was forced to tiptoe down the stairs to avoid being caught.

She hated resorting to this kind of subterfuge, but Cooper hadn't really confided in her like he'd promised. Kinda promised. In any case, he was only telling her half of the story... that half being that Mary Jo, Mom's surrogate, was on a sabbatical of sorts. Really? This close to the big day?

It sure seemed like a stinking, big pile of bullshit.

So, something was wrong with Mary Jo.

Harley's pulse fluttered. God, she hoped it wasn't the baby. They were all so excited about the impending births. Emma, especially, who had once offered to be Jamie's surrogate, but no one ever felt that was a good idea. Emma was great, but she was unpredictable. But then, look at Mary Jo. What the hell was she doing?

Harley had checked Cooper's phone when he'd left it on the counter for a time the night before, like he always did when he went upstairs to see Mom. She knew his password and had casually taken a peek at whoever he'd been texting. No name, but she now had the number. She'd been debating about calling whoever was on the other end, but that would be a big risk. Whoever it was would undoubtedly alert Cooper that she had called, and then her stepfather—the stepfather she loved and respected—would lose all trust in her.

So, no. That couldn't happen. She needed Cooper to tell her who was on the other end of the text. Then she could follow up on her own and wouldn't have to relate how she'd gotten the number.

*And if he doesn't tell you?*

As if hearing her unspoken thoughts, Cooper's phone, back on the counter, buzzed softly. Another text. She glanced at the screen and saw it was from the same number, saying Cooper could call at three. Well, okay. She could be hovering in the background somewhere when that call was placed.

*The things they make me do.*
*If they were just honest with her . . .*
*Yeah? And whose fault is it that they fear you'll take matters into your own hands?*

There was that. She wasn't known for sitting back and waiting.

But as far as she could see, that was never the right choice anyway. All it did was delay, delay, delay and there was no time to lose if Mary Jo was wandering around looking for some meaning in life while carrying Harley's half-sister or -brother.

She could wait for Cooper, or . . . live dangerously.

After a moment of thought, she pulled out her own phone and texted the number she'd gotten from Cooper's.

**Cooper Haynes, here. New phone. Can we meet at two-thirty?**

She bit her lip in anticipation, knowing she was crossing a line. But desperate times called for desperate measures.

After a few moments, the message came back. **Okay. Where?**

She shivered. Was she being hypersensitive, or did that response sound wary? Too bad. She was committed now. **How about Bean There, Done That on Lincoln?**

**See you then** was the reply.

Oh, man, she was going to be in trouble.

Sloan sat at his desk. The department was mostly empty on this cold and dreary December Saturday. He picked up the receiver on the desk phone, then replaced it. Drummed his fingers on the desktop. Thought about Veronica Quick. Picked up the receiver again and this time punched in Clint Mercer's phone number. Once again it rang on and on. Mercer might have talked to him last night, but the man was devastated. Didn't want to answer questions and apart from admitting to an affair with Melissa McNulty, and revealing that Veronica Quick had stopped by last night with his sister, he'd given Sloan nothing to help with the case. Maybe Townsend could get more out of him, although the two men were better friends than Sloan was with either of them, so who knew?

Sloan wanted to see Clint's truck tires. Wanted to photograph the tread.

*Do you really think Clint killed her?*

No . . . maybe . . . maybe . . . Love and obsession made people do crazy things. Crazy, crazy things. Dangerous things. Sometimes deadly things.

His cell rang from within the pocket of the jacket he'd slung over the back of his chair. He pulled it out and saw it was Tara. An unwelcome surprise from his ex. The divorce had been finalized nearly a year ago. He made a face and answered, knowing she would likely pester him until she had her say.

"Hi," he answered.

"Hi, yourself. I see you've been staying at a You+Me property for . . . mmm . . . two months now? Three?"

It got under his skin that she was keeping tabs on him. "Uh-huh."

"Well, I might come on down and see you, if you don't mind."

Tara was in Seattle, four hours and about two hundred miles north of River Glen. He hadn't seen her since the divorce. Had only spoken to her a few times in the last year when she'd called him. "What's going on?" he asked now.

"I've just been thinking about us . . . me . . . my . . . choices. I know they were bad. I was just so hurt and—"

"I'm not going over this again."

"—I just want to say I'm sorry. I think we could have made it, if things were different. If I'd handled things differently."

"Where's this coming from?" He cut her off. "What do you want?"

"Jesus, Sloan. Do you have to be such an ass? I'm trying to apologize!"

She'd apologized and apologized. She'd wheedled and cried and begged. Sloan had been relieved when the divorce was finalized because it had been a long, rocky road to get the final decree signed and the marriage dissolved. "Tara, we're divorced and it's going to stay that way," he said in a firm but calm voice. "No more apologies."

He heard her swift intake of breath. She hadn't expected him to be so forceful. So certain.

She exploded. "Well, fuck you, then. Fuck. YOU." She slammed down the phone.

*Perfect*, he thought sarcastically.

Suddenly he was claustrophobic.

The walls and his past seemed to close in on him and he had to get away. Get out. Without a word, he snagged his coat and left the squad room. He wasn't supposed to be at work anyway. He thought about heading to a bar and then changed his route to Clint Mercer's house.

Ronnie slipped on her jacket on her way to Bean There, Done That, a local coffee chain which had started in the neighboring town of Laurelton. The one on Lincoln was actually closest to her, but then maybe Detective Haynes knew that when he'd chosen it.

As Ronnie left her apartment, she glanced toward Angel's door. She hadn't seen him since he'd kept her from falling this morning and she was kind of glad not to run into him. She was embarrassed and didn't want a lot of explanations.

*A lot of that going around*, she thought.

Her brain snagged on Angel. Something about him.

"What?" she asked aloud. All these feelings. All these *messages*... What she needed was answers. Explanations. Something substantial that she could grab on to. Something—

*He's a private investigator.*

Oh.

As soon as the thought entered her brain she knew it was true. Was he... following her? Watching out for her? Someone had hired him. Maybe the stuff with his cousin Daria was all a lie, or maybe not. But he'd planted himself next to her for a reason. Maybe it was about Daria. Maybe she was just egotistically assuming it was about her. Maybe—

*Jesse Taft put him up to it. Returning the favor.*

Ah. She knew it as if someone had told her.

Not long ago, Ronnie had "seen" Taft's sister, Helene, his muse. Helene had a dire warning for her brother. Ronnie had passed it along, insisting that Taft be careful. Taft hadn't really believed Ronnie, but his heightened awareness had saved him. So now it seemed Taft had hired Angel to watch over her, or maybe Angel had somehow let him know about his cousin's issues with her firm and they'd worked out some kind of deal between them. But Taft was involved. She was sure of it. Keeping an eye out for her in the form of Angel Vasquero.

Did Detective Haynes know? she wondered as she pushed through the door to Bean There, Done That. The aroma of coffee and some kind of spice... Christmas spice... greeted her along with soft music, some jazzy version of "The Little Drummer Boy" emanating from overhead speakers while a blond girl in braids and an elf hat manned the register.

Ronnie glanced around the smattering of tables but there was no sign of Haynes and only a few people hanging out. She checked the time on her phone: 2:35. So he wasn't that late, yet. But she had things to do and if he didn't show up soon, she would call him and leave.

A slim young woman with dark hair rose from a table where she'd been sitting, tensely facing the door. Ronnie registered her a moment before she stopped in front of her.

"Are you waiting for Cooper Haynes?" she asked.

Ronnie had a sudden flash of insight. "You texted me."

"Yeah. Sorry. I had to find out what happened with Mary Jo, and Cooper isn't talking. He's afraid my mom will freak out and I am, too. But I have to know. I've got to find her."

"The... surrogate?" she guessed.

"You do know about her," she said intensely.

"No. I don't really. I just..."

"What? You just, what?"

"I came up with a wrong name. I didn't know her name was Mary Jo."

"What did you come up with?"

"It's irrelevant. It's—"

"What name?"

"Rebekkah. Two *k*'s, one *h*. That's what I told Detective Haynes."

That stopped her. She clearly didn't know what to do with that.

"Are you his daughter?" asked Ronnie.

"Uh, stepdaughter. But more like a daughter. I'm sorry. I'm Harley Woodward. Cooper's married to my mom. I thought you knew where Mary Jo was."

"I'm afraid not. I wish I did, for you. I think you should ask your stepfather."

"Yeah, that's worked so well so far. He wanted to meet with you, though. He was calling and texting you." She regarded Ronnie with narrowed eyes. "I don't know who you are."

"My name's Veronica Quick. I'm with Tormelle & Quick Law Firm."

"Oh. Yeah. That's right. He was going there. Did you do the legal work for him?"

"No. I'm not a lawyer."

"Oh, shit. Oh. Sorry. Um." Her eyes narrowed a bit. 'You're the psychic? I overheard him talking to someone about you."

"Jesse Taft?" Ronnie suggested.

"Maybe. You really are a psychic?" Harley asked. "You *see* things?"

"Part-time," she said in a voice laced with irony.

But Harley wasn't allowing her to get away with anything. "What does that mean?"

"It means I'm not always right."

"Like maybe you just guess at things?"

This was going nowhere. Time to end the conversation about her abilities. "I hope I helped some," she said to Harley. "Talk to your dad. He knows more than I do."

Intent on making her escape, Ronnie glanced toward the door and the wide window facing the street. A colorful van was parked directly in front of the shop. Children's handprints and a beaming sun decorated its exterior.

Her heart stopped for second. What were the chances? "Heart of Sunshine Church," she read aloud as the panel door slid open.

"What?" Harley followed her gaze outside just as a group of women and children who'd emerged from it were entering the coffee shop, the door opening, allowing in cool air and soft voices.

"Oh... fu... oh, shit... oh, holy hell... there she is," whispered Harley, her eyes rounding as several children rushed forward to the pastry counter where they pressed their palms and noses to the glass. "Mary Jo. Oh, my God."

Bustling in with two other women, a very pregnant woman entered. She was dark-haired, her face troubled. She must have felt the stares of both Harley and Ronnie because her gaze collided with theirs as if drawn by a tractor beam.

Mary Jo's face registered surprise. She gasped and faltered a step, looked panicked enough to consider fleeing as she looked at Harley, who was gazing right back in stunned surprise.

Harley muttered a quick, "Thanks," to Ronnie, then started to stride straight for the stunned woman.

"Don't," Ronnie warned, but too late, Harley was on a mission.

But she was intercepted by a man with graying hair bound into a wild ponytail... the preacher of Heart of Sunshine, maybe?

He stepped directly in front of Mary Jo.

Ronnie immediately didn't trust him. Like the image of Galen with the boss's wife, she saw the preacher in a chapel of sorts. He came up behind a blond woman and with a few whispered words and large hands he bent her over a pew and lifted her long skirt. There was a lot of desperate praying on her part, moaning on his, as they bucked against the wooden benches.

Ronnie recognized the blond was among the parishioners. She was holding tight to the hand of a boy who was about three, and she was pregnant again. Feeling Ronnie's eyes on her, the blond looked over in fear, or was it a silent plea for help?

As the throng from the church collected at the counter, Ronnie drew her cell phone out of her purse and scrolled to Cooper Haynes's texts to find his number. It appeared on her screen just as Harley yelled, "Mary Jo!" and tried get past the preacher to the woman cowering behind him. "What're you doing? My parents have been looking for you!"

Several people at surrounding tables turned to look their way.

"I'm sorry," the preacher said calmly. "There is no Mary Jo here." To the frightened woman, he suggested, "Maybe you should go back to the van, Rebekkah."

"Rebekkah?" Harley spat, then met Ronnie's gaze—the name she'd just learned—then attempted to look around the large man and catch Mary Jo's gaze. "Is that what you go by now? Well, that's pure bull... I know you! You're Mary Jo Kirshner and you're pregnant with my—"

"Hush!" the preacher ordered harshly as he waved Mary Jo outside. All the while he pinned Harley with a furious glare. "I'll not have you harassing my parishioners."

"Harassing?" Harley repeated. "Are you kidding?"

"Uh-oh," someone at a nearby table whispered.

Phone in hand, Ronnie stepped closer to Harley and sent her a warning glare, hoping to defuse the escalating situation, then Ronnie addressed the gray-haired man, directly. "She's right. We really do need to talk to—"

"Is there a problem here?" A heavy-set woman in a long white apron and hair net bustled from the kitchen and moved quickly through the tables where the few customers were ignoring their coffee to watch the drama unfold. A name tag identified her as *Tess*.

"No problem," the preacher said calmly, slipping on a beatific, and oh-so-patient smile that Ronnie found completely fake. "This girl, here, is just confused. Well, they both are," he said, indicating Ronnie as well as Harley. He let out a bit of a laugh as if he found the situation utterly inane. "Mistaking one of—"

"I'm not confused!" Harley glared at him and ignored the woman in the apron. Harley's color was high, her fists balled and she looked like she might just punch the preacher. "It's not a mistake! I just want to talk to her, that's all. Everyone's been worried sick!" Moving swiftly, she attempted to circumvent the big man again, but he effectively blocked the door as Mary Jo escaped outside and into the van.

"Rebekkah doesn't want to speak with you." His smile was tight, but he didn't budge, not even as Ronnie tried to slip past him.

"What's going on here?" Tess demanded.

"Nothing, I assure you," the preacher said, "A case of mistaken identity, that's all." His voice had taken on the pseudo calm tone Ronnie associated with some preachers and therapists. "I'm sorry for any inconvenience this . . . confusion has caused."

Ronnie told him, "No confusion. Is there a reason we can't speak with—"

"Isn't it obvious?" he snapped, losing his well-practiced cool for a second. "Rebekkah doesn't want to speak to either of you." With a tight smile, he turned his attention to the aproned woman and added, "We just came here for some refreshments. Coffee or tea and some sweets for the children."

Tess glanced back to the counter where the cashier was already ringing up orders, the line of women and children snaking past the display case.

Ronnie hit the button on her phone and placed the call to Cooper while catching a glimpse through the window, where Mary Jo pulled the sliding door of the van shut.

"I *need* to talk to her," Harley insisted.

"And I don't want any trouble," Tess warned while still eyeing the flock of women and children near the counter, all of whom were ordering drinks and donuts and scones, the girl in the elf hat collecting cash while another lanky teen had appeared from the back and was busying himself at the hissing espresso machine where he was making a growing list of coffee drinks.

"No trouble whatsoever," the preacher assured her in that supercilious tone that made Ronnie's skin crawl, just as she heard someone pick up on the other end of her connection.

Haynes!

Under her breath, Ronnie said, "Detective Haynes? Ronnie Quick. I'm at Bean There, Done That on Lincoln with Harley, and you'd better get here fast. I believe your missing surrogate just walked in with members from the Heart of Sunshine Church..."

# Chapter 16

Ronnie knocked on Angel's door. She'd never sought out his company before, but now that she had an inkling about who he was, she wanted to see if she was right. He didn't respond, so after a few minutes she let herself into her own place. He'd always been around these past few months, but of course now that she wanted him he wasn't home.

She'd waited at Bean There, Done That until Cooper Haynes had arrived. She hadn't told the detective what she'd envisioned about the younger pregnant woman. Wasn't sure it was completely accurate. But she did mention that she thought the preacher was treating his flock more like a harem, to which the detective had skewered her with a look and asked point-blank if that was a prediction on her part. "Just a guess," she'd told him, thinking the half lie would be easier to swallow than the truth.

Harley had been all about keeping Mary Jo from getting back on the bus. Stepdaughter and stepfather had eyed each other, silently promising to deal with the hows, whys and wherefores of Harley's meeting with Ronnie at some future point. Ronnie had left them to their "discussion" with the preacher, who had gotten all huffy and perturbed and threatened to call the police, to which Harley had boldly claimed, "Go ahead, you perv," which caused Detective Haynes to place a restraining hand on her shoulder.

The "perv" hadn't followed through, maybe having a little insight to how that was going to look. Instead he and Detective Haynes had shared a tête-à-tête outside, while the herd of women, and several emaciated men who also seemed to idolize the preacher, milled around the shop while curious gazes from the few other customers observed the drama.

In the end Mary Jo, i.e., "Rebekkah," had rather reluctantly left with the detective and Harley. A stopgap to what Ronnie knew would be a later raid of some kind on the church because of the age of some of the younger women who'd apparently been the ones instrumental in getting the preacher to extend their privileges to the coffee shop.

Now, Ronnie was just finishing snacking on a small cup of mixed nuts she'd heated in the microwave when her phone buzzed. Glancing at the screen, she saw it was Brandy. "I was just thinking about calling you," she answered warmly.

"What did you tell Sloan?" Brandy cut in harshly.

Ronnie's breath caught at her sharp tone. "What? About what?"

"He went to Clint's and took pictures of his tires and some debris out of the truck bed. He thinks Clint killed Melissa! Why? What's he doing? Did you put him up to it? Did you think you SAW SOMETHING?"

Ronnie's heart started thumping against her ribs. "No . . . we were . . . discussing the site, the clearing . . ." A lie, sort of. But the truth, in essence. "There were a lot of tire tracks, different ones. You saw them."

"What about the debris? What was he looking for?"

She swallowed. "Something maybe to rule out Clint?"

Brandy's breath came out in an angry rush. "Clint couldn't hurt Mel. You know he couldn't! What the hell, Ronnie? Is this just because you want to be with Sloan?"

"What?"

"You threw Clint into the fire! Pointed Sloan right at him, and he's innocent! Thanks a fucking lot." She clicked off in a fury.

Ronnie sank against the kitchen counter, her pulse still racing from the exchange. Sloan must've listened to her about the maple tree whirlies. That must be what the debris was that he'd gathered from the bed of Clint's truck.

But that kind of evidence would never hold up in a court of law. You needed a chain of custody, tech people who could vouch for where the evidence came from. A grab by a single officer didn't mean anything... except as a means to scare a guilty mind... Is that what he was doing?

She dialed Sloan before she could change her mind. He answered on the third ring. "I'm in a meeting. I'll have to call you back."

"I just got a call from Brandy. She's totally pissed at me. Thinks I sold her brother down the river because of some evidence you picked up?"

"Clint knew what I was doing."

"Have you even looked at Hugh McNulty? Checked his alibi? Or any of Mel's other relationships? Or did you just go after Clint?"

"I'll call you back." His tone was cool.

"Don't bother."

He was busy. She got that. But his actions had lost her Brandy's friendship again, and she wanted to blame somebody, *him*, for it.

She glanced at the time on her cell phone. Three hours till she was supposed to meet Marian Langdorf. Damn, she didn't want to go. She wanted... to scream!

She stalked back outside and pounded angrily on Angel's door. She wanted answers. Now! She listened at the panels but there was no sound from within. Maybe he was on a job. Or whatever.

A rush of brutal December wind chased along the covered porch and cut through her before she re-entered her own apartment, all the while thinking hard. Shivering inwardly, she closed the door behind her. She decided to call Jesse Taft, and after shedding her coat, punched out his cell number on her phone. The P.I. picked up right away, but before he could say anything, she demanded, "Did you ask Angel Vasquero to watch over me?"

He hesitated in responding for a moment; telling, in itself. "He was trying to help his cousin and there was an apartment next to yours. He's a good man." A pause. "What gave him away?"

"Oh, I'm a psychic, remember?" she retorted. "I know these things."

He didn't rise to the bait. "Why do I get the feeling you're in trouble?"

"Maybe you're the psychic. Maybe you really do see your sister."

"You're mad at me."

"Caught onto that, did ya?" She let out a long breath, then said, "I'm mad at the whole world, Taft. You're just part of it." She silently counted to ten. Still her hot temper didn't cool, despite her best efforts. "Thanks for looking out for me, but I can handle myself."

"That's what I said when you warned me," he reminded with a hint of amusement.

"Goodbye, Taft. I'll tell Angel he's off the job when I see him."

She clicked off and threw the damned phone onto the couch. A moment later she picked it up again and noted she'd received a voice mail she must've missed while she was at the coffee shop with Harley and Detective Haynes. Touching the symbol for voice mails, she realized the phone number was familiar but couldn't place it. Clicking on, she felt gooseflesh sweep up her arms as she heard Shana's voice say, "Mom said you and Sloan were looking for me. I got spooked and checked into a motel to recover. Things feel weird. Why were you worried about me, and what were you doing with Sloan?"

Shana's last words were an accusation. Oh . . . God . . . Ronnie stumbled into the living room and sank into her favorite chair. Really? Shana was okay? But . . . She listened to the message again, then once again, checking the time and finally accepting that the voice had to be Shana's by the hour that the call had come in. She was alive!

Ronnie shook her head. Good . . . good . . . that was good. Of course it was good . . .

*But you were so wrong!*

She covered her face with her hands, took several deep breaths. Dear God, her visions were making her crazy! Or . . . maybe she always had been.

No! No! She closed her eyes, forcing herself to calm down, pulling the fuzzy throw over her body again as she was still chilled to the marrow.

Images of Shana and the questions about what had happened to her swirled through her brain. Did Sloan know? Was that part of his cold remoteness? No. If he'd known, he would have ripped into her.

Five minutes later she threw off the blanket and pushed herself to her feet, a new determination driving her. Sweeping up her purse, she headed for her Escape and Aunt Kat.

"... don't want you wandering off the reservation, bro. That's all I'm saying. Not criticizing your investigative technique, just your slant." Townsend smiled thinly at Sloan. Beneath the bonhomie there was steel. Sloan had always known it was there, but he was getting a real good sense of it now. "You gotta lay off Mercer."

"You checked with Hugh McNulty. What did he say?" Sloan asked. He was seated in a visitor's chair in Townsend's office, and had been the recipient of the sheriff's ire for the past forty minutes already. The conversation had been all wrapped in "we're just two old friends workin' through a problem" and he was sick of it.

"Says he was out in the Coast Range. Nowhere near the site of his wife's demise. So far that's panned out, but you know how these things can turn." He leaned back in his desk chair, the spring shrieking as if in pain. Townsend was apparently so used to the sound he didn't react.

Sloan's ladder-back chair kept him sitting like a schoolboy, purposeful on Townsend's part, another subtle reminder of who was boss. Getting a taste of his old friend's methodology amongst his troops made Sloan determined to make the move to River Glen P.D. permanent.

"Leave Mercer to me. *Capisce?*" Townsend's eyes were hard.

"*Capisce.*"

Sloan left the sheriff's office for the scattered desks the deputies and office personnel used, but kept right on heading for the door. He didn't expect autonomy from Townsend on the investigation into Melissa McNulty's death, but he did expect cooperation. Instead, he'd been dressed down. Mercer had complained to Townsend and that's all it took.

But the tech team had the pictures of Clint's tires, and Inga Pedderson was already examining the seeds from the maple tree. If those seeds' DNA matched that of the maple seeds picked up at the site where Melissa McNulty's body was found, then Mercer, or at least Mercer's truck, had been at the homicide site and Sloan was going to get answers, Sheriff Abel Townsend or not. He just hoped Mercer had some.

He drove away from the sheriff's department, intent on checking with Hugh McNulty himself. Townsend may not like him digging where the sheriff had already dug, but Sloan didn't like the feeling that secrets were still buried.

He hadn't had a chance to tell Townsend that Clint's face had gone white and he'd staggered a bit, throwing out a hand to hold on to the porch post as he stared at Sloan's plastic bag full of leaves, grass and seeds that Sloan had retrieved from his truck bed. Clearly he'd called Townsend and complained, so Sloan had been dressed down without relaying that information. So now he was on his own. Mercer knew something about Melissa McNulty's death. He just hoped to God Clint wasn't responsible.

His cell rang. Townsend. He answered cautiously, but the sheriff barked, "Hart?" before he could even say hello.

"Yeah?"

"You didn't tell me your next move."

Sloan didn't like already being checked on. And he'd be

damned if he told the sheriff he was rechecking with Hugh McNulty. "I'll let you deal with Mercer. There're rumors that his wife was seeing other men besides Clint. I'll check with her friends. See what I can find out."

"Be careful with that," warned Townsend.

"I'll check with Brandy first. I imagine she'll be happy to widen the investigation away from her brother."

Townsend said, a smile in his voice, all friends again, "You're on her shit list."

Brandy had also called the department and complained loudly. It felt like her fierce protection of her brother might be rooted in something more than sisterly love. Desperation or fear was his guess.

"I've got this," Sloan assured him.

"Okay."

Sloan's cell rang as soon as he clicked off. He didn't recognize the number, debated about answering. Decided to, just before the call went to voice mail. "Sloan Hart."

"Sloan? It's Shana . . . I heard you were looking for me . . ."

He recognized the voice as she burst into tears.

At home, Harley was on one foot and then the other, waiting for Cooper to get back from dropping Mary Jo off at her home. Harley thought leaving the woman was a bad idea. Didn't trust that Mary Jo wouldn't just race right back to that sicko priest, or whatever he thought he was, and join the cult again. Because Mary Jo was a cultist. That was a fact. Leaving her with her husband and kids was not a good plan.

In fact, it was just plain stupid. Which was a word Harley would not normally ascribe to her stepdad. Except for today. Cooper had said something about Mary Jo being a free person, and there was such a thing as being sued for kidnapping, and all that, but hey, facts were facts, and that woman was not okay. A flight risk. Right back to the harem, as the psychic lady had said. Veronica Quick.

"Heart of Sunshine, my ass," Harley muttered beneath her breath.

Emma was staring down Twink, who was gathering herself for a leap to the counter. Harley moved into the cat's way and Twink regarded her balefully before sauntering off, tail in the air, as if she'd never had any intention of stealing any of the frozen shrimp thawing for tonight's pasta dish.

"I've seen that bus," said Emma in her flat tone.

"What bus?" asked Harley.

"The Heart of Sunshine. With the handprints. From the kids."

Harley wasn't sure where this was going. Emma could be kind of obscure at times. "Yeah? They have a bus."

"They pick up people and take them away. They asked me if I wanted to come and meet the Lord."

Harley froze. "Seriously? Where'd this happen?"

"At the thrift shop. Theo told them there was no soliciting. They told her to 'go with the Lord' and she said the Lord didn't want her and shooed them away. They said she was in their prayers."

Emma worked part-time at Theo's Thrift Shop.

"They wanted you to get in the bus," Harley said again, just to be certain.

"They said I was special." Emma frowned. "I know what that means."

"I don't like them," Harley said fiercely.

"I don't think you'll be in their prayers."

Harley eyed her aunt closely. "Was that a joke, Emma? Are you making jokes?"

"I don't make jokes."

"Yeah . . . but I think you're joking."

Emma, whose face rarely changed expression, seemed to faintly smile.

Movement out the living room window caught Harley's eye and she saw Cooper's Explorer bounce into the driveway. He was driving faster than normal. She ran to the back door to greet him, Emma at her heels. Their sudden movement caused Duchess to bound to her feet. As the dog raced by Twink, the cat arched her back and hissed, but no one paid her any attention.

"What happened?" Harley demanded, holding open the door for Cooper as he came up the back steps.

"She's with Stephen and the kids. They were all glad to see her and she got kind of emotional seeing them."

"That's good, right?" Harley asked.

"I'd say so."

"She should stay home," said Emma.

"Yes, she should." Cooper smiled faintly at Emma. Once upon a time, before Emma's accident, back when they were both in high school, the two of them had dated. Years later they'd reconnected when Cooper had started dating Mom. Like herself, Cooper was very protective of Emma.

"Do you think she will, though?" Harley asked suspiciously. "She could run right back to that creep or run off somewhere else. She needs to have that baby."

"The baby will make that decision," said Emma.

"Unless it's a C-section. Can we order a C-section?" Harley looked to Cooper.

"Not our purview," he told her as he shrugged out of his jacket and hung it on a peg near the back door. "I gotta talk to your mom."

"Maybe the baby will decide to come soon," Emma said.

"That's a very real possibility," muttered Cooper as he headed for the stairs.

Harley wasn't satisfied and admitted, "I kind of want to go to Heart of Sunshine and make sure she doesn't show up there."

"You could catch the bus," Emma pointed out.

"Nah. The preacher's already seen me. I wasn't... discreet when we found Mary Jo."

Emma blinked and said, "I could catch the bus. They want me to meet the Lord."

Harley eyed her aunt thoughtfully. A bad idea. A really bad idea. "I think the preacher has sex with the women there. That's what the psychic lady hinted at. He might try to coerce you."

Emma considered that carefully. "Is that how I meet the Lord?"

"I don't know what they mean, but I'd give that a big 'no'. I don't like it. Sounds so permanent."

"Like I'd be dead?" Emma asked flatly.

"Forget I said anything!" Harley waved her hand in the air as if erasing the entire conversation. "Don't get involved with any of them. I think Cooper's going to break up that party anyway. Something creepy about them."

"Like last summer."

"Exactly like last summer. Okay, maybe not *exactly*." Sometimes Emma took things too literally and last summer's brush with a cultish group wasn't the same. "But along those lines." Harley peered closely at her. "Don't do anything, Emma."

Emma cocked her head, which gave Harley a bad feeling. But then Emma didn't drive and she was always with people, so what was there to worry about?

Ronnie flopped into one of Aunt Kat's kitchen chairs. She was building up a head of steam, tired of feeling out of control. Tired of being pushed around by her own jumbled thoughts. "I think I'm losing my mind," she stated flatly.

"Let me make you some tea," said Aunt Kat.

"I could use some anti-psychotics," Ronnie half joked, but Aunt Kat didn't smile as she bustled around the cozy room where candles were burning and cheery Christmas lights surrounded the window over the sink.

When the teakettle whistled, Aunt Kat quickly filled two cups with the hot water and added a blend of tea leaves she called Winter Spice, which included cinnamon and other Christmas scents—pumpkin, maybe—that filled the air.

Ronnie wrapped her hands around the cup to ward off the chill that had been with her most of the day.

Aunt Kat sat down opposite her and folded her arms on the table. "Any news about Melissa?"

"I don't know. Maybe?" Ronnie told her how Sloan had obviously heard her when she'd mentioned the tire tracks and the plant DNA, forensic evidence that could possibly incriminate

Clint Mercer. She stumbled a bit when she got to Brandy's reaction, and then stumbled a lot when she explained about her vision of Shana Lloyd, how she'd also convinced Sloan that Shana was in danger, that she couldn't be found. And then Shana's call.

Aunt Kat didn't react aside from a pursing of her lips a time or two. Ronnie had never really laid out her visions to her aunt, but then she hadn't ever experienced so many, cascading one after the other, some entirely true, some entirely false, apparently.

"I thought about tracking down Patrice, wherever she is," Ronnie admitted, "but I really don't want to talk to a therapist again, any therapist. Patrice was patient, but she never got it. Not really." She took an experimental sip of her tea, found it hot and somehow calming. She said, "And Kat, you have some of this . . . woo-woo, like Mom and me. You just don't talk about it."

She shook her head, her brows tightly drawn as she avoided Ronnie's gaze and twirled her cup slowly in her hands, as if she were contemplating just how much she should divulge. If anything.

"Tell me about Mom," urged Ronnie. "Don't hold back. I need some history. And I need to know what really happened to her."

"You know what happened. It's—"

"No, I don't!" Ronnie cut in and slammed her cup down, sloshing some of the tea onto the table. She was tired of all the mind games and double-talk and innuendoes with no real answers. "I don't know what led up to her death! Dad and Mom loved each other madly, that's what you said. But what happened to them? When did it change? Jonas won't talk about her!"

Aunt Kat plucked a napkin from the holder on the table and dabbed up the spilled tea as Ronnie let all her pent-up emotions out. "Dad is all over my case these days, like he expects me to spontaneously combust, or something. Wants to nail down my future. Worse than ever. And I see things and hear things and I can't tell what's real anymore. No one trusts me! I don't trust myself! Something's happened. Something's wrong. If you know anything that can help, tell me."

Her aunt had almost flinched at Ronnie's words. Pressing her lips together, she wadded up the stained napkin and tossed it into the sink. Slowly, she turned back to her niece and Ronnie suddenly knew she was going to hear something she didn't want to know. She automatically braced herself.

"Okay," Aunt Kat said on a sigh. "You want to know, so here's the truth. Your mother started seeing things that weren't there. Worse than ever. Things that were never there. And she had a lot of fears that just intensified. She was deathly afraid of water, but kept going toward the river as if . . . it beckoned her."

Gooseflesh broke out on Ronnie's skin and her nerves thrummed. *Don't go in the water.*

"She didn't drown . . . That's not what you said."

"No. It was exposure, sickness, pneumonia complications . . ." she said painfully. "You know how I feel about your father. He's . . ."

"A trial?"

She smiled faintly at her words tossed back at her. "Yes. But he did try hard to save Winnie. I'll give him that. As difficult as their marriage was, he did love her."

"So, things got worse for her? The visions? Before she died?"

"This . . . what's happening to you is different," Aunt Kat insisted. "You're not anything like your mother," she added with sudden ferocity. "You're just confusing things, that's all."

"But didn't you just say that's what happened to Mom?"

"Not the same. You're not paranoid."

"I'm not? Don't I sound paranoid?" She choked on a laugh as she scraped back her chair and stumbled to her feet.

"Sit, sit." She waved Ronnie back toward her chair. "Take a deep breath. Separate what you know is true from your feelings, your guesses."

"How? It all runs together more than it ever has."

"Try. What do you know for sure?"

"I know Mel's dead." Ronnie sank into her chair again. "I

saw her body with other people. I don't think Clint killed her, but maybe he did. Or, maybe it was her husband. Or, maybe someone else. Brandy said she had other lovers. Mel was one of those people who is always in love with love even if it involved more than one person."

"Let the police figure that out," Aunt Kat advised, her kind eyes searching Ronnie's. "Your friend, Detective Hart, seemed very capable."

"He's not my friend. He's . . . he's just someone I know. And he doesn't believe me and I don't blame him. I don't believe me! But now he's . . ." She ran her fingers through her hair in frustration. "It's not his fault but Brandy thinks I betrayed her and Clint, and maybe I did. I just want to know what happened to Mel . . . and I want to know why I saw that vision of Shana. She was strangled like Mel. Dead. But then she called me, and it wasn't a fake. It was her."

"Are you sure?"

"Yes . . . mainly. Yes," she added, though doubt crept into her voice.

"What else do you know for sure?"

"Not much," she admitted, picking up her cup and sipping what remained of her tea. "I think I did help Detective Haynes a little."

"Who's Detective Haynes?"

"Oh . . . something separate." She explained about Sloan temporarily stepping in to Haynes's place at River Glen P.D. while the detective was on administrative leave, and how Haynes was currently searching for a missing surrogate. "At least she was found, unharmed."

"That's good."

"Yeah, but then there's Shana. Was Mom ever that wrong?" There was a telling hesitation by Aunt Kat and Ronnie answered her own question: "She was at the end."

"You are not at the end of your life, Ronnie," Aunt Kat stated fiercely. "Just try to untangle your visions, impressions. That's what Winnie did. She sang sometimes, when she was overwhelmed."

"I'm no singer," said Ronnie, but her aunt's words made her recall those times she'd felt safe in her mother's arms while Mom softly crooned to her.

"What makes you feel better?"

"I don't know. Answers. The one thing I can't get."

"There are answers out there, somewhere."

"I don't know where." As soon as she uttered the words, Ronnie realized she'd ignored the obvious. "Shana's not dead. She called me. I know I'm going to have to face Sloan, who already thinks I'm a nutcase, and try to explain why we went on a wild-goose chase, looking for her."

"And it matters what he thinks."

"Of course it does."

"Maybe a little more than what others might think of you?" she suggested and for a second an image flashed behind Ronnie's eyes. She and Sloan. Alone. Water raining down on them as they clung together . . . holding each other . . . kissing . . . his hands on her wet body . . .

*Don't go in the water.*

She blinked. Felt the heat crawling up her throat. "I—I need to talk to Shana," she said, dismissing the forbidden image. Ronnie forced her gaze back to Aunt Kat in her warm little kitchen with the twinkling Christmas lights and the reason Ronnie had come here. "I thought Shana was terrified," Ronnie said. "Strangled. I *saw* her. And I swear it was her voice on the phone, but . . ." She tossed her hands in frustration as she focused on the missing woman. "I need to talk to her in person."

Aunt Kat nodded. "That's a good start."

"And if she's okay, which I really hope she is, what then? What's my next move?"

"I don't know, hon."

"You know, the truth is I thought I was supposed to save her. That's what the psychic message was all about. I know that sounds ridiculous." She was on her feet again, needing to be in motion, the rest of her tea forgotten.

"Maybe you are supposed to save her," Aunt Kat suggested as she collected the cups. "Just not in the way you think."

She let herself recall her vision of Shana. The horror on her face as she dug her fingers into the carpet. The bluish marks of strangulation on her throat.

"Not dead. Just . . . attacked . . ."

"Possibly," agreed Aunt Kat.

"Maybe Shana's hiding from her attacker. Maybe it didn't happen at her apartment. Maybe my mind just embellished."

"It sounds like a job for the police." Aunt Kat frowned as she put both tea cups into the sink.

But Ronnie was already heading toward the door, her mind racing. "Maybe I jumped to conclusions."

"You're leaving?"

"I gotta go."

"Honey, be careful."

"I am. I will be. Thank you . . ."

She phoned Shana as soon as she was on the road again. The call went to voice mail, and she momentarily debated on calling right back, seeing if Shana would pick up on a second call, but then opted to leave a message.

"Hi, Shana. It's Ronnie. Where are you now? I want to meet with you in person. All right? I'm on the road. Give me a call when you can."

She was feeling more clearheaded, less emotional than when she'd raced over to see Aunt Kat. Not that anything Aunt Kat had said had really soothed her fears. Far from it. It was more that she felt she had a path, an explanation about Shana, and she couldn't help it if Brandy wanted to blame her for Clint's possible, maybe probable, involvement in Mel's death.

She was going to be late to meet Marian. So be it. She needed to get home and change for dinner and think things through.

She was pulling into her parking spot at her apartment when her cell buzzed back. Shana? No. Sloan.

Grimacing, she let the call go to voice mail as she got out of the car and climbed the stairs to her unit. She glanced at Angel's door. No sign of him again. No bat, though, nor other noxious warning on her mat. Maybe she should have told Sloan about the bat.

*Do you want him to come to your rescue? Wait till he hears that Shana called you. He won't believe anything you say from here on out.*

*No thanks* to that.

She changed clothes into a nicer dark red blouse and pair of black slacks. Grabbing a black blazer, she looked at herself in the mirror. Okay. Professional. She needed to convey that she was serious about not accepting Marian's job offer.

Say what you will, she still wanted to work at the law offices. She was mad at her father—more annoyed, really. His tactics for keeping her with the company needed work. Still... she was good at what she did. Maybe someday she would finish law school. Maybe someday she would step into his shoes.

She snorted at herself. *Kind of a big turnaround from a few days ago.*

But she'd learned that her father had tried to protect her mother from herself. His means might not have worked, but according to Aunt Kat, he'd never strayed from loving her.

Ronnie sensed that she was weakening when it came to her father. Was that a good thing, or bad thing? Hard to tell at this point.

She raced out the door, thinking she might not be that late. It was dark. The rain felt pent-up, waiting in the clouds, like it was about to dump in a deluge. She hurried down the stairs, expecting to be poured upon at any second, but made it to her Escape before the heavens opened.

Her cell rang as she was driving toward the Langdorf estate.

*Shana.*

Ronnie answered, "Shana."

"Yeah. I'm back at my apartment," Shana said in a rush. "Got your message. I want to talk to you, too. But I... I'm packing up. I going to leave town."

"Why? What happened?"

"I'll call you when I'm safe."

No! "Wait. If you—"

The line went dead.

"Shit."

Ronnie thought about it hard for the space of five seconds, then she wrenched the wheel at the next side street, decided to blow off Marian and go find Shana. She was alive. She believed that much and it was obvious Shana was scared to death.

Pushing the speed limit, Ronnie circled back to Shana's apartment building. As soon as she found a parking spot and stepped out of the car, the clouds burst open and a curtain of rain pelted down, drenching her in the few moments it took to cross the parking lot and get in the shelter of the stairways that led to Shana's apartment.

She hurried upward, shaking water from her hair.

Shana's door was two-thirds of the way down the fourth-floor outside corridor. As Ronnie neared the apartment, her steps slowed. There were no lights on inside, though the outside illumination was bright enough to see the door knob. Ronnie tapped her knuckles on the panel. "Shana?"

A silvery sense of premonition ran down her nerves.

Slowly, carefully, she twisted the knob, recognizing even as she did so that she was leaving prints. It turned beneath her fingers and she pushed open the door.

Shana was lying just as she'd pictured her in her vision. Mouth open in a silent scream. Eyes filled with terror. Fingers digging into the carpet.

"What are you doing here?"

Sloan's voice came from behind her, where he was striding along the corridor in her direction.

She felt her knees buckle. *I was right*, she thought despondently. *I was right.*

"I just had the time wrong," she said, and then felt his arm grab hers to keep her from falling.

# Chapter 17

The apartment building was a madhouse.

Ronnie had only heard a buzzing in her ears for a while. The crowd of techs and officers and EMTs had descended en masse before she could legitimately answer him. She told the techs about what she'd touched and where—only the doorknob—but that was about all she could manage.

Sloan had steadied her, then immediately starting firing questions. What was she doing here? Did she find Shana on the floor? When had she gotten here? Had she seen anyone else? Was Shana gone before she arrived, or still alive? Had she said anything?

*Shana's dead*, was the refrain running around her brain. *Shana's dead, Shana's dead, Shana's dead* . . .

*You were supposed to save her.*

It was hardly a positive that she'd been right about seeing Shana's dead body on the floor of her apartment before she'd actually died. It made Ronnie look guilty as hell, which is exactly how she felt.

She'd moved onto the outdoor corridor with Sloan, rain gurgling in the gutter, some dripping through the boards of the floor above that weren't caught by the overhanging roof of the top apartment tier.

Now, Sloan was as wet as she was, his hair dark and damp, rain sliding down the sides of his cheeks. He was looking at her in a way that made her want to shrivel up inside, like she was some kind of freak. At least an hour had passed. Maybe more. She couldn't tell. But the ME had arrived and pronounced Shana deceased, not that Ronnie had suffered any doubts even though she hadn't touched the body.

"Why were you here?" she demanded, realizing she hadn't asked the question earlier.

"Shana called me."

"So, you knew she was alive, too," Ronnie accused.

"How did *you* know?" he demanded.

"You asked me that already," she realized. One of his questions.

"Yeah, and you didn't answer me."

"She called me, too. And then I left her a message that I wanted to see her, and she called me back, not long before I got here, and told me she was at her apartment."

"I can check the phone records."

"Do that," she said, not bothering to mask her irritation. "Please."

"Did she say anything to you? Give an idea what was happening?"

"Just that she was scared... spooked... I never got why. She was going to tell me, I think, but she was dead by the time I got here. Strangled." She drew in a long, calming breath.

"I can drive you home," Sloan offered, once it was clear that neither of them was needed any longer.

"I can drive," she told him.

"I have a few more questions, but I'd rather we did it inside."

A few? More like he wanted an interrogation. "Fine. Follow me. I'm taking my car," she told him, her smoldering emotions flaring in a burst of indignation.

"Fine," he agreed tersely.

She wanted to fight back. Fight *him*.

She drove fast—probably too fast—and parked in the apartment's lot just as Sloan swooped into one of the few empty visitor's spots. She didn't bother waiting for him, just headed upstairs, feeling weary all over . . . but mad. Still mad. And wet and miserable.

He followed her up the steps. "I already told you everything I know," she muttered, scrounging in her purse for her key as she reached the long porch that ran the length of the building. "I didn't kill her. I just *saw* it. And it . . . sucks . . ."

"I want to talk to you about that."

"By all means."

She threw him a fierce glare as she shoved open her apartment door. She was going to cry. God. Damn. It. She was going to cry. Shana's body . . . and Mel . . .

She fought back the burning tears. She was just too tired. And deep down furious at whoever had done this. It felt like they were playing with her. Even though it wasn't about her, of course. Shana and Melanie dead. *Dead!* So the idea of the killer toying with her was ridiculous, but something was different.

Whoever was doing this was involving her, too. It was so frustrating. And scary.

Sloan closed the door behind them, cutting off the wet, winter air. They stood in the small entry space off the kitchen and suddenly the room seemed too close.

"You can hang up your coat," she said, stepping away from him and pointing to the hooks on the back of the door. She shrugged out of hers and had a moment of wondering what her hair looked like. Undoubtedly plastered to her head.

"I didn't kill Shana," she said again, hanging up her blazer.

"I don't think you did."

Was that true? He still sounded unconvinced. She pulled out her cell phone. She'd called Marian and gotten Carlton, who'd been snobby and snarly when she'd told him she had to cancel, without explaining why. Now she had several voice mails from Marian's number.

"I was supposed to meet someone for dinner," she explained,

though he didn't ask, while she walked into the living room. Without listening to them, she punched in the Langford number, but once again reached Carlton, not Marian. "Nice of you to return Marian's calls," he ground out.

"Is Marian available?"

"She's in her bedroom and she doesn't want to talk to you anymore."

"I don't know if I believe you."

That set him off. "You've jacked her around all over the place! I don't know what you expect!"

It was not the time for Carlton Langdorf to get on his high horse with her. "Tell her I'll be there at six sharp tomorrow."

"She's done with you!"

"If that doesn't work, have her call me." *Asshole.*

She clicked off, angered anew. She hadn't wanted to be Marian Langford's private psychic, still didn't, but Carlton was infuriatingly high-handed in a way that made her want to punch back.

Sloan's eyes were looking around her apartment in that cop way, cataloguing everything.

"I don't have anything to hide," she snapped. She wanted to drop into her favorite chair, pull up her fuzzy blanket and block out the world, but she couldn't, and his presence made her nervous. She was shivering, she realized, and hugged herself closely.

"Shana was in the exact position you described, but she wasn't there earlier," he said tonelessly.

"I know. I was ahead of myself."

"How did you know *at all*?"

She narrowed her gaze at him. What was he really asking? "You know how I know . . . that's what this is about."

"I don't know how you know," he came back swiftly. "Is it like a sudden inspiration? A whole picture that bursts on the scene? Something that develops slowly?"

He was exasperated, and she wasn't sure if he was being facetious or serious. She decided to take him at face value. "Okay.

Look," she acquiesced, palms out, fingers spread. "Sometimes it's like a dream. I wake up from it. And sometimes it just comes on me. If it's strong enough, it can make me stumble or fall."

"What happened with Shana?" he demanded. "How did that one go?"

"I was on the phone to you," she reminded him, "and I got a vision and Angel, my neighbor, caught me as I was falling. That's what I mean. That was this morning and then Shana called me, us, I guess."

"So, you were just off a few hours?"

"Yes!" she said, resenting his tone as she stepped into the living room and turned on a table lamp. God, she was still cold.

"You were ahead of whoever strangled her."

"Yes." She hadn't really thought about it that way, but yes.

"Did you tell anyone what you 'saw'?"

"You say it like that because you still don't believe me," she snapped back.

He threw his hands up in the air. "I don't know what the fuck to believe."

He was angry, too, she realized. At whoever had killed Shana. They agreed on that, at least. "Believe this: I want to know who did this. And who killed Mel. And if the two deaths are related. And if Clint Mercer had anything to do with either of them."

"I want to find out who killed them and rip their throat out," Sloan admitted.

She felt a thrill of fear go through her, maybe a thrill of something else. Sloan had always been so contained. So capable and cool. Shana's death had unleashed something hiding beneath the surface. "I want to, too."

"Tell me how to find them."

"I wish I could."

"Help me."

She searched his formidable gaze. "I don't have control over any of it. You don't know how much I wish I did."

"You're shivering," he said suddenly as if he'd finally noticed and wasn't completely consumed by his own frustration.

"I'm cold . . . kind of . . . not so much right now." Which was a lie, but beneath his gaze, she felt an unwelcome warmth and she couldn't help returning his stare. Was that her pulse she felt at her throat? Did he see it?

Sloan looked away first. His gaze shifting to her lips. He raked his fingers through his still damp hair. "I should leave," he said, as if arguing with himself.

"You should leave." She didn't know what was going to happen next, but it felt dangerous. And oddly welcoming. The room seeming to shrink, the atmosphere charging, a wanting starting to seep into her blood.

Neither of them moved. And she remembered her vision at Aunt Kat's, where they were holding each other in the rain . . .

*Don't go in the water.*

She dropped her gaze to his chest. She had the unlikely urge to press herself against him so much she actually swayed a tiny bit. Remembering him holding her with raindrops falling all around them. He took two giant steps forward, but she shook her head. "I'm okay. Sorry. It's just a lot."

He was close enough she could feel some of his body heat, smelled his clean, male scent. Oh, no . . .

The desire to lean in was damn near irresistible and she saw the darkening of his gaze, his pupils dilating.

Oh. Lord.

Her breath stopped somewhere in the back of her throat.

*I got this feeling that this is the beginning of something beautiful between the two of you.*

Evan Caldwell's comment brought back a bit of sanity. At least on Ronnie's part. Until she looked up and saw the smoldering desire in his eyes, how dark they'd become.

"Oh, damn," she whispered.

"Damn," he agreed.

"You're not leaving."

"Doesn't look like it."

"I haven't kissed you . . . in a lot of years," she breathed.

"You never kissed me. I kissed you."

Her heart thumped. "I don't remember."

For an answer he reached for her arms and slowly pulled her toward him. Her blouse pressed against his shirt and he wrapped an arm around her, bending her backwards just enough to make her cling to him, something she desperately wanted to do. He pressed his lips against hers and her mouth opened of its own accord. He slipped his tongue inside and she sucked hard. Everything felt on fire. Vaguely she wondered if he was in that place of awe a little bit, where Galen had been when he'd discovered that what she could do was real. Of course, he'd fallen out of that mode right away. He'd always been more interested in who her father was than who she was.

The kiss deepened and she strained to press herself against him as best she could, given her precarious position. He immediately lifted her up and she wrapped her legs around him, feeling his hardness so blessedly good between her hips. She couldn't get close enough.

"I don't want to wait." Her breath came out in a whoosh when he broke the kiss long enough to move to her ear, his tongue finding whorls and tiny crevices that sent shock waves through her.

*I'm going to marry you.*

She nearly cried out. Wanted to press the heels of her hands against her own head to stop that particular thought. It was *wrong*. That wasn't what this was. She didn't want that.

His mouth came back to hers as he carried her into the bedroom and then the bathroom. *What?*

She blinked.

"Shower," he murmured against her lips.

Ahhhh. "Yes."

He set her on her feet and they broke apart for a moment. Her chest was already heaving and his breath was coming fast, too. She kicked off her shoes and he flashed a devastating smile, something he didn't do near enough, and slipped out of his, too.

She started to unbutton her blouse but he pushed her hands away and did it for her, sweeping it off her shoulders into a pool on the floor. Her bra clasped in front, which deepened his smile.

She stopped him at the clasp and his gaze shot to hers. "My turn," she said.

A bit reluctantly, he dropped his hands and let her take off his shirt. One look at his sculpted muscles and she wanted to run her hands over him, which she tried, but he manacled both of her wrists in one palm and said, "My turn."

He unclasped her bra with the deft fingers of one hand.

"You have skills," she observed.

"You have..." His eyes devoured her breasts and his breath came out in a sigh.

She felt herself melt inside. She hadn't realized how anxious and repressed she'd been. When was the last time she had sex? Good sex? *Never?* She knew this was going to be better than anything she'd had before... it already was.

"Okay. Shower," she whispered, slipping from his grasp and turning on the spray. He was already tugging down her pants as she checked the temperature. She shivered again, but it wasn't from the cold.

By the time she turned back he'd ripped off his pants and kicked them away. He grabbed her and they both went under the water, locked in a kiss.

"I don't want to wait, either," he growled against her ear.

"Yes... yes..."

He brought her legs around him again and she eagerly settled herself so that he could push into her. She gasped, swallowed water, laughed. He chuckled, but it ended in a groan as they worked in rhythm, friction feeding each other's desire. Ronnie buried her face against his neck, so close to climax so fast she was gasping and moaning and clawing at his back to drive him closer, closer, *closer*.

"Ronnie..." he murmured unsteadily, and she closed her eyes remembering the vision of rain falling over them.

One moment she was clutching and grabbing and hugging and the next she was spiraling into waves of pleasure, crying out and loosening her grip, which made him clasp her harder, press her back into the wall as he drove deeper and deeper, reaching his own throbbing climax with a soft groan against her wet hair as his heart pounded wildly in tandem with hers.

They stayed that way for long, long seconds, minutes maybe, before Sloan slowly set her on her feet again. Her hair was in her eyes and he gently pushed it away. He looked behind them and turned off the spray. They were both still breathing rapidly.

"Is the interrogation finished?" she murmured.

His lips curved. "We could go another round. Didn't want to run you out of hot water."

In truth, what she wanted now, more than anything, was to wrap herself around him and spend the night beneath the covers of her bed.

But then a thought hit her and she felt cold again.

He immediately dragged her close. "I don't think I want to hear it yet."

"You don't. But I just remembered. I told Evan Caldwell that Shana was lying on her back on the carpet in her apartment."

# Chapter 18

Ronnie's wish was granted.

She spent all night in bed making love with Sloan.

They both turned their phones off and hardly spoke another word for hours. Even Ronnie's comment on Evan Caldwell was tabled. Only in the very early morning hours did they bring up the subject again.

"Why Shana?" Sloan asked near her ear.

Ronnie was dozing beside him. It had been so nice to dive into this cocoon of warmth, safety and lovemaking, but in her snatches of sleep she'd been plagued by dark images haunting the edges of her dreams. Shana's death on top of Mel's . . . and at a lesser level, losing her friendship with Brandy all over again.

"Do you think Evan told someone?"

His lips twisted. "He could have told any number of people, or put it on the internet. But he can be discreet when he wants to."

"He said there were no cameras around Shana's apartment."

"And he was right," Sloan reminded. "Maybe one of the neighbors will remember something by now."

They sure hadn't the night before. Even immersed in her

own shock and cold, Ronnie had expected someone to know something, have seen something, and come forward. Unfortunately there were quite a few empty units in the building. So far, those neighbors who had been home, had sworn they hadn't heard a thing.

"We need to talk to Evan again," Ronnie stated firmly.

"We?"

She was about to argue her case to be included in whatever he was investigating, but the words died on her lips when she realized there was the faintest of smiles hovering around his.

"Another shower?" he suggested with a lifted brow.

She snuggled close to him once more. "Maybe not just yet..."

Four hours and a long shower later, Sloan was dressed in his clothes from the night before, his collar open, his jaw unshaven. Ronnie had put on jeans and a thick sweater but was still barefoot as they stood together in her living room.

Sloan was scrolling through the messages on his cell. "Nadia Lloyd called me. No voice mail. I need to stop by and see her," he said without looking up.

Nadia had obviously been alerted to the painful news about Shana. "I don't think she'd want me to go with you," said Ronnie.

Sloan gave a slight nod. "Probably not. I'll talk to Roberts and then head over there around ten, maybe." He lifted his head to peer outside her window toward the highway where the first flakes of a winter snowfall were gently wafting downward.

"I want to help in the investigations."

"I know, but first let's get breakfast. I didn't get much dinner, how about you?"

"No dinner, and yes to breakfast. But you're not answering me." She wasn't about to be put off.

"You're a civilian and—"

"Who's helped the police before."

"—that's not my decision to make."

"A cop-out, no pun intended," she grumbled. "I can help. I've helped before. Just aim me in the right direction. Any job you can't do, or don't want to do, or... what?"

Something she'd said had caught his attention. "We can talk about it on the way," he said, heading for the door.

"Let me get my shoes..."

By the time she met him at the door he'd clearly thought over her plea. "There's maybe one thing you can do. Townsend told me to stay away from Clint Mercer. He thinks I headed in the wrong direction with Clint. I don't think Clint killed Melissa. It doesn't fit. But he knows something. If I'd been able to press him last night, he would have told me what that was, but Brandy was there and she was running interference. Maybe you can get past it with her."

"You forget. Brandy blames me for siccing you on Clint."

"Tell her I'm off the case. See what she says."

"If she even takes my call. A big if. But I'll do it," she added swiftly, sensing he was about to shut down the discussion entirely.

They headed out the door and she glanced toward Angel's place. Still dark. Still not home... A bad feeling was beginning to worm its way through her, but then she'd had a lot of those lately.

"What?" Sloan asked, following her gaze.

"Just wondering where Angel's been."

She headed down the steps, which were quickly being disguised beneath a building layer of snow.

"I'll pick you up around four," Harley said to Emma as she navigated her car through the streets and noticed the beautiful white swirls sweeping across her windshield, the wipers flicking off the dry snow before it had a chance to melt. Harley wasn't all that adept at driving in the white stuff, but the weather reporter had assured her it would stop by one p.m., two at the latest. It damn well better.

Emma, seated in the passenger seat, was scheduled for a shift at Theo's Thrift Shop and she was determined to go even with the change in the weather. The store wasn't normally open on Sundays, and it shut its doors at the merest hint of inclement weather, but they were having a heavily advertised pre-Christmas sale today, which was always busy, no matter if the sky rained down cats, dogs and frogs.

"I will call you," said Emma as they passed the park where kids in jackets, scarves and mittens were already trying to scoop up snowballs and chase each other.

Harley regarded Emma carefully. Since their talk about Mary Jo and the Heart of Sunshine Church, Emma had been remarkably quiet. It didn't bode well. Emma rarely, if ever, hid things, but she was certainly being careful now.

Harley said, "Don't do anything I wouldn't do. Actually, don't do anything I would do. Just stay out of it, okay?"

Emma was staring through the windshield. "What wouldn't you do?"

"Never mind. Just don't leave the thrift shop."

Emma said tonelessly, "I have a work shift."

"I know. I know. I just want you to stay on the shift the whole time."

"I will unless I see the van."

"That's what I mean," Harley said in exasperation. "Don't get in the van. Is Theo going to be there today? You stay with her."

"Who's going to follow Mary Jo?" Emma asked.

"I will. Don't worry. I'm on it. I'm going to park outside Mary Jo's house or something. She's not going back to that cult until she has our baby."

"Jamie and Cooper's baby," corrected Emma.

"That's right," Harley agreed. Geez. Sometimes Emma could be so literal. "So . . . trust me. Okay, Emma? I'll take care of everything."

"I trust you, Harley."

"Good."

Was Emma understanding the gravity of the situation? It was so hard to tell sometimes. "Just stay at the thrift shop," Harley repeated as she pulled into the store's back parking lot and Emma climbed out.

As she watched her aunt head toward the rear door in her familiar plodding walk and finally enter, Harley let out her breath. She gazed through the windshield and upward to the falling flakes. Mary Jo was supposed to have her baby late January, but it didn't hurt to ask, did it?

*God, if you're up there, would you mind bringing that baby in about a month early? No pressure, and everything needs to be A-OK. Just asking. For my mom ... and dad ... and Emma.*

For breakfast, Ronnie chose Lucille's again and she ordered oatmeal with a swirl of maple syrup and pecans, while Sloan chose an egg-bacon scramble with thick slices of wheat toast, which came with a trio of toppings: peach and blackberry jam and orange marmalade. They both dug in as if they were starving to death as Ronnie had missed dinner entirely and she'd learned Sloan's last meal was two street tacos around three p.m. Shana's death had curbed any desire for food, but after an enthusiastic night of lovemaking, they both needed fuel.

Ronnie tried not to keep looking at him across the table, but it was difficult. He was serious and the planes of his face could look harsh, but he was a warm and giving lover and she ... felt herself *blushing*, which was such bullshit!

"What?" he asked, glancing up.

"Was there anything else at the clearing and shed? Something forensics discovered?" she asked a bit desperately, trying to hide her feelings.

"I gave the residue I collected from Mercer's truck bed and pictures of his tires to my contact at the lab."

"Anything else? Something you can tell me, maybe I can use to press Clint?"

"The forensics report will likely be ready this week. Why? Are you looking for something in particular?"

"No ..." She could tell she'd piqued his curiosity, but she really just wanted to distract herself from thinking about the feel of his mouth on hers, the hard muscles beneath the skin of his back, the weight of his body ...

"You're holding something back." His eyes bored into hers as she stirred her oatmeal to keep from thinking about last night. "Did you *see* something?"

"No! Uh . . . not this time. I just want to help and thought maybe you knew something more."

"What kind of help do you mean?" He took a bite of toast.

"Are we talking in circles? I just told you," she said. "Something to help with Clint."

"You're not going to try and do something . . . extraordinary . . . are you?" A line had formed between his brows.

"You mean like . . . look into a crystal ball?" she asked before taking an experimental swallow of the warm oatmeal.

He held up his hands. "You were the one who said you don't have any control over your ability."

"That's mainly true," she admitted.

"Mainly?"

"You're still having trouble with it, aren't you?" she stated flatly.

"You think I should just accept that . . . you . . . that . . . you're . . . ?"

". . . a crazy loon? The woman you just spent the night making love to is batshit crazy?"

"Did I say that?" he demanded.

"Kinda. Almost."

"I don't understand your . . . ability. That's what I'm saying. I don't understand it at all, but there is something there," he continued, when she would have broken in. "You have *something* . . . You saw Shana's body, and you didn't have time to kill her before we both got there."

"Well, thanks for that."

"This is what a prosecutor would say, if you were ever on the stand, which you can't be, because psychic phenomena don't count in court. So, when I state a fact, like I just did, look at it from outside of yourself. Think like a juror would. If it was anyone but you, would you believe they got psychic messages?"

She hated to admit that he was right. "I'm not the only one."

"Yes, you are," he said simply, and for a moment she wasn't sure they were still on the same topic.

They finished their meal and Sloan insisted on paying, quickly overriding Ronnie's protests to put in half, and they headed for his SUV. Maybe she was being unfair, trying to root out his ingrained beliefs in one fell swoop. She just wanted him to believe in her.

*Celebrate how far he's come, not how far he has to go.*

Easier said than done . . .

"Someone killed Shana, and Melissa McNulty, and it's all happening around you," Sloan said as he turned the corner and Ronnie's apartment building loomed within sight.

Well . . . hell . . . he was right about that, too.

He found a spot near the stairs in the parking lot and seemed intent on walking her up to her unit, saying, "I'll come back after I see Nadia and before I call on Hugh Mc—"

"I'll just call Brandy and go from there."

"The more I think about it, it's dangerous for you to—"

"You said yourself that you don't think Clint could hurt Mel."

"Stop interrupting, Quick. We're talking homicide. Police business. I don't want—"

"*You* stop interrupting," she said. "And last night you called me Ronnie."

"—anything to happen to you." He stopped. Then added, "That was personal."

She narrowed her eyes at him. "And this isn't? What's the difference?"

"We've got two homicides by strangulation. Less and less I'm liking your involvement in this."

"*I* came to *you* with my vision. I've been in this from the start. And by the way, that's not how this works. You don't get to decide when I'm in or out. My gift doesn't work on your timetable."

He almost laughed. "I got that. I just don't want you to get hurt."

"Noted. And I don't want you to get hurt, either."

He'd gotten out of the car and tiny drifting flakes of white were settling on his hair, shoulders and lashes. The snow had lessened, but still hadn't gone away entirely.

"I'm good," she said, holding up a hand to let him know he didn't have to follow her upstairs.

"Yes. You are."

Even though it sounded like a joke, he looked very serious. Ronnie half wanted to give him a hug, or kiss, or something, but it felt awkward. After last night everything should be natural and *loving* . . . but instead she felt like there was something missing.

*He doesn't trust you.*

She gave him a wave and then hurried up the stairs, glancing back to see his Bronco reverse out of the lot, leaving two tracks through the building snow.

Out of the corner of her eye she thought she saw Angel, leaning against the rail to his apartment, but when she turned fully to look, there was no one there.

A lot like when she'd seen Jesse Taft's sister, Helene, except that her image had lasted more than an instant. Or, maybe she hadn't seen Angel? Maybe she just wanted to see him.

She stopped outside his apartment door, hesitating. Throwing off her misgivings, she gave the panels a few good hard knocks, but once again no one answered. For someone who'd been hanging around a lot before, he was sure MIA now. Okay, the weather had changed, but it hadn't been exactly warm and toasty before.

She withdrew her cell from her purse and texted his number.

**You around?**

Maybe he was just busy, she thought, and watched as a man walking his dog, the pug in a red and green sweater, crossed the street, then seeing no return text from Angel, she found her key. He'd text when he was ready.

Inside her own place, she stamped snow off her boots and hung her jacket on the hook behind the door. She was tired . . . and sore . . . and kind of giddy, even with Sloan and her awkward goodbye just now. And she was also filled with that twisting worry that was going to be with her until she learned who had killed both Mel and Shana, whether the perpetrator was one and the same or not. Maybe the two deaths were unrelated, but it sure as hell didn't feel that way.

She wondered if she should contact Evan.

She and Sloan hadn't really discussed whether Caldwell, with all his information resources, had been at least peripherally involved in Shana's killing, maybe telling the wrong person something key. She suspected Sloan planned to check in with Evan on his own, but Ronnie wanted to be part of that, too.

She carried her cell into her bedroom, her eyes sliding to the bed that they'd straightened but that sparked her imagination again, remembering the tossed covers, questing hands, hot mouths and tongues, hard muscles, deep rhythm. Had that really happened? Yes, of course it had! She could feel it in every movement in a good, somewhat breath-catching way.

But breakfast had been so *normal*, a world apart from a night she already wanted to repeat. And now...

*You should have gone with him to see Nadia.*

He wouldn't have had it.

She sank onto the end of the bed. She was torn between laughing and crying. Didn't know which. There was the joy she'd reveled in with Sloan, and the horror of Shana's death, and Mel's...

Shaking herself back to the present, she screwed up her courage to text Brandy: **Could we talk? Neither Sloan or I think Clint would harm Mel. I just want**

She stopped. What did she want?

*To be with Sloan. Happy. Without these questions and worries and visions.*

Well, that wasn't going to happen. She thought hard for several minutes then gave up on texting completely, placing a call to Brandy instead, heart rate speeding with nerves. Texts were too impersonal, or they sounded like nothing she wanted to convey. Know-it-all and cold. She needed to talk to Brandy, leave her a message.

She didn't expect Brandy to answer. For all Ronnie knew, Brandy could be shunning her calls, at work, busy in some other regard, so she was prepared when the call went to voice mail. As soon as she heard the beep, she said, "Brandy, I never thought Clint had anything to do with Mel's death. I just want to help prove his innocence. Would you call me?" Her throat grew hot and her last, "Please?" came out in a strangled gasp. She clicked off and tossed the phone onto the bed.

Ugh. Shit! She sounded so desperate. Not how she wanted to be at all.

"Get over yourself," she advised as she walked into the bathroom and stared at her reflection, expecting the events of the past hours to have somehow changed her, but she looked utterly the same. Pale. A few damp spots in her hair where snowflakes had melted. A bit anxious, maybe, but that was how she'd felt for days.

In the mirror, a shadow passed behind her.

*What?*

She whipped around, heart thumping. "Hello?" she demanded.

No answer.

Cautiously, she stuck her head out of the bathroom door, her gaze scouring the bedroom. Nothing. No one. Quickly she searched the rest of her apartment, throwing open closets, testing the locks on the front and balcony doors, checking the back deck itself.

Again, nothing.

This had never happened before.

This was new.

And she didn't like it.

Nerves tight, she peered out the windows and checked the latches on the door. Had she imagined the whole thing? But no, her rapidly beating heart and prickled skin convinced her that she'd seen something.

And it wasn't good.

When she had a vision, it sometimes took her over but generally only when she was sleeping. She'd stumbled outside her front door when she'd had the vision about Shana, and that first vision of Mel she'd been standing in the kitchen, but usually she was aware of her surroundings. Now, all bets were off. And she was seeing things. Ghosts. She cocked an ear, half expected to hear the dog barking again, but apart from the soft rumbling of the unit's furnace, and the hum of the refrigerator, the rooms remained quiet.

Something had changed, but what?

She felt it, a slight charge in the atmosphere.

*Your mother saw things at the end.*

Slowly, throat dry, she walked back into the bedroom, listening hard, looking around the room. What had she seen in the mirror? Movement... someone walking by? A trick of light?

It had been something, hadn't it?

Her gaze swept across the top of her small bureau. A picture of her mother, a secret smile curving her lips as she stared back at Ronnie. A shot taken from before Ronnie was born. Before Winnie's own gift had grown into a monster.

Her heart clutched. Was this how it started?

Beside her mother's picture was Ronnie's jewelry box. Nothing fancy. Something her father had given her, obviously picked out by Aunt Kat, a silver rectangle with two tiers when you opened the lid. She lifted the top, pulling out the upper, black velvety insert, which held earrings and costume jewelry. Beneath it was another level where she'd put the diamond rings Galen had given her. She needed to give them back to him. Was kind of surprised he hadn't asked for them already. They weren't horribly expensive; that wasn't Galen's way, and it wasn't hers, either, but she suddenly wanted them out of her apartment.

She dug her fingers inside for the rings and encountered a silver chain. What? Slowly she lifted it up and suppressed a surprised little cry as she discovered her third of the BFF necklace she'd shared with Brandy and Mel.

Her chest ached and she crushed the necklace in her fist, its sharp edges digging into her flesh. Mel now gone and Brandy angry with her.

Friendship... long ago friendship...

*The woman shivered and counted her many sins... she'd made mistakes... she wasn't good at reading human nature* and it was going to kill her... the dog whined... it wasn't hers but she'd taken it with her for protection.

In the shed... the smell of dirt and damp weeds... couldn't stay here... had to move... run... who to call?

Was someone here? Were those footsteps?

Her hand moved to clasp the rock... if the dog couldn't save her... last defense.

And then...? Not who she expected but the dog...

Bark, bark, BARK!

Slam. Her head hit the wall.

Dazed. Lost... but awake outside... moon glow...

Gloved hands at her neck, squeezing hard, harder!

Dog barking, frantic, tied, chewing rope... growing distant...

"Why? WHY...?"

And the answer came: BECAUSE YOU CHEATED.

Ronnie shot awake from her fugue state. A man's voice. The necklace slid through her nerveless fingers to the floor. Her heart galloped. Fear was ice in her veins. Her fear. *Mel's fear!*

*RING!* Her phone burst into song and she gasped and stumbled backward against the bed, half panicked. Was there someone here? Was she still alone, or that... *person*... that shadow? Was he here?

But she'd checked.

Panic gripped her.

The phone kept ringing, clamoring for attention. She swept it from the bed, glancing around the room. How long had she been out? Seconds? Minutes? What was happening?

She looked down at the caller. *Brandy.* Thank God...! Reaching down to the floor for the necklace, she answered the call. "Hey," she whispered, her voice strangled.

"Hi," Brandy responded diffidently. "I got your message."

"Good. Good. I'm so glad to hear from you!" Still she peered around the room, by the bureau, to the window, behind the door and into the closet where the doors were open.

"Okay." A pause. Then, "What's wrong?"

"Nothing. Nothing. I'm just... I want to help so badly. I want to help you... help Clint."

"Now?" Brandy snorted, her disbelief audible.

"I always wanted to help," Ronnie insisted. "And... Sloan doesn't think Clint is involved, either."

"Sure about that?"

"The evidence Sloan collected from Clint's truck may well exonerate him. *Will* exonerate him. I'm sure of it, but—"

"He's gone," she bit out.

"—I think we can..." Ronnie forced herself to slow down her apologetic rush. To quickly recheck the bedroom. To focus. "Gone? Gone, how?" What was she saying?

"He's gone to find Mel's other lovers," Brandy explained. "He feels he has to prove himself now. I tried to talk him out of it, but he's not listening to me. Now he's in danger, thanks to you and Sloan. If one of those guys killed Mel, and Clint goes after them, they could kill him, too!"

"Do you know who they are?" demanded Ronnie.

"No, I don't *know* them, but I've heard of them. Clint, though, he knows 'em."

"But you know their names?" Ronnie demanded.

"Well, yeah, but—"

"Give them to me. We can ask Evan Caldwell about them. Sloan probably already knows who they are, too. I could call him, but—"

"I'm not talking to Sloan!" Brandy bit out.

"I know you don't think you want him involved... which you've made clear. But you said it could be dangerous. And Sloan could help."

"You're not listening, Ronnie! All I want to do is stop Clint. That's all. And, you're right, I don't want Sloan Hart involved."

"But—"

"Do you have Evan's number?" Brandy cut in.

"Yes..."

"Will you give it to me?" Her voice was low, questioning where Ronnie's loyalties lay.

"Let me call Evan," Ronnie suggested, thinking quickly. "I'll call you right back. Are you working today?"

"Not till tomorrow."

"Good . . . okay . . . we could . . . er . . . go look for Clint together?"

She waited tensely, afraid Brandy would reject her like she was rejecting Sloan. But after a moment, Brandy said carefully, "Okay."

"Okay." Ronnie cleared her throat. "I'll call Evan and come to your place?"

"Uh-huh . . ." Brandy sounded like her mind was already far away. "You know what Clint said to me? 'She was a cheater at heart, but I loved her.' I don't know what he'll do when he sees these guys . . . what they'll do."

BECAUSE YOU CHEATED.

"We'll find him," assured Ronnie. "I'll be there soon."

She clicked off. Took several deep breaths. Felt like she'd run a marathon. She wanted to call Sloan, but stopped herself, knowing if Brandy found out that would be the end.

And he was with Nadia Lloyd.

Those dream fragments . . . they were from what she hadn't been able to recall. Had Mel . . . or Mel's spirit . . . sent the message?

She looked down at the necklace curled on the floor, picked it up again and balled it within the tight fist of her left hand. Thinking hard, she felt the sharp edges against her skin again. When she loosened her fingers, her skin was grooved where she'd squeezed the shard. Expelling a breath, she clasped the necklace around her own neck and tucked it beneath her collar.

As she was heading out the door—double-checking that it was locked tight—she put a call into Evan Caldwell and heard him click on. "Hi, Evan, it's Ronnie."

"Veronica Quick," he said and she heard the smile in his voice, as if he'd been expecting her. "I recognized your number right off." He chuckled. "You and Sloan set the date yet?"

Ignoring that, she went right to the point. "You alluded to Mel having affairs with other men. You know who they are."

"Didn't I say I did?"

"You know where they live?" she asked tightly.

"Well, yes I do. Funny, you're the second person asking for their addresses," he said, still toying with her.

"Sloan?" God, he could be irritating. She hurried down the steps to the parking lot and unlocked her car remotely as she talked.

"Well, him, too, but Clint caught me early this morning. Nice to be needed."

"I thought Clint already had that information."

"Not the addresses. I got the impression he wanted to set some things straight. Why?" he asked, with genuine curiosity. "What's your deal?"

"Can you give me those names and addresses?" Ronnie said, feeling tense, sensing that the passage of time was against her somehow. She unlocked her Escape and slid into the cold interior.

"You think one of the men Melissa was fucking killed her. Or, oh wait, did you *see* it?"

"I saw someone," she stated flatly, starting the SUV and turning on the defroster to clear the windows. "Figuring out who that is now."

"Okay, okay. Catch up with Clint and you can form a posse together." A few moments later he gave her the information.

Caldwell was still a dick, she thought, backing out of the parking space, but he was handy with information.

# Chapter 19

The first address on their list was for one Benjamin Neel. Ronnie had punched it into the GPS on her phone.

"I've heard about him from Clint," said Brandy from the passenger seat as she wound a scarf around her neck. Her hair was pulled into a thick ponytail and she was wearing a puffy jacket over a sweater and warm leggings. Ronnie had driven to her place and picked her up. "He's in chemistry... maybe a chemical engineer, I guess. Maybe? Anyway, Clint calls him Benzene. They only know each other through Hugh, I think."

Ronnie wondered about that. Had anyone talked to Mel's husband? Certainly the police, though Sloan hadn't mentioned it.

"And we're sure Mel was involved with Neel?"

"I'm not sure about anything anymore," Brandy admitted as she stared out the passenger window.

The wipers were swishing wet snow, almost rain, off the windshield. Ronnie's gaze kept sliding to the map on her phone's app to make sure she was heading the right way. The interior of the vehicle was warm, but tense. She and Brandy hadn't talked about the new rip in the fabric of their friendship. Brandy didn't seem to want to address it, and that was fine with Ronnie. For now.

"Benzene is sort of a loner. More of an animal guy, I guess. But he moved in on Mel behind Hugh's back. Clint said it was brief, but he doesn't think Benzene got over it when Mel moved on."

"When did Clint and Mel get together?" Ronnie asked diffidently. She didn't want to set Brandy off on another tirade about Clint's innocence.

"After Benzene, but before Erik Wetherly. In between them."

Wetherly was supposedly Mel's other lover, and they were going to see him next.

It was uncomfortable, dissecting Mel's life like this. Whatever choices she'd made were hers to make. No judgment. But it was all they had to work with today.

Brandy was staring out the side window at the passing cityscape as they headed west out of River Glen toward Laurelton. "Hugh's kind of wealthy. Well, he is wealthy, in my book anyway. Mel gravitated to him because of his money, at least in the beginning. But she flirted with Clint. And I guess Benzene and Wetherly." Brandy gave a sad little laugh at the memory of her friend. "Mel was a terrible flirt. I hope to God Clint isn't planning something crazy."

"You think he is?"

"Yes? No?" She shook her head. "He's been insane since Mel died."

Ronnie didn't comment.

Twenty minutes later they pulled into an older, pocket neighborhood. Tucked into a cul-de-sac with similar homes on all sides, Neel's house was a gray, shingled, daylight basement with a neat sidewalk leading to a small porch.

Clint's truck was not in the driveway, nor anywhere Ronnie could see in the neighborhood.

"He's not here," Brandy muttered on a sigh of relief. "Don't park. Let's go to Erik Wetherly's."

"Too late. There's someone coming out of the front door now." Ronnie watched as a man about their age, maybe a little older, walked out with a large, white and gray dog on a leash, some kind of "Doodle" mix.

Ronnie edged her car to the side of the road. Both she and Brandy observed the man come toward them on the sidewalk. Long-faced and frowning, he wore black jogging gear, had dark clipped hair, a baseball cap on his head and was barking orders at the dog straining on the leash. "This way. Jude. Leave it!"

"That's him," said Brandy, nodding to herself. "I've seen a picture."

"Let's ask him if he's seen Clint."

Now that they were here, Brandy seemed reluctant to move, but she opened the passenger door just as Neel reached the Escape. As she stepped onto the curb, the dog immediately veered toward her, nearly bounding while Neel, commanded, "Stop. Jude! Heel!"

Regardless of Neel's orders, the dog stretched the leash to sniff Brandy's outstretched hand.

"It's fine," said Brandy, letting Jude smell her until the dog allowed her to rub its head. "Are you Benjamin Neel? Benzene?"

He stopped short, suddenly wary, as if afraid of being attacked. "Who're you?" he demanded as Ronnie circled the Escape, stepping over slush piled near the curb and onto the sidewalk. All the while Ronnie kept her gaze trained on the dog.

"Hi, I'm Brandy. Clint Mercer's sister," Brandy said. "So this is Jude?" she asked, patting the dog's head.

Alarm flared in Neel's brown eyes. "Yes. Jude, sit!" He jerked on the leash and stepped back, his eyes leveled at the two women. "What do you want?"

"Clint's missing and we're worried about him," Ronnie put in and quickly introduced herself.

"Have you seen him?" asked Brandy.

"Have I seen him?" he repeated angrily. "You bet I have! He damn near took my head off! You find him, keep him away from me. You hear? I'll file charges! He's out of his friggin' mind! I mean it." Neel motioned to the dog. "Luckily I had Jude with me."

Jude whined and looked from Brandy to Ronnie, her legs stiff, poised.

"I'm sorry," said Brandy, clearly meaning it. "I'm sure he didn't mean to—"

"We're trying to make sure he's okay," Ronnie cut in.

Neel laughed a bit hysterically. "He's okay for a psycho! I was this close"—he held up his free hand, index finger and thumb nearly touching—"this close to calling the police. He's damned lucky I didn't. For God's sake, he accused me of killing Hugh's wife!" He shook his head in disbelief while the dog whined, anxious for the walk. "Melissa and I, we hooked up a few times. That's all it was. Well, except that she took the dog."

"What dog? You gave her a dog?" asked Ronnie, instantly on alert.

"More like she took it. A mutt. I didn't have it all that long. I swear that dog had a thing for her." And then he stopped his rant and his face instantly crumpled. "Shit." For a moment it looked like he was about to break down altogether. "Didn't we all," he added miserably, all of his earlier bravado and insistence that Mel meant nothing to him dissolving into the cold winter air.

"What kind of dog was it?" Ronnie asked, squinting against the falling snowflakes, but undeterred by his sudden display of emotion.

He blinked a few times, likely coming back from memories of Mel. "Melissa's dead. And you're asking about the mutt?"

"I just wonder what happened to it," explained Ronnie. "What's it look like?"

"Like a mutt. Medium sized, I guess. Black and brown. A stray that just hung out for a few days."

He eyed Ronnie and scowled. "What's your deal? I don't know what you're getting at but, just so you're clear about things, it wasn't Jude that bit Mercer. It was that damned mutt."

Brandy gasped.

"Whoa, wait. The dog—the one you call the mutt—bit Clint?" queried Ronnie.

"That's what I said."

"When?" Ronnie asked. "Today?"

"No! I told you she took it."

"When?"

Neel glowered at her and Ronnie felt the chill of snowflakes melting in her hair, water dripping down the back of her neck. "Who the hell knows?" Neel said. "The last time she was here."

"But Clint, he was just here?" She looked at Brandy, who seemed to be struggling to take in what Benzene was saying. "Today?"

"Hell yeah! Didn't I say so? Just about half an hour ago. Maybe forty-five minutes. Fucker was out of his mind. I should've called the police. Your psycho brother *threatened* me!" Scowling, he looked from Brandy to Ronnie. "We're done here." With that he yanked hard on Jude's leash, turning the dog around and jogging back to his house. He disappeared inside, the door slamming firmly behind him.

Brandy took a step toward the walkway, but Ronnie grabbed her arm. "That's all we're gonna get from him," she said, glancing around at the cul-de-sac to the other houses, but no one else was out, no one peering through the windows where garlands were strung and doors decorated with wreaths and strings of lights.

*Merry Christmas*, Ronnie thought sarcastically as she shepherded Brandy into her SUV again, then settled herself behind the wheel. She felt buzzy and strangely wired, with weariness crouching like a beast underneath. Her lack of sleep was a bill she was going to have to pay sooner rather than later. She wanted to confide to Brandy about her night with Sloan, but that was clearly a no-go right now.

"It's not true," said Brandy in a dead voice once Ronnie had started the Escape.

*What part of it?* Ronnie thought, but didn't ask.

"Clint's not that way," Brandy added, adjusting her ponytail, but her unhappy expression belied her words. "Why'd you ask so many questions about the dog?"

"Was Clint bitten by a dog?"

"No." Then she grew silent and a bit of color entered her cheeks. "No."

*You were just lied to, Ronnie.* She started the Escape and pulled away from the curb. As she drove around the curve of the cul-de-sac, she cast a glance at Neel's house, and thought she saw him peering through the blinds.

"We're going to Wetherly's, right?" Brandy asked, her jaw tight, her hands balled into fists.

"You sure?"

"I need to find Clint," she said sharply, glancing out the side window.

"Then, yeah." Not that there had been any doubt. She drove steadily back toward River Glen and then headed to the city's northern edge, to another older neighborhood where the streets were laid out in a grid. The snow had all but quit falling. Only a few lonely flakes drifted from the steely sky.

Erik Wetherly lived on Eagle Drive in a faux Bavarian three-story home, snow melting on the dark brown crisscrossed boards across the house's tan face. Its mullioned windows glittering in the afternoon sun, their leaded glass, beveled panes staring down at the street as if glaring at the vehicles parked on both sides. And parked in the driveway was a dirty pickup.

"Clint's truck," said Brandy, voice tight, muscles tense.

"Right." Ronnie had spotted the white Ford at the same time and was girding herself for whatever came next. By Benzene's description, Clint was in fight mode. She jockeyed into a tight parking space and glanced toward her purse, which was sitting in the console between herself and Brandy. The light from her cell phone had flashed on from inside a pocket.

A text . . . from Sloan? The ringer was on silent, but she didn't dare check it without risking Brandy's ire.

"You ready?" Ronnie asked Brandy, whose determined gaze was pinned on the house as they both got out of the SUV.

Then Brandy stopped at the front yard and anxiously turned to Ronnie. "You don't . . . think he did it, do you? You know, by mistake."

Ronnie didn't know what to think anymore. "We should call Sloan."

"No! God, Ronnie. He's the police! I need to talk to Clint.

Please." She pressed her hand to her mouth, suddenly unsure and scared, very unlike the Brandy Ronnie had always known.

A dull crash sounded from inside the house.

*Uh-oh*... Ronnie exchanged a glance with Brandy, whose face had slackened in horror.

"What was that?" asked Brandy.

"Nothin' good—" Ronnie started, but Brandy was already jogging forward, breaking into a run through the snow in the front yard, Ronnie on her heels and fumbling in her purse for her phone. She heard the sound of breaking glass just as she reached the porch and caught a glimpse of the text from Sloan:

**Met with Nadia. How're you doing?**

She didn't have time to text back as she ran after Brandy and up the short flight of concrete steps to the front door, left ajar.

Oh, God.

Angry voices reached them from the top of the stairs that ran up one wall. Men's voices. Raised in fury. Screaming obscenities.

One of the voices was Clint's.

"Clint!" Brandy shrieked at the top of her lungs, starting for the stairs.

*Thunk!*

"Fuck!" Clint yelled back. Maybe not at her.

Ronnie was trying to call Sloan when a barrel-chested man appeared at the top of the staircase.

With a glance over his shoulder, he rushed down at them.

Brandy backed up a step.

Straight into Ronnie.

Her cell went flying through the air, toppling down the wooden steps as she grasped for the railing to keep from tumbling backward.

"He's trying to kill me!" the man yelled, breathing hard, his eyes wild, his face a mottled red. "That fucker's trying to fuckin' kill me!"

"Clint!" Brandy yelled again.

"You know him?" the man demanded, stopping suddenly.

He grabbed Brandy's arm, preventing from her climbing further up the staircase.

"He's my brother! Clint! Are you okay?"

The man—Wetherly, Ronnie assumed—held a small dumbbell in his free hand, his fingers clenched around it as if it were a weapon.

"I—I had to hit him," he said, dazed, looking at the bloodied hand weight as if he'd never seen it before.

Brandy scrambled out of his grasp.

Ronnie, too, shoved past the man. He lunged for her jacket, but couldn't catch her as she scurried up the stairs a step behind her friend.

Frantic, Brandy muttered, "Oh, God . . . oh, God . . ."

From below, Wetherly bellowed, "I had to take it from him! He came at me with it! Blames me for something I didn't do!"

Ronnie stopped short at the landing.

Clint was stretched out on a faded red carpet runner, blood pooling into the fibers from a gash in his head.

"No!" Brandy screamed. She sank to her knees beside Clint, grabbing his wrist, checking his pulse. His eyelids were fluttering. Ronnie could see his chest rise and fall, rise and fall, rise and fall. He was alive! But behind her, she heard the steady, heavy tread, the labored breathing of Wetherly.

"Get away from him," Wetherly ordered as he reached the upper floor and took in the scene. "He's fucking crazy!" Frantically Ronnie scanned the hallway for any kind of weapon.

"I'm a nurse," Brandy said angrily, ignoring the fact that Wetherly was twice her size and holding the blood-stained hand weight.

"He gets up, I'm gonna hit him again," Wetherly warned, holding the dumbbell fast. "I already called the police."

Only then did Ronnie hear the sirens sounding far away, but growing closer.

"Clint," Brandy said brokenly. "Clint."

"He said I made him do it," said Wetherly, backing up a step as the sirens screamed nearer.

Good.

"You made him do it?" Ronnie gave the big man her full attention, but all the fight had apparently gone out of Wetherly as he finally dropped the weight to his side and leaned against the wall.

Within seconds flashing red and blue and white lights strobed through the beveled panes.

Thank God, Ronnie didn't need to call Sloan. The River Glen police were already here.

Sighing, knowing the police would want statements, that she would have to answer a bevy of questions, she glanced back toward Clint, who turned his head and looked her way.

*I didn't mean to hurt her . . .* he said, rising upward, his slack lips not matching the words.

This time, as she watched a ghost ascend, Ronnie managed to keep herself from screaming.

Sloan's fingers tightened over the steering wheel as he drove back to his You+Me apartment after his meeting with Nadia. *That* had been a tough meet-up. Nadia's grief had solidified to anger since she'd been told the night before of Shana's death.

"That conniving witch you brought here? She's the one responsible for my girl's death!" Nadia had blasted him, her face twisted in grief.

"What?" was all he managed to ask, he'd been so taken aback.

Nadia had pointed a finger at him. "I know she's the one you saved from drowning that day at The Pond. The psychic girl. I know who she is! Don't think I don't. What did she do to my girl, Sloan? What did she *do* to her?"

"Nadia, we don't know, yet, what happened to Shana." He'd said it quietly, hoping to calm her.

"Shana was *strangled*! And if that psychic witch didn't do it, she had someone do it for her!"

"She had no reason to hurt Shana," Sloan had tried to explain.

"She has *you.*"

Sloan had opened his mouth to deny it, but images from the night before in bed with Ronnie crowded his mind. Nadia had catalogued his hesitation with a hard, miserable smile and tears glistening in her eyes. "Go away. Leave me be. You weren't there for Shana when she needed you. You were with *that woman.*"

"I'm going to find out who killed Shana," he'd assured her.

"Tell me you're not with that devil's spawn. Tell me you didn't . . ." She'd glanced him over. "You're in the same clothes. Oh, for God's sake. You spent the night with her, didn't you?"

"Shana's murder is my priority."

"You . . . *liar.*"

So much for offering comfort to Shana's mother. He'd left feeling like he'd let her down and had sent a text to Quick, needing to make contact.

He'd planned on interviewing Hugh McNulty himself, as he'd told Townsend, but the man was meeting a friend for an afternoon of watching NFL games. Not exactly pining over his wife's death, but then everyone grieved in their own way. Sloan had run into the same thing before. Sometimes the survivor of a violent death was stricken, wailing, lost in clear misery, sometimes they were in a state of suspended shock, but sometimes, like maybe this time, they completely compartmentalized the tragedy and moved on with their life as if nothing had happened. Didn't mean they were a killer, or a sociopath. Townsend didn't seem to think McNulty was either, and maybe he wasn't. Sloan planned to meet up with the man and take his measure of him, one way or another.

But after Nadia . . . and McNulty wrapped in his circle of friends . . . Sloan had decided to head to home base for a change of clothes. Didn't need a shower. He'd had a couple of those already.

Memories of the night before peeked into his brain as he parked. Quick softly moaning as her heart raced in tandem to his . . . the tangle of her arms and legs . . . her fingers digging into the flesh of his back . . . the sweet, hot pleasure of her mouth on him . . .

Damn. It was unexpected... and breathtaking... and had unleashed a craving that was frankly new to him. The hours it would take before he could be with her again felt like a punishment.

He didn't believe in predestiny... unexplainable abilities... hocus-pocus... He'd always lived by empirical data, that which could be tested, verified...

But now...?

Now, he was under Veronica Quick's spell.

Inside his place he quickly changed into jeans, sweater and insulated jacket. The snow flurries were slowing, but it was still freezing outside and, well, he might not come home to sleep again tonight. He hoped to hell he didn't come home to sleep tonight, as a matter of fact, he thought with a smile.

Tomorrow was Monday and Detective Verbena would be back. Sloan planned to get up early, head home from Quick's apartment to change again, check in with Townsend... and quit. The way he'd been summarily told how to run his case when Townsend had told him not to interview Clint Mercer had proved to him that there would be no independence under the sheriff. No original thought or planning. He'd been grateful for the job Townsend had given him, but he was going to try for River Glen P.D. full time.

It might not work. Detective Haynes's leave would end and he would be back on the force, leaving no other spot available on the River Glen roster. Didn't matter. It was a chance he was willing to take.

On the drive back toward the RGPD station, he checked his phone to see if Quick had read or returned his text. Not yet. Was she with Brandy? And had they contacted Clint? He felt uncomfortable with them out in the field, so to speak, even while he reminded himself that Mercer wasn't a violent man and Brandy was his sister.

His phone buzzed.

Evan Caldwell.

A call, not a text. "Hart," he answered, the phone clipped to his dash as he negotiated traffic.

"Thought you'd already be at the scene with your girlfriend."

Sloan froze for a moment. Caldwell loved being able to hoard and disseminate information at his whim. "What scene?"

"Name Erik Wetherly mean anything to you?"

Was there a smile in Caldwell's voice?

"You said he was one of Melissa McNulty's relationships," Sloan answered tightly.

"Relationships? Hookups. Meaningless fucks, something like that."

"What. Happened?" Sloan demanded.

"Did your psychic sweetie have a vision, or something?" he asked curiously.

"Get to the point, Caldwell."

"Okay, okay. It looks like Mercer got himself a trip to Glen Gen after a fight with Wetherly. Brandy and your fiancée were there." He paused for dramatic effect, but Sloan didn't rise to bait. "Thought she woulda contacted you by now."

Police scanners. Caldwell followed them religiously. "Where was the fight?"

"Wetherly's house. Hey, when you talk to Madame Veronica, tell her to give me a call. I've got some information for her."

"What information?"

"Family background shit. Nothing for you to be so tense about, bro. Go. Find out what's happening with Mercer at the hospital. Talk to you later."

As soon as Caldwell disconnected, Sloan texted Quick again. No immediate response. What the hell? He hit his Favorites key, which now listed Veronica Quick among the less than ten names he considered reliable friends. Caldwell's name wasn't on it. Neither was Mercer's.

He punched in Ronnie's number and waited with growing anxiety. What had happened?

No answer.

Not good.

Twisting the wheel, he headed for River Glen General Hospital.

*Knight in shining armor bullshit, bro?*

Evan Caldwell hadn't actually said those words, but they echoed in Sloan's head as if he had.

Keeping up with the speeding ambulance, Ronnie wheeled into Glen Gen's parking lot bare moments behind it. Brandy was practically out of the Escape before it had fully stopped. Ronnie racewalked behind her as she waited on one foot and then the other for Clint's gurney to be lifted out of the back of the ambulance and snapped up to waist height before being pushed through the double doors into the ER.

They were waved toward the front of the building by a security guard stationed inside, but Brandy spit out, "Brandy Mercer. I'm a nurse here and that's my brother," and strode on past him, Ronnie at her heels.

Clint was taken down a short hallway, past a large window where the ER staff worked amongst myriads of screens. The gurney was pushed into a small room and a nurse greeted Brandy politely, but requested that they stay outside until they assessed Clint's condition.

Clint's eyes were open, but he didn't seem to be aware of what was going on . . . until his gaze drifted toward Ronnie and his attention sharpened. With effort, he said, "I followed her to that shed. You know already. Don't even need the stuff out of my truck to prove I was there. You already know it . . ."

Brandy swept her gaze from Clint to stare hard at Ronnie, then back to Clint. "Don't say anything more," she warned him.

"She already knows." His eyelids fluttered closed.

Brandy jumped forward, but the nurse, whose name tag read *Kate Centauri*, held up a hand and gently told her to go to the waiting room. Brandy really wanted to resist, but Ronnie put a hand on her back and guided her out. "Come on."

"I have a right to be there," Brandy sputtered, as she took a seat in one of the chairs near a shedding ficus tree.

"Do I have to tell you they want to make sure he's okay?"

"I don't have to listen to you." Brandy glanced around the room where under the glare of fluorescent lights, knots of people were gathered, an elderly couple in medical masks, the balding man coughing and a twenty-something woman trying to keep two toddlers under control.

Ronnie said, "You should concentrate on what's best for Clint."

"Like you did?"

There was no arguing with her. Ronnie took her phone from her purse for all the good it would do. She'd retrieved it from the bottom of Erik Wetherly's stairwell, but she had discovered it wasn't working when she'd tried to call Sloan, against Brandy's wishes. Though he would learn of the fight through his fellow River Glen officers, several of whom had taken their statements as Clint had been loaded into the ambulance, Ronnie needed to let him know what she'd learned about Clint. Brandy had been too upset and worried about her brother to give Ronnie much more than a glare, then had forgotten some of her ire in the flurry of getting Clint to the hospital.

Now, however, she'd reverted to form and was angry. "Clint's upset," she said under her breath while the beleaguered mother of the preschoolers was trying to interest them in an age-old comic book lying open on the table. Brandy worried her hands together. "He loved Mel . . ."

Ronnie didn't respond. She shut off her phone, hoping a cold boot would bring it back to life.

"He couldn't hurt her. Maybe he followed her . . . but he wouldn't have gone after those guys if he didn't think one of them killed her." Brandy shot to her feet to pace. To worry. To send nervous glances to the closed double-doors behind which Clint was being attended to. "They would let me in to see him if it wasn't for the police," she muttered. "I am his sister *and* a damned nurse."

*Well, maybe he could've killed her . . . it wouldn't be the first time a killer went after further revenge . . .*

Ronnie took a careful breath as the thought passed through her. Clint's ghost rising from his body was still vivid in her memory.

They lapsed into a tense silence.

Fifteen minutes later, Brandy had stopped pacing but was still standing when she muttered, "Oh, shit . . ."

Ronnie followed her line of sight through the ER windows to the man walking across the parking lot under a now lighter sky, the gray clouds high and moving slowly overhead.

Sloan.

Brandy's eyes blazed as they turned to Ronnie. Then they filled with sudden tears that spilled down her cheeks, and she sat down hard in one of the hard-cushioned ER chairs and covered her face with her hands.

# Chapter 20

Sloan's eyes cut to Ronnie as he strode into the ER waiting room. Brandy didn't look up from where she sat, elbows on her knees, hands over her face. She hadn't made a sound since she'd spied Sloan.

"How's Clint?" he asked tersely.

Ronnie looked to Brandy, who didn't move. "He's awake. Head injury."

"What happened?"

"We, uh, found him at Erik Wetherly's house, one of Mel's—"

"I know who he is."

Ronnie nodded shortly. "They were fighting and Wetherly hit him with a hand weight."

"They were fighting about Melissa McNulty," he clarified, glancing at the double doors leading to the examination rooms.

"It appears that way."

She wanted to tell him a whole lot more about what Clint had said, how he'd taken the blame for Mel's death . . . and how his ghost had risen up, saying how sorry he was. But it wouldn't go over well in front of Brandy.

As if reading her mind, Brandy said from behind her palms,

"Tell him. Go ahead. But Clint didn't kill Mel. He loved her too much. That's his crime."

Sloan's attention slipped to Brandy, then he looked at Ronnie once more.

"Let's go outside," she said, seeing a weak sun peeking through the clouds.

Sloan followed her back out to the parking lot, where they stood on the sidewalk that bisected the rows of designated parking spots. Ronnie's gaze settled on the thin layer of snow that was currently puddling on the tarmac. Though it was no longer snowing, the air was still cold, a bitter wind cutting through the parked vehicles as Ronnie explained, "He said that we didn't need the stuff from his truck to prove he was at the shed."

"He admitted he was there?" Sloan frowned.

"Yes." As he absorbed that, she added heavily, "Maybe we were wrong about him." She looked back toward the hospital windows to the ER waiting room. Brandy had moved from her chair and was nowhere in sight.

"I'm going to talk to the officers that were there."

"We gave them short statements," she said, rubbing her hands and wishing she'd thought to wear gloves. "I think they were taking Wetherly to the station. We left when the ambulance did and followed it here."

He nodded. "Did Mercer say anything else?"

SHE WAS A CHEATER... but that was from her dream.

*I didn't mean to hurt her*... and that was from his... ghost.

Ronnie shook her head.

"You sure?" he asked in a softer voice that sent shivers across her skin, memories of last night swirling.

"I don't want to think he did it," she managed.

"Neither do I."

His cell phone buzzed and he pulled it from his pocket, looked down at the screen. His face grew set. "Hart," he said in a cold tone.

"What the fuck are you doing?" Abel Townsend's voice sounded loud enough for Ronnie to identify him.

"Sounds like you heard about Clint," he said, and as he listened to Townsend's diatribe, Ronnie signaled that she was going back inside the hospital to find Brandy and check on Clint.

". . . breathing normally . . . MRI clean . . . but lost consciousness . . . transferring to ICU . . . animal bite on the leg . . ."

Ronnie caught most of what the doctor, a woman with smooth, mocha-colored skin and rimless glasses, had been telling Brandy as she reached her friend, but Brandy ignored her, repeating back to the doctor, "Animal bite on the leg."

"Definitely canine. Tooth marks are distinctive. I've started rabies protocol—he's had the first shot—but you will need to have the animal tested and—"

"We don't have the dog," Brandy cut in.

"—reported to the state. Okay." She stopped talking as Brandy turned away and brushed past Ronnie with as much regard as if she were an inanimate object.

The doctor—Dr. Shaw, by her name tag—asked Ronnie, "Are you a relative?"

"No."

Sloan came back through the sliding entrance doors at that moment and caught sight of the two of them. He strode forward and Dr. Shaw's eyebrows drew together. Ronnie could tell she was about to ask Sloan the same question, but Sloan pulled out his identification with the RGPD.

Dr. Shaw clearly looked unhappy that she might be obliged to talk to him. She refused to discuss what, if anything, Clint had said about the fight that had caused him to end up in the ER but did reveal that Clint had lapsed into unconsciousness fairly quickly after allowing the rabies vaccination to be administered.

"He was bitten by a dog?" asked Sloan.

"Mr. Mercer was bitten by some kind of canine and from the bruising near the teeth marks, I assume it was a few days ago."

Sloan clarified, "It didn't happen in the fight today?"

"No," Ronnie answered for her, then asked the doctor, "Did he say where it happened?"

She shot a look toward Ronnie, clearly wondering what her role was in all this. But after a long moment, Dr. Shaw sighed and admitted grudgingly, "He said that he was trying to save her, but the dog misinterpreted. Whatever that means. Mr. Mercer didn't elaborate."

"'Her'?" repeated Sloan.

"Yes, but I'm afraid that's all I can tell you, Detective. We do have a protocol here when it comes to patient confidentiality." She left them abruptly, slipping back behind the closed doors to the ER examination rooms. Ronnie sensed Dr. Shaw was sorry she'd said as much as she had.

"The dog was with Mel," said Ronnie.

"This is the dog you've been . . . hearing bark?"

"I think so. Yes."

It was still tricky talking about her gift with Sloan. If she pushed too hard, said too much, he retreated.

"Can we go back to my place?" she asked.

His attention, which she'd felt she was losing, snapped back to her. "Yes?" He quirked an eyebrow.

"Yes."

"Let me text Brandy and see if she needs a ride as she came to the hospital with me," Ronnie said, already punching in the message. Within seconds Brandy replied she planned to stay longer and could catch a ride back from one of her coworkers, and Ronnie walked with Sloan to the parking lot.

Once she'd driven home and was at the entrance to her apartment, Ronnie glanced toward Angel's door again. She didn't see any hint of him, couldn't *feel* him. Had she really seen that flash of him leaning against the rail the other night?

*Did you really see that shadow in the mirror?*

*Or is your mind playing tricks on you?*

She shivered as she unlocked her door, glancing back to the parking lot, glad to notice Sloan's Bronco pulling into a spot not far from her SUV.

When she turned back around Angel was standing in her living room, right in front of her.

She cried out, startled.

And then he, or more likely his image, *poofed* away.

She froze in place, a hand over her barreling heart. It's not real, she told herself, taking in a shuddering breath. It's *not* real. But what, then? Why did she keep seeing him? Her mind raced wildly with her thoughts.

When Sloan came in behind her she hadn't moved.

"What?" he asked, his tone tense.

"I saw Angel," she answered in an unsteady voice. "Or—I saw his image. Here in this room." She tried to keep the panic from her words. "I think . . . he's trying to tell me something. But . . ." Her throat grew so thick she could barely get the words out. "I think . . . he might be dead."

Emma Whelan stood outside Theo's Thrift Shop. It wasn't four o'clock yet, but the new woman, Annette Brown, who was in charge today, had decided it was time to close down anyway. Annette had flyaway gray hair and a frown that took over her whole face. She was a "temporary hire for the holidays" Theo had told her, and then Harley snorted and said she was "not a people person."

"We've sold everything at the sale," Annette had explained to Emma.

Emma hadn't agreed. "I see clothes. I see shoes . . . and a lamp."

That made Annette suck her pale lips into a tight line and say, "The Christmas decorations went right away, and anything in really good shape went next. This stuff isn't good."

"It is good," argued Emma.

"Not for today. They can come by tomorrow and shop. Or Tuesday, or any day of the week."

"I don't have a ride till four."

"Well, call them."

When Emma didn't respond, Annette let out a puff of disgust. "What?" she demanded. "Can't you call your ride and get whoever it is to come for you?"

Emma had a cell phone. Harley said it was "basic," which meant it was different from hers. Emma had Harley's number, but Harley was coming at four, so there was no need to call her.

Emma waited outside the thrift store while gray-haired not-a-people-person Annette locked the door behind her and pulled down the shades. Emma knew Annette would go out the back way to where her car was parked. She also knew that the thrift store was not in a good area of town and she shouldn't stand outside too long.

She looked up at the sky. No snow now. She wondered if she should call Harley. You weren't supposed to talk on cell phones when you drove the car. Harley tried to be good, but sometimes she said she had to use her phone. She scolded herself about it, but Harley did it anyway. Emma didn't want her to. She didn't want her to get arrested and go to jail. But she was pretty sure Harley was already on her way to the thrift shop to pick her up, so Emma decided to wait to call. Harley would be here soon.

She heard a scuffle and turned, just as a guy stumbled out of the side alley. Nearly falling over, he squinted at Emma. He caught himself. He looked dirty. He had dirty hair and dirty boots. He started coming her way. He didn't walk straight.

Emma wasn't sure if he was bad or not. It was hard to tell. Maybe she should call Harley.

She reached inside her pocket for her phone and that's when the bus with the handprints and the yellow sunshine turned down the street. It was going to go on by without stopping, but the dirty man raised a hand and the bus *ssscccrrreeeeched* to a stop right in front of her.

Emma wasn't supposed to get on the bus. Harley had told her not to. She was to wait for Harley.

The bus driver pushed open the door with a handle like a long arm, like when Emma was in school. Emma looked at the dirty man who'd waved for the bus. He was coming closer.

He was giving the bus "the finger." Two "the fingers."

The bus driver looked worried. He said, "Hop in," to Emma.

"FUCK YOU ALL!" the dirty man yelled. He bumped into Emma. He smelled bad. Sour.

Emma nearly lost her balance, so she grabbed on to the bar inside the bus and hauled herself onto the steps.

The dirty man wanted to come in, but the bus driver slammed the door shut. The dirty man pounded on the door, but the bus was moving.

Emma took the nearest seat, then twisted to look out the back, past the rows of women and kids and saw the dirty man give two more "the fingers" through the rear window. He then turned around, bent over and pulled down his pants. Harley had a name for that. Mooning.

Emma could tell the people on the bus were all looking at her. She kept her head down. She didn't like staring eyes.

She would call Harley when she got to where she was going. Where she would be saved.

One of the women had a big stomach like Jamie, so she was pregnant. Emma slid her a sideways look. "You're pregnant like Mary Jo."

"Who?" The woman looked kind of scared.

"I'm Emma."

"Hi, Emma."

Emma glanced around at the other women. They all looked kind of worried. She thought maybe they were all hiding something from her. Lots of people tried to hide things, but Harley and Jamie and Cooper and Theo and Marissa promised to always tell her the truth.

"Mary Jo ran away to your church with my sister's baby inside her."

"She was lost in your world as Mary Jo!" the woman said. "But she has found salvation with us as Rebekkah!"

Emma frowned at her. If Harley were here, she would say the woman was "getting all worked up." She wasn't really listening to Emma. "Mary Jo's not lost. I don't know about Rebekkah, but Mary Jo is home with my sister's baby inside her."

"It's not *her* baby. It's . . . Rebekkah's."

Well that wasn't right. Emma stated clearly, "It's Jamie

Whelan Woodward Haynes's baby, and if Mary Jo won't give it back, she's going to jail."

"Tell me about Angel," Sloan repeated. Quick's pallor had been ghost white and he'd led her to a living room chair. He'd worried she was in some kind of trance, a wild effect of his leeriness over her psychic "powers." But then he'd realized she was simply reacting to something that scared her. "He's your neighbor. What's his last name?"

"Vasquero." Her brows drew together. "He got rid of the bat for me. I didn't tell you about that."

"What bat?"

She glanced toward her front door and Sloan did the same, half expecting to see something himself. "It was left on my doorstep and Angel got rid of it for me. He's a P.I. and he was trying to protect me, I think. He moved in about the same time I did." She drew a long breath and said, "His cousin is battling a wealthy family over an inheritance. Angel asked me to help Daria, and I told him, and her, that she needed to talk to the lawyer handling the estate. But then she backed off. Didn't want any help."

Ronnie stopped for a moment, but Sloan encouraged her, "Go on."

"Angel's other purpose in moving next to me was to protect me."

"To protect you?"

"I've been envisioning him...he's been haunting my thoughts." She stood up abruptly. "And this...*bombardment*...of information I've been getting...ever since Mel...and then Shana and now Angel..." She pressed her hands to her face.

"You don't know Angel is dead."

"Don't I?" she asked miserably.

"When was the bat left on your doorstep?"

"A few days ago. I heard something early that morning. A noise outside my door. Must've been whoever delivered the bat. It was a warning. Intimidation of some kind."

"You said Angel got rid of it. Where?"

"I don't know. Probably in the trash in the back?"

For a second she thought he was actually going out to check the dumpster. Instead, he rubbed a hand around the back of his neck. "Okay. So, do you have his cousin's phone number?"

"Yes... in my files. Daria Armenton."

"I'll check with her, too."

"What's going to happen to Clint?" she asked, her blue eyes capturing his. His mind filled with images of those eyes from the night before, half closed, staring up at him...

"We're placing a guard outside the ICU."

"He needs a lawyer. Tomorrow's Monday, I can... oh..."

"What?"

"I have somewhere I need to be tonight. A dinner that I've put off too many times already."

"Put it off again." A slow smile spread from one side of his face to the other.

Finally, a bit of her spark returned as she said dryly, "That will only delay the inevitable, and I just need to get it over with."

His cell phone buzzed and he saw it was from Abel Townsend again. He ignored it. "Meet later, then?"

"Back here?"

"I'll take that as an invitation." His phone rang again. Townsend.

"Someone wants you pretty badly," she observed as she walked him toward the door.

"I hope you're talking about yourself."

That netted him a real smile. He bent down and kissed her impulsively and she momentarily melted in his arms. But then she pushed him away. "Later," she promised.

He was still smiling when he answered the call as he clambered down the stairs to his Bronco. He looked up at the sky. Clouds were gathering again as twilight descended. Maybe more snow... maybe rain.

"Hi, Abel," he answered as he pressed the remote to unlock his doors.

"Hart, you're not the only one who has someone who'll go that extra mile at the lab. We got some results back today."

"From Mercer's truck . . . ?" Even as he said it he knew it couldn't be. He'd barely sent in those samples and it hadn't been through the sheriff's department.

"The coffee cup lid from the McNulty crime scene. It's got your psychic friend's DNA all over it."

Harley was doing her damnedest not to panic. She'd shown up at four o'clock and no Emma, and now it was after five. She'd tracked down the number for Annette Brown, the woman Emma had worked with today, but she'd answered Harley's questions with a long whining tale about how it wasn't her fault Emma was missing, and how she hadn't signed up to be a handicapped person's babysitter. Harley had clicked off that call, pissed off to no end.

But Emma was nowhere to be found. Harley had left two voice mails for her. Normally Emma was really good at returning calls. The only time she delayed was when she felt something was more important, which could be something as mundane as petting Duchess first.

However, Harley had specifically told her to be ready at four o'clock and Emma had agreed. If Emma agreed to something, she followed through.

So, what had happened?

Her mind flew back to that conversation with Emma about the Heart of Sunshine Church.

*They pick up people and take them away. They asked me if I wanted to come and meet the Lord . . . They said I was special. I know what that means . . .*

But had she gone with them? Had she gotten on the bus with the people Theo had shooed from her thrift shop? Had she ignored Harley's warnings and gone with them anyway, in an attempt to keep Mary Jo safe?

*Oh, Emma . . . you didn't, did you?*

Like it or not, Harley was going to have to call Cooper.

# Chapter 21

Ronnie put a call through to Marian's cell phone as she drove to the Langdorf estate, but once again Carlton picked up.

"I don't think dinner is going to work tonight," he stated flatly before Ronnie could even say hello.

"Did you even tell Marian I would be there tonight? And why are you on her phone?" No use trying to be deferential to a client. Carlton didn't pick up on subtleties and Ronnie was annoyed, really annoyed.

"She's unable to come to the phone. She's not feeling well. Maybe you can reschedule again."

His "maybe" was tinged with "but I don't think so."

Ronnie didn't have time for Carlton Langdorf or his petty games. "Well, I'm on my way, so she can tell me herself."

"She's not up. It's not a good time," he shot back, his voice rising.

Was Carlton being a little too eager to keep her away from his aunt? With Mel's and Shana's deaths, the worry about Angel, and the vortex of messages she was receiving that almost left her with whiplash, she'd shoved Marian and Carlton Langdorf to the back of her brain. Now she wondered if she smelled a rat. Of course he didn't want Ronnie involved, as Marian was way too interested in pulling her into the inner circle, but taking over her phone? Speaking for Marian? Not allowing Ronnie to talk to her?

"You know, I've been rethinking the whole 'moving in' plan," Ronnie lied. "I know I've been lukewarm on it. It just didn't seem feasible, but now I actually think it might work out very well for me."

"You said it *wouldn't* work for you!" he squeaked.

"Crazy how these things change, huh? See you soon," she sang, then ended the call.

She had a faint smile on her lips, which slowly dissipated as her mind tripped back to Mel and Clint and Brandy and Shana and Angel and everything that had jumbled together over the past half week. It almost felt like someone or something was specifically targeting her.

"It's not about you," she reminded herself. Then again, maybe she was wrong.

Sloan ended the call with the sheriff as fast as he reasonably could. He needed time to think. His pulse was flying. Townsend had sounded almost gleeful that he could impart unwelcome news.

"Bro," Sloan muttered fiercely. He wasn't Townsend's *bro*. Never had been.

And now Sloan was behind the wheel. Driving way too fast.

*Stop. Think. Follow the investigation to its logical conclusion.*

But Veronica Quick was not logical!

But then there was the coffee cup lid . . . with her DNA . . . ?

*How?*

His thoughts flipped to her prediction about Shana's death . . . and then finding Shana's body laid out in that *exact same way*. A prediction, she'd said. A vision. But shit . . .

Still, Quick couldn't have been involved in Shana's death. She hadn't had time and *why would she?*

Now Sloan was the one who was mad. At Townsend for

bringing this to him, putting doubts in his head... no, *increasing* his doubts about Quick's ability to "see" things. Those doubts had already been there.

His chest constricted. He needed to talk to Quick, but she was at that dinner.

*Don't rush. Think it through. Work the investigation.*

Words he lived by, but then he'd never been so personally involved.

All right. Fine. Stop. What next? Hugh McNulty, but he was with his friends and Townsend had already interviewed him. Go somewhere else.

He looked down at the screen of his phone, working hard to keep focused. He'd planned to call Amy Deggars, whom Shana had stayed with just before she was murdered. Amy had undoubtedly already been notified by the police communications department, but Sloan hadn't yet interviewed her.

It was Sunday evening. In his mind, he'd planned on spending time with Quick today... Ronnie... interviewing Deggars tomorrow.

*It's got your psychic friend's DNA all over it...*

He shook his head. Science against pseudo-science.

Push that aside!

Gritting his teeth, he punched in the number he'd gotten for Amy Deggars. She answered on the third ring with a cautious, "Hello?"

"Amy Deggars? This is Detective Hart with the River Glen Police Department. I would like to talk to you—"

She gasped.

"—about Shana Lloyd. I'm sure you've been contacted regarding... her death." He slowed down at her reaction.

"She said it was because of you!" Amy charged. "Shana was scared to death!"

"What do you mean?"

"She was scared of *you*! Of everything! And look what happened." Her voice had gone from fury to fear.

He slowed for a corner and took it too fast, his Bronco slid—

ing a bit as he tried to keep the conversation on track. "She was staying with you, after the car accident." Then, "She had no reason to be frightened of me."

"She said she made a mistake! Trusted you when she shouldn't have!"

Was she sobbing?

"I-I don't trust you!" she insisted, panic audible. "I don't need to talk to you. I—I need someone else. I need a lawyer!"

He slowed for a stoplight, silently ticking off the seconds in his head and tried to calm the woman down. "I don't know what Shana said to give you the impression that—"

"I'm gonna tell them you killed her!"

Sloan could hardly grasp what she was saying. "I didn't have anything to do with Shana's death."

"She found out about you and your girlfriend!"

Trying to keep up, Sloan was rendered damn near speechless. He didn't have time to go into the whys and wherefores of how wrong she was. "She must've meant someone else," he said. "Did she contact anyone?"

"No."

"She talked to Evan Caldwell," he suggested.

"Evan Cald— No! Wait. I—I think he tried to talk her out of it!"

"Out of what?" he asked, but Amy wasn't listening.

"Evan said she was being paranoid! But it's you. *You* she was scared of!" She sobbed loudly and then clicked off.

Well, that sure went down the rabbit hole fast. But it forced him to think hard and ease off the gas. What the hell had Amy been talking about? She had to have him confused with someone else. Who?

*Not. Ronnie.* She was not responsible for Shana's death no matter what the evidence looked like.

He'd spent the night with her. That had been real. That had been . . . wonderful.

*But are you being led in circles? You thought she was a charlatan. A fake. A nutcase.*

*But she's none of those things.*
*Are you sure? Do you just want that to be true? Like Townsend doesn't want Mercer to be responsible for Melissa McNulty's death?*
*Is Clint Mercer responsible? He was there. Maybe he didn't mean to hurt her, but he was on site.*
*If he didn't do it, who did? And did it have anything to do with whoever murdered Shana?*

"Emma's at Heart of Sunshine Church?" Cooper repeated slowly.

"I think so." Harley swallowed hard. "I can't be sure, but yeah, I think so."

"Where are you?"

"Home," Harley told him as she stared at their house where the Christmas tree was visible in the living room window. "I'm parked across the street."

"Well come inside and wait. I'll be back later after I visit the preacher."

"You're here? In the house?" she asked, and at that moment she saw him shoving his arms down the sleeves of his jacket as he crossed the living room behind the lighted tree.

"And you're going to Heart of Sunshine?"

"That's right," he said, steel in his voice.

"I'm going with you!"

But she didn't know if he'd heard her. Didn't matter. She cut the engine, threw open the door and locked the car remotely as she dashed across the street to the yard. Her boots sank into the slushy ground as she ran around the corner to the driveway and caught a glimpse of Cooper sliding behind the wheel of his SUV. She sped up because whether he liked it or not, she was going with him.

Ronnie pressed the bell for the third time, annoyed with Carlton, who seemed to have control of Marian's phone and possibly Marian herself.

Faintly, she heard the sound of a dog barking. Somewhere from the back of the estate . . . Langdorf's dog? *Mel's* dog? Or a neighbor's?

The door opened and Carlton stood in front of her in a dark jogging suit, hands folded at his waist, his expression tense. "There's no dinner. My aunt isn't feeling well. I told you not to come."

Ronnie glanced around the foyer, her gaze sweeping up the stairway and then back again, settling on the umbrella stand that currently held Marian's cane, the red eyes of the wolf's head seeming to throb.

"She doesn't have her cane with her," she observed.

"There are other canes. That one's for going out."

"She used it last time I was here."

"Well, she's not using it now! She's in the den. Do you want to see her or not?"

"Yes," said Ronnie, a little surprised. All Carlton had done was try to dissuade her from contact with Marian over and over again.

She followed him back to the den. This time he didn't pose at the fireplace. This time he sat down next to Marian on the leather couch, while Ronnie remained standing.

Marian was staring into the fire, which was now mostly glowing red and orange embers. She looked up as Ronnie entered.

"Hello there, dear." Her welcoming smile was a taut line of her lips.

"What's going on?" asked Ronnie. The vibes in the room were definitely odd.

"I made you a generous offer, and you've been very . . . rude . . . about it," Marian said as Carlton patted her hand. "You've put me off and put me off, and . . . maligned me behind my back."

"*What?*"

Marian said calmly, "I'm still grateful that you saved my life, but—"

"The doctors would have found it," interrupted Carlton.

"—I think it's time we part ways."

Marian was deeply hurt, Ronnie realized, surprised. Her blood boiled as she considered the lies Carlton might be feeding his aunt. She wanted to scream at him to stop being such an asshole, but more than anything she just wanted to go. To leave Carlton Langdorf and his naked greed and go back to finding what had happened to Mel and Shana . . . and Angel.

"All right," she said. "If that's the way you want it."

Ever more faintly she heard the dog. She glanced toward the back windows and then at Marian and Carlton.

"What?" Carlton asked. Did he seem nervous?

Ronnie asked, "Do you hear anything?"

Marian waved a hand at her. "Oh. That's just the bats."

Ronnie met the older woman's gaze. "The bats?" she repeated slowly.

"In the walls. They come inside to hibernate, but the fireplace warms them and you can hear them sometimes." Her lips pinched, she turned to Carlton and said with more of her usual imperiousness, "What's the name of that pest service? You need to call them again."

Ronnie's gaze was turned to Carlton, whose eyes were fixed back on her. She said, "So when the bats hibernate, they might be easy to catch and kill."

"Well, yes, I suppose so." Marian frowned.

Carlton's pallor had bleached to white, but he looked determined. Even dangerous.

Ronnie's stomach turned sour. He'd left her the bat in a fit of pique because he wanted all of Marian's money. What a louse. The thought of his perfidy, how he'd lied, how he'd ingratiated himself to his aunt. . . . It took everything she had to say to Marian, "I'm sorry things didn't work out for us. It was a generous offer." She edged around the couch toward the double doors.

"I'll see you out." Carlton dropped Marian's hand and was on his feet in an instant.

"No need."

She was out of the room in a flash. She didn't know just how far Carlton would go, but he obviously hated her. Was he dangerous? She didn't want to take the time to find out. The dead bat was enough proof that he was more than a little unhinged. She racewalked to the foyer as she heard quick footsteps behind her.

Damn.

Carlton caught up with her and rather dramatically threw himself in front of the door. "I don't think you should leave."

"Because you left that dead bat on my doorstep?" she said, stopping.

"No... what do you mean?" he stammered.

"You sneaky... grifter. Those are your tactics? Intimidation... then run and hide?"

His face flushed. "I just think we should talk."

"I don't need to talk to you anymore."

The sudden whoosh of cold air ran through her like a blade. She blinked as there was no air movement. Then out of the corner of her eye she saw a shadow. Someone...? Something? A ghost, like in her bedroom...?

"Where's Angel?" she asked almost before the thought had fully formed.

His mouth dropped open and his eyes bugged. "Wh-what?"

"You did something to him," she said with sudden razor-sharp clarity. Just how dangerous was he? "What did you do to him?" she demanded.

"I don't know what you're talking about. You're fucking crazy... Crazy!"

Liar! "Did you hurt him?" *Kill him?* She was dizzy with the knowledge. Not a vision... she just *knew* it.

"You're... *raving!*" Carlton accused, his voice rising an octave. "You're always raving!" Gathering himself, he said, "You can't talk to Marian anymore. She doesn't believe you. She knows you're a liar... and evil!"

Ronnie started rummaging in her purse for her phone, glad it had started working again.

"What—what are you doing?"

As soon as she retrieved the phone, Carlton batted it from

her hand. It sailed across the room, hit the marble floor and spun to the far wall.

"I'm leaving," she said, lurching for her phone.

He twisted her around. "Not until I say so."

"I'm leaving," she repeated. Adrenaline spiking, she wrenched her arm free, but he caught her midsection before she reached the door and she stumbled, sliding on the slick marble.

Looming over her, he leaned forward, glaring at her from the tops of his eyes. Demented. Furious.

*He killed Angel.*

*Because of me.*

Ronnie's heart skipped several beats. Carlton was on the edge.

Though her heart was beating frantically and in her peripheral vision she searched for a weapon, something to defend herself with, she managed to keep the panic from her voice and said with far more calm than she felt, "Where is Angel, Carlton? Is he here? On the grounds?"

But he wasn't listening. He was still raving about his aunt. "You got into her head! She was all set to put you upstairs, write you into the will. She already made a stipend for you. I had to do something."

"Marian's not leaving her estate to me," she reminded tautly, her mouth dry. "We just went over that." Was her voice squeaky? Nervous? Terrified? *Keep calm.*

"I had to stop you."

"You came back again. You left the bat the first time, but you came back again, and Angel saw you."

"You've been after Marian's money for years!" he charged.

Projection. He was the one who'd been after her money. Ronnie calculated how far she was from her phone. Sloan's number was one of her most recent. She could hit the call button in a second, if she could get ahold of her phone.

She lifted her hands, as if he were keeping her at gunpoint. "I've never wanted Marian's money. I think I've made that clear."

How fast could she be to the phone? He had no weapon. But he was determined. Flight or fight? she asked herself. She was no match for Carlton, who was taller and though lean, probably had thirty pounds on her.

And she wasn't a fighter.

"Don't move," he ordered.

Ronnie ignored him. One moment she was standing still, the next she was scrambling across the floor for the phone.

He sprang.

On her instantly.

Ripping her arm back as she reached for the phone. Yanked it behind her.

Pain ripped through her shoulder.

She yelped, but lunged, dragging him.

The phone twirled from her fingers, but she threw herself forward, snagged it and pounded on the button with her finger.

Sloan!

Please, God!

"No!" Carlton growled furiously, grabbing her by the waist and flinging her across the foyer. She skidded across the marble, but didn't release her phone.

*Bam!*

Her forehead smacked against the wall. Stunned, aching, she saw past the pain. Past the fear. "You killed him," she threw out as he turned on her again. "Didn't you? You killed Angel!"

"You bitch! Why couldn't you just leave us alone?"

He leapt forward, catching hold of her arm again and hauling her to her feet.

She swayed a bit, the world spinning, and then her eyes came into focus. His grip tightened as he reached for her other arm, but she writhed within his grasp. In a move that surprised even her she suddenly stomped hard on his foot, her boot slamming into his shoe as she finally managed to wrench her arm free.

He screamed, "You're the grifter! You're the one!"

"*Where is he?*" she screamed back, breathing hard, ready for a fight. He started this and she would damn well finish it.

"Quick?" Sloan's tinny voice sounded from the phone in her hand, cutting through her rage.

"No!" Carlton cried, scrabbling in the air for her phone, but she ducked away and yelled, "Langdorf's! Three two seven Brynndal—"

Carlton grabbed her by the hair and yanked her head back, slamming it into the wall next to the stairway. She saw stars, bright flashes of light behind her eyes. Her feet sliding from beneath her she tried desperately to clutch tight to her phone.

"Carlton?"

Ronnie blinked, tried to hang on to consciousness, her head aching, Carlton still snarling and holding on to her hair. She saw Marian standing in the aperture to the den, leaning against the doorjamb. Her eyes were full of dismay. "What's going on?"

Trying to get the phone from her outstretched hand, Carlton yanked her head back as far as he could. She managed to reach behind her and she found his throat, her nails clawing at the skin hard enough for him to roar in pain.

His grip slackened.

She broke free, gasping for breath.

"She attacked me!" Carlton said frantically. "Marian. You're not safe! Get in the den! Lock the door!"

"Not true!" Ronnie yelled, but her voice was more of a rasp. She gazed around wildly.

The cane.

The wolf's head cane.

She lunged for it. He sprang after her, grabbing the fabric of her blouse. She heard it give with a sickening rip. Kicking back at him, she felt one of his arms snake around her waist again.

She stretched, fingers wriggling madly for the cane, but he was too strong. One of his hands found her neck. Began to squeeze.

"Carlton!"

Ronnie heard Marian's voice . . . She sounded far away.

Her mind fractured . . . Mel . . . Shana . . . strangled.

*Can't lose consciousness. Can't lose consciousness.* She extended her arm as far as she could reach.

The tips of her fingers felt the metal wolf's head...
A dog howled.
*Don't go in the water.*
No more stars... just an enveloping blackness trying to take over as she grappled and gasped for air.

"Quick?" Sloan, driving, answered his phone and heard: "Langdorf's? Three two seven Brynn—"
Call cut off.
"Ronnie!" he yelled. "Ronnie! Goddamn it." He recognized the urgency. Felt the danger.
He knew where Brynndalwood Lane was. A pocket of estates on the northeastern edge of River Glen. He'd driven aimlessly in the opposite direction while he'd considered his next move and now did a quick one-eighty and hit the gas.
He didn't know what was happening.
But the danger was real. Palpitating.
Oh. Jesus.
Ronnie!
He only hoped he wasn't too late.

"You shouldn't have come... you shouldn't have come... you shouldn't have come..."
Carlton's litany was a muttered mantra, over and over. *You shouldn't have come...*
Ronnie's head was still spinning, but slowly, as if swimming through mud, she was regaining her wits.
*You. Have. To. Fight. Think, Ronnie, THINK!*
He was dragging her down a hallway, her head bouncing along the hard floor, pain exploding behind her eyelids. She tried to lift her head, to open her eyes, to get free. But she couldn't. Her damned body wouldn't respond.
*Keep trying. Fight. Or—reason with him...*
"Carlton," she murmured. "Carlton, don't."
"It's your fault," he said with calm determination. "I didn't do it."

Was he talking about Angel? Or . . . what?

"Sorry, sir. She took the pills on her own," he said tonelessly.

A chill went through her. Was he talking about her? To whom? Himself. There was no other person here, no "sir." As clouded as her mind was, she was certain of that. Oh. God. Was he planning to drug her? Murder her?

"She took the pills on her own," he said again, as if testing the words to see how they played.

*Marian. He was talking about Marian.*

Slowly, too slowly, Ronnie was coming around.

"She took the pills on her own." This time his tone was threaded with tears.

*Marian . . .*

"*She* gave her the pills! My aunt realized she'd been conned and cut her off! But then *she* killed her! I had to stop her!"

Ronnie's heart clutched. *Has he given Marian the pills already?* He was creating his story, throwing the blame on Ronnie . . .

"It was an accident!" he cried out.

She struggled to think clearly, but the blackness kept dragging her backward, into the void, the pain-free void. She was fading out. And if she went out, he would kill her.

She knew it.

"Carlton?" Marian's dim voice sounded heavy and slow.

"Go sit down!" he suddenly yelled.

Ronnie heard a *hummmmmmm* building inside her.

"It was an accident!" he repeated, fake sobbing.

Sloan called for backup and bit out the address to the operator. He cut the connection and kept speeding to the Langdorf address. He didn't have lights and if he picked up a cop for speeding, all the better.

He wasn't far.

Still, how long had it been since Ronnie's desperate call? Minutes.

But minutes were often the difference between life and death.

God damn it. He pounded on the steering wheel and slid around a final corner, tires screeching. He didn't know what was happening but he'd heard her terror.

Icy fear thrummed down his nerves.

He beat the sirens to the Langdorf estate.

He skidded to a stop in the semicircular driveway in front of the mansion, ablaze with lights. As he did he spied the blue Escape, Ronnie's car.

Jaw set, he slid his Glock from his shoulder holster, and ran up the steps to the front door.

As if from another world, Ronnie heard the pounding. Her head felt swollen, maybe it was, her thoughts moving through a field of dense cotton. She sensed rather than saw Carlton leap away from her, the movement sending air currents scurrying around her.

*Get up . . . get up . . .*

Then Carlton was back, hissing in her ear. "Tell them to go away!"

He abruptly hauled her to her feet, but her knees were jelly.

When she didn't respond, he slapped her.

Hard.

Her cheek was immediately on fire, but the pain a surprisingly welcome distraction from her dull brain.

She managed to get her legs to move as Carlton half carried her to the front door. Oak, she thought. It had been oak. Too sturdy to break through.

She was mad at herself. Mad that she wasn't in control. It took everything she had to gather her wits about her.

Carlton jabbed her in the ribs with his elbow. "Tell them," he whispered harshly.

"It's the police!" yelled Sloan. "Open the door!"

Sloan. Sloan had gotten her call. Ronnie nearly went weak at the sound of his voice. But she dug down deep. With all her strength, she yelled, "Break a window!"

"Carlton . . ." Marian. Feebly calling to him.

As Ronnie turned glazed eyes in the older woman's direction, Carlton released her. She stumbled and fell to her knees.

Pull yourself together!

Ronnie, this is your chance!

"Police. Open the door!"

Insistent pounding.

"Ronnie!"

"Sloan," she said, her voice a whisper and then she heard another, chilling sound.

Frenzied barking.

The dog.

She blinked.

And saw the wolf's head cane.

Carlton was holding his head and staggering as if he couldn't make his brain work.

*Crash!*

A cudgel...

Splintering glass as Sloan broke through a leaded glass pane.

She dragged her feet under her.

"No! No! NO! NO!" Carlton's head whipped from side to side.

She lurched forward, the foyer spinning.

Her fingers wrapped around the cane.

Red eyes glowed bright.

Carlton's head snapped her way, his mouth an "O" of disbelief.

*Bark, bark, bark, bark, bark, bark, bark, bark, bark!*

She swung at his knees with all her strength.

He dropped like a stone.

# Chapter 22

The doors to the Heart of Sunshine Church were locked.

Harley watched as Cooper pounded on the panels, then looked like he was about to try to throw his shoulder at the thick oak panels or shoot his way in with his sidearm.

"Don't!" Harley grabbed his arm and shook her head.

Then, assured that he wasn't about to do himself bodily harm, she knocked urgently on the door and called, "Help! Help me!" in a sobbing voice. "I need the Lord's help!"

She kept knocking and crying loudly.

Within minutes the locks slowly clicked open and the door cracked. A woman wearing a cloak, blond hair visible, peered out from the aperture, light from behind throwing her in relief and spilling into the twilight where Harley stood wringing her hands, Cooper in shadow.

"We...we're...the church isn't open," the woman said, eyeing Harley with curious suspicion. "Our father is busy..."

"My baby!" Harley clutched her stomach. "I'm losing my baby and I can't go to a hospital. I need help!"

"Your baby?" The door opened further.

Harley didn't wait. Barreled her way in. Cooper made a

sound of protest, but Harley was already inside an anteroom of some kind. The doors to the church itself were open and though the blond woman rushed to close them, Harley had already dashed through and was running down the aisle.

"No! Stop! Don't! You can't go in there! Stop!" the woman screeched wildly while Cooper was using his most soothing voice. It never worked on Harley. Fingernails on a chalkboard.

And still the woman was screaming.

Harley raced down the row between the pews. The empty pulpit was front and center before a raised altar. Overhead a huge wooden cross had been suspended over a wide portrait of the sun, beams radiating from its golden center.

She hesitated only a second as there were doors on either side of the nave.

Left or right?

She chose left, mainly because she was leaning toward right and that felt wrong.

Something in that thought was screwy. Whatever. She just kept moving, ignoring the voices and footsteps behind her and slipped through the door to a darkened hallway with doors on either side.

Well, shit.

She hesitated, then noticed a dim light shining at the far end of the hall where a door leading to the exterior had been fitted with a glass insert.

She headed that way. The light was murky and faint but she pushed the door open. Winter cold slapped her face and the dark of dusk was creeping over a two-story barn-like building with one small window on the second floor and a few scant panes, which appeared to be covered, on the first. The long, rectangular structure seemed to end at what appeared to be a garden area.

But her eyes were drawn to the flickering illumination coming from the second story. Maybe candlelight?

Harley set her jaw. She'd come to find Emma. And she'd had enough of these fakey religious types at last summer's camp.

She exited the church and ran lightly across wet grass to the rather featureless adjunct building, her toes dampening through her Nikes. She caught glimpses of light through cracks in the curtains covering the windows on the lower floor. That illumination was steady and even, so Harley supposed the building did have electricity, if only on the first floor. As she neared a metal door, she peered through a gap in the dark, obscuring curtains and noticed at least one overhead bulb.

She tried the door.

Locked.

*Damn.*

She pounded her fist on the metal panel, then glanced behind her. No sign of Cooper, the woman or anyone else. No sign of the "father," or was it "Father"? Was their leader considered God?

And Emma was in their clutches? Not to sound too dramatic, but *hell.*

"Who's there?" a voice from within called.

Harley and Cooper had tersely gone over what they knew about Mary Jo and the Heart of Sunshine Church as a means to hold down their panic over Emma. Now, she jerked her jacket in front of her face and cried through the fabric, "Rebekkah."

"Rebekkah?" a woman's voice said with obvious doubt. Oh crap, what if Mary Jo was already inside? But the voice returned. "Sister, is that you?"

"Yes!"

Within seconds the locks clicked and the door swung open. Harley charged inside . . . to a room of woman and children of various ages sitting on wooden benches scattered over the old plank floor. And in the center of the room, the overhead light shining down on her blond hair, her braid slung over her shoulder, looking for all the world like Elsa from *Frozen* about to cast out ice fractals, was Emma.

Harley felt her knees go weak in relief.

"Hi, Harley," Emma said in her flat way, as almost everyone else in the room stayed momentarily motionless, frozen themselves. Emma continued. "They don't want to stay here anymore. They don't like having sex with him. He doesn't ask nicely."

"He doesn't ask at all," a woman with red hair and dark eyes stated fiercely.

"Where is he?" asked Harley. The door had closed behind her but she glanced back at it.

"The men have separate living arrangements off site," said a woman with a shorn head.

"Our father is preparing a room at the church," an older woman added.

"For what?" asked Harley. "Left or right side of the pulpit as you face the altar?"

"For me," said Emma. "But I don't think I'll have sex with him." She reached forward and accepted a wicked-looking utility knife from the red-haired woman. "But I won't let him cut off my hair. I think I'll kill him."

Ronnie shivered against Sloan's warmth as he held her close, standing outside the Langdorf mansion as two officers swarmed into the house and subdued Carlton, who was on the floor, clutching his knees and howling how it was her fault. Her, being Ronnie. She'd come when she wasn't invited! he'd insisted. She'd attacked him! She'd drugged his aunt after being summarily turned away. She was after the inheritance. She was a sham, a fake, a bullshit psychic!

He'd thrown out an arm and pointed at Ronnie while they were trying to handcuff him. "She's a fucking lunatic! Look at my dear aunt!" His voice had broken and he'd wept vociferously. "Look what she did to her! Arrest her! Not me! HER! Look! Look!"

They'd all glanced toward the spot where Marian had slid down the den doorjamb and was lying half in, half out of the room.

EMTs had arrived on the heels of the police and while Carlton kept screaming that they were making a mistake, arresting the wrong person, Marian had been loaded into an ambulance and it had raced down the driveway, lights flashing, siren winding up.

Ronnie had given her statement to a uniformed officer with Sloan at her side and now they were outside in the curved driveway, a cold December mist falling. "He—Carlton—must've given her something," Ronnie said through chattering teeth. "She was normal... seemed fine, but then I heard the dog... Is there a dog?"

Sloan said, "I don't hear one." He was holding her, his arm tight over her shoulders, but she felt the tension radiating from him, his muscles tight. His attention was split between tending to her and taking charge of the scene.

"Marian doesn't like dogs, so there's no dog..." she murmured. She glanced toward Carlton on his knees, hands cuffed behind his back as he forced the police to drag him to a patrol car. "He put the bat on my doorstep," Ronnie said, hitching her chin in Carlton's direction. "Ask him what he did to Angel."

Sloan glanced down at her. "He's responsible for the bat?"

"Yes." She nodded, glaring at Carlton, who was being hauled to his feet. "Marian mentioned that they have a colony roosting in the walls of the house." She glanced up at Sloan. "And he did something to Angel."

"This is something you've seen, I mean did you witness it? Or did you envision it? Or did Carlton admit it?"

"I just know it," she bit out. "And no, Carlton didn't admit it, but he was shocked and looked guilty as hell when I brought Angel up. I *know* he did something to him, but I don't know what."

Sloan's eyes darkened with concern. "You're sure you don't need a doctor?"

"I'm fine," she insisted once again. Sloan had wanted to pack her off to the hospital, and had said as much, but she'd refused.

"You could be concussed."

"Do I seem concussed?" Sure, her head ached like a monster, but she was clearheaded.

He reluctantly capitulated, saying, "Okay, then, if you're sure."

"I'm sure!"

"Fine. We'll pick your car up later." To the officers, he added, "I'll meet you at the station in a bit. I've got something to check out."

Sloan tucked Ronnie into the passenger side of his Bronco. "Sure you're okay?" he asked again and she sent him a dark, don't-go-there look. "Okay, okay," he said, palms up as he backed away from the SUV. She yanked the door closed. It warmed her heart that he so obviously cared, but she felt a restlessness, a desire to hurry, a driving, gut-clenching need to find Angel.

If they could.

For his part, Sloan, though certainly solicitous, was as intent as she, unrelentingly stern. Maybe he sensed, as she did, that Carlton Langdorf had actually murdered Angel. She hoped to God she was wrong, but the gnawing fear inside her was destroying all hope.

"Angel's car hasn't moved from our parking lot," she said as Sloan started the engine and hit the gas.

"Then that's where we'll go."

"What are you doing here?" Atticus Symons demanded imperiously as he glared at Cooper from the podium of the church. The preacher had appeared from a door on the right and crossed toward a lectern on the dais. He was wearing robes tonight, more ceremonial than the last time Cooper had crossed with him.

Some kind of rite was about to go down. Cooper could feel it. Didn't like it.

"I'm sorry, Father," said the terrified blond woman who had inadvertently let Cooper and Emma enter. She stood a few steps away from the preacher and was nearly cowering as she turned beseeching eyes at Cooper.

"Hush!" the preacher ordered and she backed up a step, nearly tripping on the hem of her cloak.

"Where's Emma?" Cooper ground through clenched teeth. He had to hold himself back from inflicting serious harm on the man.

"You're on private property. How did you get in?"

At the soft cry from the blond, Atticus turned, his angry gaze narrowing at her. "You opened the door," he accused.

"There was a girl, Father," she said in a rush, tears glistened in her eyes. "A young woman whose baby—"

"Where is she?" Cooper nearly leapt up the few steps to reach Atticus's level.

"You can't go there," Atticus said. "It's sacred ground and—"

"Stop me, then," Cooper challenged, one fist balling, the other ready to reach for his Glock, his gaze hawk-like on the preacher. As soon as Cooper found Emma, this sanctimonious prick was going down.

"I'll call the police and—"

"Call them. I'm a cop."

The preacher's eyes flickered. With anger? Fear?

"Call them. They can talk to every damned person in the flock."

For a moment, there was a standoff. Itching for the fight, Cooper mentally begged the man to come at him. "Where. Is. She? Tell me now or—"

A door suddenly opened.

Banging against the wall.

Echoing through the nave.

The huge cross above swaying a bit on its wires.

Harley flew into the church and one step behind her was Emma, incongruously clutching a knife. A crowd of other women followed them.

Thank God, she was all right!

And then, in her emotionless tone, Emma said to Atticus, "I don't like your way of meeting the Lord." She motioned broadly with her free hand to the women streaming into the nave and the pews within. "They don't like it, either."

Atticus's eyes were riveted on the knife and he paled a bit in his ornate robe. "What? *What?*" he uttered, obviously stunned for a second. Trying to gather his authority again, he started giving commands. "Go back to the dormitory. All of you! Sister Alma," he ordered one of the older woman. "Take them back. This is God's loving home!"

Harley snorted. "Arrest him, Cooper. He's been having sex with these women against their will. *God's loving home...*" she muttered under her breath as Cooper drew his weapon on a floundering Atticus.

"No, no, this is a sacred place! I won't be bullied. I only speak the word of God!" But now his gaze was fastened on the gun and the snap ties that Cooper withdrew from his pocket. Perfect to tie off a garbage bag, or use as handcuffs on supercilious dicks like Atticus Symons. "You give preachers a bad name," he said, wrapping the zip ties around Atticus's wrists.

Then as the congregation looked on from their pews, Cooper read Atticus Symons his rights. He might be on administrative leave, but he was still an officer of the law, and they could argue in the courts whether he had the right to arrest Symons, but in the moment, he didn't really give a shit.

The rain was falling in earnest, adding another chilling layer as Sloan and Ronnie pulled into her apartment parking lot. "Go over it all again with the bat and Angel," he'd ordered as he'd driven, and Ronnie had complied.

Now as they got out of his SUV, she was shivering again and he took off his coat and gave it to her, ignoring her protests that she could just go upstairs and add more layers of clothing.

"You told me he said he put the bat in the garbage," Sloan said.

"That's right."

He was already heading in the direction of the apartment building's east side, where the trash receptacles were stored. Clutching his coat over her shoulders, she hurried after him, ducking under the second-floor stairs on the far end of the balcony and crossing to a small, locked storage building.

Ronnie hesitated when she saw that the door was cracked. Sloan's gaze had been raking over the garbage receptacles, but now he looked back.

She reached out a hand to push open the door and Sloan said softly, "Don't."

She yanked her hand back as if burned.

Sloan took over.

Ronnie caught the ugly but faint scent of rotting drifting from the shed's interior.

"Oh, no," she whispered.

Sloan sent her an unreadable look, then pushed open the door and stepped inside the pitch-black interior. Heart pounding, she peeked in and saw the wall of boxes that loomed in front of him as he reached up and grabbed the string for the bare overhead bulb.

The place was instantly flooded with glaring light.

She didn't recognize any of the boxes, but then she'd only seen into the interior once when it was left open by the maintenance people.

Her nerves rippled within her skin.

Sloan turned around and hustled her out of the shed.

"Angel," she said. Her racing heart galumphed painfully in her chest.

"Someone."

Her stomach turned over, but she said, "I can identify him."

"Ronnie, I don't think—"

"Let me!"

Sloan clearly wanted to argue further, but she pressed her hand into his chest and moved past him to the wall of cardboard. Tentatively, holding her breath, she pressed against the side of one of the boxes with her elbow, pushing it slowly aside.

And there was the body.

Angel.

"Oh God," she whispered, tears burning hot in her eyes.

Angel lay on his back, eyes open, as if trained on the shed's ceiling. Blood had drained down from his crown and left a reddish-brown trail between those eyes. A bloody shovel lay beside him. Ronnie's wobbling knees gave out and she would have fallen if Sloan wasn't there to catch her.

\* \* \*

She lay on an examining table in ER, the afterimage of Angel's slain body burned on her retinas.

After finding him, Sloan had called the department, waited for an officer to arrive, then had reversed course and driven Ronnie to the ER to be checked out. She hadn't protested.

She'd felt . . . spent.

Still did.

The events of the past couple of hours crowded in her head.

Carlton had killed Angel. *Angel!* The knowledge was a heavy, heavy brick in her chest. She felt weak and responsible and angry. She'd so hoped she was wrong.

She closed her eyes against the pain of losing Angel. *He died because of me!*

Angel must've caught *Carlton* in the act of some further nefarious deed, maybe another dead bat for her, maybe something else. It didn't matter. He'd killed Angel with the shovel from the shed, then stacked the boxes to hide Angel's body before running away.

For money.

She turned her head to see Sloan pacing between her cubicle and the outer hallways. He'd told her that Marian had been examined, her stomach pumped, but whatever drug had been administered was already in her bloodstream. They'd discovered a prescription sleeping aid in her name and were giving her an antidote. Carlton had switched his plea, according to the officers who'd taken him in, to say that Marian had apparently accidentally overdosed on her own meds. This new take on what had gone down was apparently because no one had seriously believed Ronnie was at fault.

The ER staff was finished with Ronnie's test and waiting for results. They'd already concluded she was not concussed, a minor miracle, considering the way Carlton had attacked her.

"I wish Angel would have talked to me," Ronnie murmured as Sloan re-entered her cubicle. "I've seen him a few times lately, but haven't talked to him since he caught me, keeping me from falling when we first found the bat."

"Where did you last see him?" asked Sloan as he moved closer to her bedside, his phone beeping in his pocket.

"On the balcony outside our doors. Just for a second or two. It was . . . he was protecting me, but we never . . . got close again. He was . . ."

He'd checked his cell, but now he turned his gaze on her as her voice trailed off. His eyes were opaque and dark, more black than gray, and she couldn't read his thoughts.

"What?" he asked.

"Nothing. I don't know."

"Angel was . . . what?" he insisted.

*. . . like a ghost.*

In her mind's eye she could see Angel clearly as he'd been the last time she'd spotted him on the balcony. Leaning against the rail. In his usual slouched position. His head and shoulders outside the overhang, his feet and legs sprawled across the decking. It was snowing . . . It had been snowing, flakes falling all around, drifting under the overhang onto the decking, some sticking, some melting . . . only nothing was sticking to Angel. No snow. No melting precipitation.

Another hallucination of him, maybe? Not Angel in the flesh. That day it had been a quick sighting and since then she'd only seen shadows of him.

*Psychic ability, or a step into madness?*

She shivered and shook her head. Telling Sloan would only convince him that he should not have gotten involved with her in the first place. He might be regretting it already, she thought, with an aching little jolt to her heart. He might be taking care of her now, but he sure as hell was remote.

"I need to go to the station and interview Langdorf," he said, slipping his phone into his pocket.

"I'm fine. Do what you need to do. I can take Uber to my car."

"I'm not leaving you here."

"I'll take her," a familiar voice put in.

The curtain to her cubicle was swept back to reveal Brandy.

Her eyes were weary and dull and her hair was falling out of its clip.

"Hi," Ronnie greeted her, a catch in her throat. She was surprised Brandy was talking to her, had apparently sought her out. Maybe this was an olive branch? She hoped so. "How's Clint doing?"

"You're wrong about him," Brandy stated flatly to both Ronnie and Sloan. "Clint didn't physically hurt Mel. He just tried to reason with her."

"He's woken up?" Sloan fixed her with a stare.

"No. But when he does, he wants a lawyer." She returned the stare. "Leave him alone."

Sloan relaxed ever so slightly. "Townsend makes the calls on your brother."

"Oh. Right." She gave him her shoulder and turned to Ronnie. "I heard you were here. Why? What happened?"

"A long story."

"You can tell it to me on the way home."

"You're really my ride?" It lifted Ronnie's heart a bit.

"She hasn't been released yet," warned Sloan.

As if hearing his words, Ronnie's ER doc swept in again. Seeing Brandy, the young man said in surprise, "What are you doing down here?"

"Heard about a friend."

"Well, your friend is ready to go." He turned to Ronnie, but the smile that lingered on his face was for Brandy. Ronnie looked at Brandy, who rolled her eyes, but she, too, seemed glad to see the doctor.

As soon as he was gone, Brandy shot a frown Sloan's way, clearly waiting for him to leave.

He caught eyes with Ronnie for a moment, and she sensed he wanted to say something more. He hesitated, but with Brandy there, kept whatever he wanted to say to himself.

"Call me when you're free," he finally said to Ronnie.

"I've got this," Brandy reminded him.

Sloan clearly didn't want to leave her, which warmed Ronnie's heart. Although, she told herself, maybe he was just irked at Brandy's insistence. He said, "I'll call you as soon as I'm done with the interview."

As soon as they were alone, Brandy turned to her and whispered, "What Clint said? That wasn't a confession. He did *not* hurt Mel. All he meant was that he didn't mean to hurt Mel *emotionally*."

Ronnie wasn't about to take on the argument with her about Clint again. Especially with so fragile a truce between them. Instead, she agreed, "You might be right."

"You're just saying that because I'm your ride home."

Was that a faint spark of humor in Brandy's eyes?

"Maybe," Ronnie allowed. Then, "Why *are* you my ride?"

Brandy sobered immediately, her lips trembling a bit before she cleared her throat and said, "Because I lost one friend and I don't want to lose another."

Ronnie's throat tightened. "All for one and one for all?"

"Something like that."

She didn't trust her voice to answer. Instead, she found the necklace and held the broken shard out for Brandy to see. It took a moment, but Ronnie finally managed, "I found this earlier in an old jewelry box."

Brandy stared at it a long time, her lips clamped together. Never one to bend to emotion, she said, "Not only found it, but put it on, I see," she said. "God, I wonder where mine is. Don't even know if I still have it. That was a damn long time ago."

"A damn long time ago. Let's go."

They walked out to her car together and Brandy unlocked the doors. Climbing inside, Brandy hesitated before engaging the engine. She glanced in the rearview mirror, then over at Ronnie in the passenger seat. "Okay, I'll say it. It's not your fault. It's not Sloan's, either, although he and Townsend really piss me off."

"Sloan said Townsend is the one in charge—"

"I heard him. But let me finish. I hate apologizing. It's no one's fault but Clint's, okay? He's an idiot. He chased Mel down to that shed, which was apparently her hideaway. She'd go there to get away from the men in her life. Hugh, Clint, whoever else . . . Benzene and Wetherly . . . But Clint followed her to talk her out of ending it with him. They'd had some kind of fight I guess. She'd tried to break up with him. She said it was over and left, and he followed her."

"Clint told you this?"

"Well, yeah, but maybe he didn't mean to. Who knows? He's been in and out of consciousness. But when he's awake he's blabbing, blabbing, blabbing, and with that cop still outside ICU." She rolled her eyes. "For God's sake, he's not a criminal. Just a moron. I told him to shut up, but he wasn't clear enough for it to sink in." Then she said, as she started the engine, "So, where's your car? What's the address?"

Ronnie gave Brandy the address of the Langdorf mansion, and Brandy punched it into her GPS.

Once the address registered on the screen, Brandy said, "I've been thinking. I want to call that Paula, at your firm, for him."

"Paula Prescott?"

"Yes."

"She doesn't do a lot of defense work," Ronnie warned.

"She'll do it if you ask her."

Oh. "Is that what this—you insisting on giving me a ride—is all about?" Ronnie was plunged into disappointment as Brandy backed out of her parking slot and drove away from Glen Gen's parking lot.

"I just told you I don't want to lose you," she snapped. "Don't make this some nefarious plot."

Ronnie lifted her hands in surrender, but she was really starting to feel used and abused by people she knew.

Brandy slowed for a stoplight, idling behind a small sports car, and as she switched on the wipers, changed the subject. "What's with you and Sloan?"

"What do you mean?"

She slid Ronnie the "don't kid a kidder" look.

Ronnie *really* didn't want to go into her relationship with Sloan with Brandy right now.

"He seemed pretty possessive," she said as the light changed and the car in front of her didn't move. "Come on." Brandy hit the horn and the driver, startled, sped through the intersection, then made a quick turn into the lot of a strip mall. "Idiot," Brandy muttered under her breath, then to Ronnie, "Something's happened between you and Sloan. Don't tell me that long-ago prediction might be coming true."

"I won't tell you that."

"No wedding bells?"

"No. We just . . . spent one night together, that's all."

"Oh, shit. Really?" Her brows nearly reached her hairline.

"Too new to talk about. Might be nothing." Ronnie kept her gaze focused on the road ahead, her mind probing her own tender feelings. "He seems to have pulled back today."

"When you say, 'spent the night together,' not to put too fine a point on it, but . . ."

"You know what I'm saying." Ronnie half laughed as they passed by a park where a huge Christmas tree was lit and a few kids in thick jackets and rain gear were climbing on a dripping play structure. "We're not talking about this anymore. Tell me about Clint. What can I do to help?"

"Get Sloan off his back, for one thing."

"You heard him. Townsend's in charge."

"Yeah, they all work together," she said dismissively. "I want to clear Clint's name. I want to go through Mel's things, but they're at Hugh's. Maybe go back out to the clearing."

"You want to go to the clearing?"

"Someone else met Mel there besides Clint. At the shed. The person who really killed her. Right?"

Ronnie nodded slowly. There was still a chance Clint was responsible, or involved in some way. Or, maybe it was someone else.

"We need more information, but the sheriff is hiding it from us. Maybe you can talk Sloan into helping us."

Ronnie snorted.

"But you *saw* what happened to Mel in one of your visions," Brandy insisted.

"It was more like a dream," Ronnie corrected.

"Whatever. Maybe you can see it again. See who did it this time."

"That would be nice, but it doesn't work that way."

"Why doesn't it? Just try, okay? Push your brain, or whatever. Lean into it!"

"Brandy," she reproached as they passed a slower vehicle, an older Chevy where the driver was seemingly searching for an address.

"Please?"

Ronnie glanced over and met her pleading brown eyes. "All I know was the dog was there. And someone came to the shed door and Mel went to answer it, and she was surprised by someone."

"Who was it?"

"I don't know. I couldn't see."

"You see other things. Why can't you see this guy?"

"We could argue about this for hours, or do something constructive."

"Okay, okay." Brandy shook her head. "I'm working a day shift tomorrow. I'll be off around three, three thirty. Let's go to the clearing."

"I'll call Aunt Kat," Ronnie said, somewhat reluctantly. She didn't want to get in the way of Sheriff Townsend or Sloan, but she wanted answers, too.

The weight of Angel's death returned as Brandy pulled into the Langdorf circular drive. The police vehicles were gone, the windows of the house still illuminated. Ronnie's Escape was right where she'd parked it.

"Tomorrow," Brandy said and Ronnie thanked her for the ride as she got out and felt the chill of December in the rain that was spitting from the dark sky.

Driving back to her apartment Ronnie felt every bruise, bump and scrape from her fight with Carlton. As she pulled into her slot she noted the yellow tape announcing Angel's apartment as a crime scene and as she climbed the stairs to her unit, she spied more of the plastic ribbon on the shed and a few of the neighbors clustered together talking and smoking, one man in a down overcoat casting a glance her way.

Thankfully he didn't call to her, but a chill passed through her as she thought of Angel and she uttered a quick prayer before she hurried to her unit. As soon as she was inside she headed for a hot shower, standing under the spray until the water started to cool.

Then she climbed into flannel pajamas before sliding into bed, where she pulled the covers up tight to her chin. She both wanted Sloan to come over and wished to be alone with her thoughts. She needed to think. To relax. To do the opposite of what Brandy suggested. Not lean in, but lean out. She'd been too tense and upset for far too long.

It was barely eight o'clock, but she was done for the day. Not hungry, even though she hadn't eaten.

When her phone rang, she grabbed for it on her nightstand. Was disappointed that it wasn't Sloan. Realized he'd asked her to call him and she just... hadn't. She frowned at the caller ID. Evan Caldwell? She considered ignoring the call. She didn't want to talk to anyone but Sloan.

But...

"Hi, Evan," she managed to greet him.

"Hi, there," he replied. "I expected to hear from you."

"Me? Why?"

"Didn't Sloan tell you I have something for you? I told him to tell you to call me."

Did he? God, her whole day was such a mess. "What is it?"

"I did a little research on you," he said and she thought she heard his smug smile in his voice.

"What kind of research?"

"You know, some family background stuff."

Instantly she felt her muscles tense. "On my family?" she asked.

"So you've got your father and your Aunt Katarina? Right? And your mom supposedly died when you were about four?"

Her skin prickled. "Supposedly?"

"No record of her death, Ronnie, my dear. None that I

could find. And you know I can find just about anyone or anything."

Her insides churned. Where the hell was this going?

"Ever see her death certificate?" he asked.

"Well, no."

"Somebody's been lying to you," he said and his words seemed to echo in her head. "Your Spidey sense never pick up on that?"

Ronnie's nerveless fingers dropped the phone onto the bed. She could hear Evan's tinny, "Hello? Hello? You there?" but it didn't really register in her brain. Mom was *alive*? No. They wouldn't lie to her about that. Not her father. For sure not Aunt Kat.

She threw back the covers and leapt out of bed. Stood in shock in the bedroom for a full minute without moving, then swept up the cell and cut Evan off. She couldn't hear this. Not from him. She pulled up Aunt Kat's contact picture, her thumb hovering over the button to connect.

Lied to... she'd been lied to? *Mom was alive?!*

No. Don't trust Evan. It's too fantastical.

But was it? Her mind reeled. A hundred questions swirled in her head.

*Don't buy into it. Don't!* But—

She tossed the cell back onto the bed as if it were poison.

Don't call. Wait till tomorrow.

The sudden knocking on her front door made her startle and cry out. Her cell rang at the same time. She saw the screen. Sloan. She swept up the phone again and answered.

"I'm at your door," he said. "You okay? You never called."

"Sorry... sorry... I just came home and got in the shower."

"You okay?" he repeated, but his tone had shifted. She could tell he was on alert. Worried.

"I'm fine." She half laughed.

"Can you open the door?"

She hurried through her living room, feeling raw and exposed. When she let him in she wanted to throw herself into his arms. She only hesitated because he seemed so rigid and cold.

"What is it?" she asked. She sensed there was something more going on than what she knew about. That was sure an understatement! Did she believe Evan Caldwell? No. No. It couldn't be. She trusted her family more than that. Didn't she?

"You still feel okay, then?" he asked, examining her face.

"Hard question to answer right now." Her limbs were trembling and she reached for the back of one of the chairs to steady herself.

"You want to go back to the hospital?" he asked quickly.

"No, no. It's not that." She looked up at him, at the raindrops glistening in his hair and the rain-spattered shoulders of his coat—the very coat he'd placed over her shoulders earlier, but slipped on again at the hospital. "Aren't you going to take your coat off?" she asked, then, "Why didn't you tell me Evan had something for me?" At the same moment he said, "Townsend got some DNA evidence at the crime scene."

Ronnie held up a hand, took a step backward. She felt slightly hysterical. "You go first."

He frowned. "I forgot about Evan," he admitted.

She waved that away. "What DNA evidence?"

"It was on a coffee cup lid found at the scene. Townsend put a real rush on it."

"Uh-oh," she murmured, realizing by his strained attitude it must be someone he knew. "Clint's?"

"No," he said solemnly. "It was yours."

# Chapter 23

"Mine? What? *What?*"

Her brain couldn't process what he'd said. The hysteria that had been lying just below the surface bubbled upward and spilled over. She fell into the chair she'd been using for support, then bent forward, her head down by her knees, suddenly laughing like the mad woman she'd become.

He tried to outwait her, which made her laugh all the more.

It wasn't ha-ha funny. It wasn't even strange funny. But she couldn't stop herself.

"Have you eaten?" he asked as she finally climbed to her feet and shoved her hair from her eyes.

"Oh . . . yeah . . . I went to a restaurant and ordered a prime rib dinner with all the trimmings, Yorkshire pudding for sure!" Ha, ha, ha, ha. "Next, I'm going to have crème brûlée . . . No. Baked Alaska! Set the dessert on fire and bring it to me."

Sloan regarded her with concern. He moved as if to embrace her, but she shrank away from him.

"Don't touch the crazy person," she said tightly.

"You're not crazy."

"How do you know? I've done some pretty crazy things, right? I've seen it in your face."

"I don't think you killed Melissa McNulty," he stated flatly.

"Oh, well, thanks for that."

"I'll order something," he said, dragging his eyes from her as he retrieved his phone from a pocket.

"You do that," she gulped.

She wanted to scream and jump and have a full-on fit. Anything to shake up his composure like she'd been shaken to the core.

As soon as her laughter slowed down, she was stricken by hiccups that threatened to knock her off her feet. She crossed the living room to the balcony and then paced back again. She was acting like a maniac. She knew. Her head felt it was about to explode. TMI to the max.

He was ordering ramen and gyoza and rice. Japanese food. She had no appetite but realized grudgingly that she needed to eat or everything was just going to get a hell of a lot worse.

She wanted to go to bed and pull her pillow over her head for a millennium. She wanted to find her lying father and wring his neck. She wanted to hit Carlton over and over again with Marian's cane, and she wanted to make love fiercely with Sloan and make it all go away.

Her gaze was centered on Sloan, watching as he clicked off. She was a hair's breadth from throwing herself on him, ripping off his clothes, slamming him up against the wall.

He misunderstood whatever emotion showed on her face. "There's this little ramen place I found that I wanted to take you to."

"Before you decided I was a criminal."

He narrowed his eyes at her. "I don't think you're a criminal."

"Okay, no. Not a criminal. But certifiable. Bring on the 5150," she said, citing the police code for involuntary detention of someone having a mental health crisis.

Her head was still full of Evan's shocking news. She hadn't even asked him about debriefing Carlton. She didn't have room for anything more. Except . . . "DNA?" she repeated, trying to make it make any sense. "*My* DNA?"

"So Townsend said." He finally took off his coat, throwing it over the back of a chair, not the peg behind the door. A clue that he wasn't planning to stay.

Well, fine. She didn't want him to, anyway.

*Liar.*

"Food'll be here in about forty minutes," he alerted her.

"Well, good. A last meal."

She could almost feel him shrink away from her, even though he hadn't moved. She wanted him to leave. She needed to be alone with her thoughts, to calm down, to think. *Her* DNA? What the hell? Was this from that swab she'd sent off to some lab to check her heritage? Had to be.

The fact that she'd wanted to know more about her "gift" had now somehow put her on the short list for Mel's killing?

"Were you ever at that clearing before Melissa McNulty was killed there?" he asked.

"Since childhood? I don't think so. Unless . . . maybe I just don't remember. Maybe I was in a psychic fugue and went there to strangle my friend . . . from elementary school . . . and then I came to you to be the one to find her because . . . because . . ."

"How did a coffee-cup lid with your DNA end up in the clearing? Give me a way that could happen," he cut in.

*He's giving you an out. He really wants to believe in you.*

*Or, he wants you to face the fact you are a complete lunatic. You are a complete lunatic. Your mother was a complete lunatic . . . and she's ALIVE?*

He was waiting for an answer.

With an effort she forced herself to take a deep breath, trying desperately to clear out the insanity, trying to reach reality. Finally, she said, "I don't know how it got there. I didn't leave it there. If I'd set out to kill a friend of mine whom I hadn't seen in a decade or more"—she shot him a baleful look—"I sure wouldn't be sloppy enough to leave that kind of evidence that I'd been there. I'm not quite that inept."

"Ronnie—"

"Stop!" She held up a hand. "I liked it better when you called me Quick."

She saw his jaw work. Was she pissing him off? She hoped so. She wanted to feel something more than this terrible overwhelming tsunami of pain and grief and complete bafflement. "And don't ask me why I can't save myself by just 'psychically' calling up who killed Mel. I know that's what's coming next. Well, it doesn't work that way! Sometimes it just feels like I'm . . . blocked!"

"How did the coffee lid get there?" he asked again.

Cop mode. He was in cop mode. Well, fine, she'd asked for this, hadn't she? She concentrated hard on her dream of Mel and the dog, but her mind slipped to Carlton . . . and then Angel . . .

She slumped into her favorite chair, spent. Too many deaths. Too short a time. Mel . . . Angel . . . Shana . . .

Her brain fizzed. Oh. Shit.

"Shana," she said, exhaling a whoosh of breath she hadn't known she'd been holding.

"Shana?" His attention sharpened.

"She asked to stop for a coffee when I was taking her home from the hospital, so I drove through Starbucks and we each got one. She said she'd get rid of my paper cup for me. She actually seemed eager to do it." Ronnie blinked in recollection.

"A Starbucks cup with a lid?"

"I left it at her apartment . . ."

He was staring at her, but her mind was clicking away, reviewing the past. He said slowly, "You're saying she took your coffee cup on purpose? To plant false evidence?"

"No . . . I . . ."

Ronnie trailed off, grappling with the idea that Shana could have purposefully left the coffee cup lid at the clearing. But what other explanation was there? "Shana didn't know Mel. She didn't know anything about her. That doesn't make sense." *But you saw Mel's image over Shana's.* "She didn't have a car. I drove her home."

"There are other means of transportation," Sloan pointed out as he started pacing. Thinking aloud. "Uber, Lyft, a friend..."

"Shana said she didn't have any friends. Even Evan couldn't pick her up."

Sloan suddenly sucked in a sharp breath of air and stopped dead center in the middle of the living room. "Amy Deggars. I saw her today." He scoffed. "She accused me of killing Shana."

"What?" She looked up to see that she heard correctly. "Accused *you*?"

"She said Shana was spooked and scared of me."

"That doesn't make sense, either," declared Ronnie.

"I hadn't seen Shana in years." He shrugged in bafflement. "Maybe she transferred her fear to me. Or, maybe she was afraid of someone else and didn't want Deggars to know who that someone was... so she led her to believe it was me."

"Who, then? Who was she afraid of?"

"If Shana left that evidence at the scene to implicate you, then she knew something about Mel's death."

"She knew who he was. And she was a danger to them... oh!" Ronnie pressed a hand to the side of her head.

"What's wrong?" Sloan was by her side in an instant.

"No, no... nothing. More like too much information. I was just thinking: Could we be wrong? In just assuming Mel's killer is a man? Maybe there's a jealous woman out there? Someone who thought Mel was stealing her man... we know Mel had a number of lovers..."

A knock on the door heralded the DoorDash food and Ronnie got out of her chair, ignoring Sloan's protests to help as she carried the bag into the kitchen, pulled the food from the bag and set up plates and bowls for them at the table, a simple task that left her time to think.

She sat down, her spoon poised over her bowl. "Could Shana have done it?"

"Eat," ordered Sloan, pointing at her bowl.

Ronnie's mind was whirling, but she dipped her spoon into the ramen. The broth was salty and hot, and she could feel it warm her chest and take the edge off the chill that had descended upon her.

"It doesn't feel like a woman," said Sloan, thinking aloud as he dug into his meal.

Ronnie didn't respond. She sensed he couldn't bring himself to blame Shana, even though she had to be the one who'd left the coffee-cup lid with her DNA at the scene.

"I need to talk to Amy Deggars again," he said determinedly.

So, he hadn't given up on the idea completely.

"I'm sorry about my meltdown earlier," she said. "I'm really not crazy."

His smile was tender. "I know."

That desire to throw herself into his arms came roaring back.

"What was it Caldwell wanted to give you?" he asked, blunting her impulse.

She didn't want to go into her family craziness with Sloan just when he'd said he believed in her sanity. And . . . she wasn't sure she believed Evan. The man loved to play games, and maybe he really believed her mother was still alive . . . *still alive!* . . . but she needed to work it out for herself. "Evan seems fascinated by my family's psychic abilities and did some research on us."

"DNA?"

"No, this was something else."

Sloan's cell buzzed in his pocket and he withdrew it to read the new text. "Verbena. She's back tomorrow." He pocketed the phone again, then took a final bite and wadded his napkin. "I'm going to see Amy Deggars."

She saw he wanted to keep pushing on the case because it might be taken away from him entirely once Detective Verbena was back on the job. "What about Detective Haynes?"

"He's still on leave. But I could be out of a job soon, after having two for a while," he said ironically and pushed his chair back.

"Be careful," she said suddenly, following him to the doorway.

He was putting on his coat and stopped to eye her for a brief moment. "You know something I don't, or is that just a general warning?"

"A general warning, but it feels like you're getting close. Maybe I should go with you."

"Yeah, that's a good idea, with the day you've had," he said dryly. "I'll be back soon."

And then he was gone.

Harley trailed after Cooper and Emma as they walked into their house. Emma was immediately swarmed by Duchess, while Twink was nowhere in sight. Probably with Mom.

Harley couldn't take her eyes off her aunt. Emma was always surprising, but the deal with the knife? Would she have really attacked Atticus Symons? Harley and Cooper had traded looks on the way home and Harley was pretty sure he was wondering the same thing.

Well, there was one way to find out. Once inside the kitchen Harley asked, "Emma, would you have really stabbed Atticus Symons?"

"He was not their father." Emma found the bag of dog food for Duchess in the pantry, while the dog pranced eagerly about her legs.

"I know that, but, I mean, actually stabbing with a knife... that's bold."

"Cooper arrested him."

Cooper put in, "I held him for the police, and it may be short-lived unless the women of the church bring evidence against him. File charges."

Emma said, "They don't like him."

"Some of them seemed to," Harley argued. "But I'm still glad you didn't stab him. I don't want you to be in trouble."

"They would rather be on the bus," Emma explained while pouring kibble into Duchess's bowl. "That's where God's love is found."

"Not sure about that, but okay," muttered Harley. "At least that fucker's in jail now."

"The f-word will cost you a dollar," Emma pointed out, then set Duchess's bowl on the floor.

Cooper said, "I'll be upstairs with Jamie," and bounded up the steps two at a time.

Harley fought back a shiver. Reaction, she decided. There was nothing to fear any longer. The bad guy had been rounded up. "Mom should be relieved now. Mary Jo's back home and the church is shut down."

As long as the women complained about Symons. Some of them had been fierce, but some of them seemed to backslide in their resolve when they saw Symons being led away by the police.

And there was the very real possibility that Cooper's "citizen's arrest" would be challenged because he wasn't really an instated officer right now.

"Don't borrow trouble," she told herself as she went to find the dollar bills she kept in her dresser drawer, a stash started since the summer when the shit that started at the camp had changed the f-word from a now-and-again thing to a staple of her vocabulary.

It was almost eleven p.m. when Sloan banged on Amy Deggars's door. She was reluctant to answer. It took three series of loud knocks despite light burning bright in the apartment's windows.

Under threat that he would call for backup, more cops, she cracked open the door, just as far as a security chain would allow. Through the gap, he noticed a packed bag tucked near a hall tree in the entryway.

"Go away! I know who you are!" she said, auburn hair pulled into a tight topknot.

"I just want to talk to you."

"And I don't want to talk to you. I—I know my rights," she argued, refusing to budge.

"Okay, then we'll do it your way," and he raised his voice, loud enough to disturb anyone in a nearby apartment. "What do you know about Shana Lloyd's—"

"Stop!" She scrambled to remove the chain and let him into the tiny entry hall, but when he tried to question her deeper about Shana, Amy—a compact, wiry woman—fell back on Shana's supposed declaration that he was at fault, and wouldn't budge.

"Why are you talking to me, then, if you think that's true?" he demanded.

"You're the police!"

Sloan said, "You know I didn't strangle Shana."

"I don't know that!"

"Yes, you do. You know I wasn't even in Shana's life," he pressed.

"She said you were," she argued, her pointed chin jutting out.

"That's a fiction on her part. I can tell you know it."

"I don't care what's true, okay? I'm leaving! She's dead. He . . . *you* killed her."

"He?" Sloan shot back.

She shook her head, desperate to dismiss her own slip. "I don't know! I don't know!"

"Because she planted fake evidence at a crime scene."

Her mouth dropped open. "No . . . no . . ."

"Did you drive her or lend her your car?" Sloan asked.

"I just told you no!"

Sloan fixed her with a glare. "Shana Lloyd is dead. There's a reason someone killed her. You can tell me now, or tell me down at the station."

"I DON'T KNOW ANYTHING! Yes! Yes! She borrowed my car and it came back muddy . . . and that's when she got scared. I washed the car, but we were both scared. She said she was going away, so I drove her home."

"When did she take your car? What day?" he barked at her.

"Thursday . . . no, Friday morning, really early. It was still dark out. I was pissed. I had to take Uber to work at the firm. I called her on the phone and gave her hell when she got back, but she didn't care. She was scared, scared of you, she said. I took her home. That's all I know. That's really all I know. Now please," she wheedled, "just leave. If you arrest me, they'll find me and kill me. Just let me go!"

"Who are 'they'?"

"I don't know. That's what I'm telling you!" She was wild-eyed and desperate, more fragile than she'd first appeared.

He sensed she'd given him everything she knew. It was Shana who'd gone to her grave with information on who had killed Melissa McNulty. "You'd be safe at the station," he told her more calmly.

"Yeah? For how long? Once you're done grilling me, you'll kick me out. And he'll . . . they'll find me!"

"If you're not involved, you should be safe."

"And end up like Shana?" She looked panicked, glanced down at the packed bag, obviously wishing she could leave.

"Did she ever mention where she was going?"

"NO." Picking up the bag, she slung the strap over her shoulder.

Sloan suddenly wished he'd brought Quick with him. After everything that had happened, Ronnie was frustrated and scared and teetering back and forth into hysteria, but she knew people. Even beyond the psychic abilities.

"Take my number," he said, gesturing to the phone she was gripping in one hand. The truth was, Amy was right that she would be interviewed at the station and then left to her own devices. Maybe she'd infected him with her paranoia, but he thought she might also be right about getting the hell out of Dodge. "Where are you going?"

"No plans. Driving south. California. Maybe Arizona . . . maybe somewhere else entirely." She gave a half laugh. "Everything's blowing up at the law firm anyway. Sofia's been fucking around with one of the other lawyers and hasn't been discreet about it. Sofia Waters. The boss's wife. Heads will roll."

That's right. Amy worked at the Bernard K. Waters Law Firm. Along with Galen Hillyard, Ronnie's ex-husband. A small, small world was River Glen.

They both stepped outside and Amy locked the door behind them.

He memorized the license plate of the silver Subaru Outback

as she drove away. Maybe it was a fool's move on his part, but he let her go. He only hoped he wouldn't end up regretting it.

*Stay calm. Don't move. Deep breaths.*
*Close your eyes.*
*Listen to your own heartbeat.*

Ronnie tried the tricks her childhood therapist, Patrice, had used to get her to relax during a session. She stayed silent in her chair, willing herself to remain immobile, letting her mind do the moving.

What first? she asked herself.

The betrayal from Dear Old Dad and Aunt Kat.

*Is it betrayal?*

She looked at the clock. Midnight? God, how had it gotten so late?

The soft knocking on her door an hour later sent her nerves abuzz.

Then her phone *dinged* with a text.

**I'm at your door.**

Sloan.

She flew to answer it and this time she did throw herself into his arms. He squeezed her tightly as if he couldn't bear to let her go. They stumbled as one into her bedroom and said not a word as they stripped down and wrapped themselves around each other.

# Chapter 24

"We need to talk things through. Meet with Duncan. Command performance from the big man himself," Verbena said. Sloan had nearly missed the call, but picked up and tried to argue his way out of the meeting. "Why don't you bring me up to speed before we roll in."

"When?" he said, glancing down at Ronnie, who was sleeping like the dead, hadn't even woken when his phone had buzzed insistently.

"Fifteen minutes."

"Make it twenty." He stretched and rolled out of bed, hating the thought of leaving her. Melissa, Shana and Angel were all dead and she was somehow at the center of it. The woman seemed to collect homicides. Though Sloan believed Carlton Langdorf was behind Angel's murder and had tried to kill his aunt as well as Ronnie, it didn't seem likely he was behind either Shana's or Mel's death.

But someone was.

And that someone might be focused on Ronnie.

Why, he didn't know, but his guts ground at the thought of

leaving her alone. Unprotected. He bent over and kissed her cheek and she stirred, but didn't waken. She'd been through too much recently and was finally catching up on much-needed sleep.

He didn't want to wake her.

If he did, he was certain one kiss or touch would lead to another and then he'd be late for certain.

He walked through the shower and didn't bother shaving.

When he stepped back into the bedroom, he noticed she hadn't stirred, so he threw on yesterday's clothes, scribbled a note that he left near the coffeepot for her to call him before she went out, then texted the same and locked the door behind him.

As tired as she was, he might be back before she even opened an eye.

Then, with a last glance at her apartment, he climbed into his Bronco and took off. He was just being paranoid, he told himself as he saw his reflection in the rearview mirror. Because he cared. He cared too much.

Ronnie stretched luxuriously in the bed as weak sunlight invaded the room. Her mind was on Sloan and his lovemaking. And though he was gone, had already left for work, no doubt, her thoughts lingered on those pleasurable moments of the night before, for the space of about thirty seconds, then her eyes flew open. She was supposed to go into work today, too. She *was* going into work today, she corrected herself.

And part of the reason she was going in was to confront her father. She needed answers.

And part was to just *do* something. To push aside the worst parts of the last few days. Her heart ached when she thought about Mel and Angel, and her blood boiled when she thought about how Carlton Langdorf had taken Angel's life.

She threw back the covers and headed for the shower. Fifteen minutes later she dressed in black slacks, a caramel, ribbed turtleneck sweater and a black jacket, but when it came to shoes, she hesitated. It wasn't the most fashionable choice but she had a pair of pure black sneakers. She had plans to head to Aunt Kat's as soon as she could and maybe check out the crime scene herself.

She was out of coffee, but saw the note that Sloan had left. It echoed the text he'd sent her, telling her to call him immediately and not leave the apartment until he returned.

Well, that wasn't going to happen.

He knew she had a job and this morning, of all mornings, she wasn't going to arrive late. Not when she planned to confront Jonas. As soon as she had it out with her father, then she'd call or text Sloan.

She queued up for the drive-through at Starbucks on the way, ordering black coffee. She stared at the plastic lid for long seconds, thinking about Shana and what that could possibly mean. Sloan had brought her up-to-date on what Amy Deggars had said, how Shana had taken her car and brought it back muddy from some unknown destination. It stood to reason she'd driven to the clearing where Mel had died. Clint Mercer's truck wasn't the only vehicle that had been there. There had been other tire tracks, so far as she knew, unmatched to any vehicle. So, it appeared that Shana had taken Ronnie's coffee cup lid to the site after Mel was killed, but before the police found her. Either that, or Shana had murdered Melissa herself?

"Shana didn't kill Mel," she said aloud. "She showed up to the clearing after Mel had been murdered." But then she must've seen Mel's body lying there.

She shuddered. Maybe that sighting is what had terrified her so?

Had someone *directed* her to leave the coffee-cup lid?

*Someone who wanted to implicate me and used Shana to do it.*

Shana had taken orders from Galen, who worked at the Bernard K. Waters Law Firm.

As she parked her SUV, Ronnie's mind instantly flew to her image of Galen and the boss's wife kneeling in front of his desk chair. Was there anything in that? Any connection to Mel's killer? Galen . . . ? No. He was a lot of things, but a murderer . . . ?

*Didn't you think the killer was a woman last night?*

Yeah, well... maybe it was... and maybe it wasn't. The truth was, she had no idea.

For a moment she shared Brandy's impatience with her "gift." Why did she only get part of the picture? Why couldn't she see more?

"And what about the dog?" she muttered furiously as she headed up in the elevator from the parking lot to the Tormelle & Quick offices. Why did she hear the dog sometimes and other times not at all? The dog had gone crazy when she was in the fight with Carlton Langdorf, but that was the last time she'd heard it.

*It warns you.*

That thought left her bemused as she exited the elevator and spied Dawn at her desk, frantically waving her over.

"What?" asked Ronnie.

"Are you okay? We all heard Carlton Langdorf is in jail for attacking you and drugging his aunt."

"He killed a friend of mine."

Dawn sucked in a startled breath. "What? Seriously? Who? Oh, my God! Why?"

"Because he thought I was going to steal Marian's money from him."

"Fucking asshole!"

"You got that right," Ronnie said with feeling. Anytime she thought of Angel she suffered a wave of fresh anger. She hoped Carlton went away to prison for the rest of his life.

The desk phone rang and Dawn reached for the receiver, still looking gobsmacked.

Ronnie pulled herself back from her own anger and asked, "Jonas in?"

"Not yet." Dawn cleared her throat and then answered, "Tormelle and Quick."

Normally Ronnie shared everything with Dawn, but today she was almost grateful for the phone's distraction.

She headed to her office, hanging her overcoat on the hall tree inside her door and glancing out her window to the dual brick buildings next door, dull orange beneath a leaden sky today.

She wanted to call Sloan. Had to force herself not to press the buttons on her phone. Instead, she left her office and rapped on the open doorjamb to Martin Calgheny's office. "Tuesday still good for the Bentons?" she asked.

He snorted. "One more change. Dolly Benton had been keeping secret her second marriage to some ex-pat living in London, and there's a possibility of another will. Her kids are out of their minds and it looks like we're not the law firm involved anymore."

He leaned back in his chair and put his hands behind his fringe of gray hair. "Just learned that this morning."

"That's . . . unexpected."

"Family secrets." He shrugged and shook his head. "Never turns out well."

She walked back to her office, her gut churning. She thought about calling Brandy but she was at work till this afternoon.

Where was Jonas? Her impatience was growing with each passing minute. Family secrets . . .

She sat down at her desk and punched in Aunt Kat's number on her cell. It rang on and on and she was about to hang up before voice mail kicked in when her aunt finally answered. "Hi. Sorry. I was outside checking the apple trees. The sun's out, finally! Maybe it will stop hovering around freezing."

She clearly hadn't heard anything about what had happened over the past few days since Ronnie had last talked to her.

"Aunt Kat, if I ask you something, will you be completely honest with me?"

"Is this about your gift?"

"It's about Mom."

"I told you. You're not like your mother. I think we established that last time you were—"

"Is Mom alive?"

Her intake of breath sounded like a gasp.

*I should have done this in person. I should have my eyes on her.*

"What kind of question is that?" Now Aunt Kat sounded almost mad.

"Can I see her death certificate?"

"Who have you been talking to?" she shot back.

It was Ronnie's turn to gasp. It wasn't like Aunt Kat to be anything but supportive. She hadn't truly believed Evan, not completely, but oh, God...

Closing her eyes she had a flash of psychic inspiration, a moment of pure clarity. To Aunt Kat's question, she answered flatly, "Dad."

She waited for an answer, but all she could hear was Aunt Kat's stuttered breathing.

They'd planned this together, she realized. This... *deception.*

"She's not well," Aunt Kat said hurriedly. "She hasn't been well for years. She's not even reachable anymore."

"Where is she?" Ronnie demanded. She was on her feet without being aware she'd risen.

"Veronica, I know you're upset, but—"

"WHERE IS SHE?" She didn't care that her scream could probably be heard all the way to reception.

"Seagull Pointe. Outside the town of Deception Bay. On the Oregon Coast. But if you go there, she won't recognize you."

"Because I haven't fucking seen her since I was four!"

"Oh, honey, no. It's just that... that she was plagued by visions and kept heading to the beach, to the ocean. Driving like a madwoman! We were afraid she would take you with her and drive off the road, killing you both!"

"You should have told me," Ronnie ground out and felt as if her very soul had been trampled upon. How could they lie to her? Dad? Aunt Kat?

"I wanted to. We both wanted to. It just never felt like it was the right time."

"It's been over twenty-five years!" The horror of it struck deep into her heart.

"I know. I know. But—"

"I need to see her."

"Well. Yes. Yes, of course." Aunt Kat was scrambling. "I'll go with you. Yes. I'll make sure—"

Ronnie cut her off with a hard push of her thumb on her cell screen. Her hand was shaking. Her whole body was shaking from the inside out.

Her phone rang back. Aunt Kat. She ended the call and switched off her ringer.

She stood perfectly still for the space of ten heartbeats, then charged out of the office.

"Where are you going?" asked Dawn as she bypassed the elevator in favor of the exit stairs.

"To the beach, I guess," she threw back, stiff-arming the door to the stairwell that led to the underground parking lot.

Sloan waited for Verbena outside Chief Duncan's office. He had a lot to tell her and felt he was wasting time while the chief brought her up-to-date on Sloan's investigations, something he could have done himself, especially since he hadn't given Duncan all the details, mainly because it had been a pretty heavy load over the weekend.

When Verbena was finally released into the squad room, she lifted a dark brow at him, which he took to mean she was surprised by all she'd heard.

And she hadn't even heard the half of it.

She sat at her desk, her black hair pulled back severely into a bun at her nape, her brown eyes pinning him as he moved closer and leaned against Cooper Haynes's desk.

"Sit down," she said. "I've heard what Humph had to say. Now you can bring me up to speed. I know about the McNulty woman's body found in the woods, and that Clint Mercer is your number one 'person of interest.' What else?"

"Mercer's in ICU at Glen Gen."

"You think he's good for it?"

"We believe he was at the homicide site. We have tree DNA

and tire tracks that will probably corroborate that theory. He's as much as admitted he was there. Says he didn't mean to hurt her. Denies killing her. They were in a romantic relationship, but he wasn't the only man McNulty was seeing."

"Motivation jealousy? Revenge killing?"

*This was a crime of passion.* Quick's words.

"Seems that way."

"What else?" she asked.

"Veronica Quick and Brandy Mercer interviewed several men McNulty had allegedly been seeing. Each of them admitted to a relationship with her, but insisted they weren't anywhere near the clearing where McNulty died. They both pointed the finger at Mercer."

"But . . . ?"

She clearly had heard his hesitancy about putting the blame squarely on Mercer. "We have alibis to check. Sheriff Townsend interviewed McNulty's husband, Hugh McNulty. He wanted me to back off on Mercer. Said he'd handle it from that point. I haven't personally interviewed McNulty yet. Planning to do it today."

"There have been a couple other suspicious deaths?"

"Shana Lloyd was strangled in her apartment. Or, at least left there. Her apartment door lock doesn't latch properly, so the perpetrator didn't have to have a key or be let in."

"You brought up Veronica Quick, the psychic. You allowed her to investigate the death of her friend."

"I didn't stop her." Quick and Brandy Mercer had taken that on, on their own, but he didn't defend himself.

"Has she helped you? Psychically?"

Sloan wondered if this was a trick question. But Quick had been instrumental in saving Edmond Olman's wife, so maybe Verbena was being on the level. "She had a vision of McNulty's death before we discovered her body," he said carefully.

"Just the one?"

Sloan leveled a look at her. "No. As you seem to well know. Am I being interrogated?"

Verbena dropped her gaze from his and looked down at the pile of papers on her desk. "Walk with me," she said, getting up from her chair. She headed for the back door of the station.

Sloan, sensing he was under curious eyes, casually followed after, picking up his overcoat on the way out. He caught up to her as she shrugged into her own black wool coat and they strode through the rain to one of the department Explorers.

"You're driving," she said, handing him the keys to the black SUV.

"Where are we going?" he asked, as he backed around and headed out of the lot.

"Somewhere we can talk privately. Just drive."

Ronnie cracked her window as she started through the Coast Range toward the Oregon Coast, letting the air play with her hair and cool her overheated face. She'd been lied to. Lied to for most of her life. Decades. She'd grieved her mother for *years* and neither her father nor Aunt Kat had ever told her the truth.

*And they were in it together. A conspiracy of two.*

She wanted to call someone—Sloan—but reception in the mountains was spotty and the road surface was wet but could turn icy as she climbed through evergreen forests of old-growth timber.

*Mom's alive!*

Her heart jolted again. She just couldn't . . . believe . . . it!

She didn't care if her mother didn't recognize her. Didn't care what the situation was. Just to know Mom was alive . . . ALIVE.

She could kill her father for keeping it from her. And she was livid with Aunt Kat.

With an effort she pushed her fury aside and just drove.

Harley's mind was full of about anything and everything but the term final test in front of her as she sat down in her classroom at Portland State. Spanish.

All that was going through her head was: *Padre loco, padre loco, padre loco.*

Unlikely to be on the test. She softly muttered to herself, "*Delincuente sexual.*" Sex offender. She'd had to look that one up on her phone on the way in.

Crazy sex offender father, Atticus Symons, was not in jail where he should be. He'd already hired legal counsel and was spitting mad and claiming he was going to sue. Still, several women in his flock had come forward and named him as the father of their children, one of whom was just barely nineteen, so it wasn't looking good for the *puta mierda*. Fucking shit. Another lookup. One she planned to hang on to.

Feeling the proctor's eyes on her, she bent her head to her paper.

"Why do I still feel anxious?" Jamie asked Cooper, who'd told her the whole story about Atticus Symons and his Heart of Sunshine Church. She was relieved that Mary Jo Kirshner was back with her family, her pregnancy still on schedule, the baby healthy as far as they all knew, but there were other worries to consider. "You're not going to get in trouble over this, are you? Not really being with the police?"

Cooper shrugged. "Wouldn't change anything. He's been exposed."

"What about those women? His—oh, I don't know what they call them—sister wives or girlfriends or whatever. What will they do now?"

"They plan to run the church the way it should be run. And there are a few men who live on the grounds, too. They appear to want to pitch in and make the church what it purported to be all along."

"Good." She made a face and leaned up in bed, rubbing her lower back. "I think I'll get up and walk." As Cooper watched her uneasily, she assured him, "Just to the bathroom."

His cell buzzed and he plucked it from his pocket, saw it was the chief and felt a shock of worry that maybe Jamie's fears had been clairvoyant. "Haynes."

"You were busy this weekend."

Yep. "You heard about Symons."

"Verbena's back and working with Hart."

Cooper glanced in the direction of the bathroom. If he was getting bad news, he wanted to keep it from his wife. "Glad she's back." He'd spoken to Verbena just this morning. The chief probably knew that.

"I'm trying to shorten your leave, Haynes," the chief said. "Try to stay out of trouble for another week or so, okay?"

"Okay." He was flooded with relief. "What happens to Hart when I come back?"

"That guy . . ." He scoffed.

Cooper strained to listen to what his boss was really thinking. He couldn't tell if it was good or bad, where Sloan Hart was concerned.

"Three homicides over a weekend. And all of them center around Verbena's psychic friend, who, I understand, once predicted she would marry Hart."

"Where'd you get that?"

He scoffed again. He wasn't one to reveal information he felt you weren't worthy of receiving. "Just enjoy the rest of your time off. Take it easy. Hart seems capable enough, and with the homicide rate being what it is, you'll both be on full hire, along with Verbena. Oh, and say hello to that lovely wife of yours."

Verbena had mentioned it had been a busy weekend, but not that there were three homicides.

Jamie returned and gingerly climbed back into the bed, her nightgown stretching over her expanding belly. "The days speed by like molasses," she grumbled.

"Yeah, but you're still a babe."

She sent him a middle finger. "I've never been a babe. Don't want to be a babe. And will never be a babe."

"I'm heading downstairs. Can I get you anything . . . babe?"

She started laughing despite herself, then jerked and said, "Ooohh . . . ugh." Reached for her lower back.

"You okay?" he asked in growing concern.

"I think so. If you can find any tea, or juice, in the kitchen, could you bring me some . . . babe?"

"Will do."

Cooper's cell rang again as he was looking in the refrigerator. There was some cranberry juice, so he poured Jamie a glass. His phone rang again and he half expected it to be the chief again, maybe Verbena. JJ Taft's name appeared on his screen. "Hey," he started to greet him, but the P.I. broke right past him. "Angel Vasquero is dead. Killed by Carlton Langford. Veronica Quick and your new detective, Hart, discovered his body at a shed in her apartment complex."

Cooper didn't know Vasquero, but he'd recognized the name when Verbena had told him about it earlier. "You knew him?" One of the three homicides.

"You could say that. I asked him to keep an eye on Quick."

He wasn't expressing it, but Cooper understood the guilt that he was now living with. "Angel was good, but Langford managed to surprise him. Took him out with a shovel."

"He ambushed him," agreed Cooper, repeating Verbena's description.

Taft asked, "Is Quick okay?"

"From what I understand. You'd have to ask Hart."

Taft let out a harsh breath. "Damn." A beat. "I don't want Angel to be gone."

"Yeah. Bad news." Cooper heard the beep of an incoming call. Stephen Kirshner's name flashed on his cell. His attention sharpened. "I gotta go. Gotta answer this call."

"You learn anything more, let me know."

"You got it." He clicked off from Taft and answered the new call, "Hi, Stephen. Everything okay?"

"She took the car. She left, for the church. She wants to see . . . *Father*," he blurted out as if in pain.

"He's not there," Cooper said. "He should be still under arrest."

"Well, she's gone! Again!" He sounded undone, which was

nothing like the sanguine "vision quest" comments he'd spouted earlier when Mary Jo had last taken her leave.

"I'll go to the church," Cooper told him.

"Detective..."

The hairs on the back of Cooper's neck rose. Stephen had long since dropped calling him by anything but his given name.

"She's in labor," he said. "And you know her babies have a history of coming fast!"

# Chapter 25

Harley pulled up across from the house as Cooper's Trailblazer was backing out of the drive in a big hurry.

"Where're you going?" she shouted, climbing from the car and madly waving at him.

He rolled down the window as he stopped to put the vehicle in drive. "Mary Jo's in labor!"

"Shit." She ran to the passenger door before he could take off. "I'm coming with you."

"You need to stay with your mom. She's not feeling great. Back pain. She doesn't know about Mary Jo yet."

"I'll check on her, but I want to meet you at Glen Gen. That's where Mary Jo's going, right?"

"Eventually," he said tightly.

"Hey!"

They both looked toward the front porch where Emma stood with Duchess, who started barking as soon as her mistress yelled at them. "Jamie wants to know where you are going!"

Harley cupped her hands over her mouth. "We'll be back soon! Take care of Mom, okay? If she still feels bad, call us."

Twink streaked out of the still open door. Duchess gave

chase. Emma yelled at the dog and the cat circled around and shot back inside the house, Duchess on her heels. Distracted, Emma said, "I will take care of her."

Cooper muttered, "It would be better if you stayed," as Harley buckled herself in.

"I don't trust Mary Jo."

"She's on her way, or already at, Heart of Sunshine Church. Stephen called me."

"Oh, God . . . already in labor?"

He pressed the accelerator and they tore forward. No police siren on the Blazer. Didn't matter as Cooper wasn't slowing down for protocol. He was hell-bent and Harley was glad.

Verbena directed Sloan to a small park on the edge of River Glen, near the East Glen River, tucked up against some older houses. She grilled him while they drove, about the McNulty and Lloyd investigations, and he told her all he knew. She didn't ask specifically about Angel Vasquero's death, but Carlton Langford was in jail and likely to remain there, so they could go over that later.

Marian Langford had awakened. Still not out of the woods, but it was a positive sign.

"Okay," she said, as he pulled into a parking spot. They were facing children's playground equipment, swings and a climbing structure in the shape of a ship with a Jolly Roger flag atop a central post. She turned to face him. "Since my mom's illness, I use this place to clear my head."

"How is your mom?"

"As good as can be expected, I suppose," was her brief answer before turning to the case. "Clint Mercer is still in ICU. Bitten by a dog, you said. And Quick has been hearing a dog but not seen one."

Sloan nodded.

"What is your relationship to Quick?" she asked curiously. At his hesitation, she added, "Look, I don't care what it is. I just need to know."

"We're seeing each other."

Her dark eyes studied him. "You believe the coffee-cup lid was planted at the McNulty crime scene by Shana Lloyd, and that Lloyd was killed because of it?"

He nodded. "Someone set her up to do it."

"Whoever killed McNulty. But now you're questioning whether it's Mercer. What does Quick think?"

"Feels the same way I do."

"Okay." Verbena quirked a dark brow.

"I want to re-interview Hugh McNulty," Sloan told her. "Townsend interviewed him and he said he was hiking with friends in the mountains, which has been verified. But I want to meet with him and hear it firsthand."

"You don't trust Townsend? I thought you were friends, and didn't you start with the sheriff's department?"

"It isn't working out."

A smile briefly slanted her lips. "I've had dealings with the man. He runs a fiefdom out there."

Sloan was glad she held the same appreciation for Abel Townsend as he did. No more bros; they never had been in the first place. "I think Quick needs protection. Amy Deggars took off because she believes she's in danger, and I think Quick is, too."

"You should've brought Deggars into the station."

"She won't be hard to find, if we need her, but for now I thought she would be better out of River Glen."

Verbena thought about it a bit, then gave a short nod. "Call Quick. See what she thinks about a temporary security detail for her. And let's go interview Hugh McNulty."

Ronnie's ire had subsided to a low simmer as she came out of the Coast Range and down toward Highway 101, which ran north/south along the curving shoreline of the Pacific.

The drive was going to be a little longer than her estimate. She was heading south, forty-five minutes to an hour before she hit Deception Bay.

Her cell dinged, an arriving text. She'd set it in her cupholder and now she looked down and saw it was Sloan: **Everything okay at work? Verbena is thinking about security detail for you.**

"Hell, no," she muttered. She could almost feel his worry being telegraphed down the phone. Since it was impossible to text and drive, she pulled over on the nearest wide shoulder and wrote: **No security needed. Running an errand. All is well.**

Not exactly the truth, but her current mission was personal, something she wanted to delve into on her own until she fully understood what was going on.

Back on the road, her phone rang. She glanced at the lighted screen. Her father calling.

She mentally went through a string of swear words. She didn't want to answer. But she'd sure as hell wanted to have it out with him earlier, so . . .

"Hi, Dad," she answered coldly, pressing the speaker button and leaving the phone in the cupholder.

"Where are you? The receptionist said you were looking for me, but you left."

"Dawn."

"Yes, Dawn," he repeated, sounding slightly annoyed at being corrected. "You need to come to the office. Albert has taken leave of his senses and left his wife for that girl he hired. What's her name? The newest one."

"Moira."

"I fired her this morning. Told Albert he was an old fool. You need to be here and support the firm."

Ronnie thought about that for a moment. Her father was nothing if not single-minded. Then she knew what to say. "Maybe you should check with Mom. You purport to love her so much. The firm should be hers."

"Is that a joke?"

It was clear Aunt Kat hadn't told him about their phone call. Her father and her aunt may have schemed together, but they apparently weren't in total agreement. At least that's how it appeared. Maybe Aunt Kat's disgust with Jonas had been real after all.

*But they sure bonded over their lies to you, didn't they?*

She narrowed her eyes on the winding coastal road in front of her. Down the cliff to her right, the gray waves of the Pacific undulated beneath a silver sky. She set her jaw and said, "I guess I've had a psychic moment, *Dad.*"

"Do you hear what I'm saying?" He barreled ahead without listening. "Albert is going to end up in an expensive divorce that may split the firm into pieces! You need to stand with me. I can't keep making excuses for you."

Ronnie gritted her teeth. He wanted to play games with the truth? Fine. "Wait, Dad. I've got another vision! I thought I saw Mom. And she was alive! Oh, wait . . . she's fading in and out . . . I can't see . . . oh, yes, she's at an institution of some kind. Maybe a care facility? I'm not really sure. It's hazy. Not really clear. Wait! Is that the sound of waves breaking against a shore? She's at the beach, Dad! It's so real! She *is* alive!"

Ronnie waited, but there was only silence. Except for his breathing. Which kind of sounded like he was struggling for air.

"You spoke with Katarina, I see," he finally said.

"Yes, Dad, I did. I spoke with Katarina, and guess what? There's no death certificate on record for Mom."

"Where are you now?"

"One guess."

"You're driving . . . to the coast."

"To Seagull Pointe, to be exact. To meet my mother for the first time *since I was four!*"

"Veronica," he said.

"Don't. Just don't."

She clicked off and turned off her ringer.

Mary Jo's car was parked outside the church. Harley and Cooper shared a look as he threw the SUV in park. Cooper had called the station to make certain Symons was still in custody, which he was, so that, at least, was something, Harley thought.

She followed a half step behind as Cooper strode up the steps to the church's double doors and yanked one open. Not locked today.

And neither were the inner vestibule doors, which Cooper pushed open, Harley scurrying to keep up behind him.

The sight that met their eyes was enough to stop Harley in

her tracks. Mary Jo, lying in the aisle between the pews. Legs spread. Dress hiked up to her thighs.

"The baby," she gasped.

Ho . . . lee . . . shit.

Cooper turned to her and barked, "Find those other women."

Harley jumped to obey. She had to pass Mary Jo, who leaned upward, her hands planted behind her, and suddenly bore down with a loud EEEEEEAAAAHHHHHHHHH before shrieking *"The head is crowning! The head is CROWNING!"*

Harley raced to the door on the left side of the apse, yanking it open, charging down the hallway that led to the outside and back dormitory. She could hear Cooper's voice almost all the way, saying, "I'm here . . . relax . . . I've got you . . ."

Seagull Pointe was a light gray, one-story building down a long drive bordered by gnarled and skeletal, wind-stunted trees whose dark limbs waved a greeting to Ronnie as she drove by. Rain splattered her windshield in big drops, her wipers brushing them away but barely able to keep up. The weather was worse here at the coast than in the valley, which had been warmed a bit by watery sunshine.

She had no hat and her coat had no hood. She parked in a side lot and walked to the front door, bending her head to the burst of wind-driven rain that slapped her face and turned her hair into wet, lank strips.

Pulling open the door, she entered a room that was warm and light. She stood a moment, dripping on the mat just inside. She could feel her heart beat in her throat. Now that she was here she was nervous.

And there was a lump in her throat as well. Her mother. Her mother was here.

It was like she'd been resurrected from the dead.

There was no one currently at the reception counter so Ronnie walked down a wide hall that opened into a dining hall, also currently empty.

She could smell cinnamon and realized there was a tray of

sugar cookies on a platter left on the nearest table. A sign with a happy face read: *Happy Monday!* She assumed they were for anyone, but her stomach was too tense to feel hunger.

A woman hunched over a walker was working her way down the hall. She shot Ronnie a sideways look out of bright, beady dark eyes. "Hi," she said.

"Hi," said Ronnie.

"They'll be back at the desk soon," she revealed.

As she passed by, Ronnie blurted out, "Do you know . . . where I could find Wynona Quick?"

The woman stopped, cocked her head, birdlike, and cackled, "How fast do you need her?"

Ronnie choked on a laugh. She'd heard that one enough in her life to get the joke. "No, Quick's her name. Sorry."

"I figured, dear. Just having a little fun. But there's no one here by that name."

"No one?" Ronnie was crestfallen. Had she been wrong?

"We do have a Winnie DuBois, if that helps," the woman said.

Her mother's maiden name.

Ronnie shivered. "Which one is her room?"

"Down the end of the hall, but she's . . . not all there in the head, I'm afraid. Been here a long time . . ."

One of the younger women of Symons's flock, a blond whose name was Heaven—*figured*—raced back with Harley, both of them carrying blankets and towels. The others were rounding up their children, excited but staying back.

The loud squall Harley heard as they appeared back in the church, brought her to a skidding stop at the end of the aisle. Cooper was holding a wet, purple baby with a thick umbilical cord coiling from its stomach that reached beneath Mary Jo's now blood-stained skirt.

"It's a boy," Cooper said with a grin, handing the child to Heaven as she reached him and wrapped the child in a blanket before settling him back in Cooper's arms.

\* \* \*

Ronnie's throat felt like it was closing in on itself. She said to the birdlike woman, "I just want to . . . meet her."

The woman lifted one arm to point with a bony finger. "Last door next to the exit."

Ronnie looked down the long hallway. At its end was a door with a window in its upper half where she could see the sun shining through the rain, creating a faint double rainbow across a side parking lot.

"Well look at that," the hunched woman said. "You must bring good luck." She turned back around and said, "Those cookies are a menace," as she thumped her way toward them.

Ronnie walked down the hallway toward the rainbow, which was swallowed up by a gray cloud before she reached the door. She felt the buzz and tingle of an oncoming vision and placed her hand flat on the panel of the door.

"*. . . All for one and one for all,*" *the young and vibrant woman said, smiling down on a girl's light brown head.* "*And that's all for us tonight,*" *she added, closing the book.*

"*Noooo,*" *the girl moaned, but was half asleep as her mother slid her beneath the bed covers and kissed her on her forehead.*

*She opened her eyes to see her mother standing in the doorway, switching off the light. Silhouetted in the illumination from the hall, a dark, somewhat scary figure, she said fiercely,* "*I love you, Veronica. Remember that when I'm gone.*"

Ronnie came to with a gasp, her limbs trembling, her hand still on the door panel. It felt like she'd been shouted at. Was that really Mom? Had she really said that to her? Had she known she would be leaving . . . or falling prey to her disease?

"Excuse me!"

Ronnie looked back down the hall from where she'd come. A woman stood there, and something about the way she was standing, something officious and stern, fist on one hip, assured Ronnie that she wasn't welcome to just drop in.

Ronnie didn't wait. She let herself into the room, closing the door behind her.

A slim, shrunken woman with wild gray hair nearly swallowed up in an armchair, turned to look at her, through blue eyes a mirror of Ronnie's own.

"Mom?" Ronnie choked out, feeling lightheaded.

The woman stared at her for a long minute, several long minutes, as a matter of fact, long enough for the stern hallway-woman's footsteps to come striding toward the door. She knocked loudly as soon as she was there and called imperiously, "Winnie? I'm coming in."

Ronnie had just half a second to move or be hit by the incoming door. She jumped to one side as her mother winked at her and put her finger to her lips. Then the Seagull Pointe administrator, Ronnie guessed by the navy blazer, tan slacks and flat line of her mouth, entered the room and fixed her hard gaze on Ronnie. "Ma'am, you didn't sign in and you don't have a visitor's tag."

"There was no one at the desk when I got here."

"Who are you here to see?"

Ronnie hesitated, afraid if she said something wrong she would be tossed out.

*Tell the truth.*

She glanced at the woman in the chair. Had that come from her or her own mind?

"Who are you here to see?" the administrator repeated coolly.

"Wynona DuBois Quick," Ronnie answered. Then turned to the diminutive gray-haired woman in the chair whose eyes were on her.

"Hi . . . Mom," Ronnie said with a tentative smile.

"I've been waiting for you," she whispered back.

Harley felt slightly woozy and sat down hard on one of the wooden pews. "I see that it's a boy," she told Cooper.

"I'll go get scissors," said Heaven.

"Should I call for an ambulance?" Harley felt overwhelmed. She had a brother. A brother!

Mary Jo was lying flat out on the floor now. But she tilted her head back and looked at Harley from the tops of her eyes. "Could you call my husband, too?" she asked.

"Sure," Harley told her and Mary Jo gave her the number. It was surreal.

She placed both calls and told Stephen Kirshner that his wife had just given birth. His voice thick with emotion, he asked if he could speak with Mary Jo, and Harley handed the cell to her.

Harley was unabashedly listening in to their call when Heaven came back with scissors. Some of the other women hovered by the hallway door. She could hear them whispering how they wanted to be with Rebekkah. She wanted to argue that Mary Jo was not Rebekkah, but didn't really have the energy. And Mary Jo seemed to have stabilized some, which was an unexpected plus. At least that's what it sounded like for the moment.

She was almost moved by the tenderness in Mary Jo's voice as she spoke with her husband.

Which made her think of her boyfriend, who she'd been shunting aside lately, not because she didn't love him, but because . . .

She didn't know how to finish that sentence. Because she felt unsettled, uncertain, uncomfortable in her place in the family?

She shook her head and texted Greer: **Just got a new baby brother! Wanna celebrate?**

The text came back immediately. **Yes! Congrats! What's his name?**

**Not a clue.**

**When can I meet Not a Clue?**

She smiled. Everybody's a comedian, she thought, but the smile stayed on her face as the doors to the vestibule opened wide and the EMTs arrived.

"She is not your mother," Myrna Gerling stated firmly. "Winnie has no living relatives. She was placed under the care of Seagull Pointe over twenty-five years ago with a trust fund that pays for her care."

"Who's in charge of the trust fund?" demanded Ronnie. She'd been practically marched down to the reception area and Myrna, the apparent boss-lady of all boss-ladies, didn't appreciate Ronnie's "sneaking" into the facility and approaching one of their residents.

"*We* are in charge of it," Myrna made clear. "And our accountant has been very wise in his approach to keeping the trust funded and solvent."

"Who put in the seed money? Jonas Quick? Katarina DuBois? Both of them?"

"Winnie doesn't do well with visitors," she responded evenly.

They were both standing in the building foyer, squared off. "She seems to be doing okay," said Ronnie. "You heard her say she's been waiting for me."

"She says that to everyone." Gerling had traded annoyance for long suffering. "Now she'll be upset and walking the halls."

"I'm going to talk to her," Ronnie told her firmly.

"Don't make me call security. Please."

"Then let me see her."

Myrna Gerling looked pained. "I see you really believe you're her daughter. If you care what happens to her, you'll listen to me. She has dementia and she wanders. And she sees things."

Ronnie could have guessed that one. She saw things, too. "My DNA's on file," she said dryly. "If you need a test, we can do that."

Gerling's lips pursed. Ronnie knew that she was really irritating the boss-lady, but she had no patience for all the rules that were keeping her from her mother.

"Fine." Gerling spit out the word as if it tasted bad.

She led Ronnie back down the hall, taking her time on this go-around. No striding footsteps. More like a stroll along the carpeted expanse.

About ten feet from her mother's door, Ronnie was forced to stop when Gerling did. She had a small set of keys in one hand, car keys, by the look of them, and she fingered them and tossed them around, a habit that she clearly used in order to think.

"I'll go in with you. Let me do the talking. See if she responds. And we'll go from there."

Ronnie nodded. Rebellion lived inside her and she had no intention of complying, but sure. *Go ahead, Myrna. If that gets me in the door again.*

"Winnie, how are you?" Myrna asked in a saccharine voice as she opened the door, pinning a fake smile on lips that naturally formed a downward curve.

Ronnie slipped in and moved around her so she could be seen.

Mom's blue eyes looked Ronnie's way. She blinked several times as Myrna went on to introduce her as a friend who just happened to drop by Seagull Pointe and was checking in with all the residents.

"We already met," Ronnie cut in to remind her mother. "About half an hour ago. I'm your daughter, Veronica. Remember?"

"Excuse me!" Gerling glared at her.

"She doesn't want me to tell you," Ronnie went on, hooking a thumb toward Myrna. When there was no reaction, she added a bit desperately, "She thinks it might upset you. I didn't know you were even here till today, or I would have been here much, much sooner!"

"Winnie, are you all right?" Gerling moved to block eye contact between Ronnie and her mother.

"Tell her you want to talk to me!" Ronnie practically yelled, grasping at straws.

"I want to talk to her," came the clear response.

"I don't think it's a good idea—" began Gerling.

"I WANT TO TALK TO HER."

Gerling drew a disapproving breath and straightened to her full height, turning baleful eyes on Ronnie. "Ten minutes," she ordered, and moved toward the door but didn't leave.

Mom tracked Gerling's movements with slightly unfocused eyes, but said clearly, "ALONE."

Gerling looked nonplused. Clearly this had never happened to her before. "I'll be right outside the door." As soon as there was a click, Ronnie knelt down in front of her mother's chair.

"I'm your grown daughter. Veronica. Ronnie. Do you remember me as a little girl?"

"Ronnie," she said thoughtfully.

"Yes, Ronnie. Maybe you called me Veronica. I don't know. I don't know enough about you." When she didn't respond, she added, "I think I have your 'gift,' too. Or, something like it."

A frown furrowed her brow, deepening the lines across her forehead.

"It's hard for me to control. I don't know if it can be," she admitted. "I'm learning to deal with—"

"It killed me. He said it 'stole' me."

Ronnie drew a startled breath. "Who? Jonas? My father?" A dark frisson ran down her spine.

"You don't have it."

"The... gift?"

"You don't have it!" she repeated, those blue eyes suddenly cutting to Ronnie's. "You don't have it like me, but you have to be careful. You fell in the water. DON'T GO IN THE WATER!"

She said it so loudly that Ronnie jerked back, startled. "Are you the one warning me? That's from you?"

Her mother cocked a head and said, "I can hear the ocean sometimes. If you can hear the ocean, you're safe."

"You feel safe here?" That, at least, was something.

Her mother leaned forward and crooked her finger to Ronnie. A little smile hovered around her lips. Ronnie bent toward her, her pulse running light and fast.

"Tell the truth," her mother said, echoing the words that had pierced Ronnie's mind earlier, maybe a thought driven by her mother?

Ronnie was literally holding her breath as she waited to hear what she was about to say.

"You're the one who made the cookies," she whispered in Ronnie's ear.

Ronnie leaned back, disappointed. She shook her head sadly.

Her mother's strange little smile disappeared and she stared at Ronnie blankly. "Who are you?" she asked in a frightened voice.

# Chapter 26

Myrna Gerling bustled back in before Ronnie could ask further questions, but Mom had already retreated into a blank silence. Ronnie's heart fluttered as she recognized that she herself sometimes entered a similar fugue state.

Gerling pursed her lips at Mom's frozen trance and shot Ronnie an accusing look. "This could go on for weeks," she warned.

"Or last minutes," countered Ronnie.

"It's time for you to go."

Ronnie looked at her mother, memorizing her face, before allowing Gerling to escort her out.

She turned her cell back on as she headed for her Escape and saw she'd missed a raft of texts and calls: Her father . . . Aunt Kat . . . Sloan . . . Brandy . . . Evan Caldwell . . .

Evan's text read: **How goes it with the fam?**

Sloan's said: **Saw Hugh McNulty with Verbena. Call when u r free.**

Brandy wrote: **Can you come to Glen Gen. Want u to see Clint.**

Aunt Kat was a missed call, no message.

The three calls from her father had culminated in one voice mail that she started to listen to but realized was just more blame shifting, so she cut it off.

She pushed Brandy's number from her call list.

"Ronnie," Brandy answered, sounding half panicked. "Clint's come around. I don't want him to talk too much. Abel was here and I don't know what Clint said to him."

"Don't worry, Townsend's already giving him the benefit of the doubt. I'm coming back from the beach, but won't be there for a couple of hours." At her moan, Ronnie urged, "Call Sloan. You can trust him."

"He's the one who's been after Clint!" she retorted.

"He's just following the evidence. You know he's leaning away from Clint as the killer."

"Ohhh . . ." she moaned. Then, in a hushed voice, "What if Clint accidentally did it?"

Ronnie exhaled heavily. Brandy's fear kept sending her seesawing back and forth over her brother's culpability. It didn't take a vision for Ronnie to imagine her sitting tightly in the hospital alcove, seeking to talk privately. "I'll be there as soon as I can, but you should call Sloan. You have his number."

"I'm off in a couple of hours, but Clint could say anything while I'm working."

"Trust Sloan."

"I gotta go. Hurry!"

"Sloan!" she repeated.

The cat arched her back and hissed at Duchess, who was barking her head off as Harley raced into the house. Greer was coming by to pick her up and they were going to the hospital, but she had to see Emma and Mom first. Cooper had already given them the good news that Mary Jo and the baby were safe and probably at the hospital by now, but Harley needed to touch base.

Emma shushed Duchess, who only paid attention to Twink when the cat decided to react. Then, game on. When the barking slowly diminished and Twink stopped making that scary moaning sound in her throat that sounded like someone dying, Emma said to Harley, who was beelining for the stairs, "It's a boy."

"It sure is," Harley called over her shoulder. "And everything's great and I'm going to the hospital with Greer." She threw open the door to her mom's bedroom.

"Tell me everything," Mom demanded, unfazed by her charging entrance.

"He's perfect. I'm heading to the hospital. More to come."

"God, I wish I could go." Her face was pinched.

"You okay?" Harley's heart galumphed.

"I'm fine," she said through her teeth. "I will stay here and stay calm and the baby inside me will not come until he or she is fully done."

"You sure?"

Mom said, "All I need to know is that my little boy is okay."

"Better than okay!" Harley beamed. "Really!"

"Pictures! Send pictures!" she cried as Harley raced back out of the room and down the stairs to meet Greer, who had already come in by the rear door. She jumped on him in glee, so boisterously unlike herself that he fell against the wall, taken by surprise.

"Wow," he said. "I like the way you celebrate."

"Let's go," urged Harley, sliding back to the ground and grabbing his hand, yanking him back toward the door.

"He needs a name." Emma raised her voice from the kitchen.

"I'll come up with one!" Harley yelled back.

The call from Brandy came in while Sloan was at his desk, reviewing everything Hugh McNulty had said to Verbena and him about Melissa and her many loves.

"She was always on the phone," he'd told them, apparently eager to throw his dead wife under the bus. "Sneaky. Trying to hide one guy from another. It was a game."

McNulty worked from home on Mondays. Like Caldwell, he had decent computer skills that Sloan suspected could maybe trip over the legal line sometimes, according to the rather sparse report Townsend had written up after interviewing the man.

Verbena had chosen to do the questioning, which left Sloan to silently assess the man. He pegged him as one of those guy-guys who really didn't like or respect women. His massive biceps and ripped muscles suggested he spent a lot of time at the gym, and he proudly wore his shirt unbuttoned to display his abs during this December cold spell.

"We've split a bunch of times," he'd said with a shrug. "I don't want to talk trash about Melissa, but she liked having a bunch of guys hanging around with their dicks at attention. Guess one of 'em finally got fed up and killed her."

"Do you have the names of these partners?" asked Verbena.

"A few. You have Mercer and Wetherly, right? And Neel? There were always more. That's just how she was." He made a face. "You know, I ran into her, just kind of by coincidence, a month ago or so, and she was laughing on the phone to someone I could hear was talking dirty to her. Didn't seem like anybody I knew of. I thought she'd moved on to someone new. That would be like her."

"Man or woman, could you tell?"

"Oh, man, for sure. Melissa didn't have a lot of girlfriends. She'd piss them off too much. Steal their partners. Generally shit on them."

"Yeah." Verbena wrote herself a note, while Sloan had found his hands were balled into fists and forcibly relaxed them.

McNulty had then screwed up his face in thought. "She said his name . . . I think. Maybe that's why I thought it was someone new. She was being flirty with him, but it didn't sound serious, really. At least on her part."

"What was that name?"

He screwed up his face in thought, but finally shook his head. "Don't know."

"Not Clint Mercer, or Neel or Wetherly?"

He snorted. "She said she had a thing for Mercer when she was a kid. Seemed like a joke, but then she decided to act on it when she had the chance. Doesn't sound like it turned out that great." He smirked. "Maybe he didn't like being dumped."

And that was about all they'd gotten from McNulty. Sloan

had given him his cell number before they left, telling him to call if he remembered anything else.

On their way back to the station, Verbena had asked, "Did he seem credible to you?"

Sloan had a lot of things he could say about McNulty, but he'd focused in on the question. "Yeah. He seemed credible."

"So, we widen the search for her killer, who might also be Shana Lloyd's."

And that's where they'd left it as they walked in through the station's back door. Sloan had texted Ronnie several times and had heard back once with a nonspecific answer, which had left him with more questions than answers. He'd grabbed tacos for lunch from a row of food carts that assembled near the station and brought them back to the break room.

His mind had then drifted back to Clint Mercer. He couldn't make himself believe the man had killed McNulty... *and* Shana. But Mercer knew something. He'd been there, at the clearing, by his own admission. He'd known the maple seeds and tire tracks would incriminate him and he'd charged after Neel and Wetherly, taking the law into his own hands, which had landed him in the ICU.

And now the call on his cell from Brandy. "Sloan Hart," he answered.

"Ronnie said I should call you. I already think it's a mistake."

"How's Clint?" he asked, ignoring that.

"Better," she said cautiously. "Ronnie's meeting me at the hospital when she's back, but in the meantime I'm... I guess I'm checking with you."

Back from where? He desperately wanted to ask but sensed she would balk at telling him something about Ronnie that he didn't already know. "If he's awake, I'd like to talk to him."

"I'm sure," she said sarcastically. "But fine. That's why I'm calling. I'll meet you at the ICU."

Sloan looked at Verbena, who was on a long, involved call with her mother's doctor. It didn't sound good. He gave her the high sign that he was leaving, figuring she could text him when she was done, but he was glad that he would have at least a few minutes with Mercer on his own.

He headed out to his Bronco and wondered again where Quick was that she couldn't text him. He had to work hard to tamp down the worry and fear that had their teeth in him.

Ronnie was lost in thought, driving back through the Coast Range. She felt low about her mother. She'd seen for herself the state her mother was in now, but she just couldn't get over all the wasted time.

She was cruising through the eastern foothills when a call shattered her reverie. Darting a glance at the cell screen, her jaw tightened. DAD.

She didn't want to talk to her father EVER AGAIN. But... what the hell.

She clicked on. "Dad," she answered flatly.

"We had a swimming pool, do you remember?" he growled with no preamble. "You fell in and your mother went to save you and she had a sudden cramp and was gone. Dead. Considered dead. She came back under CPR, but was never the same. You were unconscious, too. That was the first time she scared us that she would hurt you, but it wasn't the last before we separated you from her."

"That was years ago, and—"

"And then, you went off to the river that day without telling me. You knew I wouldn't allow it. And you nearly died again!"

"That wasn't Mom's fault!" Ronnie protested, stunned by her father's sudden intensity. He rarely showed so much emotion.

*Combustion* ... Aunt Kat's description of her parents' love affair.

"She took you in the car and ran it off the road," he went on as if he couldn't hear her. "She was babbling, raving, when they found you both. You didn't remember it, which I thought was a godsend. The less you knew the better. She was heading to the coast. Said that's where her people came from. And that psychic... *power*... that you both seem to have? That power is a *lie*. Creates a hell all its own! I knew your mother would kill you and herself, if she wasn't locked down. That's when we put her in Seagull Pointe, near the ocean."

"I just saw her," Ronnie said tightly.

That finally broke into his diatribe. "You went to see her?" he asked, sounding stunned.

"Of course I did."

She heard him take a deep breath. "How was she?"

"You don't get to know!" she snapped back. "You and Aunt Kat... I can't *even* tell you how awful and upset I feel! You kept her from me. All these years!"

"For your safety."

*Bullshit!* "You could have told me at any time!" she sputtered. "Neither of you saw fit!"

"I didn't want you to know!"

"Well, there. Honesty, finally. I needed to know, *Dad*. And I'm sorry you're in flux at the firm... No, scratch that. I don't really give a flying fuck!"

She clicked off, infuriated that angry tears now blurred her vision. She swiped at them and gripped the wheel tighter. She breathed hard, in and out, a dozen miles passing beneath her tires before she felt in control again.

*... said that's where her people came from...*

What had that meant? Mom's people? Where had they come from? The coast?

Her mind snapped back to Evan's message: *How goes it with the fam?* He would maybe know because he'd looked up her history. He was the one who'd told her there *was* no death certificate. Maybe there was more to learn.

She punched in his number and put the phone on speaker.

"Well, if it isn't Miss Psychic."

Ronnie ignored his self-satisfied drawl. "You looked up information on my family and found out there was no death certificate for my mother."

"And?"

"And she's alive."

He started chuckling. "So they hid her from you."

"Yes, they did." She also ignored the creepy crawlies that seemed to climb up her back whenever she was dealing with him. "Did you get anything more?"

"Like what?"

"Like anything about my mother's past. I know very little about her, as it turns out."

"I could dig a little deeper, I guess."

He sounded doubtful, but she was having none of it. "Can you do it today?"

"Well . . . sure, why not? I can probably fit it in."

"I'll come by and pick up the information, if that's all right." She wanted a hard copy. Something she could hold in her hands . . . and maybe crumple into a ball, if she found something else in those pages that would piss her off at her father. "I'm sorry to push, but can you do it right away?"

"What's the big rush?"

"I've waited over twenty-five years and I'm impatient, okay?"

"Give me an hour," he said.

Ronnie checked the time. Two o'clock. Perfect. She was going to arrive around three p.m. anyway.

Clint Mercer looked like hell. White bandages around a pale face with eyes surrounded by deep purple, almost as if he'd taken punches to the face. Sloan gazed at his old friend, who gave him a crooked smile.

"I fucked up bad," rasped Clint.

Brandy muttered, "Oh, Clint," sounding more defeated than angry.

"I know. I never listen to you, do I?" He slid his dull gaze toward his sister.

"I want to know what you did," said Sloan. "The whole story."

"There isn't much of a story to tell." He sighed. "Everything was fine. Melissa and I were really connecting and she said she was done with seeing other guys."

"And she meant that she was not going to see Ben Neel and Erik Wetherly any longer?"

"Benzene and that asshole who hit me." He snorted, then lightly touched his bandaged head and winced.

"You think there was someone else?" Sloan prompted, but apparently Clint had lapsed into silence.

"Was there someone else?" Brandy demanded impatiently.

"It's all right," Sloan told her. He didn't want Brandy to stop the flow of the story.

"There was some dick she was real secretive about. I caught her talking to him on the phone once or twice. Her voice would change and she would hang up quick, act like it wasn't important. She got off on that kind of thing."

"Not Neel or Wetherly."

"Didn't seem like it. I knew about them." He made a face. "Dickhead tried to kill me," he muttered.

"You brought the barbell to his house," reminded Brandy.

"Anything else about those phone calls?" asked Sloan.

"Nah... well, mighta not been the same guy, but she got real sober on one of those calls, right before she said she was going off for a while, taking some time. I asked her what that meant and she just blew me off. Then *she* called *me* from that shed in the forest. Told me where she was. All apologetic about fucking around. Said it would never happen again. I was pissed. Was done believing her. But yeah, I went there and yeah, those are my tire tracks and the plant shit from my truck, that'll be me, too."

"And when you got there?" Sloan pressed.

"I was mad. I'd had a couple drinks. That didn't help," he allowed. "And she was all nervous, but then said I shouldn't have come. Like she hadn't been the one to call me! I just... lost it. Grabbed her." His breath expelled in a rush. "She hit me, man. Fucking hit me," he admitted in disbelief. "And that *dog!* Barking its goddamn head off! So I shook her. Grabbed her shoulders and shook."

Brandy had closed her eyes as she listened. Now her lids flew open and she snarled, "You piece of shit!"

Clint's short laugh was tortured. "I know."

"Did you put your hands on her neck?" asked Sloan, steeling himself for the answer. His belief in his friend was crumbling.

"NO," Clint shot back immediately, his gaze flying to Sloan. "I hurt her. I admit it. I shouldn't have. I left her there. The damn dog bit me in the leg and I left."

"You think the person who killed her came to see her after you were there."

"You're so goddamn official," complained Clint. "Caldwell was right. At least Townsend believes me."

"Can you think of anything else? Any clue to who she'd been talking to on the phone?"

"Look, she lied about giving up cheating. That was just to cool me off, but she wasn't changing." He turned back to his sister. "I'm sorry, Brandy. She was your friend and I . . ." He looked away, the whites of his eyes turning red from emotion. "You know I loved her."

"Like hell you did," she muttered.

"I did," he insisted. To Sloan, he said, "I don't know anything else, man." He choked out a humorless laugh. "You want information about anything, ask Caldwell. Bro knows everything."

Ronnie rode the elevator up to Evan's apartment, looking out at the café and pool. A watery afternoon sun had turned the water a cold, slate blue. The lights in the café beckoned and her stomach finally growled. She'd been running on high emotion a long time and she finally needed food.

She was at Evan's door when she heard someone approaching behind her. He was coming down the carpeted hallway, pushing a wheeled walker, deliberately picking up first one dragging leg, then the other, as he came toward her slowly, a sheen of perspiration dampening his forehead.

"Just doing a little exercise," Evan greeted her, pulling out keys to open his door, which he pushed open with one hand. "After you," he said, gesturing with that same hand.

"Thanks." It was awkward walking in ahead of him, but she could tell he wanted that bit of chivalry. She moved toward his computer.

"Take a seat over there," he ordered, gesturing away from his workstation to chairs facing the sliding glass door to the balcony. He then moved to his wheelchair, dropping into it heavily, pushing the walker away. "Excuse the sweat. Gotta keep myself in shape." He positioned himself in front of his desk as Ronnie moved toward the chairs, her gaze flickering briefly back to him and his array of monitors.

*Bark! Bark! Bark!*

Ronnie inhaled a sharp breath and jerked her gaze toward the sliding glass door. Was the dog outside? Mel's dog?

*Was it another warning?*

"Relax. Put your purse down." Evan waved a hand to her and she carefully took off the cross-body and set it on one of the chairs. But she didn't sit in the other. Her mind was racing. "I've got the file right here," he went on, swinging around to look at her. He had a manila envelope in his hand. She had to take a couple of steps closer to him to grab it.

Her eyes glanced again at the monitors, drawn as if magnetized by the glowing screens. She had to drag them back to examine the pages she pulled from the envelope. Flipping through them, she frowned. "This is a genealogical family tree."

"Sure is."

"For my mother. What's 'The Colony'?"

He shrugged. "Those are her people. Your people. Live around Deception Bay on the coast."

*Those are her people . . . her father had used almost that identical phraseology . . .*

"Have you talked to my father?" she asked.

"Your father?" He was clearly surprised by that.

*Bark, bark, bark!*

Ronnie looked through the glass door again. "Do you hear

that?" Her pulse was suddenly pounding so hard in her veins it nearly deafened her.

"Nooooo..."

Had he listened in on her conversation with her father? How was that possible?

He seemed to realize she was having trouble concentrating. "You know, I wasn't kidding when I said I have a little bit of your psychic woo-woo, too. Seems you and I come from the same place. I haven't let anyone take my DNA. Don't want it in the system, but I bet there's some distant match with yours."

She was getting a raft of strange vibes. She looked hard at Evan, those creepy crawlies morphing into the beginnings of fear. "You rely on intuition, not just hacking?"

"Is that what you call it? Okay. Intuition." His gaze tightened on her. "What's the matter? You look like you've seen a ghost." He forced a grin. "Not my ghost this time."

He swung back to his desk so she could only see the back of his head as he casually opened a drawer.

Her eyes jumped back to what she could see of the monitors and her mind went suddenly blank.

*"Call him."* *Gabrielle pointed at ten-year-old Ronnie as she moved away, her hips swaying as she sauntered back toward the house, slowly pulling her phone out of the back pocket of her cut-off denim shorts.*

*"Bitch," muttered Evan admiringly, his eyes on Gabrielle's butt cheeks in her tight jeans.*

Ronnie yanked her gaze from the monitors, her heart in her throat. But it didn't matter where she was looking anymore as another scene unfolded in her mind.

"Gerard DeLenka," she said.

Both Evan and Sloan looked at Ronnie in surprise.

Evan gave her a thumbs-up. "You have one helluva memory. One would maybe think you're psychic. How'd you hook up with Shana? She never mentioned your name before."

Her mind whirled. The dream... the barking dog... Mel in the shed, surprised at her visitor.

Evan... it was Evan... but how? How did he get there?

Her eyes jumped back to the monitors... now the desktop where Evan was slyly sliding a small bottle of clear liquid into the drawer, hoping she wouldn't notice.

*Glycerin*, she suddenly knew.

Why? What was he doing?

Drops of glycerin look like sweat... the workout was faked... the whole dragging of his feet... *faked?*

He's not as infirm as he wants everyone to think.

Her heart jolted like it wanted out of her chest. *Be cool. Don't let him know.*

*He* killed Mel?

BARK, BARK, BARK, BARK!!

The dog knew... the dog was worried... *she* was worried. She needed help. She needed help now!

Sloan.

Closing her eyes, she put everything she had into sending a sizzling message across space. *Sloan!*

His phone rang while Clint was still trying to convince both him and Brandy that he was motivated out of love, not obsession, when he attacked Melissa McNulty.

Sloan walked out into the hall to take the call, disappointed when he saw that it wasn't Ronnie.

"Hart," he answered.

"Okay, I think I've got the name for you. The one she was talking to, all flirty?"

It was Hugh McNulty.

"What is it?"

"Devon."

"That a first name?"

McNulty snorted. "I don't know. I was lucky to come up with it."

"Thanks."

Devon...

He walked back into Clint's ICU room, but Brandy met him

on her way out. "We've overstayed our welcome. He needs rest. He's such a goddamn idiot! Where's Ronnie? She's supposed to be here."

"Where was she today?" he asked, giving up all pretense. She could tell him or not.

Her lips tightened, but she answered, "She said she was coming back from the beach."

He couldn't hide his surprise.

"Clint didn't kill Mel," Brandy said, returning to her mantra. "You did get that, right?"

He nodded. "It was someone who met with her after Clint."

"Well, good. Maybe Ronnie was right about you." She shook her head. "Aren't there cameras or something? Somewhere out there? Maybe whoever did it followed Clint."

"I'm sure Townsend's on it. But there aren't a lot of cameras in the country. Not even right outside River Glen city limits, according to Caldwell," he added, but his mind was on Ronnie. He had a bad feeling about her that he couldn't shake. The beach? What had she been doing there?

"Evan's just full of factoids, isn't he?" Brandy made a face. "I've never trusted him."

"Who?"

"Evan. You're not listening," she accused.

Evan . . .

*Evan.*

Not Devon.

"Shit," he muttered, a cold spike of fear piercing through him.

"Where are you going?" Brandy called as Sloan racewalked for the elevator, but he didn't answer.

Ronnie kept her mind a blank. Maybe Evan had traces of psychic ability like he claimed, maybe he didn't. Whatever the case, she didn't want him reading her mind. And she had her hands full trying to keep her panic in check.

Gabrielle . . . she could practically see him stalking her . . . actually walking into a bar . . . following her. He'd engineered that car crash. Maybe put something in their drinks before the accident. Something that caused DeLenka to drive off the road.

Gabrielle never gave Evan the time of day, but he always wanted her. More than just a crush, more than just admiration. He killed her and her boyfriend.

And then somehow zeroed in on Mel, who did give him some attention. Just as a friend. Or, maybe some flirting? That he took to be something much, much more?

He killed her, too. Maybe from her rejection, or maybe she twigged to the fact he'd killed Gabrielle and DeLenka. Maybe she learned he could walk and he didn't want that secret known!

*That's how he killed Shana. Just walked right up to her apartment and strangled her.*

It made total sense. And the direct cause of his handicap had always been somewhat murky. She'd never heard there was some definitive, permanent problem that kept him in a wheelchair. He'd let them see his physical incapability for years. His little secret. So like him.

"You've gotten awfully quiet," he said, breaking into her thoughts.

BARK, BARK, BARK, BARK, BARK!!!!

Ronnie wanted to clap her hands over her ears. *I know, dog. I know!*

Evan said conversationally, "Those women of The Colony had all kinds of different gifts. They were around for a hundred years or so before this big fire burned down their lodge, forced them to leave. And your mom was related to them. You, too. Got it in your DNA."

DNA . . . Evan was the one who'd talked Shana into leaving the coffee cup with the DNA.

*"Stop for a cup of coffee on the way. Get her to leave the cup. I'll tell you where to drop it when you've got it in hand . . ."*

That's why he'd killed her. She was a loose end.

"I don't know, Evan. I only talked to my mother briefly."

"Oh, you know," he countered.

And he rose from his chair holding a handgun he'd taken from the drawer and pointed it directly at Ronnie. Her pulse skyrocketed.

"Like Melissa, like Shana... like Gabrielle... You've always known. I gotta tell ya. I've been worried about you. The way you just came up with Gerard DeLenka?"

*Waste time. Think. Don't let him keep the upper hand.* "What are you talking about?" she suddenly demanded, going on the offensive. She could be a good liar, when she wanted to be. "What are you doing? Is this some kind of game?"

He sent her a cold smile, not buying it. "I've followed you online. I know you. The way you can 'see.' It's fucking terrifying. I know what you're capable of."

"You can't shoot me," she said, her mouth dry. "You've no reason to. And it'll be too loud. People will know."

"I can't let you live," he said with a shake of his head. "You see that, don't you? You're never going to give me peace. I really hoped this day wouldn't come, but here it is. Sloan will be heartbroken. I think he really cares about you. I've had to keep him close, too. Never hurts to have someone in law enforcement in your pocket. And it takes too much goddamn energy blocking you."

*Maybe he's not completely steady on his feet*, she thought hopefully. But then, *oh, shit*... as he took several steps forward with ease, backing her toward the sliding glass door.

"You came at me with all kinds of accusations," he said, looking past her for a moment, trying out the lie. "You were crazed... *crazy*... just like your mother. I had to defend myself!"

Ronnie's fingers closed on the handle to the slider. She swiftly yanked it back and lurched onto the balcony. *He won't pull the trigger*, she told herself, prayed to herself. She hadn't had time to grab her phone. Bad move. Now she was trapped out here and helpless.

*Sloan! Sloan, where are you?*

Evan was on the balcony. He tossed the gun aside and

grabbed her by the hair. She kicked and scratched but his grip was intense, fingers grappling for her throat. NO!

BARK, BARK, BARK, BARK, BARK!!!

"*Where are you?*" she screamed to the dog, but Evan's fingers cut off the sound to a croaked whisper.

She flung herself away from him, but he grabbed her and bent her over the railing. The swimming pool was far below. A glimmering blue gem. Hands on her neck, squeezing. She kicked and twisted and bit his ear. He howled and his grip loosened. She gulped air but he lifted her beneath her knees and tipped her over the railing's edge. She cried out and clung to his arms. He fell forward. Momentum. One second they were balancing on the railing, the next they were both falling, falling, falling . . . and he was screaming and she couldn't breathe and . . .

SPLASH!

. . . and they were under, entangled and struggling and freezing.

*Cold . . . Killing cold . . . I can't breathe . . . CAN'T BREATHE!*

Evan's hands wrapped around her neck again. She hit at him, but was losing strength. *This is it*, she thought. He was bleeding profusely, she realized. Red wisps through blue water. Knocked his head on the side of the pool. Gravely injured . . . but still murderous.

Something rolled beneath her, lifting her upward. Something furry. An underwater shriek from Evan. He released her and swatted at whatever was in the pool with them.

Something bit into her wrists. Tugged. Pulled hard. Dragging her upward. Watery images of people . . . like last time . . . *Mom?*

She broke the surface and sucked air deep into her lungs, choking and coughing.

Beneath her in the water. Evan swirling with an animal . . . *the dog!*

And then Sloan was there, running full bore from the bistro to the pool. Jumping in and grabbing her into his arms.

"Where's the dog?" she squeaked out.

Police and EMTs burst through in a hoard, swarming around the pool.

"The dog. Where's the dog?" she chattered as Sloan pushed her into the arms of a strong EMT who pulled her from the pool and wrapped her in a blanket while Sloan splashed in and grabbed Evan's floating body.

"What dog?" the EMT asked, bending over to get a good look at Ronnie's wrists.

There were bite marks on both of them, but no broken skin.

"That dog," she said, but it was nowhere to be seen.

Sloan dragged Evan's lifeless body to the edge of the pool. He locked eyes with Ronnie, then he was out of the pool and they were in each other's arms, shivering.

"It was Evan," she said in disbelief as she was guided to an ambulance. "Evan."

"I know," he said. "But it's over now. You're safe."

*You're safe with him*, said Mom.

# Epilogue

**Two Months Later...**

Jamie lay on the hospital bed, gazing over her crowning belly at Cooper as they prepared to take her into surgery for a C-section.
*I made it*, she thought with relief. *I made it.*
All the scary moments during this pregnancy were about to be over. Like that last time when her back had been killing her and she was worried that her bed rest wouldn't be enough to hold the baby in, or that he or she would be a preemie with a very real chance of not making it.
The thought made her shudder. "You cold?" Cooper asked, concerned.
"More like excited."
He moved closer and clasped her hand, which she squeezed. He was back at work with both Verbena and the new detective, Sloan Hart. They were expanding the police force after years of contractions, and though there had been no serious complaints about Chief Marcus Duncan, it looked like he was moving on and they were looking for someone new. Cooper's name had been tossed about, but ever since their son, Christian, had arrived, named by Harley who thought it was appropriate as he

was born in a church, Cooper had decided he was happy where he was on the police echelon.

But Verbena had shown interest and Jamie, and especially Harley, and Emma, too, were voting for a woman.

Mary Jo, after scaring them all into thinking she was trying to steal their baby, had returned to her family and apparently planned to have another child, one of her own. She'd suffered panic when she'd realized she wanted another baby, knowing she couldn't have the one growing inside her. True to form, she'd sought out another church with a cultlike constituency, and in active labor had raced back to her supposed safe place, the Heart of Sunshine Church. Cooper's appearance and help when she was actually delivering, had luckily seemed to ground her.

Jamie smiled to herself. Cooper was living the dream. He didn't complain about the late-night bottle feedings. Half the time he was battling Harley and Emma for the honor. Jamie could admit to herself a little feeling of jealousy, as she was unable to do much more than hold Christian for short periods of time. Which was ridiculous because soon enough they were all going to be up to their elbows in babies.

"Ready?" Jamie's OB said from behind her surgical mask.

"Ready."

She was wheeled into the OR, smiling as she thought of the new life they were bringing into the world, a soon-to-be sibling to the little boy who was currently tucked in at home with Emma, Harley and Harley's boyfriend, Greer.

*I hope this one's a girl, so Cooper can have one of each*, she thought, pleasantly drifting from whatever was flowing from the IV.

An hour later she was holding her baby girl and marveling at her soft brown hair and long lashes. She remembered holding Harley the same way all those years ago, when her life was so uncertain. This was a whole lot less stressful.

"What are we going to name her?" asked Cooper, as enthralled as she was, looking down at their child's clean little brow.

"I was thinking Quinn," she said.

"Quinn," he repeated, surprised, as she'd never once mentioned that as a name.

"Susan Quinn, actually," Jamie said with a straight face.

"Susan Quinn? After someone you know?"

She started outright laughing.

He blinked and then grinned himself. "Suzy Q."

"I do really like Quinn, though."

"I'm good with Quinn. But you may have just nicknamed her whether you meant to or not."

"Suzy Q," she said, gazing lovingly at their little girl again. "I can live with that."

Ronnie sat across the table from Sloan, smiling in the soft candlelight from the votive flickering on their table. They were seated at a small alcove outside of a raucous Valentine's Day party going on in the main dining room. The doors were closed but there was lots of music, laughter and cheering. Ronnie had eaten most of her buttery petrale sole, but had to pass on dessert. The champagne had left a warm glow to everything. She watched the waiter pick up their check, but neither of them was making any effort to leave.

"You look . . . happy," he said.

"I thought you were going to say 'amazing.'"

"That, too."

They'd dressed for dinner. She wore a knee-length white dress with long sleeves and her BFF shard necklace, a seriocomic touch. Her hair was down and she'd added a slim silver bracelet to her left wrist, one of her mother's. She'd finally taken her ring back to Galen the week before, as it had been difficult to find him after he'd been fired from the Bernard K. Waters Law Firm for the continuing office sex with Bernard's wife, and had basically disappeared for a time before resurfacing as basically a one-man firm.

Somewhat down on his luck, his eyes had lit up when he saw the ring she was returning. She was just glad to be rid of it.

And it was good to be through the series of funerals and memorial services that had started in late December and bled into January. Her heart had ached dully throughout Mel's service, and she'd been glad for Brandy's support. Clint had managed to come, though he was still recovering from the blow to the head he'd received from Erik Wetherly. Clint was suing Wetherly, but it was hard to get reparations when you were the original attacker.

She'd attended Angel's funeral, too, though she'd sensed that some of his family resented her, maybe even blamed her. Regardless, she'd paid her respects. Sloan had offered to go with her, but he hadn't known Angel, so she'd shaken her head and insisted on going by herself. It turned out she wasn't alone as P.I. Jesse James Taft was seated in a pew near the back door and she'd slipped in beside him. They'd sat in companionable silence throughout the ceremony and afterwards he was standing beside her on the church steps when Angel's cousin, Daria, had approached her.

"It's not your fault," she said firmly. "People just want someone to blame."

It had been nice to hear and Ronnie had thanked her. She, in turn, thanked Ronnie and the firm for standing by her. Even though Daria had told Martin Calgheny that everything was taken care of in the lawsuit against her, that hadn't been the truth. She'd expected Angel to run interference with the grasping shoestring relatives trying to take away what she'd been bequeathed, but upon his death, she'd confessed to Ronnie that she was still in trouble. The firm had then stepped in again and Martin was currently making sure Daria would be able to claim the inheritance she was due.

"I'm just so sorry Angel's gone," Ronnie had told her, to which she'd swallowed hard and said, "He loved being the hero."

She'd then left them in a hurry, fighting emotions as she headed down the outdoor steps to her car. Ronnie and Taft had watched her leave, Taft saying, "For the record, I'm the one who hired him to watch after you."

"For the record, it's not your fault, either."

They'd walked to the parking lot together and he'd stopped at her SUV, a faint smile showing off the dimples that softened his rugged, handsome face. "Any visions lately?" he'd queried.

"I could ask the same of you."

"I haven't seen Helene much lately. I've been working."

She'd felt a tweak of memory, a watery vision of a young woman. Premonition, a peek into the future? Not of Helene, his deceased sister, but someone younger who was close to him. "You've been with a dark-haired woman that you're in love with."

He'd been taken aback. "No. You just described someone I work with." To which she'd replied, "It's time you took that relationship to the next level. Life is short. Don't waste it on 'should we or shouldn't we' just because you work together."

"Jesus, you're scary," was his choked response.

"You're not as hard to read as you think," she'd answered.

That had been a month ago. And after Angel's funeral, she'd attended Shana's memorial service with Sloan. Yes, Shana had tried to frame her, had been talked into leaving the coffee cup lid with Ronnie's DNA. She'd gone along with the plan as a means to earn some cash, but her real reason had been something deeper. She'd wanted to target Ronnie herself, out of some skewed notion that if she got her out of the way, she would have a clear path to recapturing Sloan's heart. Ronnie's long-ago pledge to marry Sloan must have really triggered Shana, but she'd ended up trusting in the wrong person and losing her life because of it.

"You were telling me about Jonas," Sloan reminded her now.

She hadn't forgiven her father for all his lies. Aunt Kat, too, was still on her shit list, though she'd started speaking civilly to both of them. The sad part of all of that was Mom was really gone now. She'd escaped Seagull Pointe and found her way to the ocean, where she'd drowned. Ronnie believed she'd sent her that last message, though she hadn't told anyone about it. That was between her and her mother. She hadn't attended the small service held at Seagull Pointe, though she thought her father and Aunt Kat had. She'd gone to the beach instead and said a private goodbye as the cold water lapped at her toes.

"I don't want to talk about my father. Or the firm."

"You quit in the middle of a story. Left off with Tormelle having dumped his girlfriend," Sloan protested, faintly amused.

"And crawling back to his wife. Yes, I know." She paused, then added, "And it's not going well for Albert. His wife is making him pay dearly, with shares of the company. But that's his and Dear Old Dad's problem, not mine."

"Sure about that?"

Jonas refused to accept that Ronnie had washed her hands of all things Quick, especially Quick & Tormelle Law Firm. He kept her up-to-date whether she wanted to be or not, and though she hated to admit it, she'd started listening to his reports. Between him and Dawn, she knew exactly what was going on at the firm.

Seeing Sloan's knowing smile, she said, "Hey, I'm not the only one with leftover baggage."

Sloan had moved from his You+Me rental when he and Ronnie had gone to his place after she'd been checked out at the hospital the night Evan died—the one memorial service she'd missed—to find his ex-wife, Tara, in his bedroom, on the bed with her iPad, making herself at home while she waited for him to appear. She'd shut the iPad down with a hard smack upon seeing them. Ronnie found it a wonder she hadn't cracked the screen. Tara had access to the room because she was an executive with You+Me and had apparently assumed that it would be fine and dandy with Sloan to just move in. Not so. Sloan's ice-cold demeanor had made Ronnie almost feel sorry for Tara as she scuttled away, apologizing all over the place, at the same time shooting Ronnie dark looks.

"That baggage has been shipped away for good," he stated firmly.

"Does the baggage know that?"

"Yes."

Ronnie wasn't so sure about that, but she liked that Sloan

had a more permanent abode in River Glen now. They were actually making plans like a couple. Not moving in together yet, but definitely thinking about it, solidifying their relationship, letting more people know, spending every moment they could together.

"I doubt Tara would like being called that."

He scoffed. "Come on, let's get out of here."

Just as they arose from the table, the doors from the raucous party flew open and the guests spilled out of the main room into all parts of the restaurant. Ronnie's shoe caught on the tablecloth and she tripped toward Sloan, who grabbed her hand, attempting to steady her, and ended up holding her over one arm as if they were about to dance, or embrace.

"Well, ya gonna kiss the bride, or what!" an inebriated guest declared, to which others from the party who were stumbling behind him heartily agreed. Sloan looked down at Ronnie, who gazed back at him. Swept up in the moment, he kissed her passionately while she was suspended over his arm.

Her mind made a snapshot of the moment. *White dress... candlelight... kiss...*

*I'm going to marry you!*

She didn't say it this time, but she could almost taste the words. Maybe Sloan didn't see the connection to her long-ago prediction, but she did.

"What?" he asked, when he placed her back on her feet. The crowd was clapping, hooting and hollering.

"Nothing. Let's go to my place."

"On it," he said.

Twenty minutes later Sloan walked behind her up the outside stairs to her apartment. When she stopped short he nearly ran into her. Had to reach out his hands to her shoulders to steady himself.

He looked over her shoulders to see the dog lying on her outside mat. A mid-sized mutt, by the look of it. Brown, gray and white with one blue eye and one brown.

"The dog... the dog!" she said.

Its fur was matted and dirty. It got to its feet, came over to her and put its head in her outstretched hand. "There you are," she said.

It licked her hand and pushed its head against her. She looked up at Sloan. "Mel's dog," she said in wonder.

"Your dog," he corrected her.

She leaned in to hold its head, completely uncaring about her white dress. They looked at each other. "I don't know your name, so will Mel do?" she asked him.

For years to come Sloan would swear the dog bobbed his head in agreement.